S0-ARF-400

Pride of Kings

"An eerily beautiful, sometimes frightening undercurrent to this engrossing, thoroughly satisfying novel. . . . Tarr smoothly blends a dazzling array of characters from both history and myth. . . . A totally credible delight."
—*Publishers Weekly* (starred review)

"A new tapestry of myth and magic. Gracefully and convincingly told."
—*Library Journal*

"*Pride of Kings* offers decisive proof that heroic fantasy can still be more than an exercise in fancy dress and moonbeams."
—*Locus*

Kingdom of the Grail

"Tarr spins an entertaining and often enlightening tale."
—*The Washington Post*

"Eloquently penned mythical history. . . . Drawn with depth and precision, Tarr's array of characters are as engaging as her narrative is enchanting."
—*Publishers Weekly*

"A lyrical and exciting story . . . richly woven narrative."
—*VOYA*

"A tapestry rich with love and loyalty, sorcery, and sacrifice. Tarr's ability to give equal weight to both history and myth provides her historical fantasies with both realism and wonder. Highly recommended."
—*Library Journal*

"[*Kingdom of the Grail*] is fun and exciting and was the first Arthurian related tale that I've enjoyed in a long time."
—*University City Review* (Philadelphia)

ALSO BY JUDITH TARR

Kingdom of the Grail
Pride of Kings
Devil's Bargain
House of War

RITE OF
CONQUEST

Judith Tarr

EAU CLAIRE DISTRICT LIBRARY

RoC

A ROC BOOK

T 134175

BNT 9-30-05 #7.22

ROC

Published by New American Library, a division of
Penguin Group (USA) Inc., 375 Hudson Street,
New York, New York 10014, USA
Penguin Group (Canada), 90 Eglinton Avenue East, Suite 700, Toronto,
Ontario, M4P 2Y3, Canada (a division of Pearson Penguin Canada Inc.)
Penguin Books Ltd, 80 Strand, London WC2R 0RL, England
Penguin Ireland, 25 St. Stephen's Green, Dublin 2,
Ireland (a division of Penguin Books Ltd.)
Penguin Group (Australia), 250 Camberwell Road, Camberwell, Victoria 3124,
Australia (a division of Pearson Australia Group Pty. Ltd.)
Penguin Books India Pvt. Ltd., 11 Community Centre, Panchsheel Park,
New Delhi - 110 017, India
Penguin Group (NZ), cnr Airborne and Rosedale Roads, Albany,
Auckland 1310, New Zealand (a division of Pearson New Zealand Ltd.)
Penguin Books (South Africa) (Pty.) Ltd., 24 Sturdee Avenue,
Rosebank, Johannesburg 2196, South Africa

Penguin Books Ltd., Registered Offices:
80 Strand, London WC2R 0RL, England

Published by ROC, an imprint of New American Library, a division of Penguin
Group (USA) Inc. Previously published in a Roc trade paperback edition.

First Roc Trade Paperback Printing, November 2004
First Roc Mass Market Printing, October 2005
10 9 8 7 6 5 4 3 2 1

Copyright © Judith Tarr, 2004
Excerpt from *King's Blood* copyright © Judith Tarr, 2005

All rights reserved

Cover art by Jerry Vanderstelt

RoC REGISTERED TRADEMARK—MARCA REGISTRADA

Printed in the United States of America

Without limiting the rights under copyright reserved above, no part of this publication
may be reproduced, stored in or introduced into a retrieval system, or transmitted, in
any form, or by any means (electronic, mechanical, photocopying, recording, or
otherwise), without the prior written permission of both the copyright owner and the
above publisher of this book.

PUBLISHER'S NOTE

This is a work of fiction. Names, characters, places, and incidents either are the products
of the author's imagination or are used fictitiously, and any resemblance to actual persons,
living or dead, business establishments, events, or locales is entirely coincidental.

    The publisher does not have any control over and does not assume any responsibility
for author or third-party Web sites or their content.

If you purchased this book without a cover you should be aware that this book is stolen
property. It was reported as "unsold and destroyed" to the publisher and neither the
author nor the publisher has received any payment for this "stripped book."

The scanning, uploading and distribution of this book via the Internet or via any other
means without the permission of the publisher is illegal and punishable by law. Please
purchase only authorized electronic editions, and do not participate in or encourage
electronic piracy of copyrighted materials. Your support of the author's rights is
appreciated.

EAU CLAIRE DISTRICT LIBRARY
6528 East Main Street
P.O. Box 328
EAU CLAIRE, MI 49111

*Tar
pb*

Praise for *Rite of Conquest*

"As a reigning specialist in fiction of the ancient world, [Tarr] has taken on settings from dynastic Egypt to Camelot, and her work's fascination derives as much from the solidly grounded, multifaceted backdrop she weaves as from the magical elements, inspired by a masterful storyteller's imagination, that she injects into her scenarios."   —*Booklist* (starred review)

"Tarr animates the stylized outlines of historical figures with colorful characterizations and fast-paced plotting."   —SFRevu

"Tarr continues her series of historic fantasies in which magic and the old religion play a key role. With her usual faithfulness to the period and keen understanding of human nature, she brings to vivid life her vision of the past."   —*Library Journal*

"A spellbinding historical fantasy . . . [Tarr's] unique slant on the events leading to 1066 makes for a fun and fascinating read."   —*Midwest Book Review*

"A fantastical take on the conquest of Britain by William in 1066. . . . William and Mathilda are nuanced and sympathetic lead characters, and the reader becomes emotionally invested in their success. With an interesting premise that's fully fleshed out and taken to its logical conclusion, this is a fascinating novel and recommended for fans of the genre."
                    —*Romantic Times BOOKclub*

continued . . .

YRARBIL TOIRTSID ERIALC UAE
0828 East Main Street
PO Box 328
EAU CLAIRE, MI 49111

Praise for the historical fantasies of Judith Tarr

House of War

"Tarr blends her magic with actual historical events as well or better than any other writer in the field, and her historical settings all have an air of authenticity and believability."

—*Chronicle*

"Tarr's compelling mixture of magic, myth, and history becomes a regular page-turner." —*Booklist*

"Fans of alternate history and fantasy will love this enthralling novel." —The Best Reviews

Devil's Bargain

"Meticulous historical research." —*Booklist*

"Impressive. . . . Tarr . . . brings [her story] to life . . . with believable characters, romance, and intrigue." —*VOYA*

"Delightfully mixes tales of Arabian magic with real, although alternate, history and a solid understanding of the period to create a fascinating tale." —*University City Review* (Philadelphia)

PRELUDE

❈❈❈

THE YEAR-KING

anno domini 1127

The oak was older than France, older than Gaul, and half as old as time. Charms were wound in its branches, blessings and beseechings and the odd black twist of a curse. Low on the trunk, for those with eyes and knowledge to see, a golden sickle gleamed, all but swallowed in the bowels of the tree.

Crowds of spirits and creatures of the Otherworld flocked to the oak, clinging to the charms like flies to honey. On this chill winter night, the bare branches were as thick with insubstantial shapes as with leaves in summer. They flowed up the trunk and along the twisted branches, dripping like water off the ends and dissolving into luminous mist. The mist gathered into a wheel that spun and glimmered, casting a faint, eerie light on the mold of leaves below.

Dancers wheeled in the grove, dark shapes leaping and spinning about the blaze of a bonfire. Pipes skirled. Drums beat. Voices chanted in a tongue well-nigh as old as the oak.

The young duke crouched in the concealment of a thicket. The rumor of pagan orgies had drawn him from the dubious warmth of the castle; the chanting and the flames had shown him where to go. And yet now that he had found the Druids' dance, he had no eyes for it at all.

One of the worshippers had not joined in the dance. She sat beneath the tree, bathed in its strange light. As cold as the night was, sharp-edged with frost, she seemed perfectly at ease, as if it had been midsummer and not midwinter. And yet her garment was barely there: a shift of white linen so thin that the watcher in the shadows could see every line of her body.

His breath came short. His fingers twitched, curving to fit the swell of those sweet round breasts. The music had crept into his head and filled it. She was a part of it, as if she had grown out of it, begotten of mist and night air and the shrilling of the pipes.

He did not remember rising or moving, but between heartbeat and heartbeat, he found himself under the tree. He could stoop, seize her, and run—and the Druids would never know until he was long gone.

The thought died even as it was born. She raised her eyes to him. They were wide and dark and full of dreams.

He was in those dreams. He saw glory; he saw splendor. He saw the oak above them open wide its branches and spread them over all the world that he knew.

When he swam out of the dream, he saw her lying at the oak's foot. For an instant she and the dream were one, and the oak grew out of her, sprouting from her womb.

He knelt in the fallen leaves. The music, he realized dimly, had stopped. The silence was as deep as her eyes and as vast as the world.

For the first time in his brief and headlong life, he understood the words that he had heard time and again from the bride at the church door: *With my body I thee worship.* This was holy. This was miraculous.

She opened her arms. He had no power to refuse, nor could he wish to. This was the old rite, the great rite, the marriage of king and goddess. However devout a Christian he might be, the old blood was in him. Tonight it was stronger than any priest's cant.

She was waiting. Even the stars had paused in their courses.

The breath gusted out of him. The heat rose, so sudden that he reeled. Mind and wits spun away. Only the body remained, and the fire under the skin.

He woke in the frosty dawn. Memory was vivid, almost painful. He remembered every moment, every breath, every kiss. He remembered every line of her.

Her name was Herleva. She had whispered it in his ear, sometime before oblivion took him. One other thing too she had whispered, or maybe he had dreamed it. Most probably it was a dream. "We shall bring him back," she had said, or he had dreamed that she said, "the chosen one, the summer king."

He crossed himself. The memory did not take flight; if anything, it was more vivid than before. It was nothing that a Christian gesture could banish. It was too strong and too perfectly pagan.

He rose stiffly, teeth chattering with the cold. His horse, for a miracle, was where he had left it, grazing desultorily on the sere grass. The duke pulled himself into the saddle and let the horse find its own way home.

PART ONE

❧❧❧❧

THE DUKE'S BASTARD

anno domini 1047–1048

❧ CHAPTER 1 ❧

Mathilda bent over the tapestry. The branches of an oak spread under her needle, growing swiftly in threads of green and grey and brown. Her maids' chatter flowed over her like the babble of bright water.

Her mind was empty of thought, still and clear, intent on nothing more than the thread, the needle, and the image on the taut-stretched linen. She could feel the earth's turning beneath her feet, and the dance of flames in the hearth, and the concourse of spirits all around and about and through this room in which she sat. Some of them swirled about her needle, sliding down the shaft of it into the tapestry.

The oak's leaves rustled. She caught the scent of damp earth and new-fallen snow. There were tracks in the snow, marks of shod hooves. Still empty, still pure being, she drifted above them, following where they led.

They wove through the trees of a wood, then out into snowy fields. Shadows lay long and black across the expanse of white. At the road's end was a shape of old wood and raw stone, a walled village clustered about the squat bulk of a castle. A banner hung limp from the half-finished tower; no wind caught it, to uncover the device upon it. She saw only that it was the color of blood.

The courtyard was empty of horses, though there were signs enough of their presence: trampled snow, bits of hay, a scatter of droppings. There were men in a corner, hulking figures wrapped in wool and leather, bent toward one another, conversing in a soft growl.

Because she was air and magic and little else, she heard them perfectly clearly.

"Tonight?"

"As soon as the sun goes down. He'll be up in the tower; we'll trap him there."

"He'll fight."

"The castellan's in on it," said the man who stood nearer the wall. "He's made sure there's a little something in milord's wine. He'll be out cold. Get in, slit his throat, get out—quick as carving a roast in hall."

"I hope it's that easy," the other said.

"What could stop us? We've got him away from his watchdogs. He thinks he's with friends. After all these years, he's still a wide-eyed lamb. He'll go straight to the slaughter."

Mathilda swirled upward, caught like a leaf in a sudden wind. She was no longer so empty now. This dream or vision had a purpose. She was in it because she must be. The wind was carrying her over the courtyard and up, circling the tower. Its face was blank but for narrow slits of windows.

The wind thrust her through one of the highest, into the sudden darkness of walls and the wan flicker of a lamp.

The castellan's wine had found its victim. There was a bed in the room, filling most of it, and a man sprawled across it. He was a big man, broad in the shoulders, with a strong-boned, blade-nosed face. Even though he was unconscious, she could see the strength of will in him, and what above all must have brought her here: a fire of magic that was easily the match of her own.

It had not protected him from the drug in the wine. She cast about for signs of ill workings or hostile magic, although she had not brought enough of herself into this vision for that. One thing she could see: there were no spirits here—not in the room, not in the castle. The air was empty of them, and the earth was quiet.

Too quiet. She stooped over the man on the bed. His unconsciousness was not as deep as she had thought: she saw a gleam of eye beneath the lid, and tightness in him that spoke of struggle.

Night was coming. Darkness was already in the room, and the sliver of sky beyond was dimming slowly. Mathilda gathered every scrap of will and resource that she had, and shaped it into a voice like a trumpet call.

"Messire! Wake and ride!"

His eyelids flickered. He had heard. But he did not wake, nor did he rise.

She raised the call again, though it cost her dearly in strength. "Wake! Ride! Death is behind you."

He twitched, thrashed. The drug was heavy in him. He fought it, but it was too strong.

Desperation drove her. In her hand, far outside this vision, was a needle. She tightened her fingers about it and drove it deep into linen, willing the heavy cloth to be drug-sodden flesh.

He surged up with a strangled roar, shaking his hand furiously. If there was any rational thought in him, he wasted no time with it. He burst through the door and bolted down the stair.

Mathilda hung in the air where he had been. All her strength was gone. She melted with a sigh, dissipating into the fading light.

William had a dim memory of bowling over a pair of figures on the stair leading down from the tower. He was as mindless in his stampede as a charging bull. Only much later did he recall that there had been a gleam of steel in the men's hands, and realize that they must have been coming for him.

That chill winter evening, he knew only that he must escape that place. He found his horse in the stable, threw on saddle and bridle, and flung himself onto the broad back. People were running, shouting, scrambling to shut gates and doors. He rode them down.

Night closed in, with damp and penetrating cold. The air smelled of snow and of the sea. It revived him, waking him to a preternatural alertness. His hand ached and stung where something, God knew what, had stabbed him—and thereby saved his life.

He slowed his pace somewhat from a hard gallop to a fast canter. His horse was breathing well; it was fit and reasonably fresh, and it had caught the same urgency that drove its rider. It made its way sure-footed along the narrow twisting track, through the oak wood and out into open fields, then down toward the river's mouth and the sigh of the sea.

His spine prickled. Men could not have gathered wits to follow at the pace he set, but other things than men were on his trail. They had separated him from his escort and herded him into the castle from which he had escaped. Now they were after him again, casting nets of confusion to bind his will once more and lure him to his death.

The pain in his hand was his protection. It raised a wall of clarity against which the hellhounds behind him bayed in vain.

His horse, for all its great heart, was tiring. It stumbled as it descended a long stony slope. Water glistened below, the broad mouth of a river running into the sea.

The tide was running out. The night was dark black, without moon or stars, but his eyes saw a glimmering path, straight as the track of moon on water. His heart hesitated—was it a trap?—but his mount made straight for it.

Damp firm sand steadied the horse's strides. The baying of hounds behind seemed fainter, as if they had slowed or turned aside. Water ran beyond the track, but where he rode was almost dry.

The wind rose to a gale, edged with sleet. The cold cut through hauberk and padded gambeson, clear to the bone. He crouched down over the stallion's neck, taking in what warmth he could. The hounds were close again, howling beneath the shriek of the wind.

His death was riding there, as close as it had ever been—and he was death's dearest companion. Almost he wheeled the horse about and sent it back into the hounds' teeth. But he was a coward. He pressed onward as best he might.

The track went on as straight as ever, but rose abruptly upward. The water sank away.

The hounds were waiting where the track met the dry land. How they had come there, where they had been, he would never know. He had no weapon—that had been taken away while he lay in drugged sleep. Even his eating knife was gone.

He could bow his head now and accept the inevitable. All the promises of his childhood—that he was the chosen one, the trueborn king, the lord of wood and water—had long since proved themselves false. Bastard, men called him though he had been born of the Great Marriage between the goddess incarnate and the year-king; they scorned his lineage and sneered at the circumstances of his birth. They had hunted him, hounded him, sought his blood and life and even his soul, until he had come to this: this cold winter's night with the taste and smell of death all about him.

His hand throbbed with sudden ferocity. Without thought he

flung it up. His mount pawed, steel-shod hoof ringing on icy stone. Sparks flew from the stroke.

He caught the sparks, dimly startled that there was no heat in them. They buzzed like bees in the cage of his fingers. He felt a drawing at his center, a force called up that he had not touched or even dared to think of in years out of count.

Fear would come later, and revulsion perhaps. The hounds were circling. They had the shape and form of earthly beasts, but he could see the earth through them: tumbles of rock and bramble and winter grass. Their fangs were long and white, gleaming like corpse lights. Their eyes were embers.

The sparks tugged at his hand. He sowed them like seeds, casting them in a long curving sweep. They grew as they fell, swelled and spread and darkened.

His heart sank. The sparks of magic were failing. The ghost-hounds were drawing in.

The horse snorted, an eruption of sound. The sparks swirled, now grey as ash, and coalesced into darkness.

A shadow-hound crouched at the stallion's feet, black as soot, its eyes hot gold. It growled low in its throat.

The hellhounds sprang. The shadow-hound plucked them out of the air, one by one, calmly and almost leisurely, and with a sudden, shocking snap of the neck, shook them into nothingness.

When the last was gone, William sagged on the stallion's neck, suddenly empty of strength. The shadow-hound turned and raised lambent eyes. He met them with a perfect absence of fear. If this was death, he was ready for it.

The shadow-hound grinned as wolves will do and rose up on its hind legs, resting a very real, very solid head on his knee. Slowly its tail began to swing back and forth.

His hand dropped of its own accord. The head was broad and warm. Breath gusted on his fingers. A long red tongue flicked out, licking them.

The pain was gone. Somehow it had brought this creature out of the shadows and given it substance. His blood was in it, and something else, too: the magic he had willed himself to forget.

He tensed to thrust the dog away, but caught himself rubbing the ears instead. The dog gave his hand a last lick and dropped to all fours.

He realized that he could see it almost clearly. The sky was

EAU CLAIRE DISTRICT LIBRARY

growing pale. Dawn was coming. He was alive, but how and why and for what, he could not imagine.

The horse turned of its own accord and trotted away from the water's edge. The dog loped easily ahead, as if it knew the way.

That was more than William could claim. He was alone in the world. The hounds were gone, but he knew better than to hope that the hunt was over. It would not end until he was dead.

Unless, of course, his enemies died first. He laughed as the hound led him on through the winter morning: sharp, short, but not terribly bitter. Hope was as relentless as the hunt, and as persistent in its refusal to let him be.

EAU CLAIRE DISTRICT LIBRARY

❦ CHAPTER 2 ❦

Mathilda opened her eyes on daylight. She was standing in her bedchamber while her maids dressed her and plaited her hair, as they did every morning. In her last clear memory, she had been embroidering the tapestry for the eastward wall of her father's hall. Between that and this was nothing but dream: darkness, flight, a young man whose every turn brought him face-to-face with enmity and death.

She felt as if she had slept no more than he had. A part of her was wandering astray, following him to a place that he could only pray was a refuge. She should call that errant fragment back, but it resisted either caution or common sense.

Her maids seemed to have noticed nothing odd. Jeannette was singing as she often did; she had a voice like a linnet, clear and sweet. Agnes was more than usually impatient. "Hurry, lady, hurry! Your father is waiting."

Mathilda did not remember his summons, either. It was a strange sensation, but it did not frighten her. It was magic, with a tang in it of fate—of what must be.

Count Baldwin was deep in conversation with a shape of shadow and glimmer in a disk of smoky glass. The disk rested in a cradle of bronze cast in the shape of a dragon. The dragon clutched the glass with wings and talons and fangs; sometimes, out of the corner of one's eye, it seemed to shift, its scales to ripple, as if it breathed.

If Mathilda tilted her head just so and peered sidelong at the glass, she could see a face she recognized and hear a voice she knew. She waited politely for her father to be done, paying little attention to what he said. Her mind was drifting again, following her dream to a manor house whose lord was a tall man with quiet eyes, offering a refuge from both terror and pursuit.

She sighed faintly. William was safe—not for long, most likely, with whatever was hunting him, but for long enough to rest and eat and recover somewhat of himself.

". . . Normandy." Her father's voice was loud in her ears. She started back into the world. "You are certain? You have foreseen it?"

The image in the glass was nearly inaudible, but the murmur of sound was affirmative.

"If he survives the winter," Baldwin said. "Perhaps it's time the king came to the aid of his vassal."

"It will be done," the image said. Either Mathilda's ears had sharpened or the image had spoken louder.

"It must be," said Baldwin. "If it is not—"

"It will be," said the image.

Baldwin nodded, bowing his head. The image flickered and vanished. The glass was empty, its light gone out.

The count sat for a long while, head bent, drawing in deep breaths. It was not a great effort to wield the glass, but it drew from the heart of one's magic even so. He needed a moment to restore himself, to gather his wits and strength and turn to greet his daughter.

She bowed to him as a great lord of this world and a Guardian of the magics of Gaul. He smiled and held out his hand. "Come here," he said. "Let me look at you."

She stood for his inspection. He was a man of good height and her late mother had not been small, but she was just a slip of a thing as her nurse had been wont to say. She was pretty enough, and like to be a beauty as she grew, but there was not a great deal of her. Her blood traced far, far back to the little dark folk of the hills; in her, like the magic, it ran strong.

Her father forbore to sigh and shake his head that she was still no bigger than a child, although she had nearly seventeen summers. He was not looking at the body she wore but at the spirit within; and that was so full of magic that it sent off sparks.

His eyes narrowed slightly against it. He nodded, approving. "You've grown up well," he said. "Your teachers speak highly of you."

She bent her head at the compliment. "I heard you talking to

Dame Alais. I'm to go back, then?" She hoped she did not sound too eager. "Not that I haven't been glad to be here through the winter, learning to be a lady as well as a mage. My tutors have been wonderfully patient; and you most of all. But—"

Her father's expression brought her to a halt. He was patient indeed, and amused, and somewhat perturbed as well: the hint of a frown drew his brows together. She resolved to be silent; but she could not keep herself from asking, "*Am* I going back to the Wood?"

"You may," Baldwin said, but she did not find that reassuring. "We had hoped to give you another year or two among the Ladies, perfecting your arts and powers. But Dame Alais has had a foreseeing."

A chill walked down Mathilda's spine. Dame Alais' foreseeings were not the common and ordinary flashes of prescience that any being with a flicker of magic might know. These were visions of power. It was dangerous to ignore them, but it could be equally dangerous to heed them.

"What did she see?" Mathilda asked when her father did not go on.

He laced his fingers in front of him and sighed, peering down into them as he had into the glass. "She believes that you should go to court, to the king."

"What, king of England? King of France?"

He did not rebuke her for sharpness, although he well might have. "France, of course," he said. "Your uncle Henry. You will learn the ways of a royal court, and a pupil will find you there."

Her eyes went wide. "A pupil? For me? In magic? But I'm not—"

"Sometimes," he said, "one learns best through teaching."

"Dame Alais said that?"

"I said it. She agreed." Mathilda looked down in confusion. He set his finger beneath her chin and tilted it up. He was not smiling, but his eyes were warm. "This is a great task, child. If you reckon it too great, no one will fault you."

"No; they'll only call me coward, and blame me forever after." She scowled at him. "How great is it?"

"For you," he said, "perhaps very great. The one who comes is a powerful mage, but almost completely untaught."

"A rogue mage?" She shivered. "Rogues are dangerous. They can kill."

"Yes," her father said.

"You would send me to that? To my death?"

"No one sends you," he said. "You will go of your own will, or you need not go at all."

"Why would I go? I'm not insane."

"It won't be you who dies," he said. "Dame Alais' vision is clear on that point. If you refuse the task, another will take it, and that one will pay with his life."

"And if I take it? What has she foreseen?"

"Hope," he said, "and a crown."

"For him or for me?"

"That," he said, "she didn't know."

Hope and a crown, Mathilda thought. She had been born to rule both the mortal and magical worlds; it was expected that when she was grown in both body and power, she would become a Guardian like her father. That was nothing new or startling. It must be the other whom Alais had meant.

"My uncle Henry has no magic," she said. "My mother got it all. None of his children is known to have any. Then who—"

"It's no one from the royal house of France," said Baldwin. "It will be someone else. Someone young, and maybe unexpected. Someone . . ."

He trailed off. Mathilda waited, but when he did not go on, she said, "You said Normandy. It's not one of those reiver barons, is it? They're all still Vikings at heart."

His brow arched upward. "You're quick to judge," he said.

"Am I wrong?"

"That remains to be seen," he said. He sighed. "Alais has seen the Norman lions in a field of blood. Whether that is related to the one whom you are to teach, or whether it's part of a separate vision, she wasn't able to say."

Mathilda's eyes narrowed slightly. His face was open, his voice easy, and yet in her bones she felt that he was not telling her all he knew.

She would discover it in the end, she was sure. She held her peace meanwhile, and kept her thoughts to herself.

"There is a little time to decide," he said. "Easter Court is months away yet; then it would be best, if you are going, to be in residence."

"If I don't go? May I go back to the Wood?"

"That will be for Dame Alais to say," he said.

Mathilda nodded slowly. This was already turning into the dance of courts, words delicately chosen, directness carefully sidestepped. It was obvious what she was expected to do. Whether she would . . .

"I'll think on it," she said. "By your leave, Father?"

He bowed. She bowed more deeply and withdrew.

Mathilda walked in a slow circle around the tapestry on its frame. The room was quiet; her maids were in the greater solar, listening as Agnes played the lute and Jeannette sang. The song was a pleasant trifle, a sweet descant to the silence of this place.

Yesterday when she had sat down to her embroidery, the tapestry had been simple, almost bare: a border of vines, one-quarter done, and a skein of mounted huntsmen riding through a wood. The huntsmen had been sketched on the heavy linen, the trees just begun. She had nearly finished the first of a grove of oaks, which would open on a flowery meadow and a herd of deer, stag and does and fawns, as yet unaware of the death riding toward them.

The oak, by chance, happened to be in the center of the tapestry. It had grown. Its branches spread wide, curving and twining over the sketched outlines of its fellows, reaching outward and upward to the edges of the tapestry. Beneath it, where should have been a hunter with his horse and hound and falcon, lay the figure of a woman. Her belly was swollen with child; from her womb sprouted the tree.

Mathilda peered closer. Amid the leaves and branches she saw shapes half hidden. There was a lion with a snarling face, there a blood-red wyvern, there a cluster of lilies. She saw a cross and a sword, a golden sickle gleaming close by the trunk, and a fleet of ships sailing through the branches. Deep within was a shadowy face and a glimmer of gold in the shape of a crown. The face was too dark to see, save only the eyes. Those were grey, wide-set under level brows, cool and steady.

She blinked and they were gone. Other, stranger shapes ran up and down the branches, twined among them, hid in the shadows between them: shapes of spirits such as haunted wood and water and the realms of air.

Mathilda squeezed her eyes shut. When she opened them, the tapestry had changed yet again. It was embroidering itself even as she watched, becoming ever more complex.

The heart of it was a needle thrust into the oak, and a drop of blood that sprang from no one here in her father's castle. Faery blood, she thought; fated blood, alive with magic.

Her finger tingled when she touched it. She saw in a flash of vision, the fugitive come home at last, resting in a soft bed with a lady watching over him. Her face was hauntingly familiar.

It was older, worn with years and care, but with a small shock Mathilda recognized it. It was embroidered on the tapestry, giving birth to a world.

His mother. And there he was, seeming as mortal as a man could be, and much younger than she had thought. He had been so grim and so much beset with hatred and death; but he was no more than a boy.

If this was to be a king, he was a long way from it. She paused to say a prayer for him, praying to both the old gods who seemed to watch over him, and the new God whose Church had relegated them to the shadows and the silence.

The tapestry was still growing. She should tell her father. Yet for the moment she was content to be alone, to watch the embroidery grow and change. She would remember that intricate pattern; it would fill her dreams. In time maybe she would come to understand it.

❧ CHAPTER 3 ❧

William's scouts found him the morning after he found the king. The two forces had camped side by side in a stretch of featureless country, grey-brown with winter, where the first pallid green of spring was still too faint to see.

As dawn broke over the fallow fields, William woke almost light of heart. He was further from despair than he had been when the year was new: he had his little band of men who remained loyal to him, and in their presence the shadows that had hounded him, as well as the black dog that had defended him, seemed to have withdrawn. Now the king had come with his army, a gleaming multitude beside William's travelworn knights and mounted men-at-arms.

Under the royal banner with its clear blue field and its scatter of silver lilies, William breathed as easily as he could ever remember. Henry was a small man, dark and slight and quick, with eyes that took in his vassal, assessed him, judged him, and calculated the degree of warmth to which he was entitled. That seemed to be a goodly amount, from the smile he bestowed on William as he emerged from his tent into the frosty morning.

William did not have it in him to return the smile, but his bow was deep and his gratitude genuine. He let himself return the king's embrace. "Good morning, sire," he said.

"It's a good day for a fight," said Henry. "Are you up for it, lad?"

"Always," William said.

Henry grinned. "Let's hear it, then. Are the rebels within reach?"

"Half a day's ride through the marshes, sire," said William. "They've crossed the Orne and camped near Val-ès-Dunes."

There was no recognition of those names in the king's eye, but then there did not need to be. He had generals and clerks for that. He nodded crisply to his trumpeter. "We'll meet them there," he said. "Sound the *Mount and Ride*."

William's men were already armed and on their horses. It was an interminable while before the king was ready, his camp struck, his companies gathered, his priests and hangers-on and baggage relegated to the rear. William had precious little of any of that; he was lucky to have his fifty mounted men, and horses and weapons enough for all of them.

The king had taken charge. William had expected that; it was only right. He had not expected it to gall him. This was his battle, his rebellion; his failure, near enough.

Henry had no plan for the battle. Find the rebels, ride against them, batter them into submission, was all he had to offer. William opened his mouth to venture a suggestion, but the king had ridden ahead. If William was to follow, he had best be quick, or the king's army would leave him behind.

They had numbers in their favor. His scouts were clear on that point. The rebels had gambled that the king would not meet the duke before they forced a battle. That gamble had failed.

There were still a thousand rebels, well armed, well mounted, and determined to wrest control of Normandy from its young and harried duke. William was wise enough to be wary, but he could not suppress the small flutter of hope in his belly. He could die today; or he would win the war. Either way, that would be the end of his long struggle. He would be duke indeed or he would be dead. One or the other.

Pale sun shone across the long levels and the grey fens, gleaming in the half-frozen pools. A thin wind rattled the winter-blasted reeds.

The rebels were waiting on a marshy level to the east of the river, a long line of armed and mounted men under the banners of half the lords of Upper Normandy. The other half were waiting at home to see who won; then they would decide where their loyalties lay.

Their bolder fellows were not visibly appalled to find themselves confronted with a substantial army under the lilies of France. With an exultant roar, first one company and then another surged out of the ragged line, striking toward the center and the king.

Henry's army scattered likewise into troops and companies: choosing their targets, charging toward them. In the space of a few breaths, the battle had become a melee, a roil of armed confusion.

William kept his own company together with a word, a gesture, a glance over either shoulder. They had been a hundred separate beings, men and horses, but in that moment of gathering, they flowed into one. He was the head, they the hands and body and the strong steel-shod feet.

Then he smiled, a faint upcurve in the corner of his mouth. His eyes swept across the field, reckoning the place and movement of each company, both friend and enemy, and calculating where each would go. There was a tightness in his belly, but it was not fear. He was long past being afraid of either pain or death.

He unleashed the charge. The ground was difficult, half mud, half ice, sucking one moment, slipping the next. When enemy fell on enemy, too often it was indeed a fall: horse stumbling, rider clinging desperately to the saddle.

William's destrier somehow managed to keep its footing, leaping and scrambling over frozen tussocks and patches of sudden mire. The men behind him, the parts of his greater body, kept their feet because he kept his. Spears lowered. Swords loosened in sheaths. With a roar they plunged into the rebels' line.

The world narrowed and focused on the enemy just ahead, the stab of spear and thrust of blade, the shock of blow on shield. And yet William's skin knew the whereabouts of every man in that battle. He felt the force of the stroke that flung the king from his horse; he knew how the king's guard rallied to defend him, and how the enemy pressed the attack, driving hard against the king.

They drove harder against the duke. Where William was, the fight was thickest. With a white fire of pain, one of his men took a spear in the throat. Almost, William fell himself; almost, the conjoined body of fighters broke. With an effort so strong it nearly felled him again, he shut himself off to the pain, then to the sudden emptiness that was death.

Steel flashed in his eyes. He flung himself aside. The blade of a sword sang past his helmet and dropped. His warhorse veered. The stroke glanced off his shoulder, catching in mail-rings.

He hacked at the swordsman. He was past knowing or caring who it was. Knight in mail, steel helmet, glitter of eyes behind the noseguard. Others in back of the knight, surging forward, stabbing at the duke whom they so hated.

No. Not hate. While his body fought, his mind arrived at an odd and startling clarity. William himself they neither liked nor disliked. It was the fact of his existence. He was young, he was weak in men and power, and worst of all for most of those good Christian nobles, his mother had been no man's wife when she delivered her firstborn son.

For that, he was fighting now for his life and dukedom. They taunted him even as they attacked: "Bastard! William Bastard!"

He laughed suddenly, laughter that cracked through his loyal company. They lifted their voices all together, all at once, in roaring mockery: "William Bastard! William Bastard!"

He bared his teeth at the mass of bone and steel thundering toward him, firmed his grip on his sword and balanced it, waiting for the next wave to crash down upon him.

Their taunts had stopped. They were fighting in silence now—grim; desperate, maybe.

The king's army pressed hard. Henry had mounted again, leading yet another charge, pursuing yet another company across the churned and muddy field. The rebels had begun to give ground. William saw the gleam of the river beyond them, much closer than it had been.

Once more he flung himself and his men like a spear into the ranks of the enemy. His sword, great heavy thing though it was, was light in his hands. It pierced flesh and hacked through bone. Blood sprang, steaming hot in the cold air.

The rebels' ranks broke. William at the center, the king and his scattered companies across the field, drove them headlong into the river. For the second time since the battle began, William made a sound: a roar of triumph.

The roar echoed strangely. William's ears were ringing. His men had slipped free of the unity that had bound them; they were harrying stragglers and overrunning the wounded and the unhorsed, taking captives, seizing prizes.

So were the rest of the victors of the fight. So should William be. There were rich pickings here, the wealth of Upper Normandy in armor and weapons and trained battle chargers.

It all seemed very dim and far away. The river churned with struggling bodies. Blood stained the water. Things were moving, rising up from beneath.

They were old, and they were hungry. Magic was meat and drink to them, and he was steeped in it. Blood was sweet, oh yes, and they gorged on it, but what he had was infinitely sweeter.

The rebels were broken, and a good many of them were dead. William should have been galloping through them, singing his victory. And yet here he was, clinging blindly to the saddle, while things he could not see and yet could feel with terrible intensity set hooks in his soul and tore.

No.

It was not so much a word as a conviction. He was not going to surrender. Not to anything—man, beast, or spirit of cold water and rank earth. Let it take his magic. He was better off without it. It was not going to have the rest of him.

Groaning with the effort, he lifted his sword. It was forged steel: death to the Old Things, or so he had heard. He lifted it as high as his trembling arms could bear, then let it fall.

It clove mist and shadows. They fell away with a thin high keening. The river heaved; the things beneath thrashed in rage. But they could not touch him. Not through edged steel.

Slowly the strength trickled back into his body. He mustered enough of it to sheathe the sword and turn his stallion slowly about. Men in armor were hunting down the last of the rebels. The king was taking the surrender of those who had got so far.

That should have been William's place and his privilege. And yet . . .

Why should it not still be? He drew himself up in the saddle. His horse arched its neck and stamped. That made him laugh—so rare a thing that he startled himself.

Even more than steel, laughter drove back the powers that would have swallowed him. The last remnants shriveled and died. Whether he had any magic left, he did not know. Nor did he care. He was alive. He had won this battle, he and his king. Whatever came of it, today he would be glad. And, more to the point, he would be duke.

❧ CHAPTER 4 ❧

The king had won a great victory in Normandy. His court was full of it, the men telling and retelling every rumored detail of the fight, the women fretting over who had been wounded and who, God forbid, killed.

Mathilda was not given to fretting, even over life and death. She had been at court just long enough to know all the names and faces and all the gossip, some of it so shopworn that it must have made the rounds when Charlemagne was king. She was dressed in the latest fashion, because her maids would have been mortified if she had not been, and she was learning all the things that a properly empty-headed lady should do and say and think.

In her heart she was perfectly still. It was a waiting time, a time for gathering her forces. The pupil she was supposed to find had not appeared—not yet. Maybe not ever, but she was not ready to believe that. It was barely mid-Lent. She had given herself until Easter.

It snowed the day the king came back: heavy, wet, springtide snow, heaping high on roofs and battlements and churning to mire in the streets. Paris, being Paris, either mocked or celebrated it in song. In the cathedral school, students debated the essence and philosophy of it.

She would rather have been there than here, trapped in the glitter of the court, herded hither and yon by servants in a great fuss and fret because their lord was coming home. The usual pack of would-be suitors had found her; they had been relentless since the first. The Count of Flanders' daughter was a rich prize.

Most of them assumed that she was here to find a husband. There was no disabusing them of the notion. They courted her with pretty words and small but irritating favors. They pursued her when she retreated, and plied her with songs and sweets and bits of ribbon or lace.

It was a great distraction and a considerable annoyance. On this day, when none of them was minded to brave the weather for a hunt or a round of mock battle, it was more than she could stand.

The king's arrival came none too soon. His procession through Paris had been endless. So had the court's wait in the great hall, dressed to excruciating perfection, arranged precisely in order of precedence.

Mathilda was set quite high, and therefore rather deep into the hall, near the dais and the throne. She was not on the dais, which with her lack of height meant that she could see nothing of the king or his retinue. She could hear them perfectly well: the spreading murmur, the rustle of silk and fine linen as courtiers went down in obeisance, the king's voice speaking a word here and there.

He was almost upon her, and the people around her bowing in a slow wave, before she saw him. There were knights and barons with him, most still in armor as he was, with helmets off and mail-hoods on shoulders. They looked strikingly warlike and rather rough in that glittering place.

She was not paying particular attention to the men with him, except to note that she knew more of them than not. One she did not—and yet—

She had seen that face in a dream, or in a tapestry. It was a young face, but hard and stern. Its cool grey eyes ran quickly and constantly over the assemblage, as if reckoning either the danger or the advantage that each might bring.

Mathilda's nape prickled. There was magic here. It was buried deep, walled and barred, but there was no mistaking its presence. He snapped with sparks like a cat.

Was this . . . ?

It must be. There was a sense she had learned to recognize, of inevitability. She had been guided to him, and he had been brought here where she would find him.

People were muttering behind her, trading the gossip that was the currency of courts. "Yes, that's the king's ward, the Norman duke: William Bastard. The late and not excessively lamented Robert bred him with a tanner's daughter from Falaise."

"I heard that her father buried the dead," someone else observed.

"So maybe he tanned their hides before he put them in the ground," said the first courtier, in a ripple of muted laughter. "Big ox, isn't he? He's been running this way and that since he was too young to hold a sword, thanks to his father up and deciding to go on pilgrimage to Jerusalem, leaving the duchy with nothing better to look after it than a half-hatched by-blow."

"And I heard," said the other, "that Robert got religion because his ladylove laid a curse on him: no wife, no leman, and no other child than the one she gave him. So he ran off to scour his soul and break the curse, but there was no getting away from it. It caught him after he saw Jerusalem, but long before he came home again to Normandy."

"If she were witch enough to cast a curse that far, don't you think she'd have witched herself into a duchess?"

"Who says she didn't try? But the duke took refuge in the Lord Christ, and fended off her sorceries. She had to settle for a vicomte—and that, as soon as she'd dropped the duke's whelp, she did."

Mathilda had grown accustomed to the sheer inspired venom of court gossip, but this raised her hackles. These idiots had not the faintest conception of what this man was, or what he had been born to be. They, or people like them, had thickened his skin to armor and driven him deep inside it.

She had no doubt that he could hear what was said of him here. His back had a certain stiffness to it, a certain set to the shoulders. Even in armor, a man could feel the shock of a blow.

He had passed on by. If he had seen Mathilda except as a face in the crowd, she did not know it. She was glad of that for the moment. She had much to think on, and a number of decisions to make.

William would rather fight another battle than walk through a hall full of courtiers, even with the king for a bodyguard. But walk he did, and it was no more pleasant than ever. Everyone bowed and smiled to his face, but behind his back the word was always the same.

Bastard. William Bastard.

Fighting men were more reasonable. Red death on a battlefield cared nothing for the circumstances of a man's birth, only for his skill with a weapon. William counted the moments until he could be back among his own kind, away from this nest of snakes in silk and gold.

As the king's ward and the recent victor in a famous battle, he had a room for himself and his attendants. Those as yet were distressingly few, in the king's opinion. He had sent William a pair of pages, both too tongue-tied to call their new master anything, bastard or no, and an insouciant squire who immediately saw to it that the bed was replaced with one newer, larger, and notably cleaner, and set to work arranging the rest of the room to match it.

William would have been content to bed down in a guardroom with his men—and so he would, once his new and unasked-for attendants had gone to sleep. But before that blessed moment, a third page appeared at the door. Even as William suppressed a sigh at the burden of the king's generosity, the child bowed low and said in a sweet, schooled voice, "My lord of Normandy, the lady of Flanders bids you attend her."

William's mind had gone blank. Somewhere down near the bottom of it, his memory recalled the Count of Flanders, whom he had met a time or two, and the fact that the count had married the king's sister. She was long dead. There was a son, he supposed. And a daughter? William was not the scholar of noble pedigrees that he might have been. Too much of his life had been spent simply staying alive; there had been little time for anything else.

The squire spoke before William could find words to say. "Messire, tell your lady with all due respect, the lord duke will attend her on the morrow, at a time and place of her choosing."

"Tonight, my lady says," said the page. He was even more self-possessed than the squire. There was something odd about him, William thought. Something—

"Messire," the squire said ever so sweetly, "my lord is worn out with battle and travel. He'll be much more fit to pleasure a lady after he's had a night's sleep."

The page's smile was sweeter still. "My lady's pleasure is to speak with milord duke."

William heard their exchange as if from far away. Of course he should put the lady off, and hope to evade her indefinitely. Such invitations were not uncommon at court; he had had a fair few, though never from a lady of such exalted rank.

But his eyes kept blurring and the page kept shimmering. The room was clear enough and the squire as solid as ever, but the page seemed strangely transparent. William almost thought that he saw not a human child but a black dog, plumed tail waving slowly, brown eyes laughing as he stared.

The dog that had guided him away from death that bleak winter night had vanished even as he passed the gate of a loyal baron's manor. He had let it slip from memory, or it had done the slipping for him. Now he could almost swear—almost imagine—that it was here, speaking in a boy's voice, telling the king's squire that his lady was no light-of-love and the lord duke must speak with her forthwith.

William spoke abruptly, cutting across their byplay. "I'll go. You stay. If I'm not back by morning, send a troop of guards to rescue me."

The squire's teeth clicked together. His eyes had gone wide. All the air of worldly wisdom had forsaken him. "My lord! You can't—"

William leveled a stare at him. There was no temper in it, but the boy looked ready to faint.

The lady's page, or familiar, or whatever it was, smiled a smile rather too full of sharp teeth for human comfort, and bowed bonelessly low. The flick of his hand bade William follow.

Even while he belted on his sword and did the messenger's bidding, William fended off the crowding doubts. It was late, the halls were dark, the way seemed endless. He had been betrayed far too often. He was mad to trust this creature, or this woman who had summoned him, if woman there was at all.

And yet he stalked in the page's wake, and the part of him that lived deep down, below doubt or fear or hard-earned mistrust, was unwontedly quiet. There was no harm here, it said, unless William brought it on himself. Whatever the woman wanted, it was not his life or his dukedom—and not, slightly to his regret, his fine young body, either.

He had made a point of knowing all the ways of the king's palace. It was wise warcraft, and useful on occasion. The messenger was leading him not to the ladies' apartments but toward the king's chapel. Odd place for an assignation, he thought, even if his guide were not a witch's familiar.

His hand rested lightly on the hilt of his sword. He was

tempted to draw it, but the quiet inside restrained him. All his senses were alert, his eyes searching shadows, his ears straining to catch the slightest whisper of sound. He could see in the dark; it was a gift he had always had.

There was nothing human prowling here. Mortals were safe in their beds, or struggling to stay awake while they guarded the gates. Things that were neither human nor mortal flitted down passages and hovered in the air.

They did not trouble him. They were harmless, little more than air and curiosity. There was always a flock of those about, even inside of consecrated walls.

There were more of them the closer he came to the chapel. They swirled about his guide, who ignored them. They surrounded William in a shimmering mass, so dense that it was almost translucent.

If he had been fully himself he would have batted at them, however futile that might be. But tonight they were part of everything else. In fact they were rather beautiful.

His guide set hand to the chapel's door. The thick carved oak swung open without a sound. The page bowed him through.

His back prickled with a last, fading remnant of earthly sense. He glanced back.

There was nothing left of the page but the smile, like a thin crescent moon. Then that too melted into the swirl of spirits beyond the door.

❧ CHAPTER 5 ❧

A thin skein of spirits followed William into the chapel. They were like an honor guard.

The chapel was lit by the flicker of candles about the altar, and the vigil lamp above it. Images of Christ and the Virgin and Saint Denis stood stone-still on the edge of shadows. The altar cloth was snow-white linen embroidered with golden lilies.

A shrouded figure was sitting on the altar's step. William had marked the living presence even as he passed the door, but it was so quiet and so dark and so nondescript that it had slipped out of his mind. Only after he had taken in the rest did his eyes come back to it.

It rose in a fluid motion. The hood slid back from a pale oval of face, and eyes that were dark in that light but might, in sunlight, be deep blue. The brows above them were dark, but the hair had a ruddy sheen.

She was a startling beauty to find in any place, let alone this one. And yet there was nothing seductive about the eyes that looked him up and down, measuring him as if he had been an ox she had in mind to roast. Only slowly did it dawn on him that she was barely taller than his shoulder.

"Well?" he said, knowing how rough he sounded. "Am I fat enough for the spit?"

"Not by half," she said.

What she did next, he did not exactly know. She neither moved nor spoke, and yet he felt as if she had reached into his heart and plucked the strings one by one, sounding a slow fall of notes that made the still, cold air of the chapel sing. The spirits that had followed him in streamed toward him, spiraled about him, and with a soundless shout, dived into him.

He howled from his very center, but no sound came out of

his throat. The spirits had split him open and sucked the marrow from his soul, devouring thought, sense, memory, everything that he was. They pierced to the bottom of him.

There they found what he had long since buried, thrusting it so deep that he had lost the way to it. It burned. It seared like fire.

Abruptly, as if he had plunged into cool water, the pain was gone. She had taken it. It was in her hand, glowing red like iron in the forge, and yet she showed no sign of feeling it. The skin of her palm was clear, unmarred.

She closed her fingers over it. "That," she said, "could have brought down these walls. Did no one ever teach you to use it properly?"

"I've learned to stay away from fire," he said.

"Your teachers were fools," she said.

"And you know better?"

"I know what you are," she said. "I know who you are."

His lip curled. "Everyone knows who I am."

"I don't think so," she said.

"I'm Duke Robert's bastard," he said. "What's simpler than that?"

"You are goddess-born, the year-king's child."

He went perfectly still.

She nodded as if he had spoken. "To the Church you may be a duke's by-blow, but before the old gods you are the one foretold: king once, king hereafter. Great power was born in you. Great destiny attends you."

He heard her in confusion that transmuted all too swiftly into anger. "That's all well and good, lady, but where were the old gods when I was dragged out of my mother's house and thrown into the den of wolves that was the duke's court of Normandy? I know where my mother was. She was sitting dry-eyed at her loom, where she'd just finished weaving a cloak for me. She said the same as you. 'This is fated. Go, and be strong. Remember when all others forget. Remember who you are.'"

His face twisted. "Surely I remember. I never forget. But who would believe me if I told them? Those that I did tell, either laughed at me for being a fanciful child, or threatened to set the Church on me for talking like a witch. I learned quickly enough to keep my mouth shut, lady. Would I could forget as easily as that."

As she listened, her expression changed not at all. Her eyes were as calm as ever, and as steady on his face. Every word he spoke, every shift of his mood, sank into her well of quiet and disappeared.

"Artos," she said, stilling him once more. "Caswallon. Bran. The gods have brought you back yet again, to do yet again what you have always done."

"What? Win battles but lose the war?"

For the first time he saw the glimmer of a frown between her brows. "You are a difficult person," she said.

"I'm alive," he said, "and no thanks to any gods or powers, or any magic, either."

One of those brows arched. "No?"

Her eyes bade him remember his wild ride away from death, and the forces that had guided him then.

He shook off the memory. "What good has magic ever done me? What use are all the old stories? Souls don't come back, lady. The Church says so. This life is all we have or will have, until we rise again."

"So the Church says," she said. "There is magic in you. However deep you bury it, however strongly you deny it, it's woven in the fabric of your self."

"You took it," he said with a jab of the chin toward her fist. "It's yours. Do what you like with it."

"Do you swear to that?"

His belly tightened. This was a trap. And yet he said, "Yes. Yes, I do. I give it to you."

Her fingers unfolded. The coal burned as fiercely as ever, and with as little harm to her flesh or spirit. "Then you are mine," she said, "my sworn man. Kneel!"

He had dropped before he knew what he did, under the force of that command. Her hands cupped together, still with that burning thing within them. They rose over his head, then lowered, until they rested on his head. They were a light weight, barely to be felt, but his bones knew that they were far more than that.

"William of Normandy," she said. "Your power is mine, the magic that is in you, the destiny that waits for you. You are mine to keep and mine to command. All that you are belongs to me."

He was a fool, he thought distantly. An absolute, blinding fool. Nonetheless, for all the outcry of reason and logic and hard-earned sense, his heart was inexplicably light. He had damned himself, most likely, and it did not matter. Nothing mattered at all.

Mathilda had done something that might be very wrong, or very dangerous. So had the man at her feet, but he knew no better. She had all the training that he lacked, all the knowledge and the wisdom of a thousand years of white enchantresses, and when the moment came, she had acted purely on impulse.

It was done now. The power that he had given her had melted back into him, taking his oath with it. One useful thing that had done: he felt no pain as his magic returned. He hardly seemed aware that it was there.

"Every night," she said to him, "you will come to me here. Your ignorance is a danger to yourself and to everyone around you. You will learn how to be what you are."

He might be bound, but he was not suppressed. He glowered at her with all of his old, foul temper intact. "Who are you to call me ignorant?"

"Your master," she said, "and your teacher. Did your mother teach you nothing? Or did you choose to forget it all?"

His silence was answer enough.

"You will remember," she said. "Now go. Sleep as best you can tonight, messire. You'll be running well short of that before I'm done with you."

He left with a snarl, but he would do as she commanded. Somewhere in that mass of arrogance and ignorance and ferocious defenses was a faint glimmer of natural grace. She allowed it to give her hope, after a fashion.

"Well, daughter?"

Mathilda started awake. The crystal her father had given her at parting was clutched tight in her hand; its chain had inlaid itself in her cheek. His voice from within was as clear as if he stood beside her.

"Well?" he said again.

She sat up groggily. For once there was no one else in the bedchamber. Maids and squires were gone. The light that slanted through the high barred window showed morning well advanced. The room was icy. She drew the coverlets about her, shivering hard.

Someone deserved a whipping for that, but she was not inclined to pursue it just then. She felt as if she had spent the night hacking at the pells with a sword as long as she was. Her back and shoulders ached; her head was pounding.

She knew all too well the aftermath of a strong working. It had seemed little enough while she did it, but she should have known better.

She looked down at the crystal in her hand. Her father looked up. As small as the image was, it was perfect in every detail, and perfectly clear.

"You knew," she said. "All the while, you knew."

Her father raised his hand. With the gesture, they stood face-to-face within the bounds of the crystal.

"You knew who he was," Mathilda said. "What did you gain from not telling me? Was it worth the test?"

"That remains to be seen," said Baldwin. "Your working shook the planes of the aether, and came near to bringing down the wards of Gaul."

"It did not," she said, as unwise as that was. Even as the words escaped her, she knew that he had told the truth. She could feel it in the crystal, and see it in the shape and color of his magic.

He ignored her foolishness. "If you are to instruct this great but ill-raised power, you must be the master of your own. You must not allow it to wield you."

The rebuke was sharp, and too well deserved. She bowed to it, but she said, "If I am to go on, I must know what he is. No more secrets, Father. No mysteries. Give me the truth."

"You saw the truth," he said. "*Rex quondam, rexque futurus.* This was a king and will be king again."

"Maybe," said Mathilda, "but here and now, he is a brute of a boy with no manners, no learning, and precious little sense. Who allowed that? Why was he suffered to grow up wild? He has no more trust of the world or its creatures than a hunted animal, and no more reason to trust, either."

"There was no choice," Baldwin said.

"Of course there was a choice!" she flared at him. "He's a Druid's child, isn't he? His father repented of it, but what of the mother? She has power, I can feel it in him—he's bathed in it. Why has she left him to be hunted and hated?"

"Because she must," said Baldwin. "Steel is not tempered in soft breezes and new honey. It gains its strength in the fire."

"But if the fire is too hot, it turns brittle. It breaks."

"That is the risk one takes," he said.

"Destiny is a cold thing," Mathilda said after a pause. "Now tell me the rest of it."

"You believe there is more?"

She fixed him with a hard stare. He was no more impervious to it than William had been. It was almost a pleasure to see him hunting about for words to say.

"Tell me," she said, with a snap of command that the Ladies had taught her.

He rocked as if at a blow. She braced for one in return, but none came. He said slowly, "You will teach him. What you can give—your power, but your gentleness as well—he needs more even than knowledge. He needs you, daughter, in all that you are. Fire may temper him, but in water he will find his fullest strength."

"Will even that be enough? He's had all the softness beaten out of him. Every part of him is armor, all the way to the bottom. What if there's nothing there to salvage?"

"If it is to be found," Baldwin said, "you will find it."

"And then?"

"Then you will know what to do."

"As I knew him?"

"Just so."

She closed her hand over the crystal. Baldwin's presence vanished from her awareness. The sun had barely shifted; as long as that exchange had seemed, it had consumed barely a dozen breaths of the body.

She steeled herself to venture into the cold, to dress and plait her hair and go in search of breakfast. The day would stretch long until evening—until she would know if the binding held; if William would come, and learn what she had to teach.

❧ CHAPTER 6 ❧

In the end it was Mathilda who nearly broke her word and failed to appear in the chapel. William, coming as he was bidden, found no human thing there, only curious spirits, chittering like bats in the vaulting.

Almost he turned on his heel and stalked back the way he had come, but he was too stubborn for that. He wrapped himself in his cloak and sat on the step where she had been the night before. It was colder than it had been then, a winter cold, though by the monks' calendar the year was fair advanced toward spring.

Halfway between Imbolc and Beltane, he thought.

Those words had not spoken themselves in his head since he was a child. He had hidden them away and done his best to forget them. They were old words, pagan words, words that Mother Church had long since forbidden.

He drew up his knees and clasped them, and rested his forehead on them. In the warmth and sudden darkness, the eyes of his mind opened on sunlight.

William's mother was the most beautiful woman in the world. She was also the most wonderful. She could bring down the moon and make the sun dance with her singing. Flocks of spirits followed her wherever she went; when she worked her magic, so many of them crowded about her that one would think she could barely move.

He loved to watch her work magic. He would sit in a corner, safely out of the way, and fold his arms on his knees and rest his chin on them, and watch while she made the world more beautiful. Sometimes she made medicines, filling them full of light and laughter as well as herbs and simples. Other times she sat at her loom and wove light and shadow into the threads of linen and wool, so that the cloth carried blessing and goodwill, and a little beauty, when it was made into a cloak or a shirt or a gown. And sometimes, though that was not often, she called on the great powers for some purpose that he was too young to understand, summoning the whirlwind and bringing down the lightning.

When he was very small, he had only watched, but as he grew older, she called him to her in the middle of the working, and showed him how to do what she was doing. Once in a while she would even let him do the working. She would tell him what she wanted, and he would do as she had taught him, and brew a medicine or summon a spirit or scry in the silver bowl that she kept, wrapped with great care in a scrap of silk, in her chest to which no one else had the key—because the key was made of magic.

On the morning to which his memory had taken him, it was warm for so early in spring. The sun was so bright that when he came out of the dimness of the manor house into the light of her garden, it had blinded him.

There was a fishpond in the middle of the garden, full of silver carp. They were supposed to be eaten in this season, which was Lent, but no one ever seemed to take any of them from the pond. When there was fish on the table, it came from the river that ran past the manor.

His mother sat on the rim of the pond, trailing her hand in the water. The fish flocked to her, leaping and swirling, butting their heads against her hand and nibbling her fingers. The largest one, the king, could speak in one's head like a man, though his words did not always make human sense. They made perfect sense, of course, if one were a carp.

William's mother smiled at him, dazzling him all over again. There was something odd about the smile, as if she were trying to be happy about something, but when she thought about it, it made her sad. He wondered if it had something to do with the messenger who was coming. The spirits had told him when he got up, but even before that, he had dreamed that a knight rode to the manor on a black horse.

He went to his mother and sat beside her. "Did you know," she asked him, "that the king of the carp has lived for a hundred years?"

He nodded. "He told me he remembers when you were born, and when I was born, too. The trees sang, he said. Trees sing when new magic comes into the world."

"So they do," his mother said, smiling that sad smile again, and smoothing his hair. He was growing too old for that—this year he would start learning how to fight—but today he let her do it. It made her sadness a little less.

"I have a great deal of magic," he said. "Don't I?"

"You know you do," she said.

"And I'm not to talk about it unless the person I'm talking to knows what I am."

She nodded. "You've learned your lessons well. Time was when everyone knew what we are—when magic was held in great honor, and our power was taken for the blessing that it is. But the world grew old and the Christians came, and our people were driven into the hills and the woods and the cold moors by the sea. Some of us learned to hide in plain sight, to say the prayers and sing the hymns and wear the faces of Christian people. But in our hearts we belonged to the Old Things, to the heart and soul of the earth our mother."

"In our hearts," he repeated gravely. "But we don't talk about it. It's our secret."

"The best secret in the world," she said. She brushed his forehead with a kiss, then suddenly pulled him to her and hugged him hard, as she had not done since he was much younger. He stiffened a little, but did not try to push her away.

Later that day the messenger came, the knight on the black horse. He carried a banner, blood-red, with golden lions. A dozen armed men rode with him. All together they were a fine and martial company.

William's stepfather received them with honor, as a vicomte should receive the duke's messengers. Herluin was a quiet man, nondescript to look at, with a soft voice and a gentle way about him, though he could be strong enough when he had to be. People who knew no better thought that William's mother had married him because he was rich and she wanted to climb up in the world. But people who knew anything knew that he was one of the old folk, too, and she had loved him since they were children.

He did not have the power that William's mother had, or

William himself. Still, he knew well how to use what he had. He was very wise and very calm. William had never seen him lose his temper, even at a scapegrace stepson who could drive the most phlegmatic of nurses to distraction.

Herluin was gravely courteous to the duke's man, who was not exerting himself to be courteous in return. He had come for one thing, and he wanted to get it done as quickly as he could. "We've come for the boy," he said before the ceremonies of greeting were even begun. "Have his nurse get him ready to ride."

William was watching and listening from his favorite hiding place, the space between Herluin's tall carved chair and the wall of the room in which he received guests. The door was close to it; a small person could slip from there to the niche and never be seen at all.

He knew that Herluin knew he was there. Very little escaped the vicomte's notice. For once William was being allowed to stay—though when the knight spoke of a nurse as if William were still a baby and not almost ready to go among the men, Herluin's hand slipped around the back of his chair and gripped William's arm, holding him still.

William clamped his mouth shut and let go the urge to leap up and tell the knight exactly what he thought of him. The man was rude, and he had no business talking to Herluin that way. Herluin was not a servant.

But that was for Herluin to say or not say. Herluin smiled— William felt the warmth even from behind the chair—and said in his gentle voice, "My lord William will be ready in the morning. You will of course accept our hospitality tonight."

That set the knight back on his heels, but not for long. "No, messire, I will not. The duke wants his son, and he wants him now."

"The duke is a day's journey away," Herluin said as gently as ever, "and if you ride within the hour, you will be obliged to spend the night somewhere between. I'm sure my lord William will prefer to sleep in the bed with which he is familiar, among the people whom he knows, before he leaves it all behind to honor his father's wishes. Tomorrow night he will dine in the duke's hall—as the duke has commanded."

That last had an edge to it. The knight went crimson, and for a while could not say anything at all. Herluin used the time to call in the servants, order a bed in the manor for the knight and lodging for the knight's escort in the largest and cleanest of the cattle byres, and see to it that Cook knew there would be a pack of guests for dinner.

The knight gave way with very ill grace, but even he could not win an argument with Herluin. He stayed because Herluin had told him to, and when morning came, William would go with him to the father he had never met, but of whom he had heard countless stories.

William was too excited to be scared. He had always been meant to go to his father. That had been the bargain. His mother would raise him and teach him to be what she was, then when he was old enough, his father would take him. He had thought he would be much older, old enough to be a squire, but the duke wanted him now, as a page, he supposed.

The duke did not want him as a page. William grown, gone hard and bitter as an oak-gall, slid past the memory of his mother's farewell, the last night of his childhood in Herluin's manor, even the long, fast ride through country he had never seen before. When his vision grew clear again, for the first time since he was an infant, he saw his father.

Robert, whom men were calling the Magnificent, was a splendid sight for a child's eyes. He was dressed in silk as brightly gleaming as a butterfly's wing, and his court was a wonder of gold and glitter and perfumed delight.

Even as a dazzled child, William had seen through after a little while to the mortal man beneath the splendid show. Robert was a big, broad man, very like what his son would become, and in his heart, which he hid remarkably well, he was stark with guilt and fear.

When he looked on his son, he saw that guilt made flesh. He remembered the dance and the sacred marriage, but in his mind it was all twisted, darkened and dirtied, high holiness turned into a sin. The sin was eating away at his spirit.

And the worst of it was that if he was to make the great pilgrimage that his heart told him he must, if he was to be absolved and so made clean for heaven, he had to surrender his dukedom to the consequence of the sin. There was no other son of his blood. There never had been. There never would be. Only this grave-faced child with his cool grey eyes, still stained and muddy from the road.

William was inside his father looking out. It was an odd sensation, but not unfamiliar. He could do that sometimes, if he was very close to somebody. This man he did not know at all, but they were the same blood. They looked the same—larger and smaller, but the same shape, the same size and bulk, and the same face.

This was what it was like to have a real father, a blood father. It was strange and rather sad. His father was not glad to see him at all. William was a duty—an obligation, that was the word. He was the thing that had to be put in the chair to hold it while the duke went away.

His mother loved him with all her heart. His stepfather was as fond of him as of his own two sons. In Herluin's house, William was more than welcome. He was loved.

There was no love here. For all the glory and glitter, the duke's court was a cold place, and its heart was empty. Wolves were gentler with one another than the knights of Normandy.

"I've given you everything I can," his mother had said when he left her. "Keep it; cherish it. Use it to warm you when the world grows cold."

He had not expected the cold to come on so soon. Had she? He had no way of telling. She was gone from inside him, her presence shut away. He was doing what he was born to do. She had no more part in the making of him.

That was cold, too. Fate was cold. The gods wanted what they wanted; they cared little for what it did to the mortals who were their instruments.

William opened his eyes from memory to Mathilda's face. Her hands were gripped in his: small hands but strong, and warm.

He pulled away sharply. "You have no right," he said. "You have no—"

"You belong to me," she said.

He stiffened.

"Memory is the key," she said. "Pain unlocks the door—just as, in its time, it locked it. I wish that were not so, but that's the way the gods have made us."

"The gods." He spat. "That for the gods."

"Your father cared too much for the Christian God," she said. "You care too little for the old gods who made you. Both of you would do well to find a middle way."

"My father is unlikely to do that," William said. "He died on the road from Jerusalem."

"When he's reborn, he'll have to try again," she said.

"Is this what you call teaching? Lies and twisted stories?"

"Truth is seldom what you would like it to be."

"Nothing is as I would like it to be."

"You like to feel sorry for yourself," she said. "Stop it. You're not a hunted child any longer. You're a man, and a great lord of France."

"Not according to half the barons of Normandy."

"The king says it. The other half of your barons say it—and the rest of them have changed their minds somewhat since Valès-Dunes. You've won, messire. The power is yours. Normandy is yours."

That was true. People had been telling William so since he staggered dazed from the battle, vexed with memories that none of the rest could share. They did not live half in another world as he did—as he struggled constantly not to do.

He had won. He *had* won. He could feel the power in his hands, solid as the reins of the splendid destrier that, his men insisted, he had won in the fight.

He glared at the woman—the girl—who had trapped him into remembering what he was.

"Someone had to," she said, reading him without trying to conceal it. "When you can remember, you can heal. Then you can learn."

"I don't *want* to remember!"

"Yes," she said.

When he struck, people gave way. Or they struck back. That was the lesson he had learned in his father's court, which too quickly and too imperfectly had become his. This softness, this air of sublime reason, left him with his hand raised and useless, meeting neither attack nor surrender. It was like taking arms against the air.

She regarded him with a complete lack of fear. He could strike at her with more than words, and she would turn to air and water and flow away. That was as clear as if she had said it aloud. He could not touch her or wound her or shake her spirit. She was as rooted in herself as an oak in the earth.

"Give me that," he said suddenly. "Give me what makes you like this."

"Are you asking me to teach you?" she asked.

"I'm asking you to make me strong."

"You have a master of arms," she said.

"That's not the kind of strength I meant. I meant—"

"It's not strength you need," she said. "It's knowledge. And memory."

She would drive him mad. Then he would not be in himself at all, or care what became of him.

"So do it," he said: "whatever it is you do. Just do it."

❧ CHAPTER 7 ❧

The King of the English knelt in his chapel. He had prayed until his mind was empty of thought, until there was nothing in it but singing light.

The fey clung to the roots of earth. This place had been blessed of the gods before cold iron and cold holiness had tainted it, but it was still a shattering agony to be within it. Only the power of the straight track that ran through it, and the power of the king who knelt in the middle of the track, made it possible at all.

A fey was a light and airy thing, begotten of moonlight and mist, but this fey had taken a part of its substance from the living earth of Britain. It was a fey of great power, as much as a fey could be, and it was entrusted with a great errand.

The king was perfectly empty. The forces that had labored so long and so hard to bring him to this place at this time, for this purpose, were nearly spent. The fey must act quickly or it was all for nothing.

It could feel the walls of iron closing in, the cage of ritual and prayer that would crush its fragile self and the whole of its errand into nothingness. All of Britain was bound with it, and only with the gods' help had the fey come so far or survived so long.

It poured itself into the king. There was a moment of perfect agony. Then there was flesh all about it, heavy as mud, thick as dung in a byre. The walls of iron were far away then, their deadly song muted almost to silence.

This king was not bound to the land as kings should properly be. He was bound to the word and the rite, and the spells that laid the whole of this isle under their sway. They had driven out the Old Things, slain or cast out the gods, and done their utmost to destroy any power that was not their own.

Half a thousand years had barely been enough for the Old Things to recover enough of their strength to send this messenger down a straight track into an open spirit. There would not be another half-thousand. It must be now, or it could never be at all.

The message was simple: a thought that would, once planted, grow into conviction. In the beginning it was bare of even words. It lay quiet at the bottom of the king's heart, biding its time until he would wake and find it waiting. Britain's fate was in it, and Britain's hope.

The fey's task was done. The walls of iron were too strong for it even in the stronghold of flesh. With a silent sigh it dissolved, melting into the substance that was Edward, King of the English.

The hounds started the stag at midmorning. It was cold for this late in spring, and wet: it had rained for three days. But the morning had dawned chill and clear, and Harold had rousted out his brothers for a hunt. Most of them snarled and burrowed back into their warm bedclothes, but Tosti had fretted at least as badly as Harold had at being shut up in Earl Godwine's hall. He sprang out of bed gladly enough, over the objections of the milk-skinned girl who was curled in it like a dormouse in a nest, and reached for his hunting bow even before he found the heap of his clothes.

The two of them, with a dozen housecarls and the master of hounds on foot, had left their father's house while the day's light was still clinging to the eastern horizon. Each had a loaf thrust under his tunic, still warm from the ovens, and a flask of ale to keep him warm when the bread cooled.

The long fast of Lent was past; Easter's luminous rite was done and its memory put away for another year. In a day or two, Godwine's sons would scatter from their father's house, back to their own lands and duties. For this day, while all of them were still together, the cooks would welcome whatever meat they could bring home from the hunt.

This was a wide, flat, misty country, dotted with bits of wood and copse, but most of it was open downs and the long stretch of the chalk, the green rolling hills where the earth's bones showed white through the grass. Old things, pagan things, had run wild here before Holy Church drove them out with bell, book, and candle. Memories of them lingered even after half a thousand years, flickers of light and shadow in the corner of an eye, or voices half-heard in empty places.

There were monks in abbeys all across this country, and nuns in their convents, weaving a web of prayer to trap the ghosts and the memories and render them into nothingness. Sometimes when Harold was half asleep, he fancied that he could feel the web, and hear the prayers that were said and sung. They kept the land secure and kept the powers of evil far away.

He was part of it, too, he and every man of this country who took up arms to defend it. They were the web of iron that guarded the web of prayer. It was a deep thing, a strong thing, and no one spoke of it. It clove too close to the bone for that.

All of this was on his mind as he strode across the downs in the morning. Even as abstracted as he was, he saw the stag first: a flash of white in a thicket. He did not know what it was; stags were red, every man knew that. But the hounds began to bay and the master of hounds to loose his own wild cry. The stag sprang from the knotted hazels: white as moonlight, white as snow, and its antlers carved of ivory.

For an instant as it veered away from the foremost of the hounds, Harold thought he saw a collar of gold about the stag's neck. But it was only a twist of vine, yellowed and dead.

There was nothing mythic about the beast, in spite of the cold that walked down Harold's spine. Tosti roared in glee and took off at a run, fitting arrow to string as he went. The hounds were in full cry. Harold should have been in the lead, but his legs would not oblige him with more than a slow trot. He trailed behind, bow strung but arrow loose in his hand.

The day that had begun with bright sun was turning again to mist and cloud. The stag flitted in and out of drifts of fog. Earl Godwine's good grey deerhounds were close on its heels. In the mist they seemed as pale as the stag, but their ears had an odd, bloody sheen.

Illusion, Harold thought. But he crossed himself and began a paternoster. "Deliver us," he murmured as he struggled onward. "Deliver us from evil."

The mist seemed to grow thicker, the pursuit more eerie, as if in defiance of the holy words.

Tosti's whoop was shatteringly loud in the fog. Just as he aimed and loosed, he stumbled. The arrow flew wide. The stag leaped impossibly high, impossibly far, and vanished. The hounds swirled in confusion.

Tosti had dropped to his knees. When Harold came up panting beside him, he turned a wild grin on his brother. "A wonder! A marvel! We've fallen clear out of the world."

Harold hauled him back to his feet. Tosti's breeks had split in the knees; blood ran down. There was blood in the grass, staining the chalk beneath.

The hounds were gone. The master of hounds and the rest of the company were nowhere to be seen. They stood together in a featureless expanse of grass and chalk, walled in mist.

Somewhere far away, monks were chanting, slow and deep. The earth throbbed with the power of their voices. But the mist refused to lift. Other voices were whispering in it, and one was singing: sweet, high, too pure for mortal throat.

Tosti giggled. "The Old Things are coming back," he said. "They've found a way in. They'll make it wider. Then even cold iron won't keep them out. They'll laugh at prayer and tweak the monks' noses, and make the holy nuns run naked through the hills."

Harold shook him until he stopped babbling. He was completely out of his head. His eyes were full of laughter. What was behind them was not Harold's brother at all.

Harold gauged the blow carefully. He did not want to kill, only to stun. Tosti dropped like a stone. Harold heaved him over his shoulder, grunting with the weight, and turned completely about.

The fog had closed in. Harold let his feet lead him, even knowing how dangerous that could be.

They led him through bramble and mire, down a slope of knife-edged scree, and through a stream so cold it cut like knives. The fog hung close, thick and damp. Tendrils of it brushed his face like cold fingers.

He armored himself with every prayer he knew, and every scrap of psalm. He could have sworn that the fog laughed at him.

Tosti had begun to stir. Harold dared not drop him for fear of losing him in the murk. He pressed on as best he could, wet, muddy, and beginning to wonder how much longer his legs would hold up the doubled burden. Tosti was not near as tall as Harold, but he was a good deal thicker.

Just when Harold's knees could not stiffen for one more step, he staggered out of the fog onto a stone pavement. He fell hard, but the pain was blessed—as were the stones. The scent of incense and the sound of chanting were all about him.

Hands, gentle but persistent, freed Tosti from Harold's grip. Others raised Harold to his feet, supporting him when his knees buckled yet again. Quiet men in black robes surrounded him; every one bore the tonsure of a monk.

He let them carry him within the walls of their monastery. No fog or mist of magic could follow him there.

And yet, surrounded by stones that had been blessed and hallowed and blessed again, dining on rough bread and refectory ale, Harold felt as if the world were turning to mist and water underfoot. Even in the chapel where the monks chanted their offices, each melodious word securing the web that kept the old magic out of Britain, he could feel it.

The web was fraying. Things were coming in—old things, wild things. The white ghost-stag was but a beginning.

Tosti had been put to bed in the infirmary. The prior of the monastery, a very tall and thin man of no age in particular, shook his head over Tosti's stirrings and mutterings. "We will do our best to cure him of the evil," he said, "but already it has sunk deep. You may do well, lord, to bring him to one of the holy saints, and have the demon driven out of him."

Harold opened his mouth to deny that his brother, of all people, could be possessed; but he remembered the thing that had lurked behind Tosti's eyes, and the words died unuttered. "Will it work?" he asked. "Can it be driven out?"

The prior crossed himself and murmured a bit of Latin. "God willing," he said.

God had little to do with what had taken Tosti, but Harold knew better than to say it. He had a terrible thought as he stood in that bare and saintly room, surrounded by men who lived their lives in the service of God. God was not going to be enough. His people had done their best since Hengist and Horsa first brought their people to this island, first converting the pagan Saxons, then driving the Old Things out and making all that land safe for the pure in spirit.

But the land was older by far than the people who came and went on it. The things that were bred of it, the old dark things, the children of night and ancient sin, might have suffered exile for a while, but they had come back. Whatever had opened the door, there was no shutting it now. Not if every monk and nun, canon and canoness, priest and bishop and archbishop in Britain, praying ceaselessly, day and night, had been unable to stop it.

❧ CHAPTER 8 ❧

William pummeled his forehead in frustration. "I'm never going to remember all this!"

"Bards have remembered it for a thousand and a thousand years," Mathilda said, gently implacable, "and a thousand times more than this besides."

"Bards have years to learn," he shot back. "You're giving me days."

"Months," she said.

It was a moment before he realized that she was laughing at him. He bared his teeth at her. "Wouldn't it be easier to teach me to read? Then you could go off and do whatever you do when you're not torturing me, and I could see this blasted nonsense laid out on a page. Writing's like a map, isn't it? Only it's words instead of castles and rivers. Give me a map and I can learn this."

"Writing would catch it on parchment," she said. Her knuckle rapped his much-abused forehead. "You need it in there. The powers you've been facing, and will face, won't wait for you to run to a library before they crack open your skull and suck out your brains."

William realized he was gaping. He did a great deal of that when he was with Mathilda. "You are the most indelicate noblewoman I have ever met."

"This is not a delicate art," she said.

Past their second meeting, they had forsaken the chapel for a bit of garden that the king's gardeners seemed to have forgotten. It hid in a corner of the greater garden behind a thicket of roses that had grown into a wall: a small patch of overgrown grass, the skeleton of a long-dead tree, and cascades of roses that dizzied him with their scent. He was always scratched and irritable when he made his way through the tunnel that was the only way in, but she was always there before him, and always tidily composed. There was never a scratch on her, or a smudge or any other sign that she had not flown in like a bird.

He would not have put it past her. She had the face of an angel in a cathedral and the heart of a master of arms. Every night she commanded him to learn what she had to teach. He was cruelly short on sleep. It seemed that every waking moment was full of her voice in his ear and her teaching in his head.

None of it had anything to do with magic. It was all stories and poems, lists of names and places and things, torrents of words in languages he had not even known he knew. He was learning them even as she filled his skull with them, until surely they would come streaming out his ears.

"'In the beginning was the Word,'" she said. "In words all things are contained—yes, even magic."

"But you told me magic was beyond words."

"It is," she said. Then, before he could erupt, she went on: "In the beginning is the Word. Word piles on word, just as these roses climb up their wall and spill over. Then there are so many and so complex that they tumble together into a glory of nothingness. And that is where the magic is: in the nothingness on the other side of the Word."

"That makes no sense at all." And yet in a strange way it did. "So why bother with words? Why not go straight to the silence?"

"Magic is not silence," she said.

"But you said—"

"You don't listen carefully enough," she said. "When you learn to listen, the magic will be there."

"But—"

"*Listen,*" said Mathilda.

"I don't know how to—"

"Be quiet," she said.

He went rigid—not at the command but at the sudden shock of understanding. She was not silencing him. She was telling him how to listen.

She nodded as if satisfied. "Now recite to me the four cantrips in order from last to first."

For a moment he had no memory of what cantrips even were. Then he remembered. They were verses, and she had made him learn them from first to last. "Last line to first line?" he asked her.

"Last verse to first," she said with a quelling glance.

He closed his eyes, hunting down the words in a language that bore no resemblance to any dialect of the Frankish tongue. It was an older language, full of strange trills and torrents of liquid syllables. First he had to stretch his mind to fit it, then he had to find the words in a different order than the one that she had taught him.

He was tired. His eyes were gritty from lack of sleep. He had heard some of the king's courtiers speculating that he had a woman somewhere, to disappear so often and so late, but so far none of them had found this hiding place.

He was indulging in distraction. Words, he thought. Words were the key. He found the ones he needed and recited them in the singsong she had taught him, not quite a chant, but not ordinary speech, either.

The rhythm was part of it, the tone and timbre she had enforced on him. If the words were the key, those were the posts and lintel of the gate. He could see—he could almost see—

"Steady," Mathilda's voice said, jarring him out of his half-trance. He could have hit her; but there was no lifting a hand against those cool, quiet eyes.

"Don't force it," she said. "Let it be. It will come. Now, again. Forget the words. Forget yourself. Simply be."

It was like fighting, he thought. Like riding a horse. Like running until the breath was gone and the body was past pain and the race had become the world. On the other side of that was . . .

This.

There were no words. Words, being breath, were gone. He was the world, and the world was contained in him—every living thing and every thing that once had lived or would live, and all the frame of earth and metal and stone that held them together. He could reach out a hand to grasp whatever struck his whim, and when he touched it, impose his will upon it. Water into wine, air into fire, flesh into grass.

Spirits came crowding, twittering like birds, a flutter of wings and talons and eyes. There was no escaping them when there was magic afoot.

Was this magic, then? This sense of endless possibility? He did not feel all-powerful; it was not as grand as that. It simply and wonderfully was.

He turned as the world must turn, vast and slow. His hand, trailing, left a furrow in the sea. He reached casually to level a mountaintop.

A hand blocked his. It was a small hand, but its strength was irresistible. He looked from it to Mathilda's eyes.

He was back in the hidden corner of the garden, sprawled on the untidy grass. She knelt beside him. A pale light shimmered about him, paler than moonlight, and clearer. By it he could see as if it had been daylight.

His nose twitched. "What—"

He struggled to sit up. The tree that had been merely dead was charred black. Parts of it still smoldered.

"What—who—"

"You did that," she said.

"I did not. What I was doing—"

"Your magic woke up," she said, "as it was going to soon or late. Now imagine if it had been in a battle. Or in court—and that had been one of your own men."

"I am imagining," he said through clenched teeth, "what would have happened if you had not meddled with what was best left alone."

His anger surprised her. Her eyes had widened slightly.

He pressed the attack. "Do you know why I made myself forget? Do you know why I shut it away? Because it is no use to me! The less I knew of it, the less I remembered, the more honest a Christian I seemed to be. Now my every breath will be a lie."

"There are priests among us," she said. "Bishops, archbishops. Many an abbot, and popes enough. The Church has given us sanctuary far more often than it has condemned us."

"Then they're liars, too," he said. "You're all liars. Witches, sorcerers, servants of the Devil—"

"We are no friends to the prince below," she said, "or any other force for the world's destruction."

"Including me?"

"You are no more or less dangerous than ignorance ever is."

"That's deadly."

"It can be taught," she said, "and will. I am bound to it."

"Why?"

"It was my choice," she said.

"Because you were given no other?"

"There were others," she said coolly. "Tomorrow I will teach you how to undo what you have done."

"That's not possible."

Her brow arched. He did not quite see what she did. It had something to do with a gesture of the hand, and some part of it was a slant of the eye and a turn of mind.

The charred branches stirred and cracked. Black scales fell; ash blew away in a sudden swirl of wind. Living branches unfolded, sprouting leaves as bright as the first morning of the world. They glowed in the night. Blossoms budded and bloomed, a cloud of white and palest rose. Their scent enveloped him in sweetness.

William's mouth hung open. He could barely muster wits to shut it.

"You are meant for more and better than this," she said, "but whatever you have done, you must know how to undo. It's a law of our order."

"'Our' order?"

"You are born to it, and reborn, for ages out of count."

"I am born to the dukedom of Normandy."

"You are born to more than that, and well you know it." She rose, smoothing her skirts. "You've done well, for a beginning."

That was a dismissal. He refused to submit to it. "You can't leave me in this condition. What if I blast the king, or one of his courtiers?"

"You won't," she said.

"How do you know?"

"Magic costs," she said. "Go to the kitchens first, before you sleep."

"I'm not—"

"Do it."

She had laid a binding on him. A fugitive memory told him what it was. Then the griping in his belly bound him more tightly still.

He was ravenous—starving. He was dizzy with hunger. If the cooks were not awake, he would raid and pillage on his own. Then he would sleep like the dead.

Not the worst battle he had ever fought, on the field or in lordly hall, had taxed his mind and body as this little bit of magic had. Small wonder wizards did not rule the world, if this was what it did to them to try.

❦ CHAPTER 9 ❧

"**M**y lord!"

The voice was bright, brisk, and unbearably loud. William groaned and reached for the blanket to stuff it into his ears.

It was nowhere within reach. He opened one eye, slitting it against the unbearably bright light of a guttering lamp and a lone high window. Gradually and painfully he discerned the shape of the king's squire, with another looming behind him.

"My lord," the boy said, "the king's waiting for you."

"Tell him I'm too sick to move." It was no lie, either. God's bones, what had he been drinking? His skull was like to split.

"His majesty is not in a mood to coddle drunkards." That was a different voice, a deeper one, and there was no mercy in it. "Up, messire. Your liege lord is waiting."

That was not to be argued with. William would have ventured it nonetheless, if he had had any strength to spare.

The squire and the king's man, who was wearing a guard's tunic, hauled William to his feet and thrust him unceremoniously into a basin of scalding water. He yowled and erupted, but they held him down with contemptuous ease.

They bathed and shaved him and clipped his hair close above his ears, and dressed him in the cleanest of his clothes. When they judged him presentable, they escorted him out—somewhat forcibly—and presented him to the king.

He had recovered slightly under their ministrations. His first fear, that he had committed some sin of which he was unaware, had given way to another, which was that someone had spied on his nightly trysts with the lady of Flanders. That failed to alarm him as it should. The king's summons was a reprieve from those blasted lessons, even if it cast him into prison or worse.

*　　*　　*

The king was entertaining a small company of guests in his solar. There was music—a harp and a flute—and wine, which made William's stomach heave, but neither ladies nor dancing. These were all men, high lords and prelates, with the king in their midst.

Henry greeted William with every appearance of goodwill. "My lord!" he called as William passed the door. He held out his hand. "Come, share a cup with me. You know Count Geoffrey, of course."

William peered. He was by no means shortsighted, but this aftershock of God knew what had left him groping and squinting like a blind man. The Count of Anjou he knew, oh yes; all the great lords of France were at least casually acquainted. But casual was as far as it went between the rulers of Normandy and Anjou, what with William's spending most of his life eluding pursuit and imminent slaughter.

For a man who was called the Hammer, Geoffrey Martel was remarkably small and slight, with a clever fox-face and a smile that never quite reached his eyes. He bowed, smiling that smile, as William took the king's cup and pretended to sip. The wine in the cup was strong and heavy with spices; it was all William could do not to gag.

Henry was babbling of trivialities, but William barely heard. The small hairs of his nape stood on end; a growl was trying to shape itself in his throat.

Geoffrey knew what William was. And William knew what Geoffrey was. Devil's brood, they called the lords of Anjou: black heart, black temper, and blood of old Night running black and strong.

This was the other side of what William had been born to be. This was the enemy. The smile had reached those cold eyes at last—and there was nothing mirthful in it.

William lunged, intent on wiping that smile from the face of the earth.

When he could see again, he was on his back with the wind knocked out of him, several dozen new bruises making themselves felt, and a babble of voices washing over him. Only one was clear, and it was directly above him. "He's taken ill. Here, lift him up. Sire—"

"Yes." That was the king. The other voices fell silent as he spoke. "Fetch my physician."

If William could have said anything, he would have declared that he needed no such thing. But he was too preoccupied with remembering how to breathe.

They lifted him onto a bench. He strained to see, but the Count of Anjou was not within his limited sight.

He could breathe again, after a fashion. The man nearest him was a monk in a cowl. He gripped the rough woolen sleeve. "Did I kill him? Where is he?"

The monk turned to look down at him. He was not a young man, but not terribly old, either. The fringe of hair round the tonsure was thick and silver-white. The eyes were dark, taking his measure in a way he knew too well.

His fingers tightened on the monk's sleeve. *Priests and monks,* she had said. And lo and behold, here was one. The smell of magic on him was so strong that it made William sneeze.

The monk must smell it on William, too, though he gave no sign. "Milord count judged it best to retire from the field," he said. His accent was somewhat odd, hinting of origins elsewhere than the kingdom of France.

"You know what he is," William said.

"What do you think he is?" the monk asked gravely.

William glanced about. No one was listening or seemed interested. That would have been most peculiar if this had been an ordinary monk. But where magic was, William knew too well, anything was possible.

He answered the question as directly as he knew how. "He's a devil's get. What's he doing walking like a man?"

"He is a man," the monk said.

"You know he's not."

"By the courtesy of this world," said the monk with steely gentleness, "he is. Nor is he yours to kill, however your gorge may rise at the sight of him. Would you take on the whole county of Anjou?"

"Someday," William said from nowhere that he could have explained, "Normandy will—and it will win."

"But not today," the monk said, "or tomorrow either. Patience is a great gift, my lord. Remember that."

"Patience is all I've ever had," William muttered.

The monk shook his head, smiling faintly, and blessed William's forehead with the sign of the cross.

The king's solar came alive again. People were hovering, staring, wondering aloud what had possessed the Norman duke.

To them the monk said, "A touch of fever—it sent him briefly out of his head. Mestre Chouinard will have medicines for it, I'm sure."

To William's astonishment, they believed the monk. They nodded agreement, or shook their heads in seeming sympathy; the glances they turned toward William had lost the hot edge of hostility.

It must be a spell. William felt the lure of it, to turn any mind to his will. But the ache in his head soared to a crescendo; he could only lie groaning and cursing in his heart all the uses and misuses of magic.

Mestre Chouinard's remedy was a great deal more palatable than William had feared: hot possets, cold cloths, and consignment to bed for a day and a night. The guard and the squire, at the king's command, would assure that he stayed there.

There was a sleeping draught in the posset. When William struggled free of its influence, the king was sitting beside his bed, looking as if he had been there for a while.

William suppressed the urge to slide his hand toward the dagger that he kept under his pillow. If Henry wanted him dead, William would have been food for worms long since.

"Mestre Chouinard informs me that your fever is gone," Henry said by way of greeting.

William nodded. He felt remarkably well, all things considered. He sat up carefully, but his head felt neither dizzy nor sick. "Sire," he said, "my apologies for—"

"No need," Henry said. "You were ill. Count Geoffrey wishes you to know that his bruises will heal, and he bears you no rancor. He hopes that your indisposition will pass quickly."

At the thought of that son of old Night, William swallowed a snarl. His hatred was pure instinct, strong enough even yet to startle him. Dog for cat, snake for rat—this was nothing either rational or politic.

It seemed he hid it well enough. Henry showed no sign of having seen. William said carefully, once he had his voice under control, "I'm well again, thanks to your good physician."

"Excellent," said Henry with visible pleasure. "Then you'll

be able to answer the question I had meant to ask you. Are you ready to go back to Normandy?"

William did not stop to think at all. "Yes," he said. "Yes, I am."

The king smiled, not at all offended by his eagerness. "Your company at court is always welcome, but your duchy needs settling. I've a hundred knights to offer, and such aid and support as you may find yourself needing. It's time you laid solid claim to the seat your father left you."

That was exactly what William had been praying for, but he was all out of joint. In an instant his mood tumbled from high hope to grim suspicion. He caught himself wondering what the king thought to gain with such signal generosity. Was he conspiring with the Angevin count to be rid of the duke's bastard from Normandy?

William was losing his grip if he could be thinking that of the man who, more than anyone else, had raised him since his father left him holding a dukedom he was far too young and weak to hold. "That's more than generous, my lord," he said. "I'll take it gladly."

Henry's smile was swift, with no guile in it that William could detect. "Good man! You're ready now. Go and take what's yours."

"Now? Today?"

"Whenever you wish."

"Today," William said. "My own men—yours—are they—"

"They'll be ready," the king said. "My servants are at your disposal."

William bowed as low he could while sitting up in bed. The king returned the gesture, saluting him in high good humor. "Good, then. Good! God will prosper you."

"So one hopes," William said, but he said it to himself. The king was gone.

A thought was pressing at him, a memory, a niggle of guilt. Mathilda's face; a vow sworn.

William's oath of fealty to the French king was years older than any vow he might have sworn to a sorcerous beauty from Flanders. He was bound to go at the king's command. There was nothing Mathilda could do to stop him.

It was good reasoning, and true as far as it went. William flung down guilt and set his knee in its back. The king had commanded. He was going home. And that was the end of it.

❦ CHAPTER 10 ❦

Mathilda was not surprised to hear that the Norman duke had collapsed in the king's solar. The magic that had roused in him was strong. It was no wonder his body had been too weak to bear it.

She refused to fret that night when he failed to come to her. He was asleep, drugged, under secure guard. One of those guards, the squire Remy, fancied himself in love with her. It was a simple matter to enlist him as a spy.

On the day after William's collapse, when he was sure to be safe under the king's watchful eye, Mathilda was swept up in an outing with a gaggle of ladies from the court. A merchant ship had come up the Seine; it was purported to carry silks from the distant and legendary east. There was nothing for it but that they all must go, with guards and servants, maids and pages, and discover whether the rumor was true.

They were an army, the ladies mounted, the rest afoot, protected from the sun by canopies, advancing in procession through the streets of Paris. The sun was shining; the air was warm. It was a beautiful day to raid the cloth-market, with sallies toward the jewelers, the goldsmiths, and the purveyors of sweet cakes and spiced dainties.

Mathilda seldom remembered that she was young. Today she allowed herself to be as simply mortal as anyone else. One or two of the ladies were pleasant companions, and one or two more had enough learning to make intelligent conversation.

One of these, a baroness from Poitou, proposed an excursion much more exciting, to Mathilda's mind, than a boatload of silk. "My brother is in the cathedral school," she said, "and today, he says, they will be debating the nature of the Trinity."

No one else but Mathilda would choose words over silk. If

she had been Christian enough to believe in sin, she would have had to confess the magnitude of her pleasure in that afternoon. There in a crowded, ill-lit hall reeking of unwashed humanity, she heard such disputation as she had not heard since she left the Ladies and the Wood. It was mere and mortal logic, and therefore not quite as devastating in its perfection as the debates of bards and Druids, but it had a beauty all its own.

She forgot for a while why she was in Paris. She even forgot the one for whom she had been brought here—and that, just this morning, she would have judged impossible.

Remy was sitting in front of her door in the king's palace, looking as miserable as that insouciant young imp could look. Mathilda knew what he would say even before he said it. "I couldn't help it, lady. The king commanded, and you weren't there. I had to do it."

"Do what?" Mathilda demanded, even though she knew.

"I had to help the bas—Duke William pack himself up and ride back to Normandy."

"This soon? This fast?"

Remy shrank down under the force of her temper. "Lady, it was the king's will. The duke agreed to it. He wasn't forced, lady. He said it was time."

"Time! Time to be sane, not—" Mathilda bit off the rest of it. This boy would not understand what William was, or why Mathilda should care where he went. He thought Mathilda had taken a fancy to the young duke—as a goodly number of other women had. Bastard or no, he was a fine figure of a man.

"Lady," said Remy diffidently, but with boldness enough in the circumstances, "he is a duke, and he has a duchy to take control of. He's been scrambling to do that since he was a weanling babe. Now he finally has a chance."

A chance, she thought. A chance to escape her and all the fears that she had roused; the powers she had shown him, the magic she had awakened in him; and above all, the binding she had laid on him. Of course he had run away. Any sensible man would.

But he was not a man, not as other men were. What he had, there was no running from. It would follow him wherever he went; and if he did not learn to master it, it would consume him.

"I'm sorry, lady," Remy said. "I know you liked him."

She only stared at him, but he went white and fled. She sighed. The elation of her afternoon's entertainment was long gone. She had abandoned her duty, and this was the price she paid.

There was a monk in the room she shared with her maids, none of whom was anywhere in evidence. He was sitting beside the cluster of lamps that had come down to her family from old Rome. All the lamps were lit; he was reading a book, as easy and casual as if he had been in the library of his own monastery.

That ease was deceptive. The light of magic in him was carefully damped, but she could smell as well as see it, a faint scent of roses and heated metal.

He looked up from his book as she came in. His eyes were blurred and distant, caught halfway between the words on the page and the living presence in the room, but she could not fail to see the keen intelligence behind them.

He had been much more animated earlier, when he upheld the procession of the Holy Spirit from the Father and the Son. She had seen him debating in the school, spinning elaborate threads of words and logic.

Had he seen her? There was no way to tell.

This was not an enemy, she thought under that half-dreaming stare, but neither was he a friend. He rose and bowed, which was courteous of him; as a man of the Church, he need bow to none but his superiors or his God. She bowed her head in return, keeping silent, letting him be the first to speak.

He might have turned it into a contest, but with a slight, wry twist, he granted her the victory. "Lady. Pardon my intrusion. Your squire admitted me; I would have been content to wait by the door."

"No, no," she said. "It's more comfortable here. I suppose you know who I am; I cry your pardon, but my memory is faulty. I find I can't return the favor."

There was humor in him, she realized, although it was subtle: a glint in the eye, a quirk to the corner of the mouth. "No need for pardon, lady," he said. "We haven't met. I only arrived here yesterday." He bowed again. "Lanfranc of Bec, late of Pavia, lady."

"Ah," she said. That name she knew. "Father Prior. This is an honor."

The prior of Bec, who was a famous scholar and teacher—and by her own witness, that renown was deserved—waved away her honest respect. "I'm a man like any other, lady."

She arched a brow. "Truly?"

"Truly," he said.

"There is the matter of . . ." She flicked her hand. The lamps went out. In the sudden dimness she bade a light grow, shimmering over her fingers, unfolding from them like a strange flower.

He quelled her working with a gesture. That same gesture, completed, restored the lamps to their former condition. "This too is God's gift," he said.

"Surely," she said, "but it's given to few, and to precious few in such measure as yours."

"Or yours, lady. You will be stronger than I."

"But not yet."

"You are young," he said, "and while not foolish, perhaps not granted such judgment as will be yours with greater age and maturity."

She had had enough of dancing around the point. "Yes, I made a mistake. Yes, I know what mistake I made. And what part do you play, Father Prior, in this game of arts and powers?"

"A small one," he said, "by the grace of God."

That was disingenuous. She swept it aside. "So. You're a Guardian of Gaul. Have you come to impose sentence upon me for dereliction of duty?"

"If anyone is to do that, lady," he said, "it should be your father. No; I came to offer such aid as I could, if the duke had stayed where he was put. As it is, lady, you are best advised to follow him to Normandy."

That had been her exact thought, but because it came from him, she struck against it. "How am I to do that? The lady of Flanders has no business in that duchy."

"She may," said Lanfranc, "be summoned home, where duties and kinsmen await her; but she may slip away on the road, and take another way altogether."

"As what? A pilgrim? A wandering juggler?"

He raised a shoulder in a shrug. "Whatever you please, lady."

"And if I don't please to go at all?"

"You will," he said.

"Why? Because you force me—you and the rest of the Guardians, one of whom is my father?"

"Is force necessary, then?" he inquired.

Her lips had gone tight. "Will you come with me?"

"For a while," he said. "My abbey is not far from Caen. That, I suspect, is where he will go."

"No," she said suddenly. "No, he'll not go there first—not until later. He'll go to Falaise."

Falaise, where he was born; where his mother's kin still were. Falaise, where the Old Things were still strong. William would not know why he did it, but it would draw him irresistibly.

She had to be there before him. If he came where he was conceived and born, in the state in which he had left her, the old gods knew what his wavering power would do.

"You had best go," Lanfranc said gently.

"Only I? Have you changed your mind?"

He shook his head.

"You're blaming me, aren't you? For what he's done."

"I blame no one," he said. "It was an error of judgment."

"Would you have done better?"

"Maybe not," he said. "But the sooner it's mended, the better for all of us."

That was self-evident, and damnably wise, too. But she made no move to call for the servants. "I can't just go. Too many people will talk. There's a spell—but it takes a day and a night. Otherwise—"

"There will be a summons from your father," Lanfranc said with quiet confidence. "In the morning your entourage will return to Flanders. You will be seen to travel with it. But you and I, lady, will take the straight way into Normandy."

All the crowding words had emptied out of her. This was a Guardian indeed: he took as much upon himself as her father did, and cared as little to spare her pride.

This was no time to be proud. She had misread her pupil badly—and he had fled because of it. Whatever she could do to mend the mistake, she must do, and soon.

She drew a deep breath, ridding herself of anger, fear, even resentment. "I'm in your hands," she said.

That was respect, that inclination of his head. Somehow she

did not think that his respect was ever easily earned. It did not warm her to him, but it soothed her raw edges a little.

Whatever Lanfranc said to the king, by nightfall it was understood that the lady of Flanders had been summoned back to her father. The court's gossipmongers spun a tale of his having found a husband for her at last; he wanted her home and her dowry bestowed as soon as might be. It was a little precipitous but hardly unheard of, particularly in company with the rumor that Count Baldwin had taken ill and was feeling his mortality.

She was feeling hers, even while she lent her magic to Lanfranc's so that when her escort left the palace, she would seem to be riding with it. There was a spell on her image, a spell of good grace; whatever words were said to it, it would reply with courtly politeness.

It did not speak well of courtiers that a shape of air and enchantment could mimic them so perfectly, but at the moment it was convenient. She left the image feigning sleep in her bed, and put on the clothes that Lanfranc had brought. They were very plain, dark wool and unadorned linen, such as a noblewoman's servant or a prosperous farmer's wife would wear.

She surprised herself with regret as she put aside her much softer linen and finer wool with their bits of embroidery in silk and gold. She should be above such things; but she was no better than the rest after all.

Resolutely she put silliness aside and dressed like a common pilgrim. Lanfranc was waiting near the stable, holding the bridles of a pair of mules. Both were laden with traveling packs, and looked both sturdy and unassuming, like the gown Mathilda wore.

Night had fallen some while since. The moon had not yet risen. The stars were bright and clear above the smokes and human stench of the city.

Mathilda's heart swelled in spite of itself. She had been trammeled here, playing courtier by day and teacher by night— neither of them in perfect comfort. Whatever this was that she went to, with a companion she had met mere hours past, it was right—it was meant. This was the path she was destined to take.

❧ CHAPTER 11 ❧

When William left Paris, he was running away—there was no nobler way to put it. By the time he passed the borders of Normandy, he was running toward something, though exactly what, he could not have said.

The thing that had roused in him had sunk back into torpor, except for a faint, lingering ache behind the eyes. His dreams were strange, but he could make himself forget them. He was living entirely in the body: riding, hunting, fighting. On the road or in hall or in camp of an evening, he was a man as other men were, no more or less wizardly than the rest of them.

Normandy loved him no better than it ever had. But it was his, and for once he had the force to claim it. The king's knights were his surety; the victory at Val-ès-Dunes was still fresh in memory, the deeper wounds still healing, and women mourning their men who had died.

When they called him William Bastard now, there was a crooked pride in it. He was their bastard—and little by little, village by village, he was becoming their duke.

In his dreams the land sang where he walked or rode on it. When he was awake, his body sang, muscle and bone exulting in pure motion. Men were coming to him, nobles greater and less, laying their weapons in his hands and swearing fealty in the same words and form as when he was a child, when his father had died and he was left to rule—but this time, the words came from the heart. This time it was real.

Or at least, as real as it needed to be. Without the king's men standing behind him in their fine armor and their air of royal authority, he would have had to fight his way toward Caen. But he swore an oath to himself, soon after the first baron knelt at his feet and swore to serve him as liege lord. He would make this country his own, and rule it as he pleased, free of his debt to the king of France.

The roads were infested with bandits. Nor were most of them honest robbers. These were men of rank and property, armed knights, raiding where their fancy took them, plundering and raping and stealing for the pleasure of it. Not all of them were wise enough to avoid the duke's company, as large as it had grown with newly sworn vassals.

William had hunted out a nest of them not far from Falaise, and taken their leader's head. It stood at a crossroad now, impaled on the man's own lance, to warn anyone with like ambitions that there was a duke again in Normandy.

His blood was still running high with the exhilaration of battle. The reiver knight had put up a good fight. His horse was a fine one, too—stolen, William had no doubt, from another and wealthier knight.

The stallion was William's now, a tall and robust grey with a remarkably soft mouth. The bit in it was a plain bar—hardly enough, as more than one of his following pointed out, to keep the beast from taking it in his teeth and bolting for hell and gone. But the horse was a willing servant if a man rode him light. His willingness sang through William, a giddy sensation that after a long while he realized must be happiness.

He had not felt anything like that since he was a child. Because of it, instead of passing by the oak groves and tanneries of Falaise on his way to Caen, he led his by now rather imposing army into the town.

It was the day before the eve of May, and a fine, warm, bright day full of flowers and birdsong. William had no patience for poetry, but he did love the scent of the roses that grew in tangles and thickets along the road. The oak wood rose beyond them, full of green darkness even at noon.

Through the thudding of hooves on the packed earth of the road, the jingle of mail, the rumble of men's voices, he thought he could hear the whisper of leaves. There were words there in a language that the lady of Flanders had taught him; but when he caught himself straining to hear, he dragged his mind back to the road and the army.

The stench of the tanneries wafted down in a vagrant breeze, returning him resoundingly to the mortal world. Some of the knights from France gasped and choked. The Normans taunted them. "Oh, ladies!" they warbled in high voices. "Fetch me a nosegay, do! Or by Our Lady, I'll faint dead away!"

One of them hacked a thorny branch from a rose bramble that straggled beside the road, and presented it with a broad flourish to the most obviously greensick of the French. The knight, who was young and inclined to be a hothead, struck the branch down and clapped hand to his sword.

William's hand dropped over his. The boy's angry flush turned green again; he looked honestly ready to faint. "Easy, messire," William said. "It's a piss-poor joke, but it's the best you'll find in these parts."

"No wonder," the boy said with a curl of the lip, "with all the piss pots they've got stinking to heaven."

The Normans roared with laughter. As a jest it was not the best William had ever heard, but it served the purpose. The edge of tension eased; his Normans swept the young French knight into their circle and set about educating him in the finer points of local wit.

William let go the breath he had been holding, then nearly gagged. The warmer the day, the riper the tanneries, and the wind was blowing the stink straight down the road.

A wave of dizziness washed over him. It had nothing to do with the stench, or with the warmth of spring sun on armor. It came up through his horse's body from the earth below, filling him like a draught of strong wine.

He gripped the high pommel of his saddle and squeezed his eyes shut. In a moment, to his relief, the dizziness passed. It was nothing, he told himself. A touch of quartan fever, a bit of shock at the reek of Falaise. He had been living in France too long, that was all. He was as delicate as the boy from Paris.

The road rounded its familiar bend. He looked up at the rock of Falaise and the hulk of timber and stone atop it that was the castle. He had been born there in a cramped and windowless room, with the duke's men on guard without, but servants of much older powers in attendance within.

Those powers were still here. He could feel them. They slept lightly in the earth and drifted in the air. They were waking, sensing his presence.

Dizziness struck again, this time nearly strong enough to

send him reeling out of the saddle. If he had not already been clutching the pommel, he would have fallen flat on his face.

He should not have come here. He should have gone straight to Caen. The thought was clear, but it could not seem to find its way to his tongue. The grey stallion carried him, mute and helpless, through the gate and into the town.

❧ CHAPTER 12 ❧

Lanfranc barely waited for Mathilda to settle in her mule's saddle before he sent his own trotting purposefully toward the stable gate. The way he chose led along the bank of the river, following the curve of the isle on which the palace stood, until at the prow, where the cathedral was, he paused.

Here as so often where the Christians were, one of their holy places sat atop a place of old power. The bonds of stone and prayer had been skillfully wrought here; they contained but did not constrain the Old Things. Whoever had set the wards had been of Mathilda's kind, and gifted, too. Mathilda granted her, or him, a moment's reverence.

Lanfranc was already well ahead in the starlight, circling the square widdershins, against the track of the sun. Mathilda shivered involuntarily. He should have gone sunwise, she thought. But he was a Guardian, one of the four protectors of Gaul. Surely he knew more than she.

As Lanfranc's circle completed itself, the light of stars and the rising moon gathered into a shimmering track, running down the face of the bell tower and flowing out across the square. It was a straight track, a road of magic, and the power in it made Mathilda's ears hum.

Lanfranc was already on it. So should she be. She must be in Falaise before William came there. There was no other road so direct or so short.

She stiffened her back and urged her mule forward. The beast was as reluctant as she had been, but her will prevailed. As the mule's neat, narrow hoof touched the track, a shock ran through them both.

There was always a moment of confusion as the mortal world touched the world of magic, but this was so strong that it nearly felled Mathilda. It was a great effort to gather herself, to lift her head and see that Lanfranc seemed unperturbed. It was her youth, that was all, and a weakness to which she had not known she was subject.

She let the mule find its own way. It sought out its fellow, following it with head down and long ears slanted back in mulish resentment. Mathilda's mood was much the same, but her course was set. She must follow this track to its end.

She had traveled straight tracks before, to and from the Ladies' Wood that was no longer quite in the world, but those had been smooth, well trodden, and strongly protected by the Ladies' power. This was a wild track, open to any who could raise the power to walk on it.

The hewn stone and flowing water of the Île de la Cité were gone. They rode through a field of stars, with the whisper of wind in branches below their feet. Spirits and beings of the realms of earth and heaven were all about them, doing whatever beings of their various kinds did.

Mathilda was not as wise in the ways of the aether as she would have liked to be. That would have been the burden of her teaching when she returned to the Wood—but instead she had traveled to the Île, where she had tried, and failed, to teach what little she knew.

She would mend that if she could. Meanwhile she had to trust her guide. The navigation of straight tracks was another skill she lacked. She had few useful arts, when she stopped to think. Certainly none of them had been of use with the Norman duke.

Such thoughts were dangerous on this road. She crushed them down and walled them in the steel of her will.

The road unfurled before her. The stars wheeled. The wood of the world transmuted into the surge and sigh of a sea. A stream of shining forms was passing over it, advancing toward a vast and crumbling fortress. Within the riven walls she glimpsed flashes of green, and once a standing stone, a sentinel on a hilltop, such as guarded the length and breadth of Brittany.

Her own way led crosswise to that one. Where the ways met, hers rose above and the other below, with neither touching the other. Lanfranc was already past the crossroad. She could feel his working growing weaker, the high road collapsing toward the lower.

Her mule chose just then to be a perfect mule. It stopped short as the road buckled, and with mulish wisdom, refused adamantly to move either forward or back.

Maybe she was not as insistent as she could have been. The migration of spirits intrigued her. The place where they were going, she saw with clearer eyes now she was closer to it, was a green island in a turbulent sea. The fortress about it was made of prayer and cold iron—like the wards of the Île de la Cité, but stronger, darker, fiercer. These were Christian with teeth, raised to keep out all powers that were not of the faith, and destroy those that defied the ban.

By that she knew the name of the island: the isle of Britain as it had been in the old time, before the Saxons seized it and christened it Angla-land, England. Something or someone had weakened the Saxon walls until they began to fall, and let the Old Things in.

Her road touched the road to Britain, meeting it with a soft shiver and a whisper of inhuman voices. The Old Things streamed around and over and through her.

That was a strange sensation, like a wind blowing under her breastbone. The spirit left behind a memory of warmth and a flicker of laughter.

Its fellows tugged at her, plucking her hem and her sleeves. *Come,* they cried in their thin eerie voices. *Come and dance with us!*

In those voices she heard the pain of exile and the joy of return—and fear. Fear of cold iron and colder hallows. As broken as the walls were, powers within were laboring to restore them.

Even as she stood at the crossroad, she saw a tower go up, a skeleton of cold iron overlaid brick by brick with a fabric of psalms. A company of spirits, trapped within the sudden enclosure, went up like torches at the touch of iron and prayer.

They had been harmless beings, creatures of air, whose only interference in human life might be a faint flicker as one of them flitted through a candle flame. It was cruel and wanton destruction, and there was no need for it at all.

Mathilda urged the mule toward the tower. In the lower world it must have been an abbey. The mule, for a wonder, gave way to her will. It had a surprising turn of speed, and a good leap down the glimmering track.

She should have expected the shock of bursting from the

track to the mortal world, but her mind was so caught up in outrage that she never thought to protect herself.

She was fortunate. Her body did not break; she did not go mad. The mule, like all good beasts, traveled the track without loss of self or dignity; it was unperturbed as starlight and magic broke apart into cold damp air, cold damp stone, and a circle of startled faces in dark cowls.

It was a monastery, yes, and this was its chapel. Candles glimmered about the altar. A ragged chorus of the night office thinned and died away. She in her dark clothes on the dark mule must be an apparition to strike the fear of God in the worst of doubters—and these were monks, whose faith was strong enough to destroy any creature of magic that touched it.

She could think of nothing better to do than bow to the altar and sign herself with the cross. Gasps ran round the circle. As she straightened, she found that one of the monks had flung himself at the mule's feet.

He was an awkward creature, all arms and legs, and the voice that babbled up from the floor seemed young. His babble was in the Saxon tongue, of which she knew a little: enough to guess what she could not clearly understand.

"Oh, lady! Be you saint or angel or Blessed Mother herself, you honor us with your holy presence."

Mathilda had not expected that. An exorcism would have been more to the point. But these Saxons were a strange lot. They not only denied magic, they destroyed it. Maybe they could not recognize it when they saw it, after so long within their walls of iron.

Her silence did nothing to disabuse the monks of her sanctity. One of them had begun to sing in a clear, tuneful voice, what appeared to be a hymn to the Virgin. There were hooks in that hymn, sharp-edged fragments of old workings, as vicious to magic and magical beings as caltrops on a battlefield.

"Stop," she said.

The lone Latin word cut across the stream of Saxon. It trickled to a halt.

"Sing in Latin," she said. "Sing psalms; sing the offices. No more Saxon. Saxon is not the language of angels or the spirits of heaven."

They were gaping at her, all of them: a circle of blank, astonished faces.

"When you sing," she said, "in your hearts, bless the angels; bless the living beings whom God has made, greater and lesser, armored in flesh or wrought of the living air. Praise all creation, and not only that which your eyes can see."

She had judged rightly, she thought as she looked from face to face. They did not know what the working was that they labored to sustain. It was prayer, that was all they knew. If any of them was aware of what it did, he must believe that he had banished a pack of devils.

The monk who had sung before now began a new song, the great Magnificat itself. He had taken her words to heart. She felt the walls of iron begin to crumble, the tower of prayer to weaken, laying its summit open to heaven.

A small, long-nosed spirit like a winged mouse ventured the opening in the fabric of the world, sniffing curiously. The scent of incense made it sneeze, but it did not flutter away. It drifted down a thin slant of moonlight.

Moonlight? But—

The moon had been waning to its dark when she left the Île. Now it was close to the full.

The track had taken her not only out of place but out of time—how long, she had no way to tell. She could hardly ask the monks, who were rapt in their music.

The track was waiting. She knew where she must go—and pray the old gods she had not overshot the time, and so destroyed what hope she had of repairing her misjudgment.

She had never opened a track, but she had seen it done often enough. She knew how to bend her magic just so, to fit to the track. When it was fitted, it drew her with it, up and out and into the moonlight.

To the monks in the chapel she must have seemed to dissolve into a shimmer of silver light. It would be reckoned a miracle, no doubt, and the apparition celebrated as a visitation from heaven.

The crossroad was deserted. The great riding of Old Things had passed. As Mathilda stood in the too-bright moonlight, she saw road after road branching all about her, thick as the boughs of trees in a forest. One of them was the way to Falaise. She had known which it was, until she looked closely and saw so many others.

She fought down the rush of panic. She was not lost. Time had escaped her, but she still knew where she was going. It was that road. *That* one, not the one next to it or the one bending off from it or the one behind her.

The feel of it was perfectly distinct. It was like a cord of silk, holding her to that road and no other. It was, she realized, the binding she had laid on William. He had eluded her but not his oath.

Lanfranc was nowhere within sight or sound. He was days gone, if the moon told the truth—please the gods, not months or years. The tracks were treacherous with time, she knew that. Her fault for wandering so far off her intended path.

She turned the mule toward the road that, wherever it led, had William on the other end of it. The mule offered no objection. She let its calm infect her. She was not alone or abandoned. She had a purpose, even if it was too late to do what she had planned to do. There would be something still to be done—of that she was sure.

But for the mule she could not have stayed on the track. It was slippery, constantly trying to shift, to become another way, under another's power. Forces from without, either mindless or simply malicious, tugged at her, tempting her to stray once more. But this time they had no power over her. The binding was stronger than any of them.

Something was rising ahead. She gathered her weary wits and such magic as she could into what defenses she might. But as she drew closer, she realized that it was not rising against her. It was a place of great power, a focus of magic.

If this was not the oak wood of Falaise, then she was lost, with no strength left to continue. Even the mule seemed to be growing tired. It plodded toward the shape of darkness that was the grove.

When she touched the rein in a moment of indecision, it ignored her. The bit was clamped firmly in its teeth.

She let it carry her where it would. As she drew closer she began to see the branches and the lobed shape of leaves, and to catch the rich scent of earth and greenery. The moonlight was growing brighter, bright as gold. The warmth of sunlight kissed her face.

With no shock at all, as softly as if she had walked from a

dark castle into a sunlit court, she had left the track and emerged—where?

The oak rose above her, ancient and twisted with years. Gold gleamed, sunk deep in the trunk: a Druid's sickle, still recognizable by the shape and the sheen of it.

Just outside the circle of the oak's crown, grass grew spring-thick, spring-rich. The mule stopped, lowered its head, and began to graze.

Mathilda slid from its back. Her knees buckled; she let herself crumple to the grass. It was damp with dew. Morning, then, and a fair day, warm enough already that she let fall her cloak and hood and lay in her gown, soaking in the sun's warmth and the earth's sweetness.

Little by little they revived her. The oak was deeply reassuring: surely there were not two such in Gaul, so old and so heavily imbued with power, with the sickle to mark and bind it. Here the year-king had found the goddess on the night of the winter solstice, and brought a great king's soul back into the world.

She could see it if she chose: darkness, firelight, the two wound in a lover's embrace. She could hear the pipes and the drums, and feel the rhythm of dancers' feet on the mold beneath the trees. It was here still, clear as if caught in amber.

Her body sang with music now twenty years gone. She rose, staggering a little, and caught the mule's trailing rein. The mule insisted on a last mouthful of grass, but then it sighed and submitted.

❧ CHAPTER 13 ❧

The duke had arrived in Falaise the day before. The market was abuzz with it, even if the scarlet banner with its pair of golden lions had not been flying over the castle. People here were proud of him, and not inclined to hear any ill words, either.

Mathilda paid a cracked penny for a brown loaf and a wedge of cheese and a fistful of dried apples. A lifetime of carefully schooled manners barely kept her from wolfing them down. In her awareness she had been traveling for a handful of hours, but her stomach was ready to believe that she had not eaten in more than a fortnight.

Magic and one's stomach were not the best of allies. Mathilda sat on a doorstep and made herself eat in measured bites. The mule shared the bread and half of the apples, but sneered at the cheese.

From here she could see the squat tower of the castle, and the banner unfurling in a gust of wind. Some of the duke's men were in the market: big broad figures dressed in their inevitable mail.

It was interesting to see them from below as it were, a lone woman dressed in simple clothes and holding the rein of a sturdy but unassuming mule. When she was the lady of Flanders in the latest fashion, decked in gold and mounted on a white palfrey, they seemed smaller. And less intimidating.

They were buying bread and ale and a bit of frippery, no doubt for a woman. None seemed inclined toward murder or rapine. They did not see Mathilda at all; she was common and therefore invisible.

That stung. She was accustomed to being noticed; for the first time she realized that she preferred it. As much of a nuisance as it could be, it was notably better than no notice at all.

She chewed and swallowed a last bite of cheese, then slipped it with the remainder of the bread and apples into the mule's saddlebag. Her palms were damp. She wiped them on her skirts and squared her shoulders.

Up until now, she had avoided the thought that wanted to be foremost in her mind. She was alone. She had never been alone.

From the moment she was born, there had been guards, maids, nurses. All of those were far away in Flanders. The guide who should have brought her here was lost.

Deliberately? It could be. Something was breaking down walls in Britain. Lanfranc must be part of it.

She would ask him when she found him. But for the moment she did not know where he was.

It was terrifying. The mule rubbed its head against her, knocking her half off her feet. She pulled herself back into the saddle. The mule turned without her urging and plodded toward the castle.

At mule-pace Mathilda was in a position to hear substantial portions of conversations as she passed by market stalls and doorways and taverns. She was also, as she drew nearer the castle, subject to the vagaries of wind and wandering air, which brought the reek of tanneries to her in greater and lesser waves.

It was a bracing smell. Potent, for a fact. But she had smelled no better in certain quarters of Paris. She breathed shallowly and endured until the ascent of the hill took her out of reach of the stink.

People here were used to it, clearly. Their talk was of anything and everything but the perpetual stench, and often of the duke. Normandy was not settled yet, she gathered, but they had hopes that it would be soon.

"You'd better pray, then," said a man outside a stall that offered an array of hides both raw and tanned. "I saw him ride in yesterday, and he looked ready to fall off his horse."

"He did not!" the leather merchant said indignantly. "He was looking fine and handsome, and a fair bit cleaner than he used to before the king took him in hand."

"He was as green as a spring onion, God smite me if he wasn't," the man declared. "Have you seen him since? I haven't."

"He's been up in the castle, being duke," she said, "and

you're spreading lies, Pierre Aubin, and I'll not listen to any more of them." In proof of which, she pressed fists to her ears and squeezed her eyes shut.

He thrust out his jaw regardless. "I saw what I saw," he said. "That boy's sick, and no mistake."

The mule carried Mathilda on past, but she had heard all she needed to hear. She had come none too soon, but maybe— maybe—soon enough. If Lanfranc was there before her, she dared to think that there was hope. She refused to consider the alternative.

No one in or near the castle had heard of the prior of Bec, or seen a monk who looked like him. Mathilda hardly needed to feign weariness in the castle's court, or summon a judicious tear. The guards were taken with her face and the suggestion of nubile body under the pilgrim's garb, and drew conclusions that she chose not to alter.

"Demoiselle, if your uncle comes here, we'll be sure to tell him you've been looking for him," said the captain who happened to be in the court just then. He was not as young as the others, and had the look of a man well and truly married; he had a daughter, she could guess, and a soft heart for a maiden in distress.

"You don't think," she said in a soft and tired voice, "that I could wait here a while, and maybe he'll come?"

The captain barely hesitated. "But of course! Here, demoiselle—it's a bit rough in the hall, with all of my lord duke's men in it, but there's a bit of solar where the ladies used to sit in the old days. We've kept it up, and it's clean. It's quiet enough to let you rest a bit."

"That's generous, messire," she said, "but if my uncle comes, how will he know where I am?"

"Don't you fret," the captain said. "I'll see that he's told."

It was certainly tempting, and humbling to know how eager she was to find her own heights again—even if under false pretenses. It was also, she reminded herself, a godsend. In the solar she would be well within reach of the duke.

She nodded to the captain, letting her head droop with tiredness. "That would be most helpful," she said, "and I thank you."

"No need," he said. "It's my pleasure." He beckoned. Half a dozen guardsmen leaped to be of service. He backed most of

them down with a hard glance, but one—plain, imposingly
scarred, and almost as old as he was—was granted the privilege
of escorting the guest to the solar. Another, disappointed but
obedient, led the mule away to the stable.

Mathilda turned slowly in the room. It was magnificent—it
rivaled the richest chamber in the king's palace in Paris. It was
also spotlessly clean, which somewhat surprised her, and very
tidy. And yet it had an air of distinct disuse. The style of the tapestries reminded her of those her grandmother had embroidered in her youth, and the furnishings looked older still. The
last lady who had embroidered at the frame now put away in the
corner must have left before William's father became duke.

William's mother had given birth to him in this castle,
Mathilda knew, but she had not lived there—whether by her
own choice or the late duke's, Mathilda could not tell. There
was no remembrance of her here, either personal possession or
ghost of long-gone magic.

As Mathilda debated whether to explore the room or to sink
down to one of the tall chairs set round the walls, a woman in a
servant's gown stepped briskly through the door. Mathilda drew
herself up without thinking. The woman went down in a deep
curtsey. "Lady," she said. "I'm to ask—is there anything you
would like me to bring you?"

Mathilda opened her mouth to deny that she was a lady of
rank, but the lie hardly seemed worth the effort. She inclined her
head instead, and said, "A little water to wash in, if you will."

"Of course, lady," the servant said. "Sit; rest. I'll be back
directly."

Mathilda decided to take the servant's advice. One chair
stood in a slant of sunlight; its cushion was faded where the
light fell, but rich with bright embroidery elsewhere.

The warmth was welcome on her face, and the light soothed
her tired eyes. She was almost asleep when the water came, and
with it a cup of spiced wine and a bowl of dried figs in honey.
The figs must have been the last of the old year's stores: the servant handled them as if they had been made of gold.

She tasted one. It was dark and sweet. The wine was lighter,
almost pungent. Someone who knew herbs and spices had
mixed it to keep away sleep. She almost regretted that, but here
of all places, she could hardly afford to let down her guard.

The servant hovered unobtrusively, waiting on her command. That was so familiar and so reassuring that she could not help but smile. "Tell me," she said. "I've been traveling so long, I've lost track of the days. Is it nearly Pentecost?"

"Oh, no, lady," the woman said. "It's the eve of May." She crossed herself, but then she made another sign, a subtle sign, that Mathilda knew well. "The old ones, you know, lady—they used to say that on May Eve, the doors of the Otherworld would open, and strange things would walk under the stars. Not that it's anything a good Christian should notice, lady, but it's an odd day still. You never know what will come of it."

"Indeed," said Mathilda, "one never does."

The servant was still hovering. Mathilda smiled at her and said, "I'll rest, I think, if I may."

"Of course, lady," the woman said, accepting the dismissal.

Mathilda would dearly have loved to curl up in one of those capacious chairs and go soundly to sleep, but it was terribly late—if not quite as late as she had feared. When the servant was well gone, she circled the room.

As she had thought, the tapestry of flowers and birds concealed an opening. There was a landing outside, with a steep narrow stair leading past the solar.

If she knew William, he would choose the top of the tower to lair in—and keep a rope on the roof in case of attack from below. Therefore she went up instead of down.

His door was guarded. The man who stood on the landing just below, sword drawn and at rest, relaxed but alert, never saw Mathilda come up past him. At most he felt the hint of a breeze, and saw the flicker of a shadow.

She slipped through the door into a room as bare as a monk's cell. It had been ornate once; there were traces of bright paint on the walls, and hooks from which tapestries must have hung. But for William it offered no luxury but a larger window than usual for a castle, with its shutter fastened open.

She had more than half expected to find him lying as he had been when she first dreamed of him, asprawl and enspelled, but he was sitting up on the cot with his head in his hands. He looked like a long night in a tavern and a long morning's repentance.

There was a stool by the door. Mathilda sat on it softly, gathering her skirts about her.

It was a long while before he showed any sign of knowing that she was there. She was glad of the respite; it gave her time to rest. She slowed her breathing to match his, so that he could not hear any other breath in the room, and held herself perfectly still.

❦ CHAPTER 14 ❦

William should not be indulging himself. He had a hall full of men below, and vassals coming to offer him either tribute or treachery—he doubted they themselves knew which. He had to show no weakness, if he was to take full control of Normandy.

He had been worse than a fool to come to Falaise. The illness that he had thought himself well rid of was back in force, pounding in his skull and roiling his stomach. He had got through the day before with gritted teeth and an early retreat to bed, and managed to drag himself out this morning; but by noon he had slunk out of sight to nurse his head, which was getting worse.

He had to get over it and get back down there before the tables went up in the hall for dinner. He went so far as to gather himself and start to stand up, before he doubled over, heaving helplessly.

Small capable hands held an earthen basin under his chin. He did not recognize the basin, but the hands and the face to which they belonged were all too familiar.

The rush of relief startled him speechless. No matter how she had got here or why she had come, she was here—and she would get rid of this damnable sickness.

He was already better. He could see again. His ears had stopped ringing. The knot in his belly had begun to loosen.

Mathilda neither gloated nor upbraided him. She laid the reeking basin aside and said coolly, "Get up. Get dressed."

"What—"

She hauled him to his feet and shook him until his eyes came into focus. "Listen!" she said as sharply as he had ever heard her speak. "There's no time to waste. If there are excuses you can make for being gone until morning, you had better make them. I can't spare the power to fashion an image."

He could not understand half of what she was talking about, but the other half was clear enough. "Gone? Until morning? What—"

"If you don't do as I say," she said with banked heat, "you'll be a great deal more indisposed than you have been. That was raw magic working in unprotected flesh. You don't want to know what it can do if you don't learn to master it."

"And whose fault is that?" he demanded.

"Yours," she said swiftly, "for running when you should have stayed to learn. You broke a binding and you left your magic to fester. Did you think you do either of those things without paying for it?"

"I couldn't stay. The king—"

Her cold stare silenced him. "It's not too late," she said, "yet. You know what tonight is."

"Beltane," he said unwillingly. It was as if she had dragged the word out of him, though she had done nothing but fix those eyes on him. "What does that have to do with—"

"When the gates of the Otherworld are open," she said, "and so are the gates of a man's magic . . . things can come in. Or his soul can go out. Or both. In any man that's a terrible thing. In a man of rank and power, it's worse."

William shuddered. Whether she had meant to or no, she had brought to his mind the face of Geoffrey of Anjou. "I could be—what—"

"Worse," she said.

"How could I be worse than the son of a devil?"

"*You* have magic," she said, "strong enough to draw in greater powers than those that merely lust to rule over human people. Those powers will want more than earthly dominion. They'll want heaven above and hell below."

"All they're likely to get is Normandy."

"They'll have you, whose body was begotten at the darkest time of the year, of blood both royal and ancient; whose soul came from beyond the world to rule as it has ruled before. You've been tempered in the forge, messire. Tonight, you come forth as true steel—or you crack."

"I've already cracked," William said. His head was aching again.

"You're dallying," she said. She flung open the chest at the bed's foot and riffled quickly through it, until she had found the clothes he wore to hunt in. They were plain, except for the shirt they were leather, and they were sturdy enough to thrust through a thicket of brambles. When she showed clear signs of intending to dress him in them, he snatched them from her hands.

He pulled them on quickly, but she was halfway out the door before the laces were properly tied. He reached for his sword that hung from a peg by the door.

Her hand struck his arm aside. "No cold iron," she said.

"But—" he began. "I haven't told anybody—you said—"

She gripped his wrist and drew him sharply toward the stair.

It seemed Mathilda knew this castle better than William himself did—and he had lived in it at intervals since he was born. She led him to the ladies' solar, down a stair he had not known was there, through a dank and reeking passage that skirted the kitchen midden, and out a postern gate so old and forgotten that it had had grown up thick with grass and brambles.

William was glad of his leather tunic and leggings then. Mathilda passed through the thicket as she had the one in the king's palace, without catching her skirt or ruffling her hair. It seemed as if the thorns bent backward at her touch.

He shook away the distraction. A faint track led down from the postern, steep enough that he needed most of his attention to keep from going down it headfirst.

The sun was still well up in the sky. The people of Falaise, both town and castle, went about their daily business, oblivious to their duke who crept away from them by a forgotten path.

He had done a great deal of that in his life, and usually for his life, but since he met Mathilda it had been growing stranger. This Beltane run down the rock of Falaise and through a town that did not know him without his guards and his banner, would have been exhilarating if it had not been so baffling.

They shuffled out through the gate between a farmer with an empty cart and a full purse, and a train of mules laden with tanned hides for the market in Caen. A man and a woman afoot, plainly dressed, with not even a meat-knife between them, attracted no notice.

To a man accustomed to traversing distances on horseback, it was a long and tedious trudge away from the town and toward the oak grove—the Druids' grove, people called it, whispering the name where no priest could hear. William's feet dragged as he drew closer, but Mathilda refused to let him stop.

The light in the grove was gold touched with green, sunlight streaming through leaves onto the russet and new-grass green of the wood's floor. The quiet was unnaturally deep for as close as they were to a busy road and a crowded town. The only sounds here were the whisper of leaves and the song of birds, and the chitter of a squirrel as it ran along a branch over William's head.

He could almost have sworn that the squirrel was speaking words, cursing him for an interloper. But that was foolish, and he was giddy with the sudden absence of either pain or confusion. In this place his head was clear, his body strong. He drank the light like wine.

Mathilda stumbled. William caught her without thinking. As he touched her, he staggered. Whatever pain or exhaustion he had felt was nothing to what burdened her.

She had never even hinted at it. He swept her up in his arms. She gasped in startlement but did not struggle. After a moment she let herself relax in his grip.

She was either remarkably arrogant or unbelievably trusting. Her weight barely taxed his renewed strength. There was a peculiar pleasure in the way she let her head rest against his shoulder.

He had no idea where he was going, and she seemed to have fallen asleep. He kept on walking forward, for lack of greater inspiration.

The grove could not be this large. He had been walking for an hour and still had not come to the end of it. The sun was visibly lower than it had been. The squirrel had left him some time ago; the birds had fallen silent. The only sound now was the beating of his heart in his ears and the shuffle of his feet in the mold of leaves.

Mathilda stirred in his arms. She yawned and began to stretch. Somewhat startled, he set her on her feet. She swayed, but before he could move she steadied herself. Her eyes flicked round the grove. A brow lifted. "You found your way here by yourself?"

"You were asleep," he said. If he sounded sullen, then that was no more than she deserved.

"I do feel much better," she said, unruffled as always, "and you did rather well. We're close to where we should be. Come, follow me."

He shook out his arms and rolled his shoulders, not caring if she saw. She showed no sign of having noticed: she was already in motion, striding between two trees that looked exactly like every other pair of oaks in this place. Unless maybe the sun slanted through them differently, or something about the pattern of branches was not the same as the rest. Maybe—

She was almost gone. He flung himself in pursuit.

This was still a grove of oaks, but it did not feel like the place he had walked out of. This was thicker, older, wilder. The sun that only a moment before had been some time yet from setting now hovered on the horizon; the light it cast was more red than gold.

Mathilda stood on the edge of a clearing. Four figures stood in it. For an instant William took them for standing stones, but they were alive; they breathed.

Two were men, two were women. One of the men was dressed as a noble of rank, with a golden collar and a cotte of crimson silk. The other was a monk in a plain black habit. The women seemed less of the world William knew: one all in white, with white hair streaming loose down her back, and skin like milk, and eyes as pale as water. The other was as vivid as the first was colorless, hair as bright as gold, eyes as blue as flax flowers, lips ripe and red and begging to be kissed. Her garment shimmered like fishes' mail; it clung as close to her body as if it had been her own skin.

William stopped short behind Mathilda. As small as she was, he could see easily over her head, and yet in a strange way he felt as if she shielded him from God—or the old gods— knew what.

She appeared to feel none of his unease. She bowed to each of the waiting figures in turn. "Father," she said to the man in gold, and to the monk: "Prior Lanfranc." Each of the others was merely, "Lady." Each bowed in response. It was a courtly dance, yet it fit this place.

It anchored William somewhat, as well. Now that she had

named him, William recognized the Count of Flanders. And that was the prior of Bec, whom William had met in the king's palace. He had not known the man in this light: he seemed younger, nobler, and far more powerful here than he had in Paris.

The other two apparently were to remain mysterious, but he was not going to make a fool of himself by demanding to know who they were. If that was Mathilda's game, he was not playing it.

The white lady spoke in a voice that made no effort to be heard, and yet was impossible to ignore. "It is time," she said.

Mathilda bowed again, to the ground. William refused to move. His jaw had set. He was regaining his strength but losing control of his temper. In a very little while he was going to wrap his fingers around someone's throat and shake some sense out of him—or her.

"Steady," Mathilda said under her breath as she rose.

William's fingers snapped into fists, but he did not hit anything with them. He stayed close behind her as she moved out into the clearing.

The last light of the sun was preternaturally bright there, touching each blade of grass with molten gold. They were not in the world that William was determined to live in. That was lost somewhere behind.

Things were rising in the shadows of the Wood. The four who waited stood like pillars in the gloom, gathering the remnants of light to themselves until they glowed with a pale sheen. Mathilda halted in the center of their circle, with William still close behind her.

He should not have done that. He should have stayed on the forest's edge. Better yet, he should have stayed in Falaise—locked in his room with the blankets over his head.

When he reached the center, he felt the earth shift, then steady, as if it had rebalanced under him. The Count of Flanders and his companions stood unmoving.

Guardians, he thought. They protected—what?

"Gaul," said Mathilda, reading him as easily as ever. "They are the Guardians of Gaul. Its magic is in their hands, its defense in their charge."

"Why are they here?"

"To protect," she said.

"Damn it," said William, "stop being so bloody cryptic for once and tell me what I need to know!"

"We're here for you," said a voice behind him, rich and bubbling with laughter.

It was the lady in the gown of fishes' mail. Her eyes took him in with visible approval. "I like this body better than the last," she said. "Not that it was unpleasant to look at, but it ran more toward lean and wiry. I do like a strapping figure of a man."

William fought the urge to wriggle like a child under that dismayingly frank scrutiny. Women did like him, but he had never let it go to his head—or his privates, either. But this one spoke of even less comfortable things, as if she had actually known the man he was before. As if he could have been anyone before, and not simply a mote in the eye of God.

Her eyes laughed, reading him as easily as Mathilda could, and finding him transparently amusing.

The earth began to rumble underfoot. The trees swayed. William smelled a hint of brimstone, a warning of lightning.

"Melusine," the white lady said, soft but weighted with warning.

The bold lady lowered her eyes, but there was no repentance in them. William's teeth ground together.

A blinding bolt split the sky.

"William," said Mathilda. Her voice was gentle as the white lady's, and no less ominous.

He opened his mouth to protest that he had had nothing to do with it, but she gripped his arms and shook him. She was always stronger than he expected; even though he braced his feet, she rattled his teeth in his head.

The earth quieted. The stars shone down, tranquil again. His rush of temper was gone. He should have been outraged at the liberties she persisted in taking, but somehow, through some twist of magic, she had made him see that he could not indulge in temper. Not here; not tonight.

He was going to find out how she did that. Later. Now he said, "Whatever I'm here for, there can't be much time left. Tell me what it is."

He would have expected Mathilda to answer, but it was one of the Guardians who answered, the lady in white, who reminded him rather strongly of Mathilda. They must be kin.

"The gates of the Otherworld are open," the lady said. "Your task is to shut them."

"Why? Don't they always open at Beltane? Won't they shut when the sun comes up, regardless of what I do or fail to do?"

William expected the Guardians to bridle at his roughness, but they seemed more amused than not. The lady answered placidly, "They open, to be sure, but what may run free without harm and what should remain bound are different things. When you were born, certain sleepers began to stir. When your magic woke, they woke likewise. You are a great temptation to them, and a great prize if you can be conquered."

So William had been told before. The only danger he had seen since he met Mathilda had been in his own skull. The things that had hunted him since he was a child had not come near him at all.

Well enough, he thought. He would do what he had to do to get out of this place. Then he would demand clear answers—and be intransigent until he got them. He was beginning to understand just how difficult he could be, and how badly he could alarm even such great powers as stood around him now.

Maybe there was a useful side to this magic after all. He turned slowly about, not knowing what exactly he wanted to do, but letting his body's motion guide him.

He came to a halt facing Mathilda. She started to slide away, but he shot out his hands and caught her.

She stood still. The stars were flickering. Shadows moved behind them, great slow undulating shapes. He might have heard the slide of scales; it might have been the rasp of his own breathing. Faint and far away, hounds bayed.

His nape prickled. Even good Christians feared the Wild Hunt. But it was nowhere near this place, and the sounds of it were growing fainter.

What could be worse than those skeletal hounds and that horned huntsman? What could be more terrifying than souls stripped from flesh and bound to run the wilds of the Otherworld forever, without pause, without rest?

Damned souls were still souls—still had existence in the worlds. The things behind the stars would swallow everything: stars, souls, beings of flesh and spirit, all that was or would be.

The gates of the Otherworld were narrow and strongly barred, but on this night, their substance had lost somewhat of its strength. Powers strained through, monstrous shapes and visions of terror, spreading black wings to blot out the stars.

Even if William had lived a hundred lives, each more illustrious than the last, he was only a man. His magic was a stunted thing. He knew a great deal about fighting with steel, somewhat about ruling a dukedom, and too much about running from death. This was not part of his world.

The Guardians were waiting. The grove about them was dark and perfectly silent. The stars had begun to wink out one by one. The air was suddenly very cold.

The only warmth came from Mathilda's hands locked in his, and her face glimmering pale in the gloom. The Guardians had vanished, their light quenched. There was nothing now but the spot of ground the two of them stood on, and that was none too steady.

He sensed no fear from Mathilda. She waited as the Guardians did—as they had; maybe they were gone out of the world. Everything was waiting for him.

God, what was he supposed to do? He knew nothing. He was breaking apart with ignorance. He could feel the edges of himself crumbling, the pain behind his eyes coming back.

The ground was trembling under his feet. This time, when the lightning came, it would strike them all. And it would be his fault. His stupidity. His—

"Stop it," said Mathilda. "Stop thinking of what you don't know. I taught you one or two things at least. Remember. *Think.*"

Think? Who had ever said he could do such a thing?

Her brows had drawn together. They were beginning to sink down through earth that had gone as yielding as mud. If it went on long enough, it would all turn to water, and then to air, and so to nothing.

He knew nothing. But he could open his mind's eye as she had taught him in a lesson he had thought forgotten. He could envision a door. It was a large one, broad and high, like the iron-bound gate of a cathedral, but so balanced that a man could shift it with a touch. Carvings marched up the posts and across the lintel, intricate almost beyond comprehension; but if he peered close, he could see whole worlds encompassed within the space of a handspan.

They were a distraction. He turned his mind from them to

what they opened upon: a vast expanse of shadows and darkness.

What did a man do when the night threatened his door? Could it be that simple?

It had better be. No one else was moving or speaking. Maybe they could not. Doubt niggled down deep. They would not let everything whirl into the darkness, would they? Simply to prove a point?

But if they could not stop this, if they were helpless, how in the name of the old gods did anyone expect William to do any better?

Distraction. Again. William shut off the yammer in his head. He let go Mathilda's left hand, but kept a firm grip on the right. With his free hand he reached for one of the leaves of the gate. In the same moment, she reached for the other.

A blast of wind smote them, striving to rip them apart. They clung to each other and to the gate, fighting the wind and the force of darkness. Their fingers slipped; they clung tighter. The cords of William's neck bulged. Even Mathilda seemed to have let go her wonted calm; her face was white and set, her lower lip caught between her teeth. Her eyes were blazing.

Little by little the gate yielded. The things within struck like battering rams. Somehow their joined hands withstood the assault. Mathilda never wavered. Her steadiness made William strong.

Just as the gate was nearly shut, a mighty force hurled against it. The ground rocked; the posts of the gate swayed. The wind's howling bade fair to split William's skull.

Mathilda's hand tightened on William's, tight enough for pain. With that for an anchor, he unleashed one last, desperate effort.

The gate boomed shut. The silence was as vast as the world. Stars glimmered overhead. The Guardians stood immobile behind him, and the grove in back of them.

William looked down at his hand, expecting to find the fingers stripped to the bone. They were the same as always, long, strong, with the smallest finger somewhat crooked. The white line of a knife scar traced itself across the back, distinct in starlight.

Mathilda let go a long hiss of breath. As if that had unlocked the silence, the world gave birth to sound again: whisper of wind in the leaves of the oaks, distant hoot of an owl, and far away, the belling of hounds in the Wild Hunt.

"How are they going to get back in?" William asked suddenly, deafening in the stillness.

Mathilda tilted her chin toward the place where the gate had been. There was a shimmer in the darkness, a rent in the fabric of the world. That was the gate as it should be on Beltane night, waiting for the creatures of the Otherworld to pass through once more, as they had done since this world was new.

William's knees gave way. The earth he fell to was solid. He should have had a splitting headache. He felt wonderful. Marvelous. Splendid.

He grinned up at Mathilda. She was glaring at him. He found that hilarious, even when she slapped him. He caught her hand even as it snapped back from his stinging cheek, and kissed it. Her hiss of outrage only made him laugh the harder.

❊ CHAPTER 15 ❊

"He did rather well," Lanfranc said.

William was back in the castle of Falaise, sleeping the sleep of the drugged or bespelled. And good riddance, too, Mathilda thought nastily. Her fist was still clenched over the memory of his kiss.

He could indulge in rest. She had no such privilege. The Guardian Melusine had been more than glad to spirit the young duke back where he belonged. The rest had stayed in the grove, keeping Mathilda with them.

She had no intention of defying them. She had questions, a crowding swarm of them, and here were three who could answer them, if they chose.

They were choosing for the moment to ignore her. "He might have been better taught," said the Lady of Broceliande.

Mathilda bristled, but she forced herself to keep still.

"He is a difficult pupil," said Lanfranc. "It was your choice, and the choice of my predecessor, to let him be tempered in the fire. Perhaps he was left there too long."

"Or perhaps not long enough," said Dame Alais.

"If we had let him be," Baldwin reminded them, "tonight would have ended far differently. We would not have been enough to shut the gate."

"No?" said Dame Alais.

"No," said Baldwin, gentle but unshakable. "Even untutored, barely civilized, with his memory in tatters, he is what he is. By his blood and power he did what had to be done."

"And now what?" said Mathilda suddenly. "What happens now? He's done his duty, he's finished, he can go back to being a target for every rebel and adventurer who casts his eye on Normandy?"

"His position is somewhat improved," her father said, "thanks to the king and to his own gifts. He'll find his stride now. Normandy will come to his hand."

"Well and good," said Mathilda, "but there's more to him than that. What about the rest of him? Do we just let it go?"

"Hardly," Dame Alais said. "This is but a beginning. His destiny is all before him."

"And mine?" Mathilda said. "May I come back to the Wood? Since Prior Lanfranc is here, surely I'm no longer needed to—"

"Prior Lanfranc has duties of his own," said Dame Alais. "You are the young duke's teacher still."

"He doesn't want to learn," Mathilda said bluntly. "He ran away from me. I'm not a teacher, Lady. My own learning is barely begun. There are any number of wise men to whom he may listen, who can teach him with more skill than I have ever had."

"You are his teacher," the Lady said immovably. Neither of the men contradicted her, although Mathilda glared at her father, willing him to see what she found blatantly obvious.

Apparently he did not. "So what then?" she demanded of them all. "I can't follow him about, in disguise or otherwise: he doesn't take women with him when he travels. Shall I chop off my hair and put on a page's tabard and hope no one finds me out?"

The Guardians exchanged glances. Lanfranc frowned. Baldwin and Dame Alais stared him down. He resisted, but if he had had objections to raise, he kept them to himself.

"There is a way," said Baldwin, "to keep you by him always, full in the eye of the world, and no one will stand between you."

Lanfranc stirred. The Lady's hard eye stilled him.

Mathilda's eyes widened. "You don't mean—"

"It is a logical and even desirable possibility," her father said. "Normandy is a powerful dukedom, and enormously wealthy, even after its late disturbances. Its duke is young, virile, and not given to siring bastards."

"Because in the eyes of the world he is one," Mathilda said with banked heat.

"Does that matter to you?" Dame Alais inquired.

"No!" It was not a lie, either. There was no bastardy in the world of magic; and even if there had been, there was no birth more powerful or more divinely legitimate than that of a child born to a living goddess.

"Then you have no objections," the Lady said. "It is a good match even as the lower world perceives it. In ours it is more than good; it is the union of two great houses of the old blood, and two great powers. What you did together in shutting the gate is but a shadow of what you can do."

Mathilda shivered with the cold exhilaration of prophecy. And yet she said, "I do have objections. Granted that all of what you say is true in both the mortal world and the world of power—he is still rough, raw, untutored, and frequently intransigent. If he has a heart, it's buried so deep and armored so thick that there is no coming near it."

"You may," Dame Alais said.

"Maybe once I might have," said Mathilda: "years ago, before you wise Guardians flung him from the forge into the fire. It's too late now. He's turned to steel. There's nothing left in him that I can touch."

"No?" said the Lady.

"Daughter—" Baldwin began.

"Listen to her," Lanfranc said, breaking his silence at last. "Her objections are valid. And so, as you know too well, are mine. The Church will not look with approval on this match."

"There is no prohibition in your law against the legal marriage of a man conceived out of wedlock," the Lady said. "What other impediment can there be?"

"The impediment of close kin," said Lanfranc.

"Which they are not," said Dame Alais.

"In canon law they are," Lanfranc said. "Her father's father took to wife his father's sister."

"Preposterous," Dame Alais said with a rare flash of temper. "That marriage took place after her grandmother's death, and is not in the line of her blood at all."

"Nevertheless," Lanfranc said. "Canon law is canon law, and consanguinity is a powerful impediment in this age of the Church."

"With all due respect," said Dame Alais, "we are not meek servants of the Church—nor need we be, either in this world or in the other. We will buy ourselves a Pope if need be, and if needs must, since a lord of this world must at least pretend to serve the Church."

"That, Lady, is hardly respectful," Lanfranc said so gently that one might have thought him unmoved. But Mathilda could feel the anger beneath. Guardian of the secret realms he might be, but he had given his heart and his vows to the Church. Even in its absurdities he would serve it. That was honor. For good or ill, he had it.

"I speak the truth," said the Lady of Broceliande.

Mathilda stepped between them, not without an instant's hesitation. They were greater powers by far than she, and could blast her with a glance. But she gambled that they were both still in command of their tempers, and would listen to what she had to say. "Stop it," she said. "Please, stop. In the world that mortals live in, noble marriages can be bought and sold, and neither party may be asked to consent to it. But we are not simple mortals, and we live by other laws. I must consent—and so must he."

"He will hardly refuse," Baldwin said, "or if he does, his counselors will be sure to bring him to his senses. He'll not find a better prize in the whole of Gaul. He'll gain legitimacy from it, and standing among his own vassals, too."

"I'm sure he'll see the logic of that," Mathilda said acidly, "but will I? I'm a prize to be won. Why should I surrender myself to the likes of him? Surely I can do better."

"Can you, child?" said Dame Alais. "Can you indeed?"

"If he had what Artos had, or Bran, or Caswallon, he would be worth the taking. As he is?" Mathilda shook her head. "If he were a horse I wouldn't buy him—too many vices, too little training. I'm not a horse-tamer, however dearly you may wish I could be."

"On the contrary," said Dame Alais, "you are the one hand that can tame him. We tested him tonight—but we also tested you. If he is to be taught, if he is to become what he was born to be, he will come to it with and through you."

"And if I don't want to be the one?" Mathilda demanded.

"It is not a matter of wanting or not wanting," Dame Alais said. "It is a matter of what is."

"I don't even like him," Mathilda said. "When I bound him, I bound him as a pupil, not a lover. The thought of loving him—of bearing his children—"

"Love comes when it will," said the Lady. "The rest is a matter of duty and destiny."

"No," said Mathilda. "I'll have him by the old law or not at all. It will be a free choice—his as well as mine. I'll release him from the binding if need be. If either of us refuses, there will be no marriage."

"There will be a marriage," Dame Alais said with serene conviction.

"Not in the eyes of the Church," said Lanfranc, cutting across them both.

"The Church will come round to our way of thinking," Baldwin said.

"Ah," said Mathilda, "but will I?"

She left them with that. It was terribly disrespectful, but she was too angry to care.

She could have gone anywhere from that place: Flanders, Paris, even Broceliande. It was no logical choice that brought her back to Falaise, to the room where the duke lay asleep.

He had no dignity in that position. His mouth was open; he snored. He needed a bath—badly.

That at least she could remedy. Servants, she had already observed, could recognize noble rank, even if it came dressed like one of them. His servants would have the basin ready in the morning when he woke, and would see to it that he made thorough use of it.

In the meantime they had prepared a place for her to sleep, but she was not ready yet for that. She had her mule brought out and saddled, and its saddlebags filled with provisions for a short journey. The mule was not delighted to be wrenched from the peace of the stable and the pleasures of its manger to venture out in the dark before dawn, but she was in no mood to indulge anyone, least of all herself.

She traveled by the mortal road. She had had enough of magical tracks, and she was not minded to lose the greater part of another month—or, if the old gods were in a wicked mood, a year or a decade or a hundred years—on one of them. It was not terribly far in any case; on a horse with any speed to offer, she would have been there before midmorning.

On the mule, who was not prepared to oblige her with any gait above a slow jog, it was past noon when she came in sight of the walled manor house with its patchwork of fields. It was a tidy place, the fields well tilled, the cattle and the small herd of horses fat and sleek in their pastures. The orchards were in full bloom, promising a rich harvest of apples come the autumn.

By then Mathilda was regretting the impulse that had sent her out on this of all errands when she was so desperately in need of rest. She had dozed in the saddle for most of the way, trusting the mule to take her where she wished to go. The usual dregs and vermin that would prey on a woman alone had passed her by, deflected by the wards that she had managed to raise before she let herself fall asleep.

Those wards nearly proved false as she approached the edge of the fields that surrounded the manor. An odd prickling and tingling warned her almost too late. There were wards here, and they were strong, set against invading magic as well as more mortal intrusion.

The mule, wise beast, stopped just as the boundary-wards began to hum and crackle. Mathilda scraped herself together as best she could and shut down her own protections.

Slowly the wards quieted. The mule was not inclined to test them further, and Mathilda let it be for the moment. Her head was splitting.

After a while that she did not try to measure, the ache trickled away. The mule ventured a step forward. No opposition met it. People laboring in the fields glanced up as she passed, but none seemed alarmed or particularly interested.

That could be deceptive. This place was well guarded. By the time she reached the manor's gate, she had no doubt that her presence had been marked, noted, and allowed to continue.

A man was waiting inside the gate, ready to take the mule and bring her to the stable. He walked with a lurching gait, for one leg was much shorter than the other, but he was well fed and his clothes were clean, and his greeting was soft and polite. Mathilda found nothing in him to mistrust; the mule went willingly where he led.

She was to continue into the house. She did not mind that the mule merited a servant and she did not. It seemed sensible enough. This place was nothing if not sensibly arranged.

The hall was full of people. Women were spinning and weaving; men were sharpening scythes and fletching hunting arrows and mending harnesses. There was order in it, and industry. It was admirable.

Like the workers in the fields, they acknowledged Mathilda with glances, but did not raise the alarm. Those glances directed her through the hall to the cluster of smaller rooms behind it, then out past the kitchen garden to an outbuilding redolent of herbs. Bunches of them hung from the rafters; bottles and jars stood in ranks on shelves.

The one Mathilda had come to find was sitting by a hearth, tending a pot from which came a sweet but potent odor. Mathilda's nose wrinkled; she sneezed.

The Lady Herleva looked up. She was younger than Mathilda had expected—foolish, of course; she had been no older than Mathilda when she made the Great Marriage with the year-king who was also the Duke of Normandy. There was no grey in her hair, no lines of age in her face.

Her son must favor his father: Herleva was slender, not tall, with a delicate beauty that had passed William by. But the cool grey eyes and the hair the color of oak leaves in autumn—those were exactly like his.

Likewise the power in her. It was trained as his was not, exquisitely shaped and controlled, but the strength of it, the depth and breadth, the sheer magnitude of magic, was so like William's that Mathilda caught her breath.

It all burst out of her in a word: "Why?"

She had meant to be more roundabout, to come at it by degrees, but the shock of Herleva's presence had driven all good sense out of Mathilda's head.

Herleva appeared to take no offense. "Lady," she said. "Welcome."

Mathilda had no patience to spare for niceties. "Why did you do it?" she demanded. "Why did you send him away without art or skill or even memory? Did you want him dead?"

Herleva sighed. The pot began to bubble; she stirred it slowly. Her answer was oblique. "Duty is a cruel thing. It has no heart. It knows only what must be."

"Are you that much a slave to your duty?"

"I was a slave to prescience," Herleva said.

"Would it not have been simple common sense to give him the teaching he needed before you flung him at his father?"

"I did," said Herleva. "I taught him everything he was old enough to know."

"It wasn't enough."

"He survived," his mother said.

Mathilda opened her mouth, then shut it again.

"Do not believe," said Herleva, "that I did any of it with ease or comfort of heart. I did it because I must."

"That's what you're all saying," Mathilda said. "Tell the truth. None of you judged wisely. Granted that you had to send him to his father while he was still a young child—you could have sent a tutor with him: someone who would have taught him what he needed to know."

"He went as he was fated to go," Herleva said. "He learned what he was destined to learn—as he continues to do." She lidded the pot and lifted it from the fire, setting it on the stone of the hearth. "You have passion. That's good. Anger—not so good. Temper is the enemy of understanding."

"So I have been told," Mathilda said tightly.

Herleva met her eyes. That stare was so like William's, and yet so unlike—so direct and yet so warm—that Mathilda could hardly bear it. "He has a heart," Herleva said. "Believe that. Trust in it."

"You heard us," Mathilda said. "You were there."

"I was listening," Herleva admitted.

Mathilda stared at her in sudden and devastating comprehension. "You're the other—the hidden one. The Guardian of the spirit of Gaul."

Herleva bowed her head.

"And still you let it happen? Still you let your own blood and bone be hunted like a dog?"

"Because of what I am, I knew there was no choice." Herleva sat on the stool beside the hearth. She looked immensely weary then, and far older than the count of her years.

Mathilda refused to give way to pity. She had come here out of pure rage. It had not been wise at all, but she was far from regretting it.

This woman was kin. Not by line of blood or family, although they both descended from old Druids and women of power. She was like Mathilda: the same heart, the same mind, the same magic. The same fierce devotion to what she loved.

That brought Mathilda up short. She did not love William. She was outraged on his behalf. She was not at all certain that he would survive much longer as he was—or that he could be salvaged before he shook himself to pieces. She wanted to throttle all these Guardians and defenders of the realm, for warping and twisting a rare and marvelous power.

"Listen," she said, "all of you—I know you're here; you can hide, but I know you too well. I'll make a bargain with you. Give me the summer in Broceliande. Teach me everything I have the capacity to learn, that I can profitably teach. Then I'll decide. If I give him the choice of marrying me, it's on my terms, by my will. If I choose not to take him, that's it, it's done. You'll find him another and less difficult keeper."

"You are certainly difficult." That was her father's voice, speaking from a slant of sunlight. "But so is he. An easier spirit could never manage him."

"I haven't done so well myself," she reminded him. "The summer. That's all I ask. Come the autumn, I'll make my choice."

They were there as she had thought, each of them a shadow and a glimmer. They exchanged glances.

It was Herleva who said, "That's fair enough. There's little time to spare, to be sure—but we can spare that much."

Mathilda noted with interest how they all gave way to her—not all willingly or graciously, but not one ventured to argue. Herleva was still goddess on earth, although the Great Marriage was twenty years past.

Strangely, that understanding cooled Mathilda's temper. The gods did not think as humans thought. Their mercy was colder, their compassion less calculable. It would be some while before she could forgive her father or the rest of the lesser Guardians, but this one lived in another world altogether.

"Not entirely," said Herleva, which was proof if Mathilda had needed any, that she saw as a goddess saw. And yet the warmth of her voice and glance, the strength of her hands as they clasped Mathilda's, were incontestably human. "If you do choose him, lady, you have my blessing. I believe you are a match for him."

"Ah," said Mathilda, "but is he a match for me?"

"The gods know," Herleva said.

❧ CHAPTER 16 ❧

William's headache was gone. Better yet, it stayed that way. The night in the grove faded almost to a dream, but something in him refused to let it blur out altogether. It was important that he remember it, however disconcerting that might be.

Mathilda, like the headache, had left for parts unknown. He surprised himself by missing her. At first he was simply glad to be free of her endless, relentless instruction, but as the days stretched into months, he found himself looking for her at odd moments: on the field before a fight, in the wood when the huntsmen started a deer, in the hall of an evening when the wine went round and the shadows danced on the walls.

She had bound him. The binding was tugging at him, pulling him toward her. It was not that he missed her, truly and honestly, for her inimitable self.

At first to be contrary, then because it had become almost a pleasure, he practiced the lessons she had taught him. It was difficult to find time or space for them, but he managed. It was a matter of honor. If he saw her again—when he saw her again—he wanted her to know that he was neither a coward nor an absolute fool.

Prior Lanfranc came and went throughout that summer, while William traversed the length and breadth of Normandy, putting down remnants of rebellion and making sure his people knew his face. Lanfranc never mentioned the gathering in the grove. Even so, William knew he was being weighed and judged, inside as well as out.

He hoped that he was passing muster. It often seemed as if Lanfranc was within half an instant of saying what was on his mind, but he never did.

William let it go. He had enough to think of as it was.

By autumn he felt as steady on his feet as he had ever felt, both in his dukedom and in his private exercises. He was growing a little cocky, maybe; he actually caught himself smiling with no good reason, one morning when the sun was unusually bright and the weather unusually fine.

He was in Caen then, holding court and receiving envoys from a growing number of notables who had heard that Normandy's duke had come into his own. Most came out of curiosity, to offer gifts or alliance. Some—and this was a new thing—were offering daughters.

"So," said William to Lanfranc that evening, when the hall had grown almost quiet and the lamp was burning low in the solar. "A bastard's good enough if he comes with a dukedom attached."

"A duke is a splendid catch," Lanfranc said serenely, "and as the scripture says, it's better to marry than to burn."

"Why, do you think I should take one of them?"

"One or two might be worth considering," said Lanfranc.

William yawned and stretched. "I suppose I should, at that. I won't make the mistake my father did. This family needs sons—plenty of them, and every one as legitimate as Mother Church could wish. I don't suppose you can scry a little and find me a lady who is both fair and fertile?"

Did he imagine it, or did Lanfranc actually squirm?

Of course not. The Prior of Bec was far too dignified for that. He was registering an objection, that was all.

"Never mind," William said. "That was beneath both of us."

"Still," Lanfranc conceded, "it was a point well taken. Perhaps you should consult your advisors, and bid them find you a duchess."

"I'll think about it," William said.

Dreams were a door to the Otherworld. Mathilda had taught William that. She had also taught him to walk in dreams as if they had been the waking world, and, a little, to bend them to his will.

He had had this dream before. In it he was armed and mounted, leading a company of knights through a shadowy country. There were trees; there were sudden expanses of open country, with rocky outcrops and windy hillsides. Tonight as before, they rode toward one such crag, on which a stone fort squatted like a beast. No banner flew from any of its towers. Over its black maw of a gate, an arch of skulls grinned blankly down.

Something was there that he must have. Something magical; something wonderful. Something that he never quite glimpsed and never quite understood.

As before, he rode toward the gate, but when he came to it, it melted away. His horse, his knights were gone. He stood on the summit of a white cliff, with a long roll of green downs behind him, and the roar and tumble of the sea below. He was fixed somehow in or on the cliff, so that he could not move or turn; and yet he could see all around and above and beneath him, as if every part of him were endowed with eyes.

Tonight he saw more than grass and cliff and sea. He saw a fortress of iron laid over that green country, with walls that plunged into the waves. The iron hummed in a rhythm that, after a while, he recognized as the rhythm of plainchant.

The iron was cracked in places. Rust stained it, dark as old blood. Another song wound through the deep surge of chanting. This was clear, high, and inhuman; it resonated in the earth and air.

It carried him away from the shore in a confusion of light and music, an eruption of pure sound. On the other side of it was stillness.

This body was not his own. It was taller, narrower. Older: it creaked when he moved. His face felt odd. He looked down. A fair beard spread across a narrow chest clothed in silk.

Grimly he held panic at bay. This was a dream, no more. He had worn other bodies when he dreamed, some larger, some smaller than the one he wore when he was awake. But those all in some way had belonged to him—in other lives, Mathilda would have said if she had been there to offer her opinion. This was not his.

It was thinking thoughts apart from him, a slow murmur of reflection, oblivious to the interloper. Something else was there, something that whispered, shaping this man's thoughts, guiding his will.

They were thoughts of ruling and commanding: choosing bishops, calling councils, gathering troops of fighting men. William in the waking world thought much the same thoughts.

He found these rather interesting. Most of the names were strange, but enough were not that he began to guess whose mind he might be inhabiting—and, through that, where he must be.

He was across the sea in the Saxon kingdom, in England. The tall thin man with the fair beard must be Edward the king—who, as fate would have it, was William's close kinsman. The English king was only Saxon through his father. His mother had been Norman, sister to William's own father.

Blood must be calling to blood. Certainly in Edward the Norman strain was running strong. He was pondering Norman names for his bishoprics and abbacies, and even for his court and council. And all the while, so faint it was barely to be heard, some other voice was whispering and cajoling, wheedling him into choosing Normans over Saxons.

And why, thought William, should that be? What was he doing here?

The dream was trying to pull him away. He dug in and held on. The whisper had a quality to it—it was like the singing that had eroded the walls of iron: eerie, inhuman.

Was the King of the English possessed? Or—

The rush of frustration nearly flung William out of the dream. He knew too little. He had to guess too much—and most of his guesses, he had no doubt, would be wrong.

One more thing he was sure of. This was not idle fancy. This was a true dream, a dream born of magic and the old gods' will. He was here, walking in this strangely multiple mind, because he was meant to be.

Hush. Mathilda's voice was as clear as if she stood beside him. *Be still. Let it happen.*

"Easy for you to say," he snarled, but her calm was creeping over him. Time would tell him what this meant. For now he was simply to watch and listen, and school himself to remember.

"What is it about England?"

Lanfranc was getting ready to leave again. William caught him just as he was about to mount his mule, out in the stable-yard in the dim light of dawn. Elsewhere in the castle, only the cooks were awake, baking the day's bread. Everyone else would be up and about soon enough, but for the moment everything was unwontedly quiet.

"Every dream or memory I have," William said, "I end up in England. Why is that?"

Lanfranc was a Guardian of Gaul; before that, even before he took vows, he had been a man of law in Italy. He was used to odd questions and peculiar obsessions.

He paused in tightening the girths. "All your lives before this have been there," he said. "You ruled there in life after life. It's not surprising it calls you to it."

"But I'm not there now. I'm here. I've moved on."

"Have you?"

"Do I look like an Englishman?"

Lanfranc looked him up and down, though he had not meant the question to be taken literally. "You look like a Norman reiver, with a bit of Druid stirred in."

"Not English. Not Saxon."

"No part of you ever was," Lanfranc said.

"You make no sense."

"I make perfect sense," said Lanfranc.

He slanted a glance. William scowled, but he offered his laced hands. Lanfranc set his foot in them. William tossed him into the saddle—a little too energetically; but Lanfranc caught himself before he flew off the far side. He settled on the mule's back and regarded William with undisguised indulgence. "In time you'll understand," he said.

"I want to understand now!"

"Don't we all?" said Lanfranc.

William snarled and slapped the mule's rump. The beast protested with a kick; William evaded it easily. Lanfranc kept his seat with equal ease, and had the gall to laugh. Still laughing, he rode out of the gate.

Sometimes William wished he could be the simple, untutored brawn that too many people took him for. His world would be much less complicated then. And he would get more sleep.

❧ CHAPTER 17 ❧

The tree was cloven as if by lightning, riven from crown to root, and yet the halves of it still lived. They sprouted green leaves in spring, turned russet in autumn; acorns weighted the branches, then fell to feed the Lady's pigs that rooted in the rich earth below.

A spring bubbled from the heart of the oak, pouring down into a pool that fed the gnarled and knotted roots. Fish lived in the pool, glimmering silver creatures that seemed made of starlight and swift water. There were no other fish like them on this side of the gate to the Otherworld.

Mathilda was fond of sitting under the riven oak, listening to the whisper of the leaves and water and restoring her strength of mind and magic through the power that surged up from the roots of the tree. That power had held a prince of enchanters prisoner for many a hundred years, until he was freed by an oath and a spell. He was long gone, but the magic endured, suffusing the whole of this forest and pooling here in its heart.

She had brought a small harp today and was plucking notes one by one. Each note was a memory, a key to the door of her magic.

She could hear singing not far away: the youngest students in the Ladies' school, singing the same rhymes and cantrips that she had taught William in the spring. These were all girls' voices, sweet and clear. She caught herself missing that much deeper and surprisingly tuneful voice.

Summer was fading—some would say it was already gone. The oak's leaves were turning russet and bronze. Yet she was still here. Every day she expected the Lady to dismiss her, but the days went on and no one said anything of her leaving. She continued her studies, served her turn in the kitchens, spent mornings with the weavers and spinners. If she had not had that constant awareness that it all must end, and soon, she would have been perfectly happy.

She laid the harp aside and bent toward the pool. The water was deep and clear. The fish spun a skein through it. As she watched, they joined in a gleaming circle. It turned like a wheel, at first slowly, then more quickly.

This was magic, strong enough to make her dizzy. She should not be here alone with it; it was dangerous. Yet she kept silent even as a handful of her fellows passed on the track nearby, chattering amiably. None of them glanced toward the pool or the tree, or seemed to notice that the power was awake.

This was for her alone. She tensed to rise and walk away and so refuse it, but she never finished the motion.

The wheel of fish slowed into stillness. The shape of it was like a crown. Her hand reached without her willing it, and closed about what felt like forged silver. She lifted it out of the water. It was silver indeed, set with pearls where the creatures' eyes had been.

She held it up in hands that trembled slightly. It was cool, solid, rather heavy. Slowly she lowered it until it rested on her brows. *Lady and queen,* it sang. *Be strong; live long.*

Suddenly it spread wings and flew up against the sun: a flock of white doves with eyes like pearls, fluttering through the branches of the tree and vanishing in light.

The pool was as empty as her hands. The fish, like the crown, were gone.

For all the warmth of the sun, she was cold. The breath of the Otherworld could be a deadly thing. She rose shakily. What she wanted then was completely illogical, which meant that it had everything to do with magic.

"I have to go."

Dame Alais nodded. She was not perturbed to be interrupted in the midst of a lesson. Her pupils watched in silence, eyes wide. "It is time," she said.

She did not ask what had roused Mathilda. Most likely she knew. She knew everything.

Even so, Mathilda said, "The fish in the enchanter's pool are gone."

"More will come," Dame Alais said. "In the morning you

may go. Tonight, dine with me, and dance a last dance in honor of the gods and the Wood."

Mathilda bowed. She could hardly refuse such an invitation, even if it had not concealed the steel of a command.

Now that her departure was set, Mathilda was strangely reluctant to face it. She gathered the few belongings she had here, bound them together and set them at the foot of her hard narrow bed.

The rest of the beds in the elder students' dormitory were empty at this hour. Where she was going, she would have rooms to herself and her servants, beds both capacious and soft, and as many possessions as her whim or her fancy could encompass. And yet she would be sorry to leave this bare and ascetic place.

She could have changed out of the plain white linen gown without sleeves or undergarment that was the common dress here, and put on a gown appropriate to her worldly station, but she chose to keep it for this one last day. It was the last; she knew that. Once she had left the Wood, she would not come back.

There had been a choice once, she supposed; a time when she could have stayed. That time was past. She had made her decision before she was even aware that she was doing it.

There was no extraordinary feast tonight. The fare was the same as always: strong brown bread, pungent cheese, and honey from the hives in the orchards. There were apples, tart and sweet, from those same orchards, whole or cut up in honey, and cups of sweet mead that both fuddled and cleared the head.

Mathilda sat where she always sat, among the oldest students, young women who would be passing through the shadow and the fire come the dark of the year. A few would emerge as Ladies of full power and learning. Many would die in the testing.

She could stay; she could go with them and complete what she had begun when she was a child. But in her heart she knew better. For her the shadow waited elsewhere. The fire that she would face was earthly fire, a testing of body and spirit in the world beyond the Wood.

No one spoke of her leaving, but she knew they all knew. Their silence was a gift. So was the absence of either pity or scorn. It might be a lesser life she went to, in the eyes of the order, but they did not think the less of her for it.

The sun set while they ate; the stars came out. The warmth of

earth and air gave way to a chill that spoke clearly of autumn.
Outside the hall, in a broad green bowl, a fire sprang up. Magic
had kindled it, but it burned good earthly wood: oak for strength,
applewood for sweetness.

The dance had already begun. Pipes skirled, drums beat. Not
all the dancers were women, nor were they mortal. The old ones
had come out tonight, the folk of wood and air, with their wild
beauty and their unearthly grace.

That was not a common thing, at all. Maybe they had come for
Mathilda's sake; maybe it was only their whim, on this chill night,
to revel in the fire's warmth and the pleasure of the dancing.

She danced with her yearmates in a long winding skein. She
danced with a faery lord in moon-silver and spidersilk, and a
brown bogle with ears so long they curled together above its
head, and a young fellow who seemed to be of solid mortal
stock except for his great owl-eyes. The moon came up; the
stars wheeled round. The mead flowed sweet and strong.

Toward midnight she dropped to the grass to rest. Music and
laughter rippled all around her. Dancers whirled from firelight to
shadow and back again. Someone flung a log on the fire; it leaped
up in a shower of sparks.

A figure came to stand over her: tall, broad, solid with mortality and yet bearing a great fire of magic in its heart.

"You're not here," she said to it.

"Probably not," it said. Its—his—voice was deep, a little
rough, but there was a strong music in it. "I remember what you
told me about dreams."

She was not sure that she did, but it hardly seemed to matter. "Dance with me," she said.

His hand was solid and warm. His face was as she remembered it—but clean, which made it more likely that he was a
dream or a fetch. Yet he seemed very real and present for a fig-
ment of her memory.

He knew how to dance. Some of his time at the French
king's court had been put to frivolous use, then; and she had not
even known. How much more did she not know of him?

A great deal, no doubt. As oddly matched as they were for
height and bulk, their steps matched well. He fell easily into her
rhythm, and she into his. Was that a smile? Was that actual
warmth in his eyes?

He had to be a dream. William never smiled, never laughed;

his most favored expression was a scowl. He, or this image of him, was remarkably pleasant to look at when he smiled.

"What are you grinning at?" she demanded.

"You."

"You'd never do that if you were awake."

"Wouldn't I?"

"You're like a bear in the spring."

"I missed you," he said.

"What, because I'm bracing, like a good hard whipping in the morning?"

He laughed. "More like armor after it's been on for three days and the padding's worn through. It gets to be familiar. You miss it when it's off. You don't know what to do with yourself. Then as soon as the galls have healed, you're back in it again, same old pain, new vermin."

"You could get new padding," she said.

She had not known that he had good teeth, strong and white. He had never grinned before. This was a night for novelties, clearly, or for dreaming of them. "See?" he said. "That's what I need you for."

"Mending your gambeson?"

"Reminding me of what matters."

"You have servants for that."

He shook his head. "Not like you," he said.

"I'm more than a servant."

"Much more." He bent until their faces were level. "Rule Normandy with me."

"What is this? A state alliance?"

"If you like," he said.

"Tell me why I should give myself to you, when I could have any prince in Europe."

"Because," he said perfectly reasonably, "I'm a match for you."

"What makes you think that?"

"Arrogance," he said.

"Indeed it is." She spun out of the dance, flinging herself onto the yielding turf.

He followed, stretching out beside her, propped on his elbow. "Well then," he said. "Is any prince in Europe a Druid's son? Does he need you to keep him out of trouble when what's inside him tries to get out?"

"Do you love me?"

That brought him up short. "What does that have to do with—"

"You don't," she said. "You wouldn't know how."

"Teach me."

And that, in its turn, brought her up short. She looked for the leer, the hint that he was, in his ham-handed way, asking her to seduce him. There was none. His face was open, his eyes steady. He understood what she had asked him. This was his answer.

Maybe, she thought—maybe, after all, it was not too late. Maybe he could learn.

Maybe in dreams. The man awake . . .

"Afraid?" he asked.

She bristled. He saw: his eyes glinted. She breathed deep, willing herself to be calm. "Tomorrow I am going back to Flanders. When I come there—"

"Come to Normandy," he said.

"That would not be proper."

"Is this? Is anything that we've done together?"

"That was necessary. This—"

"This isn't?"

"We both must marry," she said, "but there is no requirement that it be to each other."

"For me there is," he said. "You bound me, remember? And here's the strange thing about it. I don't mind. I barely even resent it."

"I am imagining you," she said, "and you are becoming implausible."

"I'm here," he said. "Really here. I came the way you came to Falaise."

"How—"

"That one." He pointed with his chin. Dame Alais circled the dying fire, long pale hair streaming. The one with whom she danced was improbably tall, improbably strange: man's body, stag's head, wide sweep of antlers casting clawed shadows in the firelight.

Mathilda reached. William's arm was perfectly solid and perfectly real, just as it had been when they danced.

Still, she said, "You can't be here."

"Why? Because you don't want me to be?"

"You smiled," she said.

He stared at her.

"You never smile. You never—"

"I'm learning," he said. He paused. Then: "Come to Normandy."

She sat up, drawing in a deep breath. "If you want me for your duchess," she said, "you will do it properly. You will send envoys. My father will do the same. They will discuss the matter. Then, if they are agreed—"

"Is that how I'll learn to love you? Through embassies?"

"That could be done in a cow-byre," she said. "This is an affair of state."

"But you said—"

"I want it all," she said. "Embassies and high alliances. A proper, noble wedding, with gifts and ceremonies and processions. And your heart."

He whistled between his teeth. "Well, lady. You don't come cheap."

"I most certainly do not."

For the second time since she had known him, he laughed. He saluted her, and bowed where he lay. "As you wish, my lady."

She rose to her knees. Swiftly, before he could move, she swooped down and caught his face in her hands. She kissed him hard and long.

She had meant to take him aback. She had not expected to rattle herself to her foundations. It was all she could do to pull away, scrape her wits together, and say with some semblance of coolness, "That is your first lesson. Remember it."

If he had anything to say to that, she did not stay to hear it. She was running—she admitted it. This was more than she had bargained for.

He would never know how close she was to giving in; to following him to Normandy. But that would serve neither of them in the end. If they were to do this, they must do it full and fair in the world's eyes. Anything less dishonored them both.

❈ CHAPTER 18 ❈

T he fey appeared in the rafters above Mathilda's bed, three
days after she returned to her father's castle. It was large
for a fey, and brimming with magic. When she first saw it, she
was lying awake, staring at the carved beams; for a moment she
thought it was another carving, until she realized that it had not
been there when she lay down and tried to sleep.

It hung like a bat from the beam, wings furled below its
head. Its body was smooth and sexless but distinctly human; its
face likewise, except for the eyes, which were large and round,
yellow and slit-pupiled like a cat's. They blinked at Mathilda,
slowly, amiably.

She had a brief but powerful urge to stand on her head so
that she could see that face right side up. The fey grinned, baring teeth as catlike as its eyes, and caught hold of the beam with
long fingers. It swung there, wings hanging down like a silvery
cloak.

Three maids slept in the room: a bare sufficiency to honor
her rank. One of them, Agnes who slept the lightest, stirred and
murmured.

The fey winked out of sight if not out of existence. It was
still there: transparent as a bubble of water, but if she watched
it sidelong, she could see it clearly enough.

Mathilda murmured a word in the old language, a spell full
of sleep. Agnes sighed and lay still.

After a judicious while, the fey let itself be visible again. It
was here for a purpose: not simple curiosity, or because the
winds of the world had borne it through these rafters on this
night.

It nodded eagerly. Its face blurred and shifted, shimmering
into another semblance altogether.

William looked very odd with cat's eyes. His voice sounded as if from far away—as far as Normandy. "I fight; I lead men. I don't know anything about women: loving them, or anything else. I never learned. No bastards, I said, and I meant it. Now I don't know where to begin."

Mathilda opened her mouth to speak, but the fey had melted into itself again, hanging in the air, grinning at her. That was not the message, then. The fey was simply telling her who had sent it.

She set her lips together. Feys were notoriously chancy creatures. If she pressed this one too hard, it would bolt. Then she would never know what William had sent it to do.

It was rather amazing that he had persuaded it to do his bidding. It took delicacy and skill to master a fey. Whether he had meant that to be part of his message she did not know, but her respect for him had grown. He had been carrying on with his lessons, she could see that.

With the fey hanging contentedly from its beam, she found that she could sleep. She even smiled.

Mathilda had had eerie attendants before, though always in the Wood, never in her father's house. Those few here who could see the fey either doubted their eyes or knew what the creature was. She found its presence oddly comforting as winter closed in and no envoy came from Normandy.

Other envoys did come. The presence of a young and unbetrothed daughter, who was known to be fair of face, brought out a flock of would-be suitors. Some she had known at the king's court; others came from closer to home.

Most sent dignified persons to speak for them, but a few came themselves. Those were the overeager and the desperate, younger sons or petty barons in search of a great prize. They were as inevitable as midges in a marsh, and fully as irritating.

The fey was of the same opinion. It had a strong streak of mischief in it, and a flock of companions and kin who were delighted to join it in wreaking havoc. They soured the wine that the worst of the suitors were drinking, pinched them invisibly until they were covered in tiny bruises, tripped them as they walked across a clear stretch of hall. Spiders nested in their beds, rats devoured their belongings, packs of dogs pursued them, baying and snapping.

But William sent no one, nor did he come himself. Except for the fey, Mathilda would have thought he had forgotten her.

What did come, early in the new year, was a legate from the Pope with a letter for her father. Baldwin summoned her to him so that she could read it. It was short as such things went, and in the midst of all the formulae of the Roman Curia, to the point. That point was quite sharp. *If you marry your daughter to the Duke of Normandy, you will pay such penalties as the Church may devise.*

Mathilda restrained herself with difficulty from tearing the thing asunder, pendant seals and all. "This is ridiculous," she said.

"Isn't it?" Baldwin had had time to master his temper. If anything he seemed amused. "Especially when you consider that no such marriage has been discussed on this side of the Otherworld."

"Lanfranc," said Mathilda. She spoke the word as if it had been a curse.

"It's not easy to serve two masters—as the Lord Christ himself observed." Baldwin shook his head and sighed. "These laws of blood and kinship are absurdly broad and growing broader. A time will come when no one can marry at all without incurring the wrath of Rome; for are we not all kin through Adam?"

"Then we'll have to marry among the fey folk," Mathilda said with bitter humor. Even that sobered quickly. "That's the heart of it, isn't it? That we come from the old blood, and he more than most. The Church suffers our kind to live—but they don't want us breeding with one another. It would serve them well if all magic died from the world."

"Some within the Church would be served better if it were all constrained under their law. A point which I shall make," said Baldwin, "when the time is ripe. In the meantime, daughter, what shall I tell them? That no such marriage is in the offing?"

"No," said Mathilda without stopping to think. "I'll marry him or no one."

Baldwin's brows went up.

She bit her tongue. The words had come out of their own accord. They came from the heart, which knew neither sense nor reason. It only knew what it wanted.

It was wise in its way, and remarkably politic. She met her father's eyes. "In the spring," she said, "I'm riding to Normandy. The Church can thunder all the denunciations it likes. I'm going to marry the duke."

"Will the duke have you?"

"He'll do what I tell him."

"Wise man," her father said.

She glared at him. "Don't tell me you've changed your mind."

"I have not," he said. "I see I have an embassy to send."

"Two," she said. "One to Normandy with the offer of my hand in marriage. One to Rome with whatever answer will keep the Pope out of the way until the marriage is made."

"That goes without saying," he said. His voice was cool, his expression calm, but she could tell that he was pleased. He knew better than to ask what had brought her round to his way of thinking. It should be enough that she had done it—or her heart had.

The fey was turning somersaults in the air. "It's all your fault," she said to it.

It was notably undismayed. It had done what it came to do: surely one of the most peculiar proofs of love that a man ever gave a woman.

"It's not as simple as that," she said. "Tell him. And tell him I'll see him at Easter. He had better be ready for me."

The fey transcribed one last, ornate series of loops and curlicues, then vanished with a soft but distinct pop.

William was at sword practice when the Pope's message reached him. He whirled the massive blade around his head, barely missing the pair of knights who had been trading blows with him, and sank it deep into the hacked tree trunk that was more often used for mace practice. The shock of the blow numbed his arms to the shoulders.

He left the sword embedded in the wood and whirled to face the squire who had brought the message. The boy's face was white, but he held his ground. Cowards never lasted long in William's service.

"Where's the Pope's man?" William demanded.

The boy was visibly relieved. He was safe, or so he thought, although the papal legate might not be. "He's in the hall, my lord."

William cuffed him to keep him on his toes, pushed back his mail hood but let the rest of it be, and went to confront the envoy from Rome.

Whoever claimed the Holy See this season had had the good sense to send a younger man than most, and not too monkish. He looked as if he might even know which end of a sword to thrust into a man's vitals.

William's servants had offered him all the courtesies: food, rest, comfort. He was finishing off a well-laden trencher when William came into the hall. The sight of William in armor barely widened his eyes.

"So," said William, hooking a bench with his foot and pulling it over to sit on. "Who's Pope this week? Benedict again?"

The legate crossed himself with becoming devotion. "The Holy Father Benedict sits the throne of Peter," he said. "He wishes you to know, my lord, that—"

"I know," William said, cutting him off. "The boy told me. That's mortal fast work, for Rome. Does the lady know that she's supposed to be marrying me—unless the Pope stops her?"

"You would know more of that than I, my lord," the legate said. "My message is as you heard, from the Holy Father himself."

"What, not the Prior of Bec?"

The legate looked suitably puzzled. "Bec, my lord?"

"Ah," said William: a sharp sound of disgust. He changed tacks abruptly. "You're welcome to stay as long as you like. My servants are at your disposal. Ask them for whatever you need."

"You're generous, my lord," the legate said. From his tone, he had not expected that. No one knew what to expect from William yet.

Good, William thought. He thrust himself to his feet. He left the legate staring, with the remains of a loaf in his hand and his cup of ale half drunk.

It was bloody difficult to catch a moment for himself. Sometimes William actually missed his old, desperate existence, when he ran alone or with a few men, with death on his tail and God knew what ahead of him. A duke who actually ruled his duchy was never alone, not even to piss.

William had to wait until long after nightfall, when the last devoted drinker had fallen over in the hall, and his guards were either dozing at their posts or walking the walls without. In other circumstances he would have whipped the former awake and upbraided the latter for wandering so far afield, but tonight their lapses served him well.

In Caen as in Paris, the chapel was nearly always deserted late at night. Here also as there, and in many another chapel that William had happened upon, spirits found the air congenial; they fed on crumbs of sanctity, and danced in the flames of the candles.

Odd, he thought, how they loved the chapels here in Gaul, but in Britain that same holiness was death to them. Something there turned prayer to cold iron, whereas here, it had become a part of what these beings were.

He would wager that Lanfranc could explain that.

Lanfranc. He glared at the altar. No one else in the Church could have known what was between William and Mathilda.

William liked to think that he was a good enough son of the Church. He went to Mass, he gave alms to the poor, he showed due respect to those in orders. But when it came to where and when he would look for a wife, he had no intention of giving way to Mother Church. Particularly when the cause and instigator was his erstwhile friend, the Prior of Bec.

William calmed himself with an effort. He needed quiet; he needed focus, if he was to summon the creature he had sent to Mathilda.

Just as he managed to slow his breathing, though not quite to put aside the rush of temper, the fey winked into existence above his head. It was grinning broadly, baring a fearsome array of teeth. "Spring," it sang. "Spring, she comes."

William kept a tight grip on the surge of elation. "Did the Pope send word to her, too?"

The fey nodded so eagerly that its ears twirled together above its head.

William laughed. It burst out of him like a shaft of sun through a thick bank of cloud. The fey danced in the air, leaping and spinning.

It stopped, grinning literally from ear to ear. William grinned back. "So there's her answer. And mine, too. By the old gods, mine, too. Spring, you said?"

"Spring!" the fey agreed, lilting with delight.

"Go back to her," William said. "Look after her for me. Until spring."

"Until spring," the fey said, echoing his words exactly, deep burr and all. Its wings snapped together over its head; it poised for a moment like the miniature image of a warrior angel. Then with a last, many-fanged grin, it vanished.

❧ CHAPTER 19 ❧

Winter's grip had locked tight. The river was frozen from bank to bank; the ice was sturdy enough for a horse to walk on. The novices and lay students from the abbey had taken to escaping on clear days, filching empty sacks from the storeroom, and sliding down the steepest part of the bank onto the ice. The most adept of them could slide clear to the opposite bank; then it was a slipping, sliding, perilous journey back, to scramble up to the top and do it all over again.

Their elders had decided to be indulgent. There were few enough clear days, and they all worked hard when they were not larking out on the ice. Harder, maybe, with the chance of such a reward.

For Lanfranc those bitter-bright afternoons brought their own pleasure: quiet in the schoolroom, a fire on the hearth, a new book brought up from Bologna or Milan, and the peace to think thoughts beyond the declension of a verb or the evolution of a syllogism. He could hear the shouts of glee from without, reverberating through the hush of the cloister.

One day between Epiphany and Candlemas—or between the Solstice and Imbolc, if he allowed the other half of him to speak—the cold was particularly bitter and the sun particularly bright. The river was as smooth as glass: it had rained the day before, a rain of ice. He had seen earlier how trees in the orchard were weighted down with it, and the abbey's walls were sheathed as if in diamond, glittering in the warmthless sunlight.

He was blessedly warm. A flock of small bright spirits had congregated in the fire, fluttering and chattering like birds. He set the marker in his book with barely a page read, and let his eyelids fall shut.

"Father? Father Prior?"

He woke slowly. His hands and feet were cold: the fire had died down. The spirits were gone.

One of the novices stood by his chair, cropped hair standing on end and cheeks bright red with the cold, looking as if he had run all the way in from the river. "Father Prior," he said. "Are you awake?"

"I am now," Lanfranc said, but he smiled. "What is it, Anselm? Nobody's broken his neck, I hope?"

"Oh, no, Father," the boy said. "They're all in the dormitory, thawing out. It's cold!"

"I had noticed," Lanfranc said dryly. "So what is it? Did I sleep through the Office?"

"Of course not, Father," said Anselm. His face flushed with more than cold. "I'm sorry, Father; my brain's all scattered. There's a man here asking for you."

Lanfranc sighed. Even in the dead of winter, people came to talk to him, dispute with him, beg him to take them or their sons into his school. He had had to run away from it when he first came from Italy, fleeing the crowds of would-be disciples and hiding in this abbey of Bec. But the world had found him again.

Anselm was one of his bodyguards as they called themselves, monks and novices and older students who undertook to protect the master from the importunate. Which meant that if Anselm had seen fit to relay the request, the one who made it must be out of the ordinary.

"Do I know him?" Lanfranc asked. "Is it a monk? A pilgrim?"

"It's a knight, Father," Anselm said, "and he says you know him. He's not here to join the school. He was very firm about that."

"Indeed?" said Lanfranc. He had had dreams of thunder; there was a tang of it in the air, now that he was awake to notice.

He could be alarmed, he supposed. But one knight, however fierce his temper, could hardly put Lanfranc in danger. Not here among his own, within the walls of a Guardian's power.

"Bring me to him," he said to the boy.

Anselm dipped his head in respect and turned to do his master's bidding.

The knight was waiting in the room near the gate, which was reserved for guests and visitors. The room was cold, but he seemed impervious. A pair of the lay pupils had found him; one had his sword, which was as long as the child was tall, and was straining to lift its point from the floor. The other squatted with his nose to the knight's arm, peering closely at the joining of rings in the mail shirt.

Lanfranc paused in the doorway. That was a side of the Duke of Normandy that he had not seen before: easy, patient, indulging the fancies of wide-eyed boys. He was even smiling as he showed the would-be warrior how to grip the heavy blade. His big scarred hands on the small smooth ones raised the sword up and guided it slowly, carefully, around and down.

"I see you believe in starting them young, my lord," Lanfranc said.

The second boy, who had been so fascinated by the coat of mail, squeaked and jumped, but William took his time turning to face Lanfranc. "Good day, Father Prior," he said.

"Good day, my lord duke," said Lanfranc. "Or are you here under another name?"

"No one's asked me for any," William said. "I'd say you're a congregation of holy innocents, if the place weren't so well defended."

The boys' eyes had gone as wide as they could go. This encounter would be all over the abbey within the hour. Lanfranc lowered his glance on them. "Good day, messires," he said pointedly.

They were young, but they understood a firm dismissal. Reluctant but obedient, with many glances backward, they took their leave.

Their absence left a swelling silence. William sheathed his sword in it, a swift hiss and a ringing thump. The smell of thunder was almost too faint to detect. He was actually smiling. It was not just the children, Lanfranc thought: there was an ease to him that had not been there before.

"Life agrees with you," Lanfranc observed.

"It's easier than it used to be," William said.

"Have you come to reassure me of that?"

"I've come to tell you to leave my duchy."

That, Lanfranc had not expected. Anger, yes; recrimination; outrage. But this was perfectly calm and eminently reasonable. "May I ask why?" he asked.

"You're the wisest scholar in Gaul," William said. "Don't play the fool with me."

"I can guess," said Lanfranc. "It would be courteous to let me know whether that guess is correct."

William was not a redheaded man, but he had the high color of one. That and his clenched fists betrayed him, and the barely perceptible rumble of stones underfoot. But he said with tight-drawn steadiness, "Flanders. Mathilda. The Pope."

"Ah," said Lanfranc. "And you hold me at fault because . . . ?"

"Who else knew that that was a possibility? Who would, or could, take it direct to Rome?"

"Anyone who happened to spy on your assignations with the lady in Paris."

Lanfranc never saw William move. His magical protections had no time to rise. An iron grip closed about his throat. He could breathe, just. He knew better than to move.

"Father Prior," William said, soft as a purr, "no mortal spied on us. She made sure of that. She taught me how. It had to have been you who sent word to the Pope. No doubt you provided him with the exact reference in the law—or composed it for the occasion. Why? What is there about the two of us that merits such betrayal?"

"The law—" Lanfranc began.

William's fingers tightened, cutting off Lanfranc's voice if not, quite, the last of his breath. "Spare me your cant about the law. The Church is as easily bought as any other human thing. What is it, then? Misplaced friendship? Dire foreseeing? Simple mortal jealousy?"

Just as Lanfranc wondered if William expected him to answer at all, the vise loosened just enough to permit him to speak. "Truly," he said, "that is the law."

This time William forbore to strangle him, but leaned in close instead. "Tell me why it serves you to hew to the letter of that law. God knows you break enough others, with what else you are, and what you do when your so-holy brothers aren't looking."

There was death here. Lanfranc's protections were nowhere to be found when he looked for them. He was rather disconcertingly mortal, and this was a trained fighting man, with magic both stronger and more skilled than Lanfranc had expected, and no reason to be merciful.

"Believe me or not, as you please," Lanfranc said, "but I did not send word of this to Rome."

"You sent word to someone who did." William let him go in a near-convulsion of disgust. "Get out of my duchy. Pack yourself up and go."

Lanfranc could not penetrate this depth of anger. However unjust it might be, it was implacable. He gathered what dignity he could and said, "I've done no wrong; I bear no guilt. I will not be a martyr to a misunderstanding."

"When the Pope misunderstands," William said, "lives and kingdoms break. We'll buy our way out of this—be sure of that. Then what will you do?"

"If you are given dispensation," Lanfranc said, "then that's the end of it. But if you forge ahead in despite of Rome, you are in sin and your duchy is subject to interdict. Would you do that to your people? Is one woman worth so much?"

"That woman is worth more than you can imagine," William said. "Even you, my lord Guardian. What is it? What do you see that so terrifies you?"

"I see the law," Lanfranc said. And that was the truth, however little this man of war and magic might understand it. His kind made laws, or broke them with fire and sword. William was not born to comprehend a scholar's mind—or a lawyer's.

"I'm going to marry her," William said, "whether Rome comes round to my way of thinking now or later. It will—you can bet this abbey's revenues on that."

"What," said Lanfranc, "not my life?"

"Don't push me," William warned him, "or I'll finish throttling you. I'll give you until Imbolc. Then you'd best be gone, or I'll set the hunt on you."

It was not an earthly hunt he meant. Nor, Lanfranc thought, was it an empty threat. William's magic had grown since first Lanfranc met him. Whether that was a good or a bad thing, he was not altogether certain.

For a surety, it was not a good thing for Lanfranc—not now. But he could not unsay what he had said, or change what he believed. The Church as it was would not sanction this union. No matter what the old gods or the powers might say, Lanfranc was the Church's man first. He would do what he was sworn to do.

He surprised himself with grief. This friendship he had valued, and not only because there was more to William than any simple man knew. "I'll leave tomorrow," he said. "You can send an escort if you like, to make sure I pass the border."

"I'll know when you do," William said. Did he grieve as Lanfranc did? There was no way to tell. He had learned long ago to conceal what was in his heart. His face was opaque, his eyes flat. Only one thing Lanfranc could be sure of: there was no yielding in him.

Lanfranc bowed stiffly. "My lord," he said.

"Father Prior," said William with equal stiffness.

Long after William had gone, Lanfranc stood in that small, icy room. Slowly the reek of thunder faded, and the tang of hot iron. There had been a battle here, and Lanfranc had not won it.

He refused to succumb to regret. He had done no more or less than keep his vow of obedience to holy Church.

His feet had long since gone numb from the cold. His first step was a stumble. He caught himself, and willed his feet to be steady. He had far to go before he could rest again, or indulge in either warmth or contentment.

❧ CHAPTER 20 ❧

Mathilda came from Flanders into Normandy in the full flowering of spring. Her bridal procession was royally splendid, for she was of royal blood; she had a new gown for every day of it, each more splendid than the last.

God, or the gods, favored her. All the way from Tournai to the fortress town of Eu, the sun shone; the wind blew soft. If it rained, it was kind enough to rain at night, when the procession was safe under roofs or in gilded tents.

That was the glory that the world saw. It saw also, inevitably, that the Church had not approved the marriage. There was no outright ban—not yet—but that was unlikely to last. Rome had troubles of its own, a little matter of warring Popes and bitterly opposing factions. The Duke of Normandy and the Count of Flanders had fostered this contention, but even their conjoined forces might not be enough to hold back that particular tide.

For now it sufficed. Normandy's Church was electing to do as its duke commanded. Rome was far away. William was here, in the flesh; his power was rising, his grip on the duchy growing firmer. His priests and bishops made the practical choice.

These were cold thoughts for a bride coming to her wedding, but noble marriage was, of necessity, a coldly practical thing. Or so Mathilda reminded herself. Beneath the glorious new gowns and the regal bearing, she was as fluttery as any common bride.

What if this was a mistake? What if, once the deed was done, they came to hate each other? What if he already hated her? He was bound to her. She had never released him. And he was not a man to submit tamely to any restraint.

But if she let him go, and he in turn released her on the perfectly valid grounds of the Church's objection, what then? What would come of it? How—

She stopped herself forcibly from traveling further down that road. Not while she was on the living, breathing, dust-and-earthen road from Tournai to Eu, in what seemed to be the bright morning of the world.

Somewhat to her relief in the strangeness of her mood, the brightness was not after all unalloyed. There was a sense to the earth when a realm was bound to its lord and its lord to it. It had not been there when she was last in Normandy. Nor was it now, although there was a difference. If she could have put words to it at all, she would have said that it felt like a half-broken horse, growing accustomed to bit and saddle, but still unsure of itself under the weight of the rider.

Normandy could still rebel; could still cast off its duke. And Mathilda could be the cause of it.

Again, she refused to indulge in that thought. Not until she must. What she could do, she did: gentling the land as she rode over it, soothing its raw edges with the soft stroke of magic.

The land allowed it, when it well might have turned against her. She took that for an omen. If she was to be duchess here, she was as much a part of it as the duke.

And surely, if he was going to refuse her, his realm would know even before she came to him. His land would reject her and his fey would leave her—and neither had done any such thing. Indeed the fey clung as close as ever, with no alteration in its manner, for good or ill.

Mathilda arrived in Eu three days before Easter. There she discovered with a degree of disappointment that startled her that William had not yet come.

But—and that almost made up for it—his mother had. Herleva stood at the gate, hand in hand with her husband. Herluin's smile told Mathilda exactly why and how Herleva had chosen to love him.

Herleva's own smile was brilliant, and yet Mathilda narrowed her eyes at the sight of her. She was thinner than she had been when Mathilda met her the year before; her face had a subtle pallor that Mathilda did not like.

Nonetheless she was visibly delighted to greet Mathilda. "Welcome," she said warmly, clasping Mathilda in her arms.

There was no slackening of strength, at least, in that embrace.
"Welcome, daughter."

Mathilda's throat caught. She could feel the death lairred in
the body. It was black, like rot in an apple: spreading through the
breasts and sending tendrils down toward the belly. Pain
thrummed at the edges of Mathilda's senses.

Her arms tightened about Herleva. Herleva did not waver,
but her embrace altered slightly: warning, restraining. *Say no
word of this,* it said.

Mathilda could not refuse to obey—not in front of so many
people. She made herself smile as the lady took one hand and
the lord the other, leading her into the hall.

Even without William, the festivities were elaborate, lengthy,
and for Mathilda, unavoidable. Nonetheless, for that day at least,
they ended while there was still somewhat left of the night.

The fact that it was Lent, and tomorrow was Good Fri-
day, had something to do with it. For Mathilda there was no
great power in the day or the season, but others were more truly
Christian than she. When she rose to end the feasting, they did
not object too strongly. Tomorrow was a day of fasting and pen-
itence. They straggled off to begin it.

She would have been happy enough to do the same, but
when she sought the chambers she had been given, the door
opened on another place altogether.

There had been no warning, no shifting of the earth, no
shiver in the heart of her magic. She simply opened a door and
looked out on mist and starlight.

Her colder self knew that this must be a trap. Her heart knew
no fear. There was a rightness in it, as if one could climb a stair
in a castle and walk through a door and find oneself in a
meadow under the stars. A wood all but surrounded it, full of
rich scents and soft rustles and whispers. On the far edge of it,
the trees dwindled and the land rolled down to a long stretch of
glimmering water: a river that ran into the sea.

This was still Normandy. It was near Eu, she thought. She
could feel the town under her skin, even when she turned and
found neither door nor stair behind her. The maids and escort
who had followed her from the hall were gone. Of them all,
only the fey was still with her, hovering just above her head.

Not all the mist was born of the night air. Skeins and tendrils

of it thickened into shapes very like the fey, gauzy wings and insubstantial figures drifting over the grass and through the woven
branches of the wood.

None of them ventured toward the sea. Therefore Mathilda
did, because she had passed out of the waking world. Sense and
logic had no meaning here.

At first she thought that the tall shadows beyond the last of
the trees were Guardians in hooded cloaks, but as she drew
nearer she saw that they were standing stones. They drew up
power from the earth, humming gently with it, but doing nothing else that she could discern.

She was still unafraid. In fact she was quietly happy. As odd
as this dream or waking vision was, it was restful. It soothed her
raw edges and made her doubts seem dim and faintly foolish.

One of the stones moved. After a moment she realized that it
was a living creature, a man: broad shoulders, long firm stride.

Even as she realized what he was, she knew who he had to
be. Her heart leaped. She was running before she knew what
she did.

Part of her, too small to slow or stop her flying feet, dreaded
that when they met, he would recoil. But his arms had opened.
His face in starlight showed nothing of either shock or disgust.
He was grinning crazily; as she hurtled into him, the sound that
burst out of him was, incontestably, a gust of laughter.

They spun completely about. Mathilda could not breathe:
his arms were squeezing the air out of her. But that was fair
enough. She was doing the same to him.

He was real—as real as he had been in the Wood of Broceliande. He was here, warm and solid and utterly himself. The
hardness in him was still there, the ruthless edge, the fortress
that he was forced to make of his heart if he was to come alive
and sane from the life that he had had. But for her the gates
were open wide.

The air was full of the fey and all its kin, dancing in a cloud
about them. Their joy made Mathilda dizzy—or maybe it was
the joy in herself, rich and heady as wine.

With perceptible reluctance, William's grip eased. He kept
his arms about her, but now she could breathe. As he bent, perhaps to speak, perhaps to venture a kiss, the earth shrugged
underfoot.

Things were in it. Old things, dark things—older than the

Old Things, dark as the deep places from which they rose. William's arms had tightened again; his breath hissed.

He knew these things. So did she. They had hunted him all his life. They were death that lived in the land, devourer of life, destroyer of mortal flesh that fancied it could rule.

They had come for him tonight. They had lured him here with dreams and magic, and trapped him with Mathilda.

No. This was no fault of hers. She had come because she was meant to come. Old Night had found the weakness in the lord of this land: the gate of his heart wide open, and his guard lowered.

Yet that was his strength. It was life; it was light in darkness, and warmth in everlasting cold. He was born of this, the greatest power that mortals knew, invoked in a place of great power.

So too was this. Where it was did not matter, except that it was in Normandy, poised between wood and stone and the sea.

The old dark things were all around them, coiling up from the earth and clawing for the sky. Mathilda reached for the living warmth that was William. In the same instant he reached for her. Her hands sought the fastenings of his cotte. His sought the lacings of her gown. Silk gave way, then linen beneath.

Cool air caressed them. William shivered, though not, she thought, with cold. He started to speak, but her finger pressed to his lips. No words, the gesture said. Not here; not in this. This rite was beyond such things.

The dark things could not touch the warmth between them. However wild the world without, the two of them made a world of their own.

They sank down together into the cool sweetness of the grass. The earth rocked and surged, but they were safe in each other. Blows that fell, fell on armor of air. It was a right battering, that: fierce hammer strokes that strove to crack and shatter them. But Mathilda met William's eyes, and found there all the strength she needed.

He was frowning slightly, but that was his wonted expression. The corner of his mouth curved just perceptibly upward. "I'm not dreaming you, am I?"

"No more than I am dreaming you," she said. "No; this is real—more real than anything that is."

"You've always been that for me," he said.

She could not help herself. She drew his head down and

kissed him. It was meant to be a quick brush of the lips, but once it had begun, neither of them had any desire to end it.

She was aware very dimly that the wind was howling, the earth trembling, the standing stones rocking in their places. Here where they were, there was only the beating of their hearts and the warmth of their bodies, and the blood rising in a fierce tide.

He drew a shuddering breath. His whole body was shaking.

So it was true, she thought. He never had lain with a woman. That pleased her rather immoderately.

She cupped his face in her hands. Slowly, gentle but firm, she stroked them down his neck, across his shoulders and breast, down his belly. He tensed. "Hush," she said. "Be still. Open your heart."

"I don't know how."

"Of course you do," she said. "This is magic. Old magic: the oldest of all." She rose above him. He lay almost too still, eyes fixed on her face.

"Yes," she said. "Fill your eyes. Let thought drain away. Simply be."

That was enough like the lessons she had taught him that he had begun to obey before he knew what he was doing. She pressed the advantage. Her hands had paused while she spoke to him. Now she finished what she had begun.

He gasped, but he did not strike her hands away. "Don't think," she reminded him. "Be."

"It is like magic," he said in slow understanding. "Or when I fight."

"What is it they say about love and war?"

This gasp had laughter in it: startled out of him. But that was it; that was the key. He knew how to fight—few better. She watched the tension drain out of him. The walls crumbled; the armor of years dropped away.

It was not easy. Parts of him tried to cling to resistance. The defenses were dug deep.

But she had got inside them. She had the body's own instincts to strengthen her—and him.

For the first time he moved of his own accord, until he closed his arms about her. He trembled a little, but he held on.

She slid down until they were belly to belly. The hot, hard thing between them almost frightened her.

The powers without had thrashed themselves into a frenzy. This rite would bind them, and too well they knew it. This union of magic and magic, spirit and spirit, maiden blood and maiden heart, was the most potent of any working under heaven.

It could only be wrought once. If it faltered, the dark would swallow them.

Mathilda set her teeth, hardly aware that she was doing it, and took her beloved inside her.

She had expected pain. There was seldom any pleasure the first time, everyone had told her that. She had not expected that it would hurt so much. They did not fit. They did not—

"*Ah!*" Whether it was her cry or his, she would never know. It broke off quickly, in breathless silence.

Nothing stirred, within or without. The world was perfectly motionless, as if poised on the brink of—what?

The pain was still there inside her, but it was distant. The cruel edge had gone away. Gradually she remembered that they were supposed to move, that this was a dance.

Her body knew. Even as her mind unlocked, she began a slow, surging rhythm, smooth as the swing of the sea.

They did fit. Exactly. He was large and warm and strong. The clean male smell of him, the surprising smoothness of his skin where armor always covered it, the ridges of scars on breast and arms and sides, worked their way into her memory and lodged there. They, like the rest of him, were precisely as they should be.

She was thinking too much. She took her advice to him: she let words slide away, let thought and memory vanish, until there was only the body's awareness, and the long swell and sudden breaking of pure pleasure.

Mathilda lay in William's arms. The stars were quiet; the earth slept. They were part of it, he and she. The dark things had sunk down deep or slid away beyond the borders of the realm.

Normandy was theirs—both, through this great rite of binding. They had wrought a Great Marriage, here between the forest and the sea.

Neither spoke. Words were too small for this. She knew that she must rise, find her clothes, make her way back to the mortal world; as must he. But she hated to leave those arms even for a day, even to be wedded again before the people of this realm that now was hers.

There was a little left of the night. Such as it was, they spent it together, as they would hope to do for their lives long.

William, Duke of Normandy, took Mathilda of Flanders to wife on the day of Easter, just as the apple orchards came into bloom. The crash of the sea on the shore was a distant accompaniment to the choir's chanting, as they knelt together at Mass after their vows had been spoken at the cathedral door. William reflected dimly that he should not be able to hear the waves: they were half a league away. But there was no mistaking that soft boom and sighing roar.

It was as if the sea had come to the wedding, too. Every other spirit and creature of the aether in Normandy was there; the cathedral's arches were as thick with them as a fruit tree with birds. They flocked in the aisles and tumbled together above the altar. It was rather distracting—but never as much as the warm sweet-scented presence beside him.

He had hardly recognized her when he saw her riding toward him in procession, mounted on a milk-white palfrey and dressed all in cloth of gold. His clearest and closest memory of her was altogether different: bare and gleaming on dew-wet grass, flushed with laughter and loving, and so utterly, perfectly herself that when he looked at her, he could not breathe.

Until very recently he had not been certain that he would survive to marry. If he had paused to imagine that event at all, he had supposed that he would be bound to an heiress of suitable lineage and significant property. That she would be young, or least young enough to bear children, was a necessity. He had not expected that she would be beautiful.

It would not have mattered if she was not, as long as she was Mathilda. That came to him with the elevation of the Host in the Mass. The circle of unleavened bread, catching the light, shone supernaturally white. In it, tiny and perfect, he saw her face.

He would never tell anyone what he had seen. Even Mathilda might reckon it blasphemous. But there it was; she meant that much to him. God would understand, surely. Or else why had He made them for each other?

PART TWO

✤✤✤

THE SUMMER KING

anno domini 1051

❈ CHAPTER 21 ❈

Herleva was dying.

It had been a long, slow death. The darkness that Mathilda had seen in her before the wedding at Eu, three years past, had grown little by little until it was near to consuming her.

Her body was riddled with it. Magic had no power over it; it grew out of the body itself. What arts Mathilda had learned in the Wood had eased the pain at least, and Herleva had arts and powers of her own, as did her husband; but those were failing.

She rested now in her husband's manor near Conteville, where Mathilda had first met her. Herluin had built her a bothy in the old fashion, a little house of wattle and thatch. Its windows were wide, looking out over the fields and woods of the demesne. There was a soft featherbed for her to lie on, and coverlets woven of air and light and a handful of swansdown.

Mathilda had come the day before with as small a retinue as she could escape with, answering a summons from the vicomte. His expression as he met her at his gate had told her all she needed to know. When she saw Herleva she knew there was no denying it. Herleva was slipping away.

Herleva could still speak. She had insisted, this morning, that she see her grandchildren; nor could Mathilda dissuade her with the fact that Robert had entered into his second year with a grand show of rebellion and the baby, Richard, was teething. Their nurses brought them in at Herleva's command, ready to snatch them away the moment they began to misbehave.

A long, wet spring had given way to a cool and lovely summer. Herluin had planted a rose-briar to twine up over the bothy's roof; blossoms from it scented Herleva's bed. She lay in soft sunlight, looking no more substantial than an image made of glass.

The children stared at her with wide eyes. They were a bit of a disappointment to their mother: neither had a scrap of magic, nor was either of them anything more than the robust young Norman that he seemed. But they were alive and vigorous, and they served their purpose admirably.

William professed himself delighted with them. Normandy most certainly was. Legitimate heirs, at last, although the Church was still proving difficult on the matter of the duke's marriage.

Herleva smiled. Robert was a small and sturdy image of his father. Richard showed signs of growing up to be much larger than his brother, and also rather fairer: he favored his mother for face and coloring.

They both seemed to find their grandmother fascinating. Richard leaned out of his nurse's arms, reaching for her. Robert broke free altogether and clambered up on the bed.

Both the nurse and his mother sprang to pluck him out, but Herleva stopped them with a glance. "Let him be," she said.

He settled against her with gentleness that Mathilda had never seen in him, tucked his thumb into his mouth, and lay perfectly quietly, eyes fixed on Herleva's face.

Mathilda should know better than to gape. When great enchanters' bodies failed, their magic grew purer, stronger; it shone out of them. Robert had none of his own, but it seemed he was of the old blood after all. He could see what his grandmother was.

"Death is a door," Herleva said. It was not clear to whom she was speaking: maybe Robert, maybe Mathilda, maybe no one at all. "One walks through, and there is the Otherworld, whole and complete, just as this one is. And one lives there until one's life is finished. Then there is the door, and there is this world. Over and over, time and again, worlds without end."

She nearly sang the last of it. Her voice was losing its humanity, gaining the purity of that other world.

"Listen," she said. "Listen, daughter. Can you see? The door is opening. The time is come. Look and see."

"What?" said Mathilda. "What should I see?"

"Destiny," said Herleva.

Mathilda set her teeth. Death was making Herleva as cryptic as Dame Alais could ever be; and that was a maddening thing.

She willed herself to be calm. Neither Herleva nor the Lady

could help themselves. Prophecy was cryptic; that was its nature. "What destiny," she asked, "and whose?"

"Yours," said Herleva. "His."

No need to ask who the other was. "And that is?"

"King once," Herleva said, "and king to be."

"Indeed," Mathilda said: "But king of what? All the thrones I know of are occupied."

"You will know," said Herleva. "Soon."

That was as clear an answer as Mathilda had ever heard from a seer. She did not press further: Herleva had slid into the light sleep of the dying, with Robert still curled against her, visibly and quietly content.

The castle of Domfront crouched on its steep jut of rock, stark against the sky. William had been glaring at it for weeks now, willing it to surrender; but the gates remained stubbornly shut and the castellan refused equally stubbornly to yield his charge. The last time he deigned to come out of his hole, he had stood over the gate and sneered down at William fifty man-lengths below. "I am not the Norman duke's dog," he had declared time and again. "My lord pays fealty to Anjou. Therefore so do I."

That alone would have been enough to set the blood pounding in William's skull. His purely instinctive hatred of Geoffrey of Anjou, which had awakened while he was at the king's court in Paris, had ripened into a thoroughly reasonable loathing of an invader and trespasser. Geoffrey was claiming castles in William's own duchy—and this one, just over the border in the county of Maine, belonged to William's own vassal. Or so William had thought, until the man's castellan informed him that milord's allegiance had changed.

That was the devil spreading lies and deception, clouding minds and creeping like a mist through the borders of William's country. When William let himself feel the earth, he could feel the rot in it. It was insidious, and vicious. It tightened his gut and threatened to blind him with rage.

That too was devilry. He forced his mind to clear and his temper to calm. He must be cold; he must fight with deadly clarity. No dark things would creep into Normandy while William lived to rule it.

Four siege towers surrounded the rock of Domfront. It rose

notably higher than they, but they had their uses. When they were not battering the castle with stones, they inundated it with showers of arrows. The latest flights were fire arrows: those kept the castle's garrison at the run, putting out eruptions of flame in the wooden floors and roofs of the stone towers.

That was not likely to go on much longer. Domfront was stubborn, but William was more so—and he had a larger army, with clear supply lines. The besieged were living on salt meat and water from the cistern by now, if reports were true; soon enough the meat would be gone, and then William would make sure the starving defenders looked down on his men eating fresh meat and new-baked bread every day. With the way the wind blew here, the smells of roasting and baking would waft very nicely up to the walls and into the keep.

"My lord!"

William woke at once from his reverie. "Ah, Guibert," he said to one of the more intelligent of his knights. Guibert could think as fast as William could, now and then; and that was not common.

Guibert was out of breath now, and the horse he sat on looked hard ridden. He had gone out hunting this morning with a handful of knights and squires. There was no sign of the rest. His hunting bow was still in its case; no quarry dangled from his saddlebow.

"What is it?" William demanded, coming to full alert. "What's happened?"

"Anjou," Guibert said. "Riding this way. Five hundred men."

William felt his lips stretch back from his teeth. "Geoffrey's coming? You're sure of it?"

"I saw him myself," Guibert said. "He had his helmet off and his banner flying. We were in a thicket, trying to flush out a boar. He came riding by. I heard him say, "We'll flatten the Bastard against the rock, and pound him to a pulp."

"Oh, did he?" said William in a dangerous purr. "He's ambitious."

Guibert had got his breath back, and a good part of his usual humor. "You could say that, my lord. He only wants to rule the whole north of Gaul."

"Not on my watch," said William. He was already moving, calling for his horse, his weapons, and two hundred men.

"Only two hundred?" Guibert asked behind him.

"That's all he deserves," William said.

Guibert offered no further argument. William had not expected him to.

It was not altogether foolish to go against an army of five hundred with one less than half the size. William knew the country well by now; he had hunted every covert for ten miles around. Through that sense of the land, he willed himself to sense the invader on it.

That was not as simple as it might have been. Maine was Geoffrey's, and it was William who in strict truth was the interloper. But Normandy's nearness and William's finely honed hate gave him the power he needed.

He sent another hundred men by ways he knew, and drew up his own ranks down the broad valley from Domfront but well within sight of it. Geoffrey, riding in, would see a wall of lances, a loom of siege towers behind them, and Domfront rearing up over them all.

William bestrode the grey charger he had won at Val-ès-Dunes; the beast was the steadiest he had, but also the best fighter. William took the place he liked best, somewhat in front of his men. All his weapons were in as good order as his squire could make them.

He settled to wait. The grey lowered its head and dropped its hip and went sensibly to sleep. Only the flicking of its ears betrayed the alertness within.

William could feel the devil's get coming. It was like the slow seeping of blood from a wound.

That blood could be contained—controlled. There was power in the world to do it. But William neither had it nor wanted it. He wanted Geoffrey dead and gone.

The place he had chosen for the fight was a stretch of open field, but hills closed in beyond. They captured sound like a trumpet, magnifying it. He heard the army long before it came in sight.

Geoffrey's men would have heard nothing but the thudding of rams on Domfront's gate. William's army was as silent as two hundred men and horses could be.

Just as the first of them rode through the hills, the hundred of William's men who had gone out ahead swarmed down from above. William began to smile.

He glanced to right and left. His knights lowered spears.

Geoffrey did not ride in the front. He kept to the middle: the prudent place, where a commander could judge what lay ahead before he reached it, and be protected from whatever might attack from behind.

William knew about prudence. Other people had it. They expected to outlive him, too, but some had already proved that false. The rest would learn it when their time came.

These men of Anjou advanced slowly: a wall of shields and lowered spears. William's outriders harried their flanks.

The men with him were growing restless. Horses pawed and champed at bits. William's will held them. Not yet, he thought. Not quite yet.

Just out of bowshot, the Angevins halted. Their shields swung back; the armed knights veered aside. Men on foot ran out from behind them, unfurling raw hides and pelts of moth-eaten fur. They flung those on the ground and dropped their breeks and pissed on the hides, mocking and jeering: "Piss pot! Tanner's get! Bastard!"

There was a buzzing in William's ears. The world had gone the color of blood.

He was moving. His men were moving with him. They were shouting—flinging the word back as they always had. "Bastard! William Bastard!"

Never, he thought. Never again.

The charge did not come as far as the Angevin line. It swept up the parade of mockers with their furs and hides, hacking with deadly precision: hewing off hands and feet. But not heads. These men would live. They would remember. No one would ever fling that word against William again.

The Angevins broke and scattered. Geoffrey was running, darting like a fox for his hole. William howled and spurred his horse in pursuit. But the ranks of his own men barred him, and the wounded and maimed lying shrieking underfoot.

He fought his way through them as best he could. The grey destrier fought as fiercely as he, attacking with teeth and hooves even as William wielded sword and spear.

They were gaining on Geoffrey. William could see the whites of the man's eyes, and the sweat streaming down the stubbled cheeks below the nasal of the helmet. He firmed his grip on his sword and gathered the grey for one last, triumphant leap.

The leap ended abruptly. The stallion must have seen the spear: he bunched and veered. But there was another spear waiting, braced against the earth.

The spearman died with William's blade in his heart. But the spear had pierced the great grey body even as it wheeled; the stallion's own weight drove it deep, full into the heart.

William fell as lightly as a man could in armor and on a battlefield, flinging himself away from the dead weight of the horse. For a stretching moment he thought he would land on his feet; but the fallen were too many, rolling beneath him. He stumbled and overbalanced and fell.

The grey horse was dead. William was bruised and winded but unharmed—but that would not last long. He lurched upright. He still had his sword, clutched in a death grip, but his spear lay broken beneath the horse.

Geoffrey was gone. William cast about fiercely for a mount, but there was nothing within reach. The battle had passed him by—and so had the man whose blood he wanted most.

He harried the stragglers, as little good as it did: none of them was bold enough to stand and fight. Even in a white fury he could not stoop to stabbing knights from behind. It was Geoffrey he wanted, and Geoffrey was deep in the mass of his army, retreating as fast as his horse could gallop.

It was a victory, however unbearable the cost. The enemy was driven off. The castellan of Domfront, seeing his supposed liege lord bolting back to Anjou, had an attack of sudden wisdom. He cried surrender.

Or maybe he feared for his own hands and feet; he had been open in his contempt for the tanner's son from Falaise. William charged him with caring for the maimed men, as a reminder, but the flush of anger was past. He was thinking again.

He needed this castle, and its castellan knew best how to manage it. He took the man's oath of fealty—heartfelt for once— and left a handful of knights to make sure the castellan kept it. He had other business, even more grievous and pressing than this.

❧ CHAPTER 22 ❧

The morning after Geoffrey of Anjou fled and Domfront surrendered, William took the road back into Normandy. It was another splendid day, bright and clear, with a light wind blowing. His men were singing as they rode; some could even carry a tune. They were calling it a victory, and letting themselves rejoice in it.

William's mood was oddly changeable: from sudden uprush of elation and a turn of song, to silent brooding. He mourned the horse who had carried him so bravely for so many battles. The one he rode now was fine enough, a lovely bright bay with a soft mouth and good paces, but it lacked both the fire and the intelligence of the one who was gone. But even more than that, he grieved for his mother, for whose sake he rode away from his siege before it was properly dismantled.

She was still alive. He needed no messenger for that: he could feel her inside him, waiting for him to come to her before she left the body.

Sometimes he simply grieved. Other times he was angry—deeply, abidingly, for all the things she had done to him, from sending him to his father to dying years younger than she needed to. More than once he stopped just short of ordering the lot of them back to Domfront.

Someone was waiting for them just outside of Normandy. It was a man alone on a brown mule, dressed in a monk's habit, with his knee hooked over the pommel of his saddle and a book propped on it, reading peacefully in the shade of a tree.

Lanfranc raised his head as the duke's company approached, and smiled the sweet, vague smile that William too well remembered. It was pure deception. There was nothing vague about that mind, and precious little that was sweet, either.

William's banked anger flared and suddenly, unexpectedly, died. Between Geoffrey and Herleva, he had worn it out. "Testing your limits?" he asked Lanfranc as his stallion drew level with the mule.

"Good morning, my lord," Lanfranc said, as quietly insistent as ever on proper forms and protocols.

"Is it?" said William. "What are you doing here?"

"Reconsidering my position," Lanfranc said.

That gave William pause. But he knew better than to assume anything. "On what? Your sins? One of your theologian's arguments?"

"In a manner of speaking, my lord," said Lanfranc. "May I ride with you?"

"I'm riding into Normandy," William said.

"Yes," said Lanfranc.

"You're asking me to revoke your exile."

"Yes."

"You've changed your mind about the marriage? Or has the Church changed it for you?"

"In a manner of speaking," Lanfranc said again.

William was growing interested in spite of himself. It had been three years; the edge was off that grudge, and Lanfranc was not offering either arrogance or bluster. William made a quick decision. "Ride with me," he said. "If you cross me again, you'll have a swift escort back here."

"That's fair enough," Lanfranc said, closing his book and putting it away in his saddlebag, and lowering his foot into the stirrup. The mule sighed hugely but fell in beside William's bay stallion without further objection.

"I made my way to Rome," Lanfranc said that night. They were camped by a wood not far from the road, where a little river offered water for men and horses. There were towns near enough, and a castle within reach, but on such a fine night, it had seemed much more pleasant to sleep under the sky.

One of the men had shot a fat buck for their dinner. They ate it round a fire that was welcome even in the warmth of the night. When they had had their fill and most of the men had wandered off to sleep, Lanfranc leaned toward William and filled his cup with wine. "Falernian," he said.

William drank a draught, finding it strong and sweet. "It's good," he said.

"The old Romans sang songs of it." Lanfranc set down his own cup and let his eyes rest on the fire. The light of it filled his eyes.

"You went to Rome," William said.

Lanfranc nodded. His face had gone somber. "I was a lawyer in Pavia. I never reckoned myself an innocent. But one always dreams—one hopes—that when one takes vows to the Church of God, that Church will be as pure as it is holy."

"You believed that?"

"I wanted to." Lanfranc sighed, sounding remarkably like his mule. "Even the wise can succumb to folly."

"So what happened? They changed the law?"

"Worse. There was great debate in the Curia as to whether the connection of blood existed at all, and whether relation by marriage constitutes blood relation. Stimulating in its way. It could have been illuminating. Instead it degenerated into a squabble over power and precedence."

"Doesn't it always?" said William.

"You are young to be so jaded."

"And you are old to be so gullible." William cocked a brow at him. "So? What broke you down?"

"Reality," Lanfranc said. "The truth came out. The Church is deeply divided over our less . . . common gifts—which I knew. But there is a faction which would obliterate us from the earth. If they could kill us all, they would. Failing that, they will do whatever they may to prevent us from procreating. There are monasteries, my lord; nunneries full of us. There is nothing holy about them, or about the monks and nuns and priests who are sworn to seek out any of our kind and either bind us or kill us. That binding is not only words, my lord. There is magic in it. If the Devil may quote scripture, one of them said to me in honest conviction, then why not use the Devil's own arts against him?"

William looked at him in dawning understanding. "One of them got at you. That's why—"

"I have a vocation," Lanfranc said. "The call was in me before anyone encouraged me to answer it."

"But someone did." William frowned. "What does that have to do with me or my duchess? None of them ever got at us. Rather the opposite."

"They anticipated you. They wrote the law to keep you apart. Each refinement of it, each broadening of the definition, was aimed at you—at us, at everyone like us. There is nothing sacred in it, no law of God, no defense against human frailty. Its only purpose is to put an end to this gift that God Himself made. Not the Devil. We are not the Devil's own."

"Is that what they think?"

"If it were fear," Lanfranc mused, barely seeming to have heard him, "or simple misunderstanding, I could forgive it. But this is mere greed and grasping for power. They envy us—covet what we have, hate us for their lack of it. They will take us, use us, then scour us from the earth.

"One of them offered me a bishopric, my lord. In return, he asked a few simple favors, nothing at all difficult, a spell or two, a few uncomplicated words: but all of them aimed at filling his coffers and raising him up in the world. He wanted to be rich, and he wanted to be Pope. He also, just incidentally, wanted certain human obstacles removed. 'After all,' he said to me, 'your whole existence is a sin. What's a little more of it, when you're damned from the beginning?'

"When I begged to differ, he mocked me for an innocent; but then he reassured me. 'Don't fret yourself,' he said. 'When you've made me Pope, I'll grant you an indulgence. Then all your sins will be forgiven.'"

William whistled softly. "Now there's a man who knows what he wants in the world."

Lanfranc did not appear to see the humor in it. "The world is brief. Death is everlasting. Hell has a place for any man who turns both magic and holiness to his own ends."

"So you don't believe souls are reborn from world to world."

"That one does not deserve rebirth. He deserves the Pit." Lanfranc shook himself hard. "No; I shouldn't say such things. He made me angry, but he was far from the only one. Greed and venality are rife in Rome. And so are men who twist the law of God to fit their own purposes."

That was the worst sin of all in his mind, William could see. To William the law was whatever it needed to be; men made it to keep one another in hand. To Lanfranc clearly it was more;

God was in it, and the order of the universe. It was a loftier way of looking at it than William could manage, but if it served his purpose, then he had no objection.

"You could have gone anywhere," William said. "Why did you come back to Normandy?"

"I prayed," said Lanfranc, "and called on the Powers to show me what I was meant to do. They sent me back here to you— and yes, your duchess. My fate is here; I'm meant to serve you. If, of course, you will accept me."

"That depends," William said. "If you're here to break our marriage because it's against your personal interpretation of the law, you leave tonight and never set foot again in any domain I rule, or pay with your life. If you're honestly here to serve, with your whole heart and all your arts and talents, I'll welcome you. We can use you, Father Prior, but only if you can give us everything you have to give."

"I won't break my vows," Lanfranc said, "to the Church or to that other half of me. But those are bound with my service to you. God and the gods have sent me here; I came willingly. If it's apology you want, I'll give it. I only did what I believed I was bound to do."

"You're honest at least," William said, "and I know you'll never lie to me. If we can stay on the same side of more fights than not, we'll do well."

"I do think so, my lord," Lanfranc said. There was a pause. Then: "There's more. You should hear this before you go further, even with me."

William tilted his head and waited.

"It's not simple venality that besets Rome," said Lanfranc, "and it's more than a general desire to rid the world of us. You in particular have enemies, my lord. They've read the stars and consulted the Powers, and seen what is foretold for you. Their purpose is to stop it. They will do whatever they can to prevent you from becoming what you are meant to be."

William raised a brow. "It goes that high, then? How long has it been going on?"

"Since before you were born," Lanfranc said. "They failed to prevent your conception, but they hounded your father through guilt to his death. They did their best to destroy you. That failed because you were guarded—but I am Guardian now because my predecessor died defending you. I knew that there were enemies; that was impossible to miss. But none of us knew how deeply they were rooted in the Church of Rome."

"That shocks you?" William asked. "It makes sense to me. What is the greatest single power in this part of the world? The Church. Power seeks power. I'm sure my enemies believe, or talk themselves into believing, that I'm a great evil in this world. It stands to reason that they would be determined to destroy me."

"It's not even that noble," said Lanfranc. "There are factions within factions, men defending nations, tribes, and lesser powers of this world. Those have a great objection to your past and present existence."

"What, are the Saxons still holding their grudge after five hundred years?"

Lanfranc's glance was sharp. "Would it take you aback if they did?"

"Very little surprises me," William said. "They have a great dislike of the magical world in England, or so I'm told. I can't always say I blame them."

"It's more than a dislike," Lanfranc said. "It's a great hatred. They've perverted the prayers and rites of the Church into wards and traps against all powers but their own."

"So I heard," William said. "I've also heard that their wall is breaking down. Someone in the Church must be fighting them."

"Not in the Church," said Lanfranc, "though somewhat of it."

"You?"

"Among others. But there is opposition, and it grows stronger. There may be war."

"War in heaven?" William said. He knew better than to smile; it would be taken for mockery.

"War between kingdoms," said Lanfranc. "Earth and blood and cold iron against the powers of air and magic."

"I wish them well of it," said William. He yawned. "You'll have to pardon me; I'm asleep where I sit. You'll ride with me in the morning, and tell me more if you like."

Lanfranc seemed somewhat put out to be cut off so abruptly, but William had been telling the truth. It was late; he had been in a battle the day before. While he had no wounds, he had bruises enough, and grief on him that ate at his strength. He needed sleep.

* * *

And yet once William had lain on the war-cloak that was all he needed for a bed in the sweet grass, his mind would not stop yammering at him. It leaped from thought to thought, memory to memory. Lanfranc's voice murmured through it, repeating words and phrases, but nothing whole or complete.

It was not a spell. William would have known. It came from inside him. He was being called to his mother, that he knew. But there was more. Something else was calling. Something stronger, fiercer, but also more distant. When he tried to grasp it, it faded away.

The only word that stayed with him might be a threat, or might be a promise. *Soon.* Nothing more than that; nothing less. Simply the one word.

❧ CHAPTER 23 ❧

Herleva died in William's arms. She had let the priest from the village perform the last rites over her; they were a cleansing and a consecration, and for that they were welcome.

When she let go, only William was there. Vicomte Herluin had gone to rest for a little while; he had been awake for longer than he could remember. Mathilda was tending Richard, who would not sleep unless she rocked and sang to him. Lanfranc had gone away, apparently to pray. The servants were asleep.

It was midway between midnight and dawn: the time when sleep was closest to death. William had dozed off, but caught himself. Herleva's breathing was coming slower. Words were beyond her, yet her eyes were open and aware.

He sat on the side of the bed and drew her into his lap. She seemed to have no weight at all. Her head rolled, coming to rest in the hollow of his shoulder. She had held him so when he was small, and rocked him—as, in the manor house, Mathilda was doing even now for her younger son.

William closed his arms about his mother. Death was inside her; he could not protect her from it. But against the rest of it—the dark, the cold, the stillness—he could do a little. He gave her what he had: warmth, sound of heartbeat and breath, brightness of life and magic.

There was no agony; no rush of final terror. One moment she breathed. The next, she did not. She slipped out of the flesh as easily, as lightly as if it were a garment she had put aside.

In his world, men left life hard, and often screaming. This gentleness took him aback. He did not know what to do, except stay where he was, cradling her as if her body could still feel his presence.

He had been grieving before—to the point of rage. That was

gone. He was empty; if he felt anything, it was a kind of remote elation.

That was her joy, far away now beyond the walls of the world. "Odd," he said, "how different it is from what one would think."

Mathilda slipped her arm about his shoulders. As if her touch had freed him to move, he laid his mother's body gently in the bed. He settled her limbs with care, in the way she had liked best to lie, and drew up the coverlet to her breast.

Mathilda's hand still rested on his shoulder. He brought it to his lips. It turned, cupping the palm about his kiss.

Herluin would come soon, then the rest of them: priests, servants, the embalmers with their shrouds and unguents. But for a little while there was quiet.

The night air was soft, blowing through the bothy. It was nearly Midsummer; spirits were flocking, drawn by the magic that had been so strong in this place. Remnants of it lingered like mist.

Mathilda drew William to his feet. She knew this place as well as he: she had spent a goodly amount of time here since she became duchess in Normandy.

There was an orchard near the bothy, rows of trees growing heavy with green fruit. Deep inside it, William gathered Mathilda in his arms and lowered her to the grass.

No word had passed between them. This night was beyond words.

Mathilda lay glimmering in starlight: dark cloud of hair, pale oval of face. Her eyes were wide and dark and full of stars.

She was still a wonder to him, and a sort of miracle. That she had chosen him, that she had come willingly and stayed gladly— he could not fathom it. Nor, most of the time, did he try.

Her body by now was as familiar as his own, and yet he always found something new to marvel at. Tonight it was the moonlight pallor of her skin, and the fullness of her breasts, her deep belly and splendid hips. He drank in the scent of her; it went to his head like wine.

She took him as she often did, fierce as he had been told a man should be. He laughed, more for release than for mirth, and let her have her way with him.

It was a celebration: a rite of life to honor the one who had left it. Herleva would have been glad of their gladness.

William took comfort from the thought. He would grieve that Herleva was gone, and that grief would pass slowly; but for her he felt no sorrow. She was well rid of the body that had betrayed her.

Herleva had made her wishes clear. She would not be buried in stone within the cold hallows of a church. She had asked to be taken back where she was born, to the oak grove of Falaise, and laid to rest in the green silence.

The procession did not begin as a royal progress. There were her husband and her two legitimate sons and their households; her son the duke and his duchess and their household; then, as they took the road, people fell in with them. They were of all ranks and stations, even laborers from the fields and beggars from the villages: all following the bier under its pall of green silk. The device embroidered in silver might have been a crescent moon, or it might have been a Druid's sickle. There were no crosses on it, no emblems of the Christian faith. But no one said a word.

The silence should have been eerie, but to William it seemed more fitting than singing or chanting, and far more respectful than idle human chatter. Because there were so many, they went slowly, at walking pace. When it came time to rest, there was food and drink for everyone, and the animals, too: horses, dogs, falcons on the fists of a hunting party, a flock of sheep, an assortment of mules, a sow and her piglets, a gaggle of geese with their goosegirl, and a spotted cow heavy with calf.

The cow calved that night: a snow-white heifer and a coal black bullcalf, and on the heifer's brow was a coal-black crescent and on the bullcalf's was a rayed star. They were up and walking with the rest in the morning, slowing them even further, but it felt as if the procession had shifted out of time. They hovered between the living and the dead, moving from world to world.

William had lost count of their numbers. He could reckon up an army in a glance, but this procession stretched back into a mist and a blur. Not all or even most of it now was mortal. The closer they came to Falaise, the more of the Old Things came to walk and ride with them. In sunlight they were a shadow and a shimmer, but in moonlight and starlight they were an honor guard fit for a daughter of kings.

She had been a goddess on earth. William heard the Old
Things whispering as they slid glances at him. Some of their
speech, thanks to Mathilda's teaching, he understood. *Goddess-
born,* they murmured. *Summer king.*

They laid Herleva to rest in the heart of the grove, within
sight of the oak that had been sacred since the morning of the
world. She went into the earth wrapped in white linen, strewn
with blossoms and green leaves: oak, ash, and thorn. Prior Lanfranc, both priest and Guardian, spoke the words over her, com-
mending her flesh to the earth and her soul to the Otherworld.

The procession circled her grave three times, casting on it
whatever gifts they had to give. Most cast blossoms or boughs of
oak or willow or yew; some scattered the feathers of hawk or
goose or white dove. And some offered bits of prayer, snatches
of song, or fragments of poetry, scattering words like bright petals.
Last of all the white heifer lay on the grave, and her brother stood
above her, while their mother grazed nearby.

By then all the rest had gone. Only William was left, and
Mathilda coming to lace her fingers with his. The grave was
heaped high with gifts and blessings; the cow and her calves
seemed to stand guard, in their quiet way.

He could not feel his mother there at all. She was gone—
truly gone. But there was peace here, and the blessing of memory.

He knelt and laid his hand where her heart would be, beneath the earth and the flowers. "Rest well," he said. "When
your time comes, be reborn to gladness. May your death and
life be joyful."

The procession had scattered when William came out of the
grove. Herluin was still there, and William's half brothers—Odo
in his priest's gown and Robert in the livery of the Count of Mortain, whose squire and fosterling he was—and Lanfranc with a
book in his hand. A stranger was waiting with them, a tonsured
priest in a traveling cloak, but beneath it William saw a flash of
violet. That, and the heavy amethyst on his finger and the silver
pectoral cross, told William that here was an archbishop.

William peered. There was magic in the man; not the roaring fire of it that was in Lanfranc, but enough to be easily
apparent.

His name, as was all too common in Normandy, was Robert.

He had a Norman face and a Norman accent, but he had come from England; he was on his way back from Rome, where he had received the Pope's blessing on his new office. "The king has seen fit to set me over the see of Canterbury," he said.

William allowed his eyes to widen a fraction. "He's raised you high," he said. "Pardon me if I offend, but aren't you from Normandy? Were there no Saxons to take the position?"

"Several hundred, if you inquire in certain quarters, my lord," the new archbishop said dryly. "The king has in mind to expand his kingdom's horizons."

"Where? To Normandy?"

The archbishop raised a hand against the lash of William's temper. "No, my lord! Not in the way you may think."

"Why not?" said William. "His mother is my father's sister. He was born legitimate. What's to stop him from claiming my duchy? That's what you're here for, isn't it? To bring me his ultimatum?"

"I do bear a message from the king," the archbishop said. "I suppose you could call it an ultimatum. He asks you to come to him to receive a gift. If of course, my lord, you will take it."

"Let me see if I understand," William said. "I'm to leave my dukedom in the midst of a threatened invasion, travel to a kingdom that has no reason to love me or mine, and accept a gift from my cousin, who has a certain claim to the rule of Normandy. Would that gift be made of iron and sheathed in my heart?"

"You have a quick mind, my lord," Archbishop Robert said, "and a thorough grasp of the darker aspects of logic. But then you studied in a hard school."

"Am I right?" William demanded. The quiet of his mother's death had drained out of him. The anger was coming back, the deep sense of outrage at the injustice of the world.

The archbishop, despite his magic, seemed unaware of the thunder rumbling beneath William's words. He spread his hands. "You are logical, my lord," he said. "But—"

"What my lord archbishop is trying all too gracefully to say," Lanfranc interjected smoothly before William could strangle the man, "is that your cousin Edward has a proposition for you. He does not want Normandy. England is trouble enough—and one of those troubles is that the wife forced upon him by a certain faction of his earls has proved to be barren. There is no heir of his body."

"What, not even a bastard?"

William watched the archbishop decide not to take offense. That was a man of tact—rather excessive in William's mind, but maybe it served too well to let go.

"My lord," said archbishop. It was clearly a great effort for him to be direct. "His majesty the King of the English has sent me to ask whether you will consent to be named his heir."

William stood in the dappled sunlight, eyes fixed on that smooth-shaven and rather nondescript face. He had not expected this at all—and yet he had. It was like the notes of a harp falling one by one, until suddenly they became the verse of a song.

"I would think," he said after a pause, "that there would be Saxons in plenty with more claim to that throne than I."

"Do you think so, my lord?" the archbishop inquired. "In this life you are the king's close kin. In your lives before, you were king. Over and over, my lord, you ruled in Britain."

"That may be," William said, "but in this life my claim is tenuous at best."

"His majesty may choose whom he pleases," Lanfranc said. "You were born to be chosen."

"Tell me why I should want it," said William.

"Why, my lord," said the archbishop, "doesn't every man want to be a king?"

"That depends on what he'll be king of," William said.

"Britain," said Lanfranc. "Not England, my lord—not the Saxons' crushed and trammeled kingdom. Britain is older by far, and steeped in magic. Your spirit has been born of and for it since the oak in this grove was a sapling."

"My lord," the archbishop said, "there are songs and prophecies; promises, if you will, that although the Saxon yoke has lain heavy on the isle for half a thousand years, one will come who both was and will be king. The chains will break; the Saxons will be overcome. Britain will wake to herself once more."

William's heart stirred in spite of himself. The archbishop was right as far as he went: it was a splendid thing to be a king. But William said, "That's all very glorious, but in this life I'm bound to Normandy."

"May you not rule both?"

"At the moment," said William, "I'm barely managing the one. I won't abandon it. I've fought too long and hard for it."

"King Edward is still a fairly young man," Lanfranc said. "He could live another twenty, thirty, even forty years. Surely that's time enough to secure Normandy before you take the rest of it."

"If that's so," said William, "then I have time to think about it. I can promise to do that much. Whether I take it . . . I don't know. I have to think."

Lanfranc looked as if he might have had more to say, but the archbishop nodded even as he sighed. "As I said, my lord, you are a logical man. Reasonable, too, and sensible. I'll tell his majesty that you will consider it."

"But not too long," Lanfranc said.

❧ CHAPTER 24 ❧

Summer's heat lay heavy on the narrow streets and in the market squares of Dover. The white cliffs were shrouded in haze; the smell of the sea was strong, sharp with brine.

The fish in the market were already going off, although they were scarcely half a day out of the water. Wise sellers brought out braziers and proceeded to grill as much as they could, trusting to the fragrance to bring in the hungry. Prudent ones hastened to pack them in salt, with hope of selling them later. The rest raised their voices in a cacophony of entreaty, begging passersby to take their wares off their hands.

Normans ran in packs—and there were more of those in England, it seemed, with every passing year. This one was larger and somewhat more obstreperous than most. They were all in armor, and armed; the man who led them swaggered as the lords of that country liked to do, remembering too well that hardly more than a hundred years ago, his ancestors had been wild Vikings.

One of the fish-sellers who resorted to neither brazier nor salt happened to be young and buxom. She committed an error: she met the glance of one of the Normans even while she sang her entreaty: "Fish! Fine fish! Sweet and fresh!"

The Norman's eye sparked in response, but not at the wares she intended to sell. He swung smoothly out of the street, over and around the stall, and had her in his arms before she could have seen him move. He did not think to stop her mouth. As her skirt went up, so did her voice.

Years of crying her wares had strengthened that throat and lungs amazingly. The market square rang with her bellowing. Her attacker reeled back in shock, stumbling into the stall next to hers and shattering it to kindling. The seller, a much brawnier woman than her neighbor, laid into him with one of the larger fragments.

That was a tidy brawl, but the Normans turned it into a battle. Some of them had paused to cheer their comrade on; when he went down and the second fishwife raised her makeshift club, a sword hissed from its sheath.

The sound was oddly distinct. The blade swung, aimed for the fishwife, but the knight who wielded it had failed to consider that he was in a market square and not on a battlefield. The edge caught a townsman who had stopped to watch the brawl, and split him nigh in two.

The weight of him, going down, twisted the sword in the knight's hands. He wrenched at it, heaving it free. Blood and bile dripped from it. As he stood staring at it, the fishwife's club struck him just behind the ear. He went down like a felled ox.

"Two knights dead," King Edward said. "Four wounded—my kinsman among them. Is this the hospitality we show to guests in England?"

"There were a dozen citizens hurt," said Earl Godwine, "and one killed. And an accusation of rape against one of the knights."

"Two knights—two guests—are dead," the king repeated. He was a remarkably mild-faced man, with his long features and his pale blue eyes, but when he was angry, those eyes turned almost white. "There must be a reckoning. Dover is yours, my lord. You will go. Teach these upstart commoners that noble blood will not be mocked—and above all, it will not be maimed or killed."

"No."

The king's mouth hung open. His hall had gone perfectly silent.

Godwine let the silence stretch. If it broke, the king must do the breaking.

The king was no match for the grey wolf of Wessex. His cheeks flushed; he struck the arm of his tall chair with a narrow fist. "You will go."

"I will not," said Godwine. "Your guest attempted to rape one of my people. He was punished as he deserved; as were the rest, for inciting a battle in a peaceful town. Poor hosts my people may have been, but they were richly provoked."

The king rose. There was not much breadth to him, but his

height was considerable. He towered over Godwine. "Are you refusing a direct command?"

"Yes," Godwine said. "I will not punish good Saxon townsmen for defending themselves against a Norman attack."

"Those were my guests!"

Godwine set his lips together.

Edward was several kinds of fool, but he was not blind. "This is rebellion."

"I am a loyal man," Godwine said. "England has my heart and soul."

"I am England. I am the king."

"England," said Godwine gently, "is Angla-land. Our land. Saxon land. We are not a province of Normandy."

The king gaped like a fish. Words had failed him.

The mood in the hall balanced on the knife's edge. A word, a glance, could turn deadly for either Godwine or the king.

Godwine turned on his heel. His sons strode out behind him—and with them a notable fraction of the earls of England. Those who remained were no friends to Godwine, or were the king's Normans. Far too many were both.

"The wind is shifting," Tosti said.

It was an odd thing to say in hall of an evening, when the sky without was sublimely calm, and not even a whisper of breeze stirred the smoke of the hearth as it rose through the smoke-hole in the roof. But Tosti was given to saying odd things. He had been odd since the day the brothers hunted the white stag; no amount of prayer or chanting had shaken the oddness out of him.

He professed to be greatly amused by their father's rebellion. While the rest of them gathered in a corner, conferring in low voices, he stretched on a bench near the fire. Sometimes Harold caught him running his fingers through the flames. They never burned him.

Harold should have been sitting with Godwine and the rest, plotting the uprising against the king. He found himself beside Tosti. "I'm getting married," Tosti informed him brightly.

Harold's brows went up. "Truth?" he asked.

"Truth," said Tosti. "You were out being an earl. Father was thinking ahead again. The king's too Norman for comfort. Normandy has a Flemish duchess. Therefore, says Father, I need a

Flemish countess. The count has a sister—she's not too old, she's not too ugly. It seems she's willing. So there we are. When the king banishes us, because we're earls and he's the king and it is true that he is England—when he sentences us to exile, we'll have a bolt-hole. We'll hide in plain sight behind our noble kinsman the Count of Flanders. He is a great power. Very, very great."

"You're babbling," Harold said.

Tosti grinned. "Father is thinking ahead. Dear sister Edith's lost her grip on the king. He's going to send her away, and she won't be queen any more. So Father will marry me off to a Flemish witch—a beautiful one, of course—and she'll keep us safe once Edith's failed."

"Edith is not going to fail," Harold said. His jaw ached with clenching. "We are not going to lose. The king's Normans will go back where they came from. England will be English again—and its king will set aside the half of him that comes from Normandy."

"Normandy," sang Tosti. "Normandy, Normandy. You'll see more of it than you ever thought to see, and do things in it that you never thought you'd do. If you could see what I see . . ."

"You're mad," Harold said. "Stark and raving."

"But I'm a happy madman," said Tosti. "Are you happy, brother?"

"We'll all be happy in heaven."

"Now that's a grim thought," Tosti said. "Have you ever thought, brother? Before the priests came, all we had was the light of life between the dark and the dark. Now it's a sin to love the light, and what do we get in return? A promise. How do we know they're telling the truth?"

"Someone is going to burn you for a heretic," Harold said.

"Oh, no," said Tosti. "I'll die by the sword like a good soldier. But you—" He peered. "You will die by—"

Harold clapped a hand over his brother's mouth. "Enough! You're raving. Come back here and pretend to be sane. We're supposed to be planning a war."

Tosti subsided, to Harold's relief. The manic light faded from his eyes. It was as if something left him, some spirit other than his own.

He had been exorcised more than once since the madness fell on him, but nothing had ever come out of him. If he harbored an evil spirit, it was not anything the Church could command.

Harold did not like that thought. At all. Strange things had been happening in England: things rising up out of the grass that should have been well and truly conquered. The wind was shifting, as Tosti had said.

Harold paused. The hall was warm with firelight, full of his own people: his family, his friends, his allies, and his servants. He said nothing aloud, touched no relic or holy book, but in his heart he swore an oath. He would defend them. Whatever it cost, whatever came of it, he would stand between his people and the dark.

✿ CHAPTER 25 ✿

Herleva had been laid to rest just before the day of Midsummer. Thereafter, as the apples ripened in the orchards and the acorns in the groves, Mathilda knew that she had conceived again.

The two before had been ordinary enough, as miracles went. This was different. Instead of morning sickness, there was a sense of dizzy delight. The world was brighter, the colors clearer, the magic more sharply distinct, than they had been before.

Was this what Herleva had felt when she carried William?

It was Mathilda's secret. Even William did not know. He was settling the aftermath of Anjou's ill-made invasion. She had ample duties of her own, between keeping the ducal household in order and maintaining those parts of the duchy which were neither rebellious nor under threat of war.

The matter of Britain had sunk beneath the surface of her awareness, as it seemed to have done in William's. She knew that it was urgent, but the long drowsy days and the brief warm nights tempted her to forget.

In the late summer, England intruded upon her whether she would or no. Among the dispatches that came in to the duke's household were an increasing number that spoke of affairs across the narrow sea. The king of the English had been filling his court and his Church with Normans. Certain of his earls had taken a dim view of this; they were brewing rebellion.

Normandy knew too well the sound of that. Mathilda would have preferred to take note of it and set it aside, but her father was not minded to let her do that. The crystal through which he most often spoke to her was locked in a box amid her baggage. He sent his message by a slightly more earthly way: a letter bound to the leg of a dove.

The bird had been hatched in no mortal nest. It found her by moonlight, fluttering through the window of her chamber in Caen and coming to rest in her hand.

It was warm, like a gust of breath; it had no more weight than that. The letter unfurled without her touching it, a spool of cream-pale parchment. The letters on it glimmered as if written in fire.

At her touch, they settled into the semblance of mortal ink. The message was written in a dialect of the old runes, one that she had thought only the Ladies of the Wood knew.

It was brief, but it said a great deal. *Your aunt Judith has taken one of Earl Godwine's sons for her husband. England is ours, if Godwine is. Now let your husband consent to his fate, and Britain will rise again out of ash and cold iron.*

The parchment crumpled in her hand. The dove melted into moonlight. Mathilda drew herself into a knot, palms pressed to the life swelling slowly in her middle.

This was not inevitable, not yet. There was still a choice. William could go on in Normandy, confirm his rule there, live long and die in the rank his father had given him.

Or he could reach out and grasp this fate that had been his so many times before. He could fail: it could kill him. It might be the death of him even if he succeeded. That was the price laid on all his lives: that the crown was never simply given him. He had to earn it.

It was his choice to make. Mathilda had her own thoughts in the matter, but she had not been a king in every life that she had lived. She could not tell him what to choose.

William had not seen his wife since his mother was buried. That was past two months and heading up for three. There was no other sensible choice—Normandy was too large and still rather too headstrong for its duke and duchess not to divide their forces—but he did not have to like it.

It was harder to be away from her, the longer they went on. She had fascinated him from the first, even when he wanted to strangle her. Running away from her had only bound them more closely. Now he understood that she was . . . necessary. Life, breath, sustenance, and Mathilda. That was the world.

The other thing, the thing in the back of his mind, was beginning to fester. The message from England; the outrageous, preposterous thing that the king had offered him.

It all came together as summer ripened into the harvest. His borders were as safe as they were going to be. He had put down an uprising or two, hunted out half a dozen nests of titled bandits, and taken time to hunt a boar that had killed a man outside of Rouen.

He was losing himself in mortal things: letting magic go, letting the rest of it slip into forgetfulness. He needed Mathilda. She kept the rest of him alive, and made him remember what else he was.

He left the town feasting on the boar's flesh, and took only a dozen men. The rest could follow at their leisure.

He saw the glances and the half-hidden grins. "Time to make another son," someone said.

William pretended not to hear. People liked it that their duke was so obviously enamored of his duchess. It was a pleasant scandal, the sort that was almost a sin, but even the priests could smile at it.

They had stopped calling him William Bastard, even for pride. And no one—not one man in Normandy—ventured to call William's sons by that word, even though the Pope still refused to sanction his marriage. William had won that victory.

He had also won the right to go hunting for his wife when he could not stand to be away from her for one day longer. There were still a few hours of daylight left when he began. Then there was a moon, bright and nearly full.

He knew where Mathilda was—always, just as he knew where his hand was, or his foot. She was in Avranches then, not far from the sea.

It was a long way from Rouen. He commandeered fresh horses twice, once from his own stables in Falaise, and again from the count in Mortain. By then Mathilda had moved on from Avranches toward the sea.

She was riding toward the wild coast, the fierce and stony country on the borders of Brittany. Where, as William knew too well, was the Wood where she had learned so much of her magic, and the innumerable tribes and ridings of the Old Things that once had lived in Britain.

Sometimes as he rode, he tormented himself with the thought that she was leaving him; she was going back to the Ladies in the

Wood. He knew he was being a fool: she would no more leave him than he could leave her. But his mind had too little to do while his body did its best to come to her.

He found her on a windy headland not far from St. Michael's Mount. Nearly all her escort had lodged in the monastery; she had with her a handful of armed guards, a single maid, and two Guardians of Gaul: Lanfranc and her father.

William had not been aware of them at all. Their power was all drowned in Mathilda.

The place where they had paused in their riding was a giants' dance: a ring of standing stones like a crown above the sea. The power of the stones rocked William in the saddle. His horse snorted in mild surprise.

Mathilda sat her mule in the center of the circle. The beast was unprepossessing to the eye, but William had good reason to know its quality. She favored it over any of his fine horses; and he had to admit that it suited her exceptionally well. It even had a turn of speed, when it chose.

Magic did not trouble the mule at all. Horses in the stone circle were wide-eyed and skittish. The mule grazed with a signal lack of concern.

Mathilda's head was bent, her veil hiding her face. William recognized the deep thrumming of her magic. She was aware of him: that was all that mattered.

She raised her head. Her beauty always surprised him—not that there was so much of it, but that it had chosen to belong to him. She smiled. The world dropped away; she was all there was, and all there needed to be.

He left his mount to graze and sprang from the saddle. She came into his arms where she belonged. Her kiss was long and sweet and only slightly preoccupied.

He set her down reluctantly. Her hands were still clasped in his. She turned, drawing him with her.

On the seaward side of the circle, two stones formed the posts of a door, and a third rested atop them like a lintel. The door opened, as it should, on grey and tumbled sky.

The sound of the sea was suddenly very loud: a long, hissing roar. The wind keened through the stones. The fitful sun was barely warm, though it was still high summer in the inner lands of Normandy.

The door of stones had done nothing that William could sense—and his senses by now were well attuned to magic. And yet the sky within had changed. It was still windblown, still heavy with cloud, but the clouds boiled over a rolling green country.

As he stared, the open and treeless downs gave way to a tangled wood, then a stony moor much like that in which the stone circle stood. Then he looked on a country that he knew, if only from dreams: green grass shot through with the white of chalk, and a sudden drop of cliff—cliffs as white as bone, falling sheer into the restless sea.

"Britain," he said. He did not say it lovingly.

"It's time," said Lanfranc behind him. "The king is waiting for an answer."

"And if that answer is no?" William asked without turning to face either Guardian.

"You should ask yourself," Lanfranc said, "why you resist this so strongly. You were born for it. Your heart and body are made for it. You have every gift that makes a king."

"I have no charm," William said. "I have precious little patience. I'm a fighting duke, not a king in council."

"Artos was not a king," Lanfranc said. "He was *dux bellorum*: leader of battles. If you were born to this time, with what you were and are forever destined to be, then this time needs you. Britain needs you."

"I was born to Normandy," William said.

"You were born to power." Count Baldwin's voice was soft. One would have thought it would be inaudible above the pounding of the sea. "Is it that you are afraid?"

William was supposed to bristle at that. He smiled instead, a mirthless baring of teeth. "If I weren't, I'd be an even worse fool than you all take me for."

"Well struck!" Baldwin said.

The door had shut, or the vision had ended. The stone door showed only the sky of Normandy again.

It made no difference. William had that cursed isle under his skin now. He could feel it bulging and shifting, trying to fill him until he had no thought of anything else.

Normandy's earth held him up. Normandy's magic shivered through him. But what was in this place was older by far, and immeasurably stronger. It went down to the heart of things.

"That's what's happened," he said. "Hasn't it? Britain is cut off from the roots. It's dying inside."

He turned to face the Guardians. They were as somber as he had expected.

"The magic of the isle is dying," Lanfranc said. "We thought that we had won a victory when we were able to break through the walls of iron. Some of the Old Things have returned and done their best to settle. But the earth is tainted; they struggle to live and breathe, and their magic flows turgid and slow. The land must be cleansed and the walls of iron destroyed. Britain needs its king."

"Or?"

"Or the island will die into a wasteland. Then the poison of cold iron will spread, and hearts will grow cold and magic will fade. Normandy and Brittany will suffer first. The rest will follow."

"And you think I can stop that. After five hundred years, when no one else obviously has even bothered to try."

"We have tried," Baldwin said. "Year after year, power after power. Guardians have died and lesser powers been destroyed in the trying. We begged the gods to send us a champion; to give us one who had some hope of succeeding. You were their answer."

"If I was who you say I am," said William, "I lost Britain to the Saxons to begin with. What makes you think I won't fail again?"

"We hope you will not," Baldwin said.

William turned back toward the door of stones. Although it opened only on the sky, he could feel the island on the other side of it. The walls of iron closed like bands about his heart. The rot in the earth tried to lair in him, a creeping shadow, a pestilence of cold and nothingness.

By that he knew that it was true, what the Guardians had said. Not that he mistrusted them, but he was a man who needed to see for himself.

"I'll give you this," he said. "I'll go to England—for a price. You stay here, both of you, and help my lady make sure Normandy is waiting for me when I get back, intact as I left it. And keep that devil from Anjou away from my borders."

"We can do that," Baldwin said.

"I'm not promising anything," said William. "I'll go. I'll see what there is to see. I'll talk to the king. What happens after that, I'll tell you when I know myself."

"Fair enough," said Baldwin. "When will you go?"

"Soon," William said.

They glanced at one another. William refused to be swayed. He had obligations. When he had met them, he would go.

❧ CHAPTER 26 ❧

"You're not going alone," Mathilda said.

"Of course not," said William. "I'm taking a decent escort. This might not be enemy country, but it's not friendly, either."

"I'm going with you," said Mathilda.

William opened his mouth to say the first thing that came into his head, but she stopped him.

"Don't," she said. "I'll win the argument and you know it. Let's not waste the time."

He shut his mouth. All the way back to Rouen, she had left him to think his own thoughts. Then there had been a crowding mass of duties and obligations. A month had passed before he knew it. Summer was fading, going to seed. In the cool of dawn now he could taste the bitter edge of winter, just perceptible beneath the golden sweetness of autumn.

England had not waited peacefully for him to come to it. There was rebellion among the earls, troops marching and battle brewing.

William knew too well the way of that. Nonetheless, however he might resist, the call was growing stronger. Every night in his sleep he walked those green hills or lost himself in forests that echoed with emptiness. Magic should have pervaded them; their knotted branches cried out for lack of it.

All of this came together in the words he chose. "It's not that I don't want or need you, but if this goes bad, you're my regent for Normandy. We can't afford to risk us both."

"For this we will," Mathilda said. "I told you not to argue. I'm going. Don't try to lock me up, either, or trick me into a trap. It won't work."

Nor would it, if she said so. William growled at the inevitability of it, but there was nothing he could do to change it.

She nodded approval of his good sense. Sometimes he wondered if she thought of him as anything but a troubled child—one she loved dearly, but no more capable of looking after himself than one of their sons.

He let the flash of temper fade. His heart was glad that she insisted on going with him. Not that he was a coward, but he liked to plan his battles beforehand. This was a blind venture, a leap into the dark. Mathilda was his best man as it were, his good right hand.

They sailed on a mortal ship, riding the tide across the narrow sea. William had chosen to travel in as little state as possible: a maid, a squire, half a dozen guards, and the rest he left to the defenses that he and Mathilda between them could raise. A larger company might have been more respectful of the king who had summoned him, but William was given to trusting his gut. That warned him not to vaunt himself unless he must.

The ship's captain was a practical man. He knew who they were, but he was well paid to keep quiet.

They had fair weather for the crossing: not so common as the autumn advanced. They brought luck, the sailors said; particularly the beautiful lady as they called her, bowing and grinning and worshipping unabashed at her feet. Not even the large and glowering husband could deter them.

William trusted nothing and no one outside of Normandy, and precious little within it. His hackles were up, all his defenses armed. The quiet sea, the soft wind, reassured him not at all.

Mathilda's hand slipped into his. Her fingers were cool. Calm radiated from them. William tensed to pull away, but stopped before he moved.

He drew a deep breath. His senses were as sharply alert as ever, but the edge of panic was off them. This was a battle he went to. Battles were familiar. His whole life had been spent in or around them.

The green swell of Britain rose out of the grey swell of the sea. Then William's senses jangled; but it was an alarm he had expected. The walls of iron were strong and high. Even from so far out to sea, the force of them nearly flung him to the deck.

Under his breath he spoke the word of power that Mathilda had taught him, that raised his own walls: wards she called them, protections of magic against magic. The sense of quiet thereafter shocked him, even when he had been expecting it.

So warded, holding to calm with most of his strength, William watched the land draw slowly nearer. He wanted it to matter nothing; to be no more to him than anywhere else in the world that was not his own dukedom. But the closer he came, the more strongly aware he was of this place, this island above all others that were in the world.

He felt the walls of iron as he passed through them. It was not pain, not precisely. It was something beyond pain. It was cold agony; it was the terror of dissolution.

None too soon, the ship had sailed within. No one else seemed to have noticed the barrier. They were all mortal but Mathilda, and she was warded as strongly as William.

The other side seemed no different than where they had been, and yet there was something odd about it. The sun was the minutest fraction less bright. Each breath needed to be a fraction deeper in order to fill the lungs as before. When William looked unthinking for the flutter of spirits that were always in the corner of the eye, there was nothing. The air was empty. There was no magic above the earth of Britain.

The king was in London. So were all his earls, both loyal and rebellious. William arrived without fanfare, riding up the river with a cargo of tanned hides. He had enough humor, after three years of Mathilda's devoted labor, to appreciate the irony.

The Archbishop of Canterbury met him on the quay. There were two others with him: a veiled and silent woman, whom one might have taken for a nun of a strict order, and a man in a monk's habit. Archbishop Robert himself was no more elaborately dressed. Even his episcopal ring was hidden.

Their greeting was brief. The monk's name was Wulfstan; Robert did not name the woman, but Mathilda bowed low. "Lady," she said.

The veiled lady bowed in return, with equal respect. Mathilda arched a brow at her. "Only three?"

"The fourth is lost," the lady said. Her voice was low and sweet. She must sing more than she spoke, William thought; there was a strong rhythm in her words, a lilt that came close to music.

"My sorrow for you," said Mathilda: a little to William's surprise, with the same lyrical accent.

"She was old," said the lady. "It was her time. The fourth will come when the need is greatest. For now we are enough."

Mathilda bent her head. Those two understood each other.

Good, William thought. He had noticed that men like him, men of war and the world, were rare in the ranks of witches and sorcerers. They were all monks or scholars or both, or women of most peculiar power.

These were eyeing him oddly: looking for Artos in him, or for any kind of king. He did not know what to offer them except his unvarnished self.

If he disappointed them, they hid it reasonably well. "The king is waiting," the archbishop said.

The three of them had come on foot. Three of William's guards were prepared to give up their horses, but only the Norman archbishop accepted. The others preferred to walk.

William's instincts rebelled to see the Lady, at least, trudging through the streets, but she was obdurate. She walked at the shoulder of Mathilda's mule, conversing softly with Mathilda.

These British were all mad. William had a brief thought of dismounting and walking, but that would be a surrender. He was what he was, and that was a Norman and a knight. Therefore he kept to the saddle, though they proceeded at walking pace, plodding slowly along the river to the hulk of wood and stone that was the king's palace.

Even as large as it was, it lacked many of the defenses of a castle. William could not help eyeing it as he approached, measuring the length and breadth of it, and considering what use it had as a stronghold. If he had had anything to say about it, he would have raised a tower of stone, and made it strong enough to resist an army.

If he did this thing—if he could even think of succeeding—there would be changes. Notable ones, from what he had seen on his journey.

But that was years away, if it happened at all. His cousin Edward was not young, but neither was he in his dotage. The man who sat enthroned in the hall had an ageless look to him, as if time could not touch him as it did other men. In face and body he favored his Saxon ancestors: he was tall, thin, fair of hair and beard, with a long comely face and mild blue eyes.

William, who had a fraction his years, felt much the older. Edward seemed unperturbed by the scene in the hall, but William's hackles rose at the sight of it.

All the earls must be here: the broad high space was full of them. There were as always factions, but two stood distinct.

One surrounded the king. The other stood at the back of a man who was tall, even for a Saxon, and older than the king: a lean grey wolf, scarred and battered but strong. Some of those behind him must be his sons; they were strikingly alike, and strikingly like him.

William, entering unregarded, took note of the men on both sides. One in particular caught his eye, one of the younger versions of the grey earl. That one stood straight, light on his feet. The others were visibly tense, but he was easy, relaxed, and quietly watchful.

It was obvious why no one noticed a troop of Normans arriving in the midst of an English council. William recognized half the faces in the king's faction; some half of the rest were like enough to certain families in Normandy that William could be fairly certain that these were cousins or bastards or younger sons.

But even more than that, anything short of a full-blown invasion with cavalry and lances would have gone unmarked. William knew little of the Saxon tongue, but he knew battles, and this was a heated war of words. If weapons had been allowed in the hall, they would have been drawn. There would have been blood.

William cared little for the cause of the fight. He kept his eyes on the fighters. The grey earl must be Godwine, of whom William had heard a great deal. Even more than the king, this was a great power in England.

Edward was no match for Godwine in sheer force of presence, but the throne wielded a power of its own. Even some of Godwine's men were swaying toward it, falling under its spell.

William was hardly impervious to it. The thought that this could be his struck much harder than he had expected. Did he want to be a king? Maybe he did. Even knowing what it would cost, he had begun to feel the lure of the crown and the power.

He turned abruptly, not caring who saw or who followed, and left the king to his fight.

❦ CHAPTER 27 ❦

The day's battle of words ended without a victory on either side. Earl Godwine withdrew outside the walls of London, where his army was camped, secure under safe-conduct. King Edward sat to the day's meal with every appearance of contentment, despite the rebellion that festered in his kingdom's heart.

Then he proved that he was more alert than he seemed. He sent a messenger—a young knight of good Norman stock—to ask if William would share the meal with him.

William was well housed near the palace, and well looked after. The king's hospitality was generous and his servants skilled. They offered every comfort, from a bath in a basin of copper and silver to a troupe of musicians who would, if the lord and lady of Normandy were so inclined, play and sing them to sleep.

William had no sleep in him. The sense of dullness, of some deep lack, had grown worse as he traveled through Britain. The sooner he ended this and escaped, the happier he would be.

Mathilda declined the king's invitation. She and the Lady, who came from the west country, had forged a firm alliance. They seemed barely aware of William at all, or any other male or mortal.

Even so, William did not go alone. The monk Wulfstan and the archbishop accompanied him. He left his men to rest and to guard their lady, left his armor and weapons with them, and went as if he had any possible reason to trust his host.

There were more Saxons in the hall than William had expected. Some of Godwine's followers had indeed turned back to the king. They were sitting subtly but visibly apart from the Normans, who held places closer to the king.

There was a faint but distinct odor of lightning, and a further strangeness that, after a moment, William recognized as the first, faint, creeping tendrils of magic where none had been in half a thousand years. They were growing from the throne where the king sat. But the cause of them was in himself. William's coming into that hall on this day had awakened something that had been asleep, waiting, for the old gods knew how long. There had been no hint of it before, but he had not come so far in, nor come so near the king.

He almost turned as he had then, and walked away, all the way to the sea and thence to Normandy. But he had not come so far in order to turn tail at the last.

Something else woke in the hall as he strode down the center of it: something much more earthly. People stared and whispered. The Normans knew who he was; the Saxons might not, but he had put on a cotte of scarlet silk embroidered with golden lions. As the king's foreigners rose one by one and then all together, and bowed as men should to their duke, Saxon eyes sharpened; Saxon brows rose. One said it for them all: "The Duke of the Normans? Here?"

King Edward took no notice. He rose as William approached, smiling in what seemed to be honest pleasure. He went so far as to come down from the dais, moving carefully in his silken robe and heavy crown, and take William's hand when he bent his knee as a duke should to a king—even one who was not his own. Edward raised him before he could complete the gesture. "Cousin!" the king said, speaking French without accent: after all he had had a Norman mother and Norman nurses. "Welcome to our kingdom. Was your journey pleasant? Are you well looked after?"

"Very much so, majesty," William said.

Edward nodded, visibly pleased. There were gifts, which William's companions carried: a heavy collar of gold, a gold-washed helmet, and a mantle of crimson silk lined with vair. The king seemed delighted with them, particularly the mantle, which he insisted upon putting on then and there, laying aside that which he had worn before.

When that brief ceremony was over, Edward led William up to the dais, setting him at his right hand. William's escort had melted into the crowd in the hall. He was alone, unguarded—abandoned.

He crushed down the thought and sat on it. The upwelling of magic was growing stronger. As servants came forth with fanfare, bringing the first course of the king's banquet, the air seemed both brighter and less heavy. And yet, William noticed, the shadows were darker now that the light was shining as it should.

No one else seemed to notice what was happening. William ate, but never afterward remembered what it was. People spoke; he answered. He did not remember what he said, either. It must not have been excessively peculiar: no one stared as if he had lost his wits, or rose up in a rage.

Edward said nothing that day of the summons that had brought William here. William had no love for the game of indirection, but today he was more glad of it than not. He was a guest, he was welcome. People were speculating as to why the Duke of Normandy should appear unannounced in the midst of Earl Godwine's rebellion, but neither the king nor the duke was inclined to enlighten them.

William's presence had not driven away Edward's new allies. They watched and listened and spoke to one another in their own language, but they held to their altered allegiance.

And all the while, the magic grew and twined and put forth buds that bloomed into a tentative exploration of spirits. They crept out of the space between the shadow and the light, owl-eyed and bat-winged and all but transparent. If the magic thrived, so would they. If it withered and died within the walls of iron, they would dwindle into nothingness.

Whatever sustained the walls seemed as yet unaware of what was rousing in the king's hall. All the priests who were there, William realized, were Norman. The blessings that they laid on the hall and the feast seemed of a piece with the power rising there. Their prayers had no taint of cold iron.

That could not last. William's hackles were up again. He had been in danger of sliding into complacency, but no longer.

The feast ended without so much as a dropped knife or a flung insult. William swayed somewhat as he made his way out of the hall, though not with the English mead that he had drunk.

The walls of iron rose before the door. It was a physical effort to force himself through them. Once they were past, the world was dulled again; he gasped for breath, sucking in the insufficient air.

He swam through it as through turgid water. He remembered vaguely how to find his lodging. It was pure luck that he came to it after only one wrong turning and a circle or two.

Mathilda was still closeted with the Lady from the westlands. William crawled into bed, pulled the coverlets over his head, and tried to shut out the trapped-beast panic that had risen in him since he came from the hall.

William went hunting in the morning. The king's servants provided him with guides, bow and boar-spear, and provisions for a day outside the city's walls. They asked no questions and expressed no surprise that their charge should be so eager to escape the city not even a day after he came to it.

It would be remarked on. That was the way of courts. But he could not sleep, could not sit still, and above all could not endure a day in court. If he brought back a boar or a fine buck or a brace or two of fowl, that would be a gift to the king.

The sense of oppression was no better outside the city. In a way it was worse. The city was full of people, and their mingled thoughts and feelings gave life to the dead air. In the fields and forest and along the river, there was life enough—birds, fish, a herd of roe deer, a fox in the hedge—but the land was mute. Drifts and veils of mist wafted across it; the sky was clear above, but the valley of the river was thick with fog.

William let the deer go, though his men eyed him strangely. They decided he wanted to find a boar; with that in mind, they forged ahead, following the hounds and the huntsman. These dozen men of Normandy knew what William had been born for; they came from old families, families that remembered the old ways and the old stories. But even they did not seem to understand how wrong all this land was—how dead it was, stripped of the powers that should have made it wonderful.

And yet, as he rode, he began to feel things bubbling up from beneath. The walls of iron were not impregnable after all. There were gaps and broken fragments, places where magic could seep through. Whether enough of it was magic that could make and heal rather than sicken and destroy, William could not tell.

Down along the river in a marshy thicket, they found the spoor of a herd of wild pigs. The boar, they knew, would not be far from the sows and the farrows. They set out along the track, eager but wary.

The baying of hounds wafted down the wind. Their own hounds belled in response. The fog had not burned off as one might expect; if anything it was thicker than ever. The hounds led them; they could barely see past the foremost horseman.

Trees loomed and passed. They crossed expanses of meadow, a stretch of fallow field, and another beyond it stubbled with mown stalks. The baying swelled and faded as the land rose and descended.

Suddenly it boomed loud, smiting the hunters with a wall of sound. The horses veered and shied. Shapes loomed in the fog: men on foot and one or two on horses, and in the midst of them a snarling melee.

The boar was brought to bay. Another party of hunters had it surrounded. Even in the fog it was obvious they were Saxons; their cries were Saxon, and their narrow height, and the flash of a blue eye or the gleam of long fair hair through gaps in the murk.

The boar was huge: a bristling black bulk. Its hooves dug deep in the earth. Its shoulders brushed the low sky.

Hounds harried it, leaping, ripping, tearing; being ripped and torn in return. Blood sprayed, eerily vivid in the grey light.

Men with boar-spears hovered beyond the milling pack of hounds, braced for the moment when the pack would withdraw and the boar would be open to the kill. One pressed in close; he laughed in headlong delight.

The boar squealed in rage and swung its great head. Hounds flew helpless through the air, trailing blood and entrails. The boar charged.

The laughing madman stood full in its path. The man nearest him cried a warning, but he only laughed the harder.

William clapped spurs to his horse's sides. The beast wheezed in shock and sprang full over the outlying tangle of hounds. The man who had cried a warning was running, but far too slow.

William had no spear. Somehow he had omitted to claim one from the king's armory. He had his sword and dagger, and no more. He dropped the reins on the horse's neck and drew the sword. The beast, brave heart, never veered or faltered, balancing lightly between William's knees.

The madman had stopped laughing, but he had not found enough wits to get out of the boar's way. An arrow flew over

William's head, embedding itself in the boar's rump. The boar took no notice at all.

William judged the moment carefully. It was a mad thing he did, almost as mad as provoking the boar to begin with. He had to trust the horse under him and his arm's strength, and above all his courage.

The rank scent of boar mingled with the stench of blood and voided entrails. The stallion blew hard at it but did not waver.

The world slowed to the pace of a dream. Bloody foam floated from the boar's shaken head. The Saxon in its path stood at ease, smiling slightly. As William charged toward him, he looked directly into William's eyes. His smile widened to a grin.

The boar was fixed on him, oblivious to the horse closing in. William measured with his eye. He had one stroke, one instant, to pierce that thick hide, slip through muscle and bone, and stop the boar in its tracks.

He gripped the sword in both hands. It was weighted to hack, not to stab, but God knew it was heavy enough. He stood in the stirrups. The stallion dropped from a gallop to a rearing halt. At the top of the rear, William aimed as best he could, and struck.

The massive blade plunged straight down, just as the boar surged toward its quarry. Steel met flesh and sank deep. Bone grated, but the sword slid past it, twisting as the boar swerved, flinging itself toward its attacker. The hilt wrenched itself from William's grip.

The horse swung up and away, snapping a kick at the furious, tumbling mass of the boar. William heard the crack of bone. The heavy body overbalanced and rolled end over end.

The boar was dead before it struck the ground for the last time. William's sword was sunk deep in its neck. Its skull was cloven by the steel-shod hoof.

Silence spread outward from the crumpled body. William's horse pawed at it and snorted. William smoothed the thick black mane on the red-gold neck. The stallion settled slowly.

They were all, Saxon and Norman alike, staring at him as if they had never seen his like before. Even for a man accustomed to being stared at, that was more than William could easily bear. He swung down from the saddle, with nothing in his mind, quite deliberately, but a desire to repossess his sword.

The madman who had begun this deadly dance was standing in front of him. They were nearly of a height and nearly of a width, and as William met those bright wild eyes, he saw too much that was familiar.

This one had magic—was bubbling over with it. But he lived in this country among these people who had done their best to crush out every vestige of the Otherworld from their spirits. No wonder he was out of his mind.

Just as William pondered the best way to remove him, he stooped at William's feet. A knife flashed in his hand. William tensed, but the blade was not meant for him. It stabbed earth where the boar's blood had spattered, cutting out a clod of it.

He lifted it, earth and blood and green grass of Britain. Then he bowed, half mocking, half somber, and thrust it toward William.

William took it before he stopped to think. The blood was still hot, the earth cool. He caught the faint sweet scent of grass.

"Now it's yours," the madman said.

As he spoke, he rose lightly and stepped aside. The boar's carcass lay hulking and ungainly in death, with the hilt of William's sword protruding from its neck. Its blood seeped slowly still, pooling on the trampled grass.

Out of nowhere that he could discern, and too well aware of the madman's knowing glance, William dropped to one knee. The clod of earth was still clutched in his hand. He reached with the other and dipped a finger in the boar's blood. It was warm, tingling with the memory of life. He brought his finger to his lips.

Something flashed. The pain was much slower to make itself known. William saw the blood dripping from his arm, and for a numbed moment thought it belonged to the boar. Then he knew it was his own. It mingled with the boar's blood, scarlet on scarlet.

The madman's knife snicked softly into its sheath. The cut was bloody but shallow. Even as William reflected that he should rise up in wrath, the bleeding slowed and stopped. The earth in his hand had turned to crimson mud.

This had been a rite, high and holy, however brief and sudden it might have seemed. It was a binding. It was done, and there was no undoing it.

William was not as angry as he might have expected. By

now it had the inevitability of a long fall down a steep hill: end over end and God help him when he struck bottom.

"Good," the madman said. He was not speaking French, or Latin either, and yet William understood him. "Now that's done. Here's my brother, noble lord. There's fate on him, too. Speak sweet to him; you'll be needing each other often enough before the dance is over."

"Tosti," said the man who had been too slow to save him. William recognized him: he had stood at Earl Godwine's back while they all defied the king. This was the earl Harold, and this was his brother Tosti, who had made a splendid marriage with Count Baldwin's sister in Flanders.

William had not heard that the bridegroom was mad. His brother at least seemed sane enough. Harold was taller than Tosti and leaner, and much fairer: the kind of milk-skinned, flax-haired, sky-eyed fairness that could lead a Pope to call these people not Angles but angels.

Fortunately for William's sore-stretched tolerance, there was nothing otherworldly—in any sense—about the glance that took him in or the voice that said, "I have you to thank that my brother is alive."

"I couldn't die," Tosti said perfectly reasonably. "He couldn't have failed. This was supposed to happen."

"Tosti," Harold said with a note of warning.

Tosti laughed at it, but he stopped his babbling. Harold turned back to William. "I owe you a debt," he said. "Tell me how I can repay it."

"That can wait a while," William said. "The hunt was yours, though the kill is mine. What say we split the spoils? I don't think you'll be wanting your half feeding the king's men."

"The kill is yours," Harold said with no evidence of disgruntlement. "We'll bring a back a deer, and my brother alive and unharmed. That will do."

"Oh yes," said Tosti. "It will do. It's already well begun, but this makes sure of it. Your blood's in the land now, my lord. It's bound to you, and you to it."

Nonsense! William wanted to snap, but he was not that much a fool. Not only was it not nonsense, it was true. Tosti's twofold stroke had completed a working so subtle and yet so potent that William barely understood what it had done. But that it had done something, he had no doubt whatever.

They parted amicably, with the boar in William's possession and the Saxons agreeing to accept a quiver of hunting arrows. Some might say they were treating with the enemy. William called it good sense. These were not his enemies—Tosti was his kinsman, now that he had married Mathilda's aunt. In time they might prove useful. One never knew in this world.

❦ CHAPTER 28 ❦

Two days after the hunt for the boar, Godwine and his allies faced the king and his pack of turncoats and Normans. This time Godwine had declined to enter the city. They met in an open field to the west of it, beyond the palace and the monastery of St. Peter.

It was a raw, grey day, with rain hanging heavy in the clouds but not yet choosing to fall. Godwine drew up his forces in as good order as possible, but there was no concealing the fact that they were much smaller than they had been when his rebellion began. The king's men were notably more numerous.

Harold would have been willing to fight. It was his father, after all, and his kingdom that was dribbling away toward the king's Norman favorites. But Godwine was a wise old wolf; his heart was colder and his mind less eager to settle everything with steel.

His men came armed and in armor, but they kept their swords sheathed. Edward had come with mounted Normans, hulking figures who loomed over the Saxon foot soldiers.

Harold recognized the Norman closest to the king, with his big bay horse and his cool grey eyes. Tosti was alive because of him. Today he wore much finer clothes than he had in the hunt, and his shield was painted red, with golden lions.

So this was the Norman duke, who everyone knew was guesting with his cousin the king. Tosti had to have known who he was on the day of the boar hunt; much of what he had said then made sense now.

Harold had liked the man, Norman or no. In other circumstances they might have been friends. But who knew? They were kin by marriage; they might yet stand on the same side of a battlefield.

There would be no such amity today. The king's usual mild

expression had gone stern. As he came to the field, his line of forces spread and curved. It did not surround Godwine's diminished army, but the threat was clear.

Godwine's face was perfectly still. Tosti was smiling as if this were the most delightful diversion in the world. The rest of the men whom Harold could see were standing firm, but he could feel the power shifting from Godwine to the king.

"I think," Edward said gently, "that this has gone on long enough. Will you surrender and repent of your sins?"

"While there are men of foreign blood in the heart of your council and at the head of our Church," said Godwine, "no."

"Ah," said Edward. "Such principle. Is my memory faulty? Did you not first rise to power under the rule of foreigners? They were Danes, to be sure, and not Normans—but surely a northman is a northman."

"Once was enough," Godwine said. "Canute was no threat to the soul of England. Normandy is another matter. The old gods are still worshipped there, however cleverly the people may conceal it."

"Normandy is as Christian a realm as there is in Europe," Edward said coldly. "So. You will not reconsider?"

"Not unless you will," said Godwine.

Edward bent his head. His men drew in closer about Godwine's diminished army. On both sides, spears lowered; arrows nocked to bowstrings.

"No," Godwine said. He sounded ineffably tired. "I won't shed blood over this."

"Is this your surrender?" the king asked him.

"I give way to superior force," Godwine said. He laid down his weapons where he stood—not coming to the king, not bowing to him.

The king's cheeks flushed, but he maintained his air of serene self-confidence.

Once Godwine had made his move, Tosti stepped lightly forward to do the same. Others followed, some with sorrow, some with poorly concealed relief.

Harold was not among the first, though not precisely the last. It galled him and grieved him, even though he knew his father was right. If they fought now, they would be slaughtered. This gave them hope of succeeding later and by another way. With Godwine, there was always another way.

"Flanders," Tosti said in Harold's ear. He was laughing. "Go on, make the gesture. We'll be back soon enough."

Harold moved stiffly, but he did as he was told.

Unarmed, stripped of their armor, but not bound—that indignity was spared them—Godwine's men accepted dismissal from their lord's service. He was left with his sons and his personal guard, and a handful of his levies who refused to leave him. If the king was minded to sentence him to death, they would die with him.

But the king, now he had what he wanted, was prepared to be generous. "Tomorrow," he said, "you will leave these shores and not return, on pain of death. Tonight, break bread with me. Let us part without hatred, at the very least."

It was a royal command. Godwine assented to it. He had no choice, but neither did he protest.

The old wolf had a fox's quickness of wit. Whatever he had in mind, this neither troubled nor frightened him.

Harold glanced at Tosti. His brother was radiating contentment. The thing that possessed him was well pleased.

They heard Mass together, celebrating the king's bloodless victory and the rebels' surrender. After Mass they gathered in the hall of the palace with all appearance of goodwill, and shared a feast that warmed them admirably as the cold and the rain closed in.

William was there, and for once, so was Mathilda. She had come out smiling from her long council with the mysterious Lady, put on her best gown, and commanded her husband to escort her to dinner.

Her presence comforted William even more than he had expected, though what little she said was not what he would call comforting. "It's Solstice night," she said. "Blood's been spilled, walls mined until they've begun to crumble. Watch Godwine, my lord."

"Not his sons?"

She arched a brow at him. "All of them," she said.

William watched them. They were eating and drinking like all the rest. He could not see that they were terribly cast down by either defeat or sentence of exile. They seemed like men who had prepared for the worst and were pleased when events fell short of it.

None of them, even the mad one, was working magic. It was a perfectly earthly gathering, and completely mortal. For some reason that made William twitch.

He was at the king's right hand again. The king was as expansive as he could be, in his prim monkish way. He insisted that William have the best portion of everything. William was being singled out in front of rebels and loyal men alike. They were noticing: glances darting, whispers running from table to table.

Tonight instead of Saxon mead they were drinking French wine—and very good wine at that. Midway in the feast, Edward called for all cups to be filled, and rose, lifting his own.

Dark had fallen early on this bleak evening, but the hall was warm with crowded bodies and bright with lamps and firelight. The king's long waving hair shone like gold; his robe was crimson, and his face and hands were ivory. He looked like an image in a cathedral.

He spoke in French, and then in Saxon: the same words, William supposed, in two languages. William watched to see who understood which language, and who seemed to understand both.

"My lords," the king said, "and ladies, and men of God, tonight we celebrate more than a victory. My most patient guest, who has endured with grace while we settled this regrettable contention, receives at last the acclaim to which he is entitled."

Edward paused. William was still watching faces. They were listening calmly enough, some with boredom, others with mild interest. A few had already wandered back to their wine and their trenchers. Edward, it seemed, had not made them privy to his intentions.

He had not said a word of them to William, either. Until this moment, William had been treated like an honored guest, but no more.

Edward was presuming a great deal. But William held his tongue.

"You know," the king said, "that the queen whom I was given is sadly barren. There is no heir to the kingdom; not even a daughter to match with a strong husband. That is grief, but God be thanked, we are blessed in our kin. I have prayed and I have pondered, and God has advised me."

His hand fell on William's shoulder, drawing him up with surprising strength. William had serious thoughts of refusing, but he had come too far and seen too much to turn back now.

"My lords and ladies of England," Edward said, "I present to you my heir, who will be king after me: my uncle's son, proven in war, proving himself well in peace, well and faithfully wedded, father of strong sons, William of Normandy."

The silence was absolute. William could not believe that they were all shocked speechless. Yet no one spoke or even seemed to breathe.

He was not a man for speeches, but this silence needed something desperately. Edward was waiting for God knew what. William's eye, scanning the hall, happened to fall on Earl Godwine's son, the tall fair one, Harold. The mad one, Tosti, was beside him, clapping his hands with glee, but Harold wore no expression that William could discern.

William spoke to him as if they were alone. "Yes, I thought it was odd, too. But why not? I'm close enough kin. I was born and bred to rule. I've been doing it since I was barely knee-high."

That face gave him nothing—not hostility, not friendship. It was blank, swallowing the words as soon as he spoke them. It was not that Harold failed to understand: he knew a fair bit of French, and Edward himself rendered it into Saxon as William paused.

Still, William had more to say. "It's beautiful, this island," he said. "It deserves to be well ruled. That's my promise to you. England will be the better for your king's choice of heir."

"So indeed it shall!" Edward declared. "To balance strength with justice, generosity with prudence, and to fill the palace with strong heirs—those are a king's most sacred duties. In you we will have it all, and more besides."

Flattery was the currency of courts, but William had never let it turn his head. He nodded gracefully enough, he hoped, and said, still with his eyes on Harold's face, "When the time comes, and God grant it be a very long while before that happens, I'll do my best. You have my oath on it."

Did Harold nod ever so slightly? If he did, maybe he was not even aware of it. But William chose to let it be enough.

❦ CHAPTER 29 ❦

The Lady of the Lake had a secret. It was nothing mortifying or dangerous, but it might have caused difficulties if certain persons discovered that behind the veils was a maiden younger than Mathilda. Mortals, especially men, needed to see an aged face before they would believe in either power or wisdom.

Her name was Etaine. It was not something she shared with the world, any more than her face or her manifest youth. When she walked abroad from the lake of Avalon, she walked veiled, stately, and mantled in mystery.

Mathilda did not make the mistake of discrediting her wisdom because she had, at the most, fifteen summers on this side of the Otherworld. She remembered who she had been. Her knowledge passed from world to world, life to life, Lady to Lady, back beyond Morgaine and Rhiannon to lives so ancient that even bards had forgotten them.

"Forgetfulness is a gift," she said once as they sat together with maids and servants locked out and cups of honey mead between them. They were not drinking the mead; conversation was heady enough. "Those who can forget are blessed. The weight of memory is enormous. I remember my birth in life after life; I remember my death, over and over, sometimes in peace, more often in pain. Don't curse the gods who close the doors of memory. They're wiser than any mortal can imagine."

"Even when memory might make this life more bearable?" Mathilda asked.

"There are dreams," said Etaine.

Mathilda felt herself chastened, though she was sure the Lady had not meant any such thing. It was a moment before she could get past the sharpness of it. "I wish my husband could remember," she said.

It was blunt, but they were past either politeness or indirection. Etaine sighed, then yawned. It was late and she was young, and young things needed sleep. "Not you?" she asked.

Mathilda shrugged slightly. "What I was before doesn't matter. Not as it does for him."

"He remembers as much as is good for him. Mostly, he just is. That's what he needs to be."

"What, all brawn, no brains?"

Etaine's eyes glinted. "You said it, not I."

She had a streak of wickedness, that one. Most particularly she loved to prick pretensions, and Mathilda had a few—more than she knew or wanted, once they were made painfully clear to her.

Mathilda was losing the habit of humility that she had learned in the Wood. She told herself to be glad that this Lady of a kindred order had undertaken to remind Mathilda of her old lessons. It was an honor, however much it might sting.

On the night when the king finally named William his heir, duke and duchess left the hall together, hand unobtrusively in hand. Mathilda was in a mood for something other than a quiet night's sleep. William shot her glances that assured her of the same inclination.

There was someone in their bedchamber, sitting upright and still in the middle of their bed. Etaine's veils were wrapped about her, but her face was bare.

William stopped short. He was as shocked as anyone else would have been to see that delicate flower-face within the veils of the august Lady.

He recovered quickly, gathering his wits and setting himself subtly but distinctly in front of Mathilda. Etaine appreciated the gesture: she smiled. "Good evening, lord and lady," she said. "Your baggage is packed and your mounts saddled. It's time to go."

"What—" William kept his temper. That was a feat in itself; Mathilda was proud of him. His voice, once he had got hold of it, was steady. "We can't just up and abandon the field. The king will take it as a bitter insult."

"The king knows," she said. Her voice was soft, but its core was steel. "He has done what he was fated to do. The rest is ours."

"Ours?"

"Come and see," she said.

"Not blind," said William. "With all due respect, and every apology, I don't trust easily."

"You never did," she said with the hint of a sigh. "Very well. You hunted the black boar of Britain and mingled your blood with his, binding yourself to the earth by rite of seizin. The reigning king has spoken your name as his heir. Now, as in all great workings of our people, a third rite and test remains."

"Test?" said William. "What is it, a duel to the death?"

"Seven alone returned from Caer Sidi." She sang the verse in a voice so sweet and strong and high that it shivered Mathilda's spine.

"No," William said. His voice was flat, like a door shutting. "I'm not going there of all places, with or without an army. You'll get me when the time comes, and I'll be ready for you then. Tonight, we sleep. Tomorrow we take our leave of our royal cousin. Normandy is waiting, and it needs me."

"So does Britain," Etaine said.

"Britain has a king," he said. "It also has you. The Old Things are creeping back. I can feel them. They never left the outlands: Wales, Scotland, the far coasts of Cornwall. This island is much stronger than I was led to believe, and the magic is still in it. You're going to need me when Edward dies, but until then, this is your duty. You do it. I have my own, which I've left too long undone."

Mathilda held her breath. Whether he knew it or not, that was a king speaking—haughty, arrogant, and utterly unafraid of this most powerful of the enchantresses of Britain. She could blast him with a look, and well she might have done, if she had not quite clearly remembered what he was.

"You had better manners when last I knew you," Etaine said.

"Maybe I had time for them then." William began to unlace his cotte. It was breathtakingly rude. "Good night, Lady. Rest well. Will you ride with us tomorrow?"

Etaine fixed him with her gaze, long and steady. He ignored her, pulling his cotte and shirt over his head and reaching for the fastenings of his trews.

For a moment Mathilda thought Etaine would win that battle of wills, but she seemed to have decided against going to war. She retreated with dignity.

*   *   *

"That was not wise."

William pulled off his trews and tossed them after the rest. He knew better than to swagger, but he was in a mood that made Mathilda want to slap him.

"You can't afford to make an enemy of the Lady," she said. "You're going to need her."

"She needs me more," said William.

He was distracting her, standing there naked, and she could tell he knew it. She did love his body, big as it was, and rock-hard with riding and fighting and hunting from year's end to year's end. It had more grace than one would expect; he was light on his feet and agile, and he could move fast when it suited him.

She was in his arms even as the thought crossed her mind. The familiar smell of him was all around her; he was radiating warmth. William was like one of his horses: as long as he was dry and out of the wind, he never felt the cold.

She did her best to resist. "You can't do this. She's offended or worse. Get dressed and go and do whatever you have to do to make amends."

"No." His voice had a growl down deep in it. "If I'm the king she's served for all her lives, she should know better than to make decisions for me."

"How do you know—"

"Some things I remember," he said. "I remember Caer Sidi. I am not going there. I don't care how perfect a test it would be. Once was enough."

"You're afraid," she said.

"Of course I'm afraid. I'd be an idiot not to be. But believe me, I'd be a worse one if I did what she would have me do."

"You don't even know what it is," Mathilda said in some heat.

"I know," he said grimly. "Cross the dark lands, attack and take a castle full of shadows and blood, take away the precious thing in its heart. It was a cauldron then. It doesn't matter what it is now. Its power is the same. It brews death."

"This won't end well," she said.

"For once," said William, "let me worry about that. Tonight we are going to sleep, eventually. Tomorrow we'll go home."

"If we are allowed."

"We will be," he said. "Be sure of that. We will go home."

❧ CHAPTER 30 ❧

The night passed without further disturbance. In the morning William asked the king for leave to go. Edward seemed both unsurprised and unoffended. "Of course you have Normandy to look after," he said. "You go, be duke. Grow strong and wise, so that you can, in the end, be king."

William almost admired his cousin then. They were pretty words, but they rang true. Edward understood something of all this strangeness, though how much, William was not at all sure.

For himself he was glad to be escaping from the deadness of spirit that was Britain. Its bright places were few and far between. Its empty places, airless and suffocating, were far too many.

He was not ready to bring down the walls of iron. He knew that in his bones, which had never yet been wrong. He did not regret his refusal of the Lady's test, either. It was foolish and dangerous. He had no time for it.

She was nowhere to be seen as his escort mounted and rode out of London. It was a fine day, a golden day, with dew on the grass and not a cloud in the sky. No doubt, this being England, it would be raining torrents by nightfall, but this morning was lovely.

He could have taken a boat on the river, but he was in a mood to ride to the sea. They were well provisioned, with a baggage train and remounts: good stock brought over from Normandy, none of these hairy island ponies. The king had been generous.

Edward saw them off at the gate of his palace. William refused to look back as he rode away. The next time he saw those walls, he would be coming to his crowning.

That was more than a vow. It was prescience.

He shivered as he always did when magic caught him un-awares. Especially here—the earth and air were dead, and the day's beauty was blunted the more, the farther he rode from the king and his glimmer of the Old Things in the midst of nothingness.

William never knew exactly when the Lady joined the riding. At some point he realized that Mathilda had gained another maid; then he recognized the face in its dark frame of veil.

He sensed no hostility in her. When she met his glance, she smiled.

That smile put him on his guard. He had not won that war at all. He was not even sure, on reflection, whether he had won the battle the night before.

The best he could do was to ignore her as if she had been the maid she pretended to be, and focus on the road ahead of him. His inner defenses were up and armed. So were Mathilda's, he noticed. Out of the corner of his eye he could see the shimmer on her, the armor of light that marked magical wards.

The sun rose toward noon. There were people in plenty on the road, and a good number of them made no secret of what they thought of a troop of Normans: they spat in the dirt, or scowled and muttered in Saxon. That language always sounded like a spit of curses, but this had a particular edge to it.

William smiled without mirth. He was no stranger to hatred. If he had to bring this kingdom around as he mostly had in Normandy, so be it.

Shortly after noon they came to where the road bent round a low hill. Walls rose on the other side of it: a monastery of imposing size, with heavyset square towers.

It was not the first house of religion they had passed, and would be far from the last. England was full of them, and they were full of Englishmen, praying as they thought for the souls of their kin.

Where Edward's Normans had been sent as abbots and priors, that prayer was as salutary as it should be. But this was a Saxon abbey. The closer William drew to it, the more suffocating its presence became.

The road ran straight past its gate. By the time William thought that it might have been better to veer off overland and try to make his way back to the road farther on, it was too late. The binding was on them all. Even the Lady seemed caught in chains like iron, a spell so strong that the thought of resistance was pain.

It was a pretty trap. It only sprang when one tried to leave this island. One could come as far into it as one liked, and fancy, especially in the king's presence, that the danger was blankly unfocused: walls to close one in and crush the spirit, but nothing immediately deadly. With strong will and well-wrought wards, one might think, one could make one's way out again, and be unscathed.

This was different. It was focused. It had a stink of the things that had pursued William in his youth through Normandy: cold breath of graves, and carrion stench. Here was death, jaws opened wide, sucking him in.

It knew him. It knew why he was here.

The abbey's walls were blank, its gates shut. That was not the common thing at all; such gates were meant to stand open, to welcome guests and offer alms.

The bay stallion had carried William ahead of the rest. He could hear them behind him but not feel them. The spell had cut them off.

Mathilda was gone from inside him. It was as if he had lost a limb. He groped for it over and over, blindly, but it was not there.

He tried to turn his horse about and ride away. But the horse plodded forward, bound as tightly as he. He could not even turn his head to see how far behind his companions were. Too far: their hoofbeats were ominously faint. The road was twisting, distorting. The walls loomed above him, higher by far than they had seemed as he rode toward them.

Seven alone returned from Caer Sidi.

The verse shrilled in his skull. This was not the black strong-hold of dream or memory. It was a Christian abbey with a cross on its tallest tower, built of grey stone with a red stripe of Roman brick, where maybe it had been a villa long ago. Yet to the eyes of the spirit, it was a tower of iron. It roots were sunk in the earth, drawing up darkness.

He gathered every scrap of will and power to stop and turn and, for the sheer release of it, rage at the Lady who had tricked him into this madness. The spell on him stretched and strained. He almost had it—almost—as the gate opened to receive him.

He smelled stone and incense, unwashed humanity and sour ale: familiar smells, which combined told him what he already knew, that this was a monastery. In the distance, a choir was chanting, a slow roll of sound that crept into his bones and made him shiver.

They had twisted the words and rites of the Christians' faith and transformed them into magic as dark as it was dangerous. Whether the monks knew what it was or what they had done, he reckoned unlikely. But someone must know—must understand. Otherwise the working would have shaken itself to pieces long ago.

The horse halted in the courtyard. William had been expecting the clustered buildings of a Saxon abbey, but this was older. Its pillars were taller and more slender than the style of later days, the arches more graceful, the walls and paving still bearing traces of paint and gleaming mosaic.

The pool in the center must be the abbot's fishpond. Lilies floated on it, bearing here and there a late bloom. William saw the flicker of a fish beneath the surface.

The power in this place was strong enough to make him dizzy. He slid from the saddle. His knees buckled; he pulled himself up by the stirrup strap. Once he had his legs under him, he let go. He wanted to be on his feet for whatever was coming.

It was, eventually, twofold: the Lady, with Mathilda close behind, entering through the gate that had admitted him; and a man in a black robe coming from within the villa or monastery or whatever in truth it was. The closer he came, the more William felt as if claws of iron had closed inside his chest, choking the breath out of him.

"Stigand," said the Lady behind him. "Stop that."

William sucked in blessed air. That name—it meant something. A bishop. This was the man whom the Saxons had wanted for Canterbury, but the king had chosen Robert the Norman.

The man was not wearing any marks of his rank, if William's memory told him the truth. He looked like a monk of the abbey. Maybe he had retreated here to pray away his disappointment.

And maybe William was a plain mortal man who happened to be Duke of Normandy. If anyone knew what the walls of iron were, and even more, how to sustain them, he would wager that it was this man.

As for the Lady . . .

"We thank you for bringing him here," Stigand said to her. "It makes matters much simpler."

"Does it?" the Lady said.

Not friends, William thought. But not necessarily enemies, either.

Others were coming in behind Stigand, men likewise in black, cowls shadowing faces. William thought of the Guardians of Gaul. There were three of these, coming to a halt at Stigand's back. Two had the height and stance of men. The third, though tall, moved with a graceful sway.

If the Guardians he knew were pillars of light, these were pillars of iron. The earth groaned under them. The fish fled deep into the pond. The lilies withered in the bud.

The Lady moved ahead of William. Mathilda was beside her. *No,* he thought. He thrust between the two women. "Let us go," he said.

He knew how rough he sounded. Clumsy bull of a Norman, that was all he was. He was very careful to let them see that.

"Clever," said Stigand. He spread his hands. The air hummed.

That was not William's death, hovering between those soft white hands. It was worse. It was William's dissolution. What had been done to the king, a spirit inside him that possessed him to do and be things that in his own mind he would never dream of, would fall on William.

"Is it not just?" said Stigand. "A soul for a soul. A king for a king."

"Not to my mind," William said. The outer walls of his mind were allowing themselves to be blankly terrified. Within the bailey, he was gathering together everything that he knew, everything Mathilda had taught him, and all that he had discovered for himself.

This tainted and spellbound earth was still, deep below, the earth to which his soul had been born through lifetimes out of count. Strange that he had to stand at the heart of the walls of iron to know what still lived beneath. It was the binding, the rite of blood and earth. Tosti, or the spirit in him, had wrought well.

William could feel Mathilda again, as if through thick veils. The one with her must be the Lady: a banked fire of magic, a spark of satisfaction.

Damn her, he thought.

If England's Guardians expected anything, it was a frontal

assault: a headlong attack, physical as well as magical. William would have been happy to oblige them. But he was too seasoned a soldier for that.

Never do the expected.

William reached through the veils, draining strength as he did it, but he cared nothing for that. Mathilda was waiting. She fit like a sword hilt in his hand. There was another, not Mathilda, not the Lady, but . . . other. It leaped willingly into his grasp.

He asked no questions. There was no time. The Lady laughed as he took control of her. She was delighted with him.

He had cursed her once. That was enough. He opened the way through her, secure within the others' protection.

A shaft of sunlight shot through the tumble of cloud, direct to his feet. William set foot on it.

The walls of iron clanged shut. But sunlight was subtler than iron. It crept through cracks and pierced gaps that widened infinitesimally even as William's magic touched them.

He stood on the worldroad, the straight track between the worlds. Iron walls barred the way behind. They were all there: the Lady, Mathilda, even the bay stallion. But it was not the horse who bolstered William's strength, feeding it until the road was solid underfoot.

Mathilda's hand settled on her middle. It was barely rounded yet, but what was inside it took his breath away.

There was no time to wonder at what the two of them had wrought. The road ran glimmering through a wood darker and wilder than any he had known. Things moved there. Voices cried out. Something shrieked, abruptly cut off.

The Lady was gone. William was in no way surprised. He swung into the saddle and reached down, too fast for Mathilda to object, and pulled her up behind him.

There was no way to go but forward. The bay as always was unperturbed, although when the road softened underfoot, the beast went on gingerly, balancing its doubled burden with perceptible care.

The wood closed in. The trees were moving, snaking out tendrils. Eyes gleamed in the darkness.

Cold iron was no use against this. Magic sank into it and died. The road was melting, dissolving behind. The bay slipped and scrambled. Its breath was loud in the silence.

Panic would only speed the dissolution. William held on

grimly to the calm he cultivated in battle. He kept two things clear in his mind: Mathilda's warm arms about him and her strong presence inside of him, and the blessed earth and clean air of Normandy.

He focused on the place where he most longed to be: the oak wood of Falaise, where the bonds of body and power were strongest. His soul had come through from the Otherworld there; that memory gave him light and strength. Sunlight on leaves, russet with autumn; sweet scent of grass; richness of leaf mold and damp earth.

The road melted into nothing. The dark crashed down.

The bay dropped from a considerable height, tumbling end over end. William felt himself leaving the saddle. He went limp, the more easily to break his fall.

Something swept by overhead: a shadow that smelled of blood and iron. He struck earth that was his, his own, from the moment this body began.

A heavy weight struck him, knocking the wind out of him. He lay wheezing in a rustle of leaves. Mathilda stirred on top of him. Stiffly, with a distinct presence of knees and elbows, she creaked to her feet.

She was unharmed. So was the child. William had no breath to sigh in relief, but he could close his eyes and let the air trickle slowly back into his lungs.

Metal chinked nearby. Something large blew out an explosive snort, stamped once, twice, three times, and began to crop grass with single-minded determination. The bay had found its feet again, none the worse for the fall.

They were all home, safe, basking in sunlight, in Normandy where magic was free to flow as it would. When William looked in his mind toward Britain, its walls were higher and stronger than ever, its gates irrevocably barred.

"Not irrevocable," William said aloud. "We'll break them down. When the time comes, we will destroy them."

"Not yet," said Mathilda. "Not for years, maybe."

"Good," said William. "All the more time to settle things here—and learn to use this magic I've been cursed with. I thought I knew enough. I don't, not even close. I need to know everything. All about Britain—all its arts, its powers, who guards it, why they laid that cursed binding on it, everything."

"That's a great deal to ask for," she said.

"You think it's too much?"

"Would it matter if I did?"

"You don't," he said. "Let's hope it's enough. Don't think I don't know how I got out of that trap. I found the way, but she, whoever she is, gave me what I needed in order to make it happen."

"It was a test," said Mathilda. "You passed it—just. You don't know how close you were to failing."

"I have some small suspicion," he said dryly. "Now, lady, as to what you were doing risking both of you for what amounted to precious little—"

"It tipped the scale," she said. "Without us you would have failed."

That was damnably true. He was not about to admit it. He mounted with a snap of temper and held out his hand. "Get up," he said. "Back on the horse. We'll have a pleasant time explaining to the castellan how we could be in England one moment and in Falaise the next. And my men—God! They're dead by now. Or they think we're dead. If they send a message to Rouen that we're lost—"

"We'll be in Rouen before the message can arrive." Mathilda swung up behind him on her own, ignoring his offered hand. "But first, Falaise. And dinner. And rest. I could sleep for a month, now my dreams are free again."

"We'll be lucky to get a full night in, if we want to get to Rouen in time," William said, but some of the knots were loosening in his belly. God, it was good to be home.

Well then, he thought as he persuaded the bay to leave off grazing and start off toward Falaise, what of Britain? Would it ever be home?

"Knock down the walls of iron," Mathilda said, riding in his mind as she so often did, "and raise up walls of air, and who knows? The soul may not remember its lives from day to day, but deep memory, memory rooted in earth, does pass from life to life. You know that; you felt it."

"Here and there," he said, "for a moment or two, I felt something. But the land is too badly scarred, the damage too deep. We may never be able to—"

"Never think never," she said. "You've been given a gift: time to gather your forces, and knowledge of what those forces will have to be. Wasn't that worth the test?"

"If test it was," he said. "It was too easy. I was let go. If there's another trap laid—if I missed anything—"

"If you missed anything," she said, "you'll find it."

She believed what she was saying. He reached down and took her left hand where it clasped the other at his waist, drawing it up to his lips. "I'm glad you came," he said. "Even if it was a damned foolish thing to do."

"It would have been much more foolish for you to have gone alone," she said. She never had let him have the last word.

Here, today, in sunlight, free and safe and presumably sane, William could not hold on to his resistance. He had turned to glower at her, but at sight of her face, he could not help but let a smile escape—startling her into one so brilliant that he blinked. That made him laugh; and that was so rare a thing that they both dissolved in it, riding out of the wood and back to their familiar world.

PART THREE

❀❀❀

RITE OF CONQUEST

anno domini 1065–1066

❧ CHAPTER 31 ❧

The duke's castle in Rouen was in a state of perfect uproar. The duchess and her ladies had marshaled the servants to turn it upside down, shake it hard, and clean it thoroughly. The duke, being male and by nature a coward, had taken as many of the men and boys as could escape and gone hunting.

That suited Mathilda perfectly. Men were never any use for real cleaning. If she knew William, he would stay away for days. She was planning on it. When he came back, the castle would be in perfect order, gleaming from top to toe.

This morning they were excavating the storerooms. A battalion of servants was sweeping, dusting, and tidying while Mathilda and the most trusted of her maids went through the boxes and chests and cupboards. Her younger daughter Adela had charge of the lesser maids; she marshaled them handily to carry out the culls, the ancient linens and moth-eaten bits of tapestry, bent or broken spoons, chipped crockery, and unidentifiable lumps that might, in their day, have been treasures.

Cecilia had disappeared again. Mathilda spared a moment for a sigh. Her elder daughter had been born to the full measure of magic, a power and talent of remarkable strength; even the Ladies of the Wood professed themselves impressed with her gifts. But those gifts had not come with any noticeable leavening of practical sense. Adela had inherited all of that, just as Cecilia had got all of the magic.

Cecilia was a drifter and a dreamer. She drove her nurses to distraction—"Not even enough sense to come out of the rain," they said.

They meant it literally. She would forget where she was in the fascination of some new spell or vision or discovery: a bird, a leaf, a flower. If she was presentable at all, it was thanks to the hard work of her nurses, and her mother's insistence that no child of hers be a wild thing.

The last Mathilda had seen of her, she had been rummaging in a cupboard like the rest of them, with her fair brown hair caught up in a kerchief and a smock over her gown. She was also barefoot, scratched from the brambles she had galloped through the day before on her brother Robert's warhorse, and sunburned from the same adventure. If it had been left to her, she would have gone hunting with the men, but Mathilda had put her foot down. Cecilia was nearly a woman. It was time she learned to act like one.

To her credit, she had not sulked too terribly. She did love to go digging for treasure, and there were chests in these rooms that had been put away in Rolf the Viking's day. Mathilda had to presume that she was somewhere in these rooms, engrossed in some dusty delight.

Cecilia could feel her mother thinking at her. It was almost as loud as Adela's voice, ordering maids about with the same crack of command that made people jump when they heard it from the duke. Adela was a good general. Entirely unlike Cecilia, as people never failed to remark. Cecilia could work a spell or muster an army of spirits as well as any Lady in the Wood, but when it came to matters of the lower world, she was fair-to-middling useless.

She found it difficult to care. Like her mother before her, she divided herself between her father's various houses and the Wood. She should have been in the Wood now, but this year, for one reason and another, she was late in making the journey.

The corner she had found to rummage about in was dark, dusty, and cobwebby. Bolts of wool wrapped in crumbling linen filled most of it. One seemed newer than the others, and was larger: taller than she was. She tugged it out of its place, vaguely aware that her fingers tingled when they touched it. Something wonderful was inside it.

Everyone else was in the outer storeroom, where the light was. This room was almost empty, with a clear stretch of floor, not too dusty as such things went. She unrolled the bolt on it, and caught her breath.

Wonders indeed. It was a tapestry embroidered on well-woven linen and backed with wool. She had never seen anything like it: so intricate, so complex, stitched with such skill in so many colors.

It began with a tree—an oak, with its lobed leaves and a scattering of acorns. She laughed softly as she saw what was sunk in its heart: a sickle embroidered in golden thread. It was the oak of Falaise, where her father had been born, and she, too.

That was the start of it, at least. The oak had grown, and grown, until it filled the whole of the tapestry. There were faces in its branches, forms of men, beasts, spirits, and things she could put no name to at all.

As she bent over it, fascinated, she began to see patterns, winding skeins of figures. They were doing things that seemed to shift as she watched, as if they were alive: men riding, women weaving or spinning, children playing, dogs gamboling around and through them.

One skein caught her eye. The people in it did not look like Normans. They were tall and narrow, and their hair was most often red or gold. The men wore their hair long and grew their mustaches. When she saw them in battle with swords and spears, most of them were fighting on foot.

One figure was taller and fairer than the others. His skein told a story. First he stood next to a lean grey wolf of a man, wielding his sword against a king with crown and scepter. Then the king struck them both down and cast them out, and they took ship on a blue curl of waves toward a castle that she recognized: it was one of her grandfather Baldwin's in Flanders. A little while, and the two men sailed back; and this time they overcame the king. But they did not kill or exile him. They stood beside him instead, hovering slightly, so that she knew they were telling him what to do.

The older man died soon after that. She saw how he lay, shrunken and dead, and more than life had gone out of him. Whatever it was that he had given up, the younger man had it, and another with him, whose shadow was strange—as if it belonged to someone else. Maybe they were brothers, and the old man had been their father. They took up arms and fought, and men bowed to them, setting them each in a high hall with a golden collar about his neck.

The one with the strange shadow set his foot on the necks of his people. Cecilia could see how they hated him, even while they obeyed him. The other ruled with a lighter hand, and he stood beside the king as often as not, wielding the king's will as his own.

There was more, but a shadow had fallen across the tapestry. She looked up into her mother's face. Mathilda seemed surprised. "That's my tapestry! It made itself before I even met your father. I left it in Bruges, with wards on it and a perpetual guard. Where did you find it?"

"In the corner," Cecilia said. "It looked as if it had been there for years."

"That's not possible," her mother said, but her voice trailed off. She knelt on the floor across from Cecilia and peered at the tapestry. "It is the one. Here, do you see your grandmother? There she is, giving birth to your father. And there is his father. The golden dome is Jerusalem. And here—"

Cecilia listened with half an ear. She was looking for the skein she had followed before, but she had lost it. There were others in multitudes—her father was in most of them, mounted on a horse she had not seen before, an iron grey with a silver mane. Or else he rode in a lovely deep-bellied ship with a graceful billow of sail, riding blue waves toward a fortress of iron. But the others were nowhere that she could find.

They mattered. How or where or why, she did not know yet. But she would. She was as sure of that as of the magic that lived in the tapestry.

❧ CHAPTER 32 ❧

Edward the king sat on his throne, side by side with his queen. She was tall and fair, with a beauty that had grown finer with the years; whereas he was fading. His beard was white; his hands on the arms of the throne were bone-thin.

Harold looked at him and saw death beneath the translucent skin, written in the blue runes of veins. He was slipping the bonds that Godwine had laid on him after the great return from exile and the crushing victory, bonds that had endured long after the great earl was gone. Mortality stalked him. In a little while it would bring him down.

His mind was still as clear as it ever was. "Go to Normandy," he said. "Tell my heir: it's time. Before Easter comes again, I'll be laid in my tomb. You, my good friend and loyal servant, will see that he is there to take the crown from my hands."

Harold bowed as much to conceal his expression as to make a show of respect. Grief—that was strong enough. He had served this king because it was his duty. Loved him? Not to any great extent. But he was the king.

As for how Harold felt about the Duke of Normandy, or the prospect of a foreigner on the throne . . .

For the moment he satisfied the king with obedience. Edward dismissed him to attend to his departure. He left in no little relief.

Edith the queen knelt in her chapel, praying devoutly as she did morning and night. Her prayers had shape and form, a beauty of melded word and spirit, carved and pointed with precision like the walls of a cathedral. Like those walls, they held holiness in, and kept out the ills of the world.

She heard the soft step behind her, felt the familiar presence at her back. It lifted up her cathedral of prayer and opened it wide over the whole of England, power so beautiful that she could only kneel and wonder at it.

Archbishop Stigand knelt beside her. Canterbury was his as it should have been from the beginning, and with Canterbury was the sacred power of all England. Robert the Norman, Robert the interloper, was over ten years dead. He had died in exile, crushed in defeat.

She could still remember the glory of those years, when her father and her brothers came back from exile with great fleets of ships, and she was freed from the nunnery where she had been imprisoned, and raised again to the title and office of queen. Her time in the cloister had been a quiet joy, but her destiny was to stand at the side of a king.

She closed her eyes. When she thought of Edward without his crown or his power, she saw and felt nothing: not love, not hate. In her heart was profound indifference.

It was the same for him. He had tried at first to do his duty, to make a son and have done, but she had lain still, trying not to shudder at the touch of those soft, faintly damp hands. After a time or two and no response on his side, either, he had given it up. Then he left her alone except for state appearances, and that suited her well.

When he put her aside, her first thought was relief. Even knowing that she had failed of her duty to her kin and kingdom, that her father Godwine was defeated and might be killed, and their power in England had toppled from the height, she had been glad to escape her husband. Likewise when Godwine came back more powerful than ever, so powerful that his body could not sustain the weight of his spirit, she was sorry to leave her sweet peace, and sorrier still to return to Edward's presence.

It was her duty. She was trained, honed for it. In the year of Godwine's return, she had been needed more than ever, to bolster the king's wavering mind and protect him against the evil things that strove to possess him.

And possess him they had. Her heart still remembered the battle for his soul, when she and Stigand and the whole of St. Peter's abbey, from the youngest novice to the abbot himself, fought against the power of the Old Things in him. She could feel them even yet, striking again and again, until she was sure that the king's mind was broken.

A night and a day they fought over his tormented body. He fought back as the possessed will, not with curses or foulness, but with soft words and temptation. He sang sweet verses in a babel of tongues, he called on the spirits of air and water to defend him, he went so far as to cry out to old gods whose names should have been struck from mortal memory.

But in the end he gave way. He surrendered to the power of God and His Church, bowed before the altar, and submitted to penance: cold water, lashing with wands, and long vigil on the stones of the chapel, dressed only in his thin linen shirt. It was a beautiful mortification, a great sacrifice. When it was over, he rose up clear-eyed and quiet. Thereafter for the most part he was as a king should be; and he put an end to the placing of Normans over Saxons in his kingdom.

Now he was growing old. There was no heir of her body, and none of his. He had never spoken of the one he had chosen at the time of Godwine's exile, and no one else had spoken of it, either—until this night, when, perfectly matter-of-factly, he sent Godwine's son and heir to Normandy.

God would provide, she told herself, but deep in her heart was a quiver of doubt. It roused memory of grief that was still fresh after nigh on a dozen years. Godwine, having won back England with great show of force both in the body and in the spirit, had gone out like a lamp whose oil is exhausted.

One day after the great festival of Easter, he had strode from Mass to the hunt to the council to the king's table. There, as the trays and platters went round and the mead ran thick and sweet, he half-rose in the midst of a jest, with a look of great surprise on his face; then he toppled.

Three days he had lingered in twilight between the living and the dead. All the prayers and tears of those who loved him were of no use. He slipped away in the night, as soft in death as he had never been in life.

Edith had been with him when he died, but she was rapt in prayer. Harold was beside him. When the quality of the silence brought her to herself, she found her father dead, and her brother bending over him, wearing an expression that she never forgot.

Something had passed to him. What it was, she did not

know. It hovered there for only that little while, then it sank deep and was gone. Harold was himself again, drawn with grief but still the brother that she knew.

On the day when Edward revealed that he had not after all forgotten his naming of an heir, Edith wondered anew what had passed between Godwine and his son. The world she had thought familiar, in which she had reckoned herself mistress and queen, was turning strange.

She crossed herself, promising a penance for the wandering of her thoughts away from prayer, and turned to Archbishop Stigand. His face was calm as always.

"I cry your pardon," she said, "for my lapse with the king. I never imagined that he would hold to that of all mad choices."

"Madness is persistent," Stigand said. "We'll gather again to pray, and invoke the Lord's mercy upon his majesty."

"And my brother?"

"That will be seen to," said Stigand.

Edith frowned. "What do you mean by that? If any harm comes to him—"

"None will," the archbishop assured her. "Trust in God, my daughter. And pray."

It was wise advice. She would do well to follow it. The doubt in her was mortal and fallible, and the shiver of foreboding was foolish. Christ and his saints would not suffer the Old Things to overrun England.

❧ CHAPTER 33 ❧

The sky was lowering as the ship set sail for Normandy. It would clear later, the captain assured Harold. The weather across the narrow sea was always chancy; this was no more than bluff.

Harold had his doubts, but although he had commanded fleets, he had not lived his life at sea. The ship was sturdy enough if somewhat ungraceful, solid and well built, with a crew that seemed to know what it was doing. Even if the captain was proved wrong, they would ride it out. No one who sailed the narrow sea was a stranger to storms, sudden or otherwise.

The wind was blustery and cold. Harold wrapped himself close in his mantle and kept out of the way. He would pull an oar later if he was needed, but for the moment his best course was to leave the crew to it.

Even with the cold and the lash of the spray, Harold slipped into a doze. He felt strange, as if he was half in the world and half not. That feeling had come on him now and then since his father died: odd, floating, neither here nor there. Edith insisted that something had happened to him at Godwine's deathbed. Apart from the rush of grief and the crushing sense of emptiness and loss, he never had known what she meant.

Maybe it was this. It had no purpose that he could discern. Sometimes, as now, it seemed that he could rise up above himself and see the world with a hawk's eyes, high and clear.

The storm was not dissipating. Clouds were heaping on clouds. The sea was rising.

The captain and his crew seemed unperturbed. Harold drifted back down into himself, pulled his hood over his head, and let himself fall asleep.

*   *   *

When he woke, the wind had risen to a roar. Good English wool kept out the wet, but when he peered out from beneath his hood, all the world was water.

He was well situated where he was, braced between bales amidships. The outer bale sheltered him somewhat from the wind. His grey hound Brego pressed against him, radiating warmth.

The dozen thanes of his escort had had the sense to huddle under a hide tent nearby, with the hawks and hounds that they had brought for gifts and for the hunt. He could hear Aelfric praying. He should do the same, he supposed, but his heart was a singing stillness.

When the mast went down, Aelfric's prayer rose to a shriek. The snap of the timber breaking was deafening even above the wind. The gale snatched the furled sail and rent it in tatters, flinging the splintered mast far out over the sea.

The ship rocked drunkenly. Water poured over the prow. The captain was bellowing orders to his crew, but Harold could discern no words through the howl of the gale. He held on blindly to the dog and the gunwale, and hoped to God and all the saints that he would come out of this alive.

Maybe God heard him. The wind's shriek diminished somewhat. The ship found its balance in the swell. Maybe Aelfric's prayers did it; maybe it was the captain clinging for dear life to the rudder, steering as steady a course as he could through the madness of wind and water.

The storm died away as the day waned. The crew rigged a makeshift mast and a scrap of sail, not enough for great speed, but better than oars in those heavy seas.

As they set about making such repairs as they could not put off, the captain swung over the bale that sheltered Harold and dropped down beside him. "We're staying afloat," he said, "but we won't make harbor at St.-Valéry. We'll have to try for landfall wherever we can."

"Do you know where we are?" Harold asked.

"Somewhere south of England," the captain said with dry wit. "The wind's blown us west. We'll turn up on the coast, but maybe not in Normandy."

There was little Harold could say to that. He was feeling strange again. This time it almost meant something, but when he tried to grasp it, it escaped.

His men and beasts were wet and shivering but safe. The ship limped toward the shore. There at least would be dry land and shelter from the wind, and wherewithal to build a fire. God was with them, Harold told himself. The rest would come as it would.

Armed men found them at dawn. The ship was drawn up on the shingle; they had made a fire of driftwood and shattered timbers, and slept in the shelter of the hull.

The men on watch failed of their duty, and the hounds, exhausted by cold and wet, raised no alarm. Harold opened his eyes on a towering figure in mail. There was a cold pressure on his throat: the edge of a sword.

The man standing over him growled in French. His brain was all fuddled; it was a moment before he could make himself understand the words. ". . . Saxons. This one looks rich. Maybe he's worth something."

There were men already looting the ship, while the captain and the crew stood helpless, with their hands bound and men with spears surrounding them. Bales of wool and leather tumbled out on the sand; chests were pried open and rifled, boxes split and their contents flung aside. Two men held the leads of Harold's three braces of hounds. Of the hawks there was no sign. Whatever there was of any value, these knightly robbers took.

They did not, for a wonder, lay hand on Harold, though he wore rings of gold on his arms and wrists and fingers. The swordsman in mail kept a close eye on him.

He made no move to escape. He would be dead before he ran a furlong. Better to be still, be fearless, wait.

It was hard. He was trained to fight; he had spent his life doing it. But he was also trained to be wise.

When the ship was stripped of its treasures, its captain and crew were allowed to embark on it again, with a warning not to stray from their wonted course. Harold and his escort were not so fortunate. They were loot, and they belonged to the lord of this country, which was called Ponthieu.

The ship's booty rode on horses and mules. The men and hounds walked. Their captors seemed to reckon this a punishment, but Saxons were not the inveterate horsemen that these French were. As long as they were allowed to keep a sensible pace, and were given food and drink at appropriate intervals, they were content to go afoot.

The Count of Ponthieu sat in his high seat. His hall was drafty and cold, his castle of Beaurain bare of either beauty or grace, but clearly he had expectations of remedying that.

Harold ran his fingers over the hilt and pommel of his sword. Count Guy had ordered it returned to him—in earnest of good faith, he supposed. With Normans, one never knew. His men and beasts had been taken away, he had not been able to discover where. He was alone here.

Well, he thought, if it came to it, he had his sword. He could take a few of them with him before he died.

He let none of it show on his face. Count Guy was looking him up and down as if he were a horse in the market. Harold stood loose, easy, ready to speak or fight, whichever was necessary.

"So," said the count. "You're an earl, they tell me. That's like a count, yes?"

"Like a count," said Harold, "or a duke."

"And your name?"

"Harold," said a voice behind him. "Harold Godwineson."

Harold refused to turn. The voice he did not recognize, but something in it told him that this was a priest. God knew, there were enough of them who had run freely across the narrow sea, though not as many since Godwine won back England for the Saxons.

The priest went on with didactic precision. "Earl of Wessex, brother to the Earl of Northumbria, right hand of the English king. It can be argued that he is the wealthiest man in England."

The count's brows rose. "Indeed? You're sure of this?"

"Positive," said the priest. As he came into Harold's view, Harold was sure he had not met the man before. But priests all looked alike with their robes and tonsures.

The priest bowed with evident respect. "My lord," he said to Harold.

Harold inclined his head.

Count Guy had a tight rein on himself, but there was no mistaking the gleam of pure greed. All Normans had a look of the wild boar about them to the Saxon eye, but this one more than most, with his heavy cheeks and his narrow eyes, somewhat deep-set and bloodshot. Little red eyes, Harold thought, drinking him in more avidly than ever.

"Father Mauritius," the count said, "what do you reckon is the worth of this noble earl?"

The priest spread his hands. "My lord, I don't—"

"That much?" the count said. "Then I can ask any ransom I like. Can't I? His king will want him back—yes?"

"Certainly he is of great value to the English king," the priest said, "but, my lord—"

Count Guy waved him to silence. He leaned forward, bracing his hands on the arms of his chair. Harold could imagine the curved tusks of a boar, the bristling mane and beard, the rank, wild odor that could drive a boarhound mad.

"I shall think on this," the count said. "You, my lord earl, will rest here while I consider how best to go about it. You may consider yourself my guest."

Harold bowed. There was nothing else he could do. In its way this was his fault. He could have ordered the captain to anchor offshore for the night, then try to row to a safe harbor. Now the ship was gone and its cargo taken. His men, no doubt, would be sold as slaves; his hawks and hounds would fetch good prices. And so, all too obviously, would he.

The room in which he was kept was not exactly a prison cell. It was in a tower, to be sure, but it was as well appointed as anything in this drafty barn of a castle. He was well fed, his bed was not too thick with vermin, and the ale was not bad at all.

He supposed he should be content. He was alive. He could certainly pay the ransom; he doubted this provincial notable could imagine a sum large enough to strain his resources.

It was humiliating. The king might see the humor in it—Edward was odd that way—but Harold had rather more pride in him than a good Christian should. He had to struggle to appreciate the absurdity of his position.

The bed was too short. He had to lie crosswise on it, and even then it was awkward.

That did make him laugh. Weakly at first, with a conscious effort. Then the full ridiculousness of it overcame him. He lay back and roared, laughing until tears streamed down his cheeks, until his sides ached and his face hurt and he had to lie hiccoughing, completely given up to mirth.

❧ CHAPTER 34 ❧

The boggart perched on the end of Cecilia's bed. She had been aware of him even before she woke: he was part of her dream. In it, he crouched behind a pillar in the bleak and smoky hall of a castle. A great boar of a man sat in the high seat. Another faced him: tall and fair, with long narrow hands and a long comely face.

Cecilia knew that face. The memory was very old, very strange: as if it had come from another life. But this man was very much a part of the mortal world.

What was on him was not precisely magic. It was power, but where magic flamed outward, this had the iron rigidity of a shieldwall.

There were chinks in it. Through them she saw the spirit, strong and clean.

She had not expected that. Saxons were slayers and destroyers. The Old Things had died or been driven out from their ancient places; the magic in Britain was crushed into nothingness, because of this man and his kind. And yet he had no evil in him. He was a man of honor as his people reckoned it.

That was more than she could say for the lord who held him prisoner. Guy of Ponthieu had neither honor nor restraint. He would strip the greatest earl in England of his wealth and pride, and never stop to ask if it was either right or just.

She opened her eyes to the boggart's face. He was the most human of his kind that she had seen. His shape was still peculiar and his face was strange, but her eye wanted to call him a dwarf, black-bearded and heavy-shouldered, with massive bandy legs and broad, thick-fingered hands. At first she thought he must be at least part mortal, but the magic in him was pure boggart: bright and wicked and unusually strong.

The boggart rose and swept an elaborate bow. His voice was like stones shifting, but he spoke French with a cultivated accent, precise as a priest. "Great lady, your light blazes in the darkness."

"A fair morning to you, messire," Cecilia said politely.

The boggart grinned. There was nothing human about that grin. It split the boggart's broad skull in half, and his teeth were numerous and very, very sharp.

Cecilia blinked, but she had been rocked to sleep as an infant by beings stranger than this. There was nothing in the boggart to fear. "I saw you in my dream," she said. "Do you belong to the earth of Beaurain castle?"

"You recognized it?" the boggart asked. He seemed surprised.

"In my dream I did," she said. "So. Do you?"

"I belong to the king who was and is to be," the boggart said.

"You didn't come to him," said Cecilia.

"Your light distracted me, great lady," the boggart said, "and your dream enthralled me."

Talking to the Old Things could give even a strong mage a raging headache. Cecilia tried not to wince as she said, "If you're too shy to speak to my father, I can take your message to him."

The boggart drew himself up to his full half-fathom. Cecilia could almost hear the far cry of trumpets and the beating of battle drums. "I am not shy," the boggart said with enormous dignity. "I am fascinated. You are beautiful in all the worlds."

Cecilia's face was hot. She looked like her mother, everyone said, and Mathilda even in middle age was a great beauty; that had never turned Cecilia's head, or troubled her unduly. But that her magic was beautiful—that reduced her to a speechless lump.

The boggart had taken his revenge for her impertinence. He slid from the high bed to the floor and ruffled himself into tidiness. His odd edges smoothed away; his plethora of teeth concealed themselves behind full lips and luxuriant beard. A quite human-seeming creature bowed to her once again and offered his hand.

Cecilia could choose to refuse it. She had that power.

But the dream was still clear in her. It was a true dream, and it touched her with a sense of urgency. She let the boggart, in his guise of gracious dwarf, escort her from the room.

Her father's hall struck her with a sense of dream laid on dream. Here was warmth, light, stones scoured clean and fresh rushes on the floor, and woven hangings to keep out the chill of this grey day. Her father was a big man as the lord of her dream had been, seated in his high carved chair. But he was much cleaner and much more splendid in his scarlet cloak and his golden collar, with his great sword cradled in his arms.

Her mother was sitting beside him. They were not together often enough, in their estimation; duty kept them apart more than it brought them together. But they were here in Rouen for the feast of Pentecost, side by side and hand unabashedly in hand.

Cecilia saw how their fingers laced together, Mathilda's slender white ones in William's big brown ones. Their hearts were woven even more tightly, their spirits twined.

They were not one single being; they were too fiercely themselves for that. But they fit into each other's empty spaces.

Cecilia took great comfort from them. She had some of the sight; she knew that this wedded union would not be for her. She was meant for the divine solitude of the Ladies. But it was a good thing to have in the world.

They were hearing petitions this morning, which was somewhat of a reproach: it meant that she had slept through morning Mass. She should be more careful with her observances; that had been drummed into her since she was small.

She would have crept quietly to her usual place behind her mother, but her youngest brother caught sight of her and called out, "Ceci! Where've you been? The caravan from Spain is here!"

Young William was impulsive. It went with his fire-colored hair and his high coloring; he was as restless as a flame, and he had not learned even yet, at nine years old, to keep himself under restraint. It mattered little to him that a prelate of splendid rank and bearing was in the middle of a lengthy peroration. He ran out from between his two elder brothers, slantwise down the hall, and came to a dancing halt in front of his sister.

She suppressed a sigh. Everyone was staring. Young William, whom people called Rufus because of his red hair, was blissfully oblivious. "You've got to see," he said. "The king sent gifts. There's a charger for Father and a mule for Mother and—"

"I'll see them in a little while," she said. "There's a messenger here, see. Father will want to hear what he has to say."

Rufus looked the boggart up and down. He had no more magic than either of his brothers, but he had a clearer eye. He could see what others could not.

He did not, mercifully, unmask the boggart in front of all these mortals, most of whom would have been appalled. That much he had been able to learn. Instead he said, just as Cecilia had, "Good morning, messire. Did you have a pleasant journey?"

"Pleasant enough, young lord," the boggart said. He was as respectful of Rufus as he had been with Cecilia, which irked her to a surprising degree. She told herself not to be foolish. He was courteous, that was all; he was hardly slighting the strength of her magic.

The boggart shot her a glance but forbore to speak. The hall had fallen silent. Even the Pope's legate had noticed, rather belatedly, that he had lost his audience.

The boggart walked down the center of the hall in that silence. He held himself proudly, as a boggart of lineage and beauty should do, and bowed before William and Mathilda with grace that one would never have expected from such a thick, short creature.

They knew what he was, of course. Mathilda inclined her head. William leaned forward. He recognized the boggart: he said, "Messire Turold. Welcome to Rouen. Is all well in Ponthieu?"

The boggart, who enjoyed the luxury of a name, bowed even lower and said, "That's a matter of opinion, sire. There's been a shipwreck; the count has taken the spoils as he's entitled to do. There's somewhat among them that might, my lord, belong to you."

William raised his brows. "Is there indeed? What might that be?"

"It was an English ship, my lord," Turold said, "and Englishmen on board. They were coming to find you, my lord, but now they're held for ransom in Beaurain."

In a smooth, breathtaking motion, William swung his great

sword round and grounded it point-first between his feet. His hands clasped the guards; his eyes stared over it, fixed on the boggart's face.

When he was at rest, those eyes were the color of rain. Now they were as coldly gleaming as the steel of the sword. "Who is the English lord?" he asked, soft and calm.

"Earl Godwine's son," Turold answered him: "the heir. They call him Harold."

"So they do," William said, as quiet as ever. "Well then. And he comes to me?"

"With a message from his king."

"So he would," William said. "Did you happen to discover what Guy is asking for him?"

"As much as he can imagine," answered Turold, "and then as much again."

"Oh, is he?" William smiled. It was a smile of human dimensions, with teeth of human number and sharpness, but it was no more comfortable to look at than the boggart's grin. "We'll see about that." He raised his voice slightly. "Well, my lords and ladies, it seems I'm riding to Beaurain this morning. My lady stands regent as always. Look for me in a day or two, with a noble guest."

Even the papal legate could not object to that. Mathilda, who might have minded that her husband could escape so easily and leave her with all the dullness of the ducal court, nodded at his words. He took her hand and kissed it. "I'll be back as soon as I can," he said.

"It's begun," said Mathilda. "Be careful."

He did not ask her what she meant, only kissed her hand again and held it for a moment to his cheek. Then he turned, choosing swiftly from among his knights and men-at-arms, gathering a company that was not so large that Count Guy would reckon it an invading army, but not so small that anyone would reckon it weak.

William in action was an irresistible force. He had not chosen any of his sons to ride with him, but when he came out armed and ready to ride, Cecilia was mounted on her grey mare. A judicious distance away, William's squire held the rein of a horse who, people declared who had been with William before Cecilia was born, outshone even the splendor of his legendary and still much mourned grey charger. It was a young stallion, tall and proud, so dark a grey as to be almost black, but the mane flowing to his shoulder and the tail rippling to the ground were gleaming silver.

He was no witless beauty, either. The dark eye that fixed on William was vivid with intelligence. His nostrils flared; he snorted and pawed lightly, imperiously, commanding this new master to mount and ride.

William clearly was eager to obey, but his cold glare had fallen on his daughter. Just as he opened his mouth to speak, Turold rode between them on a small and sturdy but mettlesome horse. The horse was a horse in the same way in which Turold was a man: slantwise, and with scrupulous care.

The boggart smiled at them both, almost as a human man would—with a few more teeth than strictly necessary, but not so many as to be alarming. "The lady is most welcome," he said. "Will my lord lead us, or will he follow?"

"My lord will ride beside you," William said after a slight but noticeable pause. His glance promised Cecilia that their discussion was not prevented, only put off.

It was a reprieve, however brief. Cecilia was not packed off to her room, and that was all that mattered just then.

Her father could still mount a tall horse from the ground, in the full weight of armor, without touching the stirrup. This horse shifted slightly but visibly, the better to receive him. She began to wonder if it was of the same kind as the boggart's black devil-pony, but to her senses it was a mortal animal. It was like her brother Rufus: just a little out of the ordinary.

So was this ride, which she had joined because she could not do otherwise. She was a part of it somehow, through her dream and through the boggart's coming.

Something was beginning, as Mathilda had said. Mathilda knew what it was. Cecilia was not sure that she did, but in time she would. Of that she was certain.

❧ CHAPTER 35 ❧

I f Harold had learned nothing else in his life, he had learned that it did no good to rage against ill luck. He was a captive, and his captor was still in a quandary as to how much of an unimaginably vast estate he should demand as a ransom.

Count Guy's indecision was a blessing of sorts, in that it gave Harold time to contemplate escape. But while the count's greed was a great weakness, there was nothing weak about the guards who stood watch over Harold by night and day. They even followed him into the garderobe; when he slept, they surrounded his bed. As long as they mounted their guard, the golden goose would never fly.

By the fourth day of his captivity, he had discovered that if he moved to explore the castle, no one stopped him. A bulwark of mailed bodies stood between him and the outer world, but within these walls he was free to go where he pleased.

Therefore he was in the hall when the messenger came in great haste and flung himself at Count Guy's feet, babbling so rapidly that Harold could not follow his French at all. The count apparently could: he said, "Get up. Pull yourself together. You're sure?"

·The man crossed himself fervently. "By my hope of heaven," he said.

The count scowled formidably, but to Harold's eye he seemed slightly green about the edges. Something was coming that did not please him at all.

He snapped a command at Harold's guards. But when they moved to shuffle Harold back to his prison, he dug in his heels. "I am quite content here," he said sweetly.

He watched the count consider violence, then remember what was coming and go even greener. It spoke for the count's greed that Harold was not cut down where he stood. He was more valuable alive than dead, that much was obvious.

It was a long wait. Guy half rose a dozen times as if to leave the hall, rest, hunt, anything but stay where he was. But each time he sat down again.

Harold amused himself by challenging the count's chaplain to a game of chess. The priest was a middling fair player, although he lacked guile. He gave Harold a decent match before his king fell defeated.

As they restored the board for another match, trumpets rang without. Count Guy lurched to his feet.

Harold stayed where he was. He could very well guess who had arrived with such fanfare. It was a rescue, but the cost would not be slight.

It was God's will. Sometimes, he reflected, it was useful to be a good Christian.

The ringing thud of armed feet on stone, the measured tread of a sizable company, grew louder as the arrivals drew nearer to the hall. Count Guy's face had drained of color.

The Duke of Normandy came in like a storm breaking. Even Harold found himself briefly breathless. The hard-faced boy he had met in England was grown into a man. The face was still hard, the eyes cold iron, but the heart had a taste of fire.

The count's pretensions shriveled in his presence. William offered him a thin blade of a smile and a dangerously pleasant word. "Ah! My lord. I see you've kept my guest well. You'll be recompensed, of course—Walter here will see to it. My thanks to you; he'd have been in poor case elsewhere, with so many robbers about. If any of them had got wind of him, who he is and what he's worth in ransom . . ." William shook his head and sighed. "God be thanked, he found an honest rescuer."

He played it well. The count could not get a word in, nor, once William had spoken, could Guy confess the truth. William's men had spread through the hall, amiable, smiling, but massive and well armed. They were guests, those smiles said, but the hands on sword hilts and spear hafts warned ever so gently that they could turn in an instant to an invading army.

Some lords of Harold's acquaintance would have challenged them, but this one apparently knew his duke too well. The bitterness of disappointed greed had a taste of gall in Harold's own throat, but Guy put the best face he could on it.

He got a little out of it at least: a purse that weighed heavy and rang sweet, as gold should. Harold could suppose that it would keep its form after the duke left. William had never been accused of dispensing faery gold that turned by morning into leaves and stems of grass.

It was a quick rescue, and blessedly bloodless. By noon Harold was mounted, with his men behind him and his hawks and hounds all recovered, riding away from Beaurain.

"To Rouen?" he asked as the castle dwindled behind them.

"Eu, first," William said. "It's closer." He rolled his wide shoulders under the mail, then stretched. His mount danced under him; he rode it easily, with none of the heavy hand and jabbing spur that Normans were so much given to.

Harold was not too badly mounted himself. The horse must be one of William's own: it was a grey, much lighter than the duke's, and taller. It fit him well.

Freedom was heady, like wine. So was the change of company. This was more dangerous than Count Guy's captivity, he knew, but for the moment he was safe enough. He had never heard that William killed or maimed without provocation.

Now that they were on the road out of Beaurain, Harold had time to notice the rest of his escort apart from the duke and his second in command. Most of them were scarred and battle-hardened Normans as one might expect, but two were different. One was a dwarf, thickset and massive, with a black beard. The other rode in tunic and breeches like one of the servants, but the plait of fair brown hair that brushed the grey mare's rump, and the clear oval face with its wide grey eyes, belonged to neither a servant nor a man.

Harold observed how the men near her kept watch, making no great performance of it, but there was no doubt as to her value. She had the carriage of a queen, light and proud; for all her manifest youth, her eyes were wise and deep.

It happened, one way and another, that she came to ride beside him. The dwarf settled in her shadow, as watchful as the rest of the guards.

There was something odd about that one. Harold would consider it later. The young woman was of more pressing interest.

She did not speak as she rode beside him. She hardly seemed aware of him. And yet she must be: he looked nothing like a Norman.

"You don't ride like one, either," she said, still without seeming to have noticed that he existed. She might have been speaking to her mare's ears, or the branches of the tree that shaded the road.

It was a moment before it dawned on him that she was speaking to him. Startlement made him say the first thing that came into his head. "That bad, am I?"

"Different," she said. Then after a pause: "You may call me Cecilia. Your name I know."

"Ah," said Harold, more to himself than to her. "The duke's daughter."

It was not a question, but she answered as if it had been. "And the duchess's. What did you think I was?"

"Something unusual," he said.

"I am that." Her voice was as serene as her face. "I saw you in a dream, but Turold led my father to you."

Harold blinked. A shiver ran down his spine—not an unpleasant sensation, but not precisely comfortable, either. Whenever he was out of England, he had to remember that magic could run wild. The rest of the world was not protected as his green island was.

He had heard of the Norman duke's eldest daughter. People called her a beauty, and she was. They had not mentioned that she was a sorceress. The story was that she had been given to a holy abbey in her childhood, and dedicated to the Church. But there was nothing of the nun in this preternaturally composed young woman.

This was magic. It made his skin prickle and his heart beat faster. He crossed himself without thinking, but she did not fly shrieking into the aether.

Not that he had expected her to. These sorcerers had the Church in their power. They moved freely within its laws, and twisted its rites to their purposes.

He should be yearning for the protection of his English Church, his own kind and people, but he found himself fascinated by both the daughter and the father. The dwarf, too, now that his eyes were opened. The creature was not human. What it was he could not have said, but its edges were strange. When he blinked and peered, they were even stranger.

There was corruption here. He had spent his exile in Ireland, where there was magic, too, but wilder and odder and much easier to resist. His father had warned him of the subtleties of Gaul: the holiness that was not, the priests who worshipped more than one God, the lords who ruled other realms than the earthly.

Now Harold was in the midst of it, and it did not horrify him at all. It intrigued him. He wanted to see more; to know what it was that had been shut out so long from the Saxon kingdom.

Dangerous ground, his father would have said. But Godwine was long years dead. Harold was forewarned. He knew what had been done to his king, and far worse, to his brother Tosti. He would be wary.

So he told himself as he rode between the sorceress and the faery creature, with the Norman duke's broad back in front of him, and Normans all around him. He shot glances at them. Their edges were solid. They were as human as Normans ever were. It was only the dwarf, and the duke's daughter. And . . .

Yes. William, too.

Lords who ruled other realms than the earthly. This was one—a great one. There was no question about that.

Harold was beginning to understand what the king had done. That too should appall him, but it did not. There was a spell on him, he supposed, so strong that he could not even will to resist it.

He should have brought priests instead of thanes; monks instead of hawks and hounds. Fool that he was, sallying forth like the blindest innocent, without defense, with no warning but the words of a man over a dozen years dead. He knew what Tosti was. He should have known.

"Steady," Cecilia said. Her soft voice went deep inside him and rested there.

More magic. Harold found his feet, so to speak; his whirling thoughts stilled, and his heart left off its furious pounding and settled to a quieter rhythm. He was not going to go mad as Tosti had. He was not possessed. He was not—

"Hush." Her lips did not move at all. She was speaking within.

He drew a breath, then another. His sight cleared. This time he was truly calm and honestly steady. He could live in this world. He had a message to convey. He would convey it. Then he would be done. He would go back to England, to safety and sanity, and a world cleansed of all this strangeness.

CHAPTER 36

"There's your destiny," Lanfranc said.

He had been waiting in Eu when William came there, visiting as he often did. He said he did it to inspect the offspring—testing them for signs of magic, which so far only Cecilia, and to a small extent young William, had inherited. The baby, Agatha, was as mortal as the others, and of little interest to him except as a doting uncle.

He doted shamelessly on them all, magical or not. Mathilda professed to find it charming. William was less easily impressed, but it did speak well for the man that he saw the quality of the ducal heirs.

They were all in bed now under the eyes of guards or nurses. Mathilda was still in Rouen, settling matters that needed settling, but she would come to Eu in a day or two. William caught himself missing her ferociously.

Lanfranc was watching the Saxon earl. Harold had been quiet and rather strange on the ride from Beaurain, but once within the walls of the city, he seemed to come to himself. He had been at the high table until the last of the day's meal was taken away; then, while the wine went the rounds, he had excused himself to step down into the hall.

He was listening to the singer who had come with the king's gifts from Spain, a man entire and no mistake, but he had been trained to sing as sweet and high as a woman. The sound was rather like the yowl of mating cats, but Harold seemed to find it pleasing.

"That's the heart of England," Lanfranc said, "sitting there, looking as innocent as a man can be."

William grunted. "He seems ordinary enough to me. There's no magic in him. Quite the opposite, I'd say."

"Exactly," said Lanfranc. "That could be your bitterest enemy. But if you can make him your friend . . ."

"As I did the Popes in Rome?"

Lanfranc shook his head reprovingly. "You, my lord, are a hopelessly worldly man."

"I call it practical," William said. "We bought our way out of an interdict and into a divinely sanctioned marriage with a pair of monasteries, and now we're beloved of the Curia. It should be simple enough to win over a single man who's already in our debt for his rescue."

"It may not be as simple as that," Lanfranc said. "Behind that milk-and-water face is a mind as keen as any in England. The last time you saw him, he was a rebel sentenced to exile. Now he's the greatest earl in his kingdom."

"So he is," said William. "I wager he'll pay well to keep that office."

"You're going to take what his king offers."

"You ever thought I wouldn't?"

Lanfranc shrugged. "I know you hate to be predictable."

"I've had fourteen years to think about it. Normandy's solid. I've heirs for it and anywhere else I might be called to. Then I wasn't ready. Now, or whenever Edward goes to his God—which I wager will be soon; he's not a young man and I hear he's not strong—maybe I will be. It's worth the gamble."

"To be a king?"

"To break those bloody bedamned walls that are choking the breath out of Britain."

Lanfranc seemed a little startled. William did not see why. It should be obvious. King was a fine thing to be, but not if the kingdom was unlivable.

"It's . . . good reason," Lanfranc said after a pause. "That one can hinder you immeasurably, or he can help."

"He'll help," William said. "I'll make sure of that."

His eye rested on Harold as he said it. He was aware of the others around the earl, as a good soldier should be: marking each one, his expression, where he sat and what he did.

There was one who must have come in while he spoke with Lanfranc, or who might have been there all the while. She was plainly dressed, and she was practicing an art with which William was familiar: vanishing into the crowd, so that one's eye slid past her face. She seemed to be listening to the singer, but her body tilted ever so slightly toward the earl. She was watching him without seeming to watch.

William was notably more comfortable with magic than he had been when Mathilda first took him in hand, but this child of his was rather out of his reckoning. Even as an infant she had not been like other children. She never cried; she sat and watched, and kept her counsel.

She was still very young, but that was not a child sitting there. It was not a silly girl yearning after a handsome man, either. William did not know what it was, and that set him on edge.

Harold at least he could understand. Harold was a man who ruled men. He was here as an envoy; he had his duty and his honor, and loyalty to the kingdom from which he came.

There was nothing unusual about that. Cecilia was a duke's daughter; she had seen a hundred of his like. If she yearned after the exotic, there were the dark and sweet-tongued visitors from Spain. And yet this one man seemed to fascinate her.

Very little ever rocked Cecilia's composure. A late summons from her father had not done so, nor had his hard stare when she appeared, and his brusque question. She seemed to have expected it. Her answer was perfectly serene. "He doesn't know what magic is."

"Precious few of us know what magic is," William said testily. "What makes him different?"

"Destiny," she said.

"You were listening to Lanfranc."

She raised a brow—just like her mother. "He says it, too? Of course he would. He is what he is."

"You had better tell me what you see," William said. His voice had softened in spite of itself. More than anyone else but Mathilda, this incalculable child could melt his heart. There was no explaining it, but there it was.

She had been standing like a squire called to account for an infraction. Now William's glance and tilt of the head bade her sit. She obeyed as composedly as always, sitting at the end of his bed and tucking up her feet. Her back was very straight, her hands folded in her lap.

"Tell," William said.

For the first time her composure wavered. Her fingers laced

tightly; the line of a frown appeared between her brows. "I'm not sure what I see. It's all clouded and strange. The only clear things are two: you in armor, covered in blood, and him the same. You could be fighting side by side, you could be fighting against each other. I can't tell. Then there's a crown, but I can't see who wears it. It hangs in the air above the green hills of Britain. I see a white tower and a fleet of ships, and sometimes they're full of Vikings and sometimes they're manned by Normans. A battle below a bridge, a battle by the sea—men falling and dying, but whether one of them is you, or him, I can't say. I can't see."

She was shaking; her lips were blue as if with cold. William moved quickly to wrap her in blankets, pulling her into his lap and holding her close until she stopped shuddering. Then at least he understood her. Magic could wreak havoc with the body's defenses.

She was still trying to speak, though her teeth chattered so badly that no words came out. "That's enough," he said with rough gentleness. "You've said all you need to. It will all make sense in time."

"But will it be soon enough?" She peered up from her nest of blankets, ruffled and childlike, but her words were clear and hard. "That's why I study him. I need to know. Will he be for us or against us?"

"For us," William said with confidence. "I'll make sure of that."

"I hope you can," she said.

"Are you saying I can't?"

"I don't know," she said. "Am I?"

"You're getting cryptic again," he said.

"No," she said. "I'm really asking. I don't know anything. I thought I did, but he makes me all confused."

"If I didn't know you," William said, "I'd think you were in love with him."

"Oh no," said Cecilia. "Not in this life."

"Not in another, either?"

She did not answer that. William gusted a sigh. "Here, lie down. I'll send someone for a posset."

"I don't need a posset," she said, for once as irritable as any other child. "I'm confused, not sick."

"You still need sleep," William said, "and I'm not letting you out of my sight until you get it."

She frowned, but her eyelids were already drooping shut. William laid her in the bed and covered her warmly. He stayed where he was, sitting beside her, back against the wall. It was chill, but not unbearable. His feet were warm; that was enough. He leaned his head back and closed his eyes.

❧ CHAPTER 37 ❧

"Come fight a war with me," William said.

Harold had been a week in Rouen as the duke's guest, and he was growing visibly weary of feasting and hunting. He did not, however, seem weary of the duke's company. The sense William had had when they first met, that they could be friends, had grown into certainty.

Everything about them was different: looks, upbringing, perception of the world and its magic. And yet when they met of a morning or sat to dinner of an evening, they were never lacking for things to say to each other. Harold was not the rider William was, nor did he pretend to be; but he was a strong fighter, a canny hunter, and a commander who thought past the confusion of the melee. He understood the shapes and patterns of a battle; he could see both how to fight and how to command his troops.

And now there was a convenient little war, a matter of rebellion in Brittany, with beleaguered rebels calling on Normandy for help. Harold knew as well as William that a strong country on one's borders was much less to be preferred than a weak one. Weak countries did not make a habit of invading strong ones, or causing undue trouble for them.

What William did not happen to mention was that if Normandy was rife with magic, Brittany was mad with it. There most of the Old Things from Britain had gone, and most were still there, haunting its hills and its wild coast.

It was a gamble. Harold might flee in horror and lose all the goodwill that William had worked to gain. But William was wagering that Harold would wake to the fascination of it.

It would be a fast war, a raid to be precise: get in, do the necessary, get out. William's troops were ready and waiting. He was somewhat surprised, as they rode out at dawn, not to find Cecilia anywhere among them. She was standing beside her mother, towering above Mathilda, limned in the light of torches. Her brothers were at her back, all three: Robert sulking, Richard philosophical, young William frowning at the dwarf who was still, without apology or explanation, playing escort to Cecilia.

There was still no understanding her, but for once she was being incomprehensible away from the affairs of men and war. William was less comforted by that than he would have liked to be. The old gods knew what she would do while he was gone.

Mathilda could handle her. William turned his mind away from her and toward the raid on Brittany.

The border of Brittany was the mouth of a slow river, a broad stretch of mud and marsh that sank into the sea. On the edge of it was the sudden rock of St. Michael's Mount, humming with power, sucking in the tides and hurling them back again. Beyond was the deep magic of Brittany and the citadels of the Old Things.

There was a ford, or so their scouts said. It wound from trickle to tussock to blessed bit of shingle, where the horses slipped and clattered but did not sink.

They were dismounted and leading the horses, feeling their way foot by foot. The horses stamped and shook their heads and lashed their tails, driven half mad by swarms of stinging flies. Men were luckier in the main, with mail to cover most of them; but flies that crept into cracks and crevices stung unmercifully.

Somewhat past the middle of the ford, the channel suddenly deepened. The horses scrambled and wallowed. Those in the lead struggled to find a shallower passage.

"Damned lucky we didn't bring baggage wagons," William said to Harold. "They'd have been mired a mile back."

Harold's smile flashed under the fair mustache. He was much happier afoot than ahorse; what for the Normans was muddy misery was for him almost a pleasure.

William opened his mouth to growl at him for it, but sudden cries ahead brought him up short. The men in the lead had come through the channel to a stretch of seemingly solid sand that had, as they set foot on it, turned abruptly liquid.

The earth melted under them, rippling toward the men behind. Even as William stared, taken aback, one of the horses sank as if it had been swallowed. The man who had been leading it clung to a bit of solid ground, a small spur of rock; but it was slick with mud, and the sand about it was tilting, opening to suck him down.

William surged ahead with such speed as he could. Harold, longer-legged and more adept off a horse, sprang past him. Men were shouting, screaming. William bellowed to the lot of them to halt and stand.

Those that could obey, did. "Up!" he roared at them. "Up toward the mount! It's solid there."

They did not ask how he knew. Nor did he, as he took his own advice. Memory was stirring: another river, another time, another roil of dark and groping things deep underfoot. Death was here, now, as it had been then—but the stakes were much higher. More than his life alone was in danger.

Once he could trust the earth he stood on, he waded as quickly as he could through the mingling of mud and shingle. Harold in his crimson cloak, vivid among the browns and greys and greens of the lesser knights, ran light-footed toward the struggling men.

All the rest had escaped but those. William cursed his leaden feet. But the footing even here was too treacherous to inflict his weight on his horse.

Harold sprang to the rock to which one of the knights was clinging, and swung the man up and over his shoulder, even as he stooped toward a hand that strained out of the muck. The man to whom it belonged was nearly gone.

Harold heaved him up. The mud clutched like hands, clawing, striving to pull him down. With an effort that made the cords of his neck bulge, Harold plucked the man free.

He all but toppled over, burdened as he was with the man on his back. By a miracle he kept his feet and made for the high ground.

The earth was not done with him. Tendrils like dark mist curled up from it, nigh invisible in the clear daylight. But William saw them.

Harold lurched within reach. William got a grip on him and flung him up and onto unyielding shingle.

Both men were alive. Harold lay between them, breathing in gasps.

The rest of the army roared. William felt the mist recoil. Mortal joy was death to it. He gave it the full, fierce strength of his own relief, that withered it like a blast of cleansing fire.

No men lost. One horse—that was grievous; trained warhorses were a valuable commodity. But that expanse of sucking sand, as innocent as it seemed to be, could have swallowed them all.

"I owe you for this," William said to Harold, clasping his hand and pulling him to his feet. Harold had his breath back; he was dripping with mud, but William cared nothing for that as he clasped the Saxon earl in a strong embrace.

"It's small repayment," Harold said when he was free and could breathe again, "for rescuing me from Beaurain."

"It's well paid," said William. "Now, up. We'll ride from here. I see a way that won't suck us to perdition."

Harold barely blinked at the shift. Nor did he ask what William saw or how he saw it. William doubted that he would want to know.

Even yet, after all these years, magic did not come easily to William. He had left most of it to Mathilda; although she had insisted that he continue his tutelage as he could when he was apart from her, he found it simpler, more often than not, to put it out of his mind.

But it was there, always. Sometimes, as now, it ambushed him.

At least here it was useful. If he slanted his sight just so, and opened a corner of his mind that was usually shut, he could see a clear track.

He should have done that before any of them ventured the ford. It was no credit to him that their losses had been so small.

This was a lesson. Mathilda would not have failed to point that out—or to warn him to be careful.

The path that he could see meandered like the river, but it was solid; it supported the weight of horses. His men followed him without undue grumbling. Harold rode close behind, unwontedly silent. Worn out, William thought; and no wonder. That feat of his would reverberate in songs and stories.

It was a great thing, born of a great heart. This was an ally worth winning.

*   *   *

Ever since he hauled two of William's knights out of the sucking sands, Harold had felt strange. It was nothing he could put a name to. Mostly it was a sense of shadows just beyond the edge of vision, and voices on the other side of silence.

He rode and fought as well as he ever had, and no one remarked on any oddity in his manner. William's army, with Harold close by the duke, took back the castle of Dol for the rebels, and drove the Breton count's forces all the way to the city of Rennes.

That was a bloody fight, and seared with fire. The Bretons had burned the crops and fields. There was nothing to forage, and precious little to eat without running back toward Dol.

It was victory, but a hungry one. William withdrew his troops—wisely, in Harold's estimation. No one on that side was calling it a retreat.

Dol was well provisioned and well fortified. They rested there a night, and then another, before riding back to Normandy. Those who were wounded were glad of the respite; those who were merely exhausted ate as much as they could hold, drank rather more than that, and slept like the dead.

Of all strange places in this strange country, this to Harold seemed the strangest. William seemed to notice something odd: he had a distinctly prickly air about him, and if anyone spoke or touched him unexpectedly, he lashed out. But his men needed to rest and eat, and he was not one to give way to formless fear.

Nor was Harold, or so he would have said before he came to Dol. The men seemed unperturbed, except for one or two who shied away from shadows.

The first night in Dol, Harold succumbed to exhaustion; he remembered nothing from lying down to getting up. The second night, he lay in a corner of the hall, wide awake, twitching like a nervous horse.

The others were manifestly asleep. A fair fraction of them were snoring. Between the snuffling and whimpering of the dogs and the rasping and rumbling of the men, the bare stone chamber echoed like a sea cave.

The sea was sighing beyond the walls. It had a strange, sad sound, as if it chanted dirges in a language Harold did not know.

In this country, that was altogether likely. The place was crawling with magic. He could feel it under his skin. He had heard men speak of seeing spirits, conversing with demons, walking in woods where the trees spoke and the birds sang in human voices.

Tomorrow they would be leaving it—and none too soon. Tonight they rested.

Harold rose without undue care to be quiet. He would have had to gallop through the hall on an iron-shod destrier to attract these men's notice. He was careful not to step on anyone on his way to the door. Even the dogs barely twitched at his passing.

He had meant to pray in the chapel, but somehow he was turned about; where he had thought to find the passage to it, he found a postern gate instead, and a steep slope sparsely scattered with sea grass. A track ran down it and out to a stretch of sand that glimmered in fitful moonlight.

There was a bulk of darkness beyond the sand: a stony isle to which clung a stunted and wind-gnarled tree. Harold had seen it when they rode in, when it was girdled in turbulent water.

The tide had gone out farther than he might have thought. The path he followed was distinct under the moon, and rather unusually straight considering how rough the ground was. He walked dry-shod across the sand and climbed up amid the rocks, with no aim in mind but to be closer to the sky.

The strangeness was in him again. A mist wound through the rocks, pungent with salt and the sea. He saw none of the demonic beings that the Normans spoke of, but someone was sitting beside the tree.

It was a human shape—no doubt of that in the moonlight. He saw the glimmer of mail and the gleam of eyes. As he drew closer, the figure came a little clearer, though the mist was thickening, blurring his sight.

The voice that spoke out of the mist seemed perfectly solid, a man's voice, high and rather harsh, speaking French with a somewhat different accent than Harold had heard in either Normandy or Brittany. "Good evening, messire. It's a fine night to be out and about."

"Many would tell you, sir, that the night is full of demons and dead souls that suck blood," Harold said.

"Oh," said the man under the tree, "I'm not thirsty tonight."

He was laughing, but Harold could not help a shiver of the spine and a quick sign of the cross. The man, or whatever he was, neither flinched nor puffed into mist. If anything changed, it was the gleam of his eyes, very bright in the gloom. The moon seemed to have come down to fill them.

"My lord of Wessex," the man said. And at Harold's slight start of surprise: "You are hard to mistake, messire, although we've never met. I knew your father; our paths crossed while he was in Flanders. You look like him."

That was courtly and polite. Harold bowed to it. "I fear, sir, I cannot return the favor."

"No matter," said the man. "Call me Geoffrey; it will do."

"My lord Geoffrey," Harold said.

"I hear you've won a pretty little war," said Geoffrey. "The duke must be pleased."

"The duke has made his point," Harold said.

"Has he indeed?"

Harold moved closer. The mist was very thick; it pressed against him, clasping him with clammy fingers. Yet through it he saw that the man was wiry and dark, and chained to the tree. His wrists and ankles were ringed in darkness, and heavy links wound about the trunk.

"Sir!" said Harold in shock. "Who did this to you?"

"Why, my lord," Geoffrey said as amiably as ever, "I'm sure I deserve it."

Harold signed the cross over him. He was no more perturbed than he had been before.

That was enough. Harold drew his sword and balanced it in his hands, breathing deep, making himself a prayer. With sudden force, he smote the chain just past the trunk of the tree.

The forged steel cut through the chain like butter. Geoffrey fell backward; the shackles melted from his wrists and ankles.

The point of Harold's sword came to rest over his breastbone. He had been about to rise; he stayed where he was, smiling, unafraid. "I thank you," he said.

"Use your freedom well," said Harold, "and work no evil in the world."

"Why, do you think I would?"

"I think," said Harold, "that people hereabouts tell stories about this island, how the Devil came here after St. Michael drove him from the greater Mount. Some say he was driven from here as well; others that he was bound to its rock, sealed with chains of adamant."

"Chains of air and darkness," Geoffrey said, "and not the Devil; only the Devil's grandson."

He rose through the metal of the sword, wincing slightly as it passed through his body, but it left no wound and shed no blood. He bowed low, with the grace of a courtier. Even as he straightened, he rose up from the earth, wreathed in mist and shards of shadow. "We shall meet again," he said. "Be well, my lord of Wessex, and be watchful. Much that you are about to do will seem inevitable at the time, but later inevitability will render it to nothing."

Harold opened his mouth to ask Geoffrey what he meant, but even as the last words faded, so too did Geoffrey, melting into the moonlight. There was nothing left of him, not even the chains that had bound him.

The isle was empty, the moon sinking in the west. Its track was dim; Harold slipped and stumbled on it. Below the sheen of it, he could see the turbulent race of the tide.

He had long since decided that he was dreaming. But when he woke in the hall, there was sand in his shoes and salt dried on his mantle, and the hem of it was damp.

❧ CHAPTER 38 ❧

The men came back from their war on the eve of Midsummer. It was a restless day, full of clouds and wind and the grumble of thunder.

William's castle of Bonneville was ready for him. The women and the servants had been up all night, but it was a matter of pride to welcome their duke in their best clothes, clean and combed and as fresh as if they had slept the night through.

Cecilia was as restless as the weather. She began beside her mother in the hall, but by the time her father had ridden into the castle and handed his horse to the groom, she was there to take Earl Harold's bridle while he dismounted, then let the groom lead the horse away while she shadowed him into the hall.

There was an oddness in him, as if someone else rode inside of him. But when she looked as far as she dared, she found nothing.

He was wearing Norman armor. It was very fine, and newly polished; the device on his shield was freshly painted, a blood-red wyvern with elaborately curling tail. He walked into the hall beside William, with William's arm around his shoulders.

It was friendship, but it was possession, too. William had won more than a brief border raid. Something was agreed between them, but Cecilia caught herself wondering if Harold knew what he had agreed to.

That evening in hall, at last, William commanded Harold to complete his embassy: to say what he had been sent to say.

Harold rose from his seat at the high table. He had a cup in his hand; he raised it as he bowed to William and Mathilda and the rest of the high ones, then to the lesser folk in the hall.

That delighted them. It was a while before the cheering and pounding of tables muted enough that he could be heard.

He waited them out, smiling, at ease. When there was something resembling silence, he said, "My lords and ladies; my lord duke. I bring you this word from the king of the English: 'In the evening of my life, God speaks to me. He names in my heart the one who rules after me. William, Duke of the Normans, cousin and heir, the time is coming. Be ready; be strong. Prepare to be king.'"

There was a long silence. Harold had spoken in the strong rhythms of his people's songs, even through the lighter cadences of the French.

There was no telling who began it. It came from everywhere, reverberating through the hall: a roar of pure, bloodthirsty delight.

Normans at heart were Norsemen still, Viking reivers who set out in ships to conquer the world. Cecilia could feel it in herself, in the part of her that was Norman. It made her heart swell and her head go dizzy with dreams of conquered splendor.

Grimly she brought it under control. By blood she was more Druid than Viking. By magic she was pure Druid.

Harold, she thought out of nowhere that she could discern, was half a Dane. For the first time she could not tell what he was thinking. The smile had left his face. It was blank; she could not read it at all.

There was a coldness in the pit of her stomach. It was foresight trying to get out, but when she left a way open for it, it ran away and hid. She was as blind to what might come as anyone else.

Sunlight shone through the high windows of the duke's hall. It was a glorious morning of Midsummer, warm and bright. Even within the cold stone vault of the hall, the light was like liquid gold.

It washed with splendor the ritual upon the dais. Harold knelt between two glittering golden shrines, miniature temples studded with jewels. In each lay a relic of the Christian Church.

He was nearly as splendid as the reliquaries, with his white-gold hair and his crimson cloak and his rings and collar of gold. William above him, enthroned in full armor, cloaked and crowned with the ducal coronet, had a darker, stronger splendor. It was his will that ruled in this hall, and every one of them, Harold most of all, knew it.

.If it had been left to Cecilia, she would have made him swear on oak and ash and thorn. But her mother and father said they knew better. Harold was incorrigibly Christian; he would never submit to a pagan rite. This, with bones that might have belonged to saints but more likely had been scavenged from an old tomb, struck him with holy awe.

He was neatly and terribly trapped. She did not think he knew yet how terrible it was. He had drunk late and deep last night, matching William cup for cup—which was not a wise thing; people had been amazed that Harold lasted as long as he did.

His face this morning, beneath the glamour of light, had a bruised look. She wondered if he even remembered what he had agreed to in the heat of wine. "Swear," William had said. "Swear to stand behind me when I claim the kingship."

Harold, bright red and swaying—unlike William who was still almost sober—had laughed in a high giggle and said, "I'll swear to anything if you pass the winejar again."

"Will you be my loyal man? Will you serve me faithfully when I am king?"

"Anything!" Harold had declared, pulling the jar toward him and filling his cup to overflowing. Strong wine stained his tunic and dribbled on the floor.

Now in the morning light, William held him to his promise. The wine was still in him, maybe; he seemed calm enough, kneeling in his panoply that William had given him, with a hand on each of the reliquaries.

It was not a bishop or archbishop who administered the oath, but Prior Lanfranc come up from Bec to bind the Saxon earl to the heir of Britain. This had been William's plan since he brought Harold out of Beaurain. With the greatest earl in England bound to him, the rest would be harder put to resist.

Cold walked down Cecilia's spine as Harold spoke the words that Lanfranc gave him. They were simple, and spoken first in Latin and then in Saxon and finally in French. "In the name of Father, Son, and Holy Spirit, by my hope of heaven and my soul's salvation, by Saints Gervasius and Protasius whose hallowed bones lie beneath my hand, before God and man I swear that I shall serve my lord William with heart and hand, with life and sword and soul's fidelity. Whatever he loves, so shall I love; what he loathes, I shall loathe also, in accordance with the laws of God and the world of men. Nor shall I ever in thought or action, through word or deed, give him cause to repent of me. So let him hold to me as I to him, and be my lord and liege, in true binding while both our lives endure."

Harold brought his hands together. William came to stand before him, clasping the joined hands in his. Lanfranc laid a blessing on their heads. It was Latin and strictly canonical, but the hum of magic beneath spoke another blessing altogether.

The planes of the world were shifting. The air was full of spirits, Old Things and things older than old. It was a great oath by any mortal standard, but in that other world it was immeasurably more.

Worse for Harold perhaps, but much better for William, was the fact that with the binding, Harold's defenses against magic had crumbled away. There had been cracks in them since he came back from Brittany; those cracks had grown to consume the whole.

And that was exactly as Lanfranc had wished it. Cecilia could feel his satisfaction, and his sense that now, at last, the world would go as it should for William.

Cecilia was not so sure. Harold rose to be enfolded in William's strong embrace; then came the feast to celebrate the swearing of William's first vassal among the Saxons.

She slipped away before the first course came out in procession from the kitchens. She should have been rejoicing with the rest of them, but the part of her that she most trusted was deeply uneasy. This would not end well for someone—though whether it was William or Harold, she could not tell. Maybe even the gods did not know. They left the world to find its way, most often, and sometimes there were two ways to find.

England's king would die soon. Of that she was sure. As to who would wear the crown after him, or how he would come by it, they all would know when it came.

William sent Harold home on one of his own ships, sunk nearly to the gunwales with gifts. What Harold did not see but Cecilia could see very well indeed were the insubstantial guests who swarmed over and among the boxes and bales and barrels. A great army of the Old Things had chosen to venture the walls of iron, protected within the orbit of William's liege man.

They were nothing that the Saxons could see, but Harold had

the look of a man who hears voices where should be silence. As the speeches of farewell wound down and the chanting of the choir drew to a close, Harold moved toward his ship.

Cecilia caught his hand. She did not care who saw or what he thought. "Be careful," she said.

Harold started, but he did not pull away from her. "I . . . thank you, lady," he said.

"Don't just recite words," she said. "Listen. Be wary. You've done a thing that can't be undone—no matter how hard you try."

He stiffened. "My honor is my soul," he said.

"Just so," said Cecilia.

He did not understand. The ship's captain was calling; her father was glaring. She let fall her hand in a kind of despair. But there was one more thing she could, and must, say. "We'll meet again, my lord," she said.

"I do hope so, my lady," he said, and for all his confusion, he was telling the truth. He bowed to her as if she had been a queen. Very straight then, with his head up and his eyes already full of England, he strode toward the ship.

❧ CHAPTER 39 ❧

Tosti was mad.

That had been so since before Earl Godwine died; Harold had believed then that his brother's condition was grievous, but no one else seemed to find it worthy of remark. If anyone had anything to say, it was that Tosti was somewhat given to excess—in words, in actions, in the passions of his heart.

After Godwine was dead and the queen's grip on the king assured, Edward made Tosti earl of Northumbria. It was a great holding and a high honor. Tosti had laughed when it was given him, but that was taken for elation; people indulged him, because he did have a way about him, a brightness that drew lesser spirits and made them eager to serve him.

That was ten years ago. Harold had been hearing rumors since, rumbles of discontent; messengers to Harold or to the king, bearing tales of arrogance, cruelty, and disregard for either mercy or justice. Of late those messengers had been more frequent and their outcries more heated.

While Harold was in Normandy, matters had gone from bad to worse. He came back to a clamor of outrage and the beginning of rebellion in Northumbria.

In the autumn the peace broke beyond recall.

"Murder!"

That was the charge in the king's hall. "He slew two honest men who had come to him under promise of safety, sank blades in their hearts in his own chamber. And when even his lady wife cried out against him, he said to her in a tone of sweet and perfect reason, 'There were devils riding on their shoulders. Surely you could see them.'"

*   *   *

"Really," said Tosti.

He looked the same as ever: eyes somewhat too bright, smile somewhat too broad. But there was an edge to him that had not been there before.

"Devils," he said. "Devils everywhere. You brought them back with you, brother, from across the sea. They've swarmed through England; they've met their kin in Wales and among the Scots, and bred like flies in a carcass."

Harold had found him in his hall in Durham, after a hard ride and a near escape from an army marching on the city. Tosti was singularly unconcerned by the news, or by Harold's demanding to know what had come over him.

"There are no more devils in England than there have ever been," Harold said with all the patience he could find in him. "Those were men of good family, rich in kin and land. Now your earldom rises against you. They're coming to kill you, brother."

"They won't kill me," Tosti said. He beckoned to one of the servants, who scuttled forward with shoulders hunched and head low. "Mead for the lord of Wessex. Be quick! Or I'll snip your ears."

He smiled as he said it, but the man clapped hands over his ears and ran.

Harold's heart felt cold and small. He had ridden here with some wan hope that there was something to save. But as he met those eyes, he saw nothing. Whatever had taken Tosti had taken him completely.

The mead came at a run, overflowing the rim of the horn. The boy who brought it was not the one who had been sent for it. This one was even whiter and more shaken than the other. When Harold reached for the horn, he ducked, spun, and fled.

Harold would have preferred an ordinary cup. He could have feigned to drink from it more easily, without fear of drowning himself in the backwash of mead from the horn. As it was, he took as small a swallow as he dared.

It was ordinary mead as far as he could tell, sweet with honey and the memory of apples. It made him no dizzier than it should; he felt nothing untoward after he had drunk.

Tosti's mind had already wandered. His clerk was trying to read him the rolls of one of his domains. Tosti rose and walked away in the midst of the recitation.

That was not, apparently, an uncommon thing; the clerk left off reading and waited, as wary as the rest, until he should receive some signal to begin again. From the way he braced his shoulders, that could be a blow as easily as a word.

Still with the mead-horn in his hand, Harold eased away down the hall. Tosti seemed not to notice. He was intent on something in the rafters, now frowning, now smiling, as if whatever it was happened to be holding a conversation.

In spite of himself Harold followed his brother's gaze. Almost he thought he could see—

There was nothing there. He was not mad, no matter what had happened to him in Brittany. He did not see devils, and he most certainly did not give way to antic moods and flights of perilous fancy.

Harold had left the hall with intent to discover what he could from those who dared to speak, but as he made his way past the door, he saw a man waiting by the wall. It was a priest in a plain gown, simple and unpretentious, but Harold knew the face too well to be deceived. "My lord archb—"

Archbishop Stigand clapped a hand over his mouth. "Not here. Come with me."

Harold wasted no time in nursing the slap to his pride. He followed Stigand to one of the outbuildings, a storehouse that in this season should have been full of provisions for the winter. It was dusty and nearly bare.

Harold shook his head at that. "Surely the lady could see to this, if the lord can't."

"The lady has good reason to let her husband run unchecked," said Stigand. "Remember who she is."

For the second time in a difficult day, Harold felt himself chastened. He set his teeth and made himself say coolly, "Whatever her allegiances to Flanders or, God knows, her brother's daughter in Normandy, she has always been faithful in her obligations to her husband's people."

"Why, so has he," Stigand said. "There's something in the wind. More to the point, there's something in your brother. Would you have him be free of it?"

"You need to ask?"

"Nothing is certain in this world," Stigand said, "even the loyalty of Harold Godwineson."

And that was a third stroke, careless and stinging sharp as the rest. "So," Harold said with an edge that he did not care if Stigand heard, "what brings the primate of all England to the wild north without the escort suitable to his rank?"

Stigand sat on a bale of moldy straw, as straight and tidy as if he had sat on his episcopal throne. "Time is growing short," he said. "Your brother has grown dangerous. Word is that he has been treating with the Danes: enlisting their aid against his rebellious people."

"I'm sure he has," Harold said. "That doesn't explain your presence here."

"The Danes are mortal enough," said Stigand. "Swords and spears can hold them off—and you'll lead the army, no doubt, if it comes to that. It's another matter that concerns me. This thing that is in your brother—if it's driven out, he may be sane again. Then I have no doubt that he'll be loyal to you if not to the king."

"An exorcism?"

Stigand inclined his head. "I've come with the means to do it, and priests to assist me. But we must have him in our presence, secured and guarded. His lady watches him constantly. He has his own fierce wariness, as the mad do; what is in him will protect itself at all costs."

"Tell me where to bring him," Harold said, "and I'll get him there."

"The cathedral close," Stigand answered him, "after the night office."

"Tonight?"

"Soonest is best," said Stigand.

"You'll have him," said Harold.

Harold had never yet made a promise that he had not kept. But when he returned to the hall, where Tosti had lost patience with the endless fiddle of clerks and scattered their parchments in ribbons across the floor, Harold began to wonder if he had reached the limit of his capacity. He could deal with the reckless, the traitorous, the furious. But the mad lived in a different world altogether.

Harold had men enough with him to effect a quick capture. It would have to be after the day's meal, when the hall was quiet and the lord and lady had gone up to bed.

The lady could present an obstacle. He would have to capture her first, or lure her away—if one of the maids could be persuaded—

"No need."

He looked up startled from his ruminations. Tosti was in front of him, smiling a sweet, wild smile. "I'll go," he said. "It's terribly dull here. An exorcism might be entertaining."

There truly was a demon in him. "Will you go bound?" Harold asked it, for his brother was nowhere in those too-bright eyes.

"Any way you please," the demon in Tosti said.

"Swear to it," said Harold.

"On holy relics? In front of a duke?"

Harold stiffened.

Tosti laughed. "I swear! By Our Lady and the Child she bore, and any other saint or hallow you please."

The Devil, as everyone knew, could speak the Lord's words as if he had a right to them. Harold trusted nothing that this creature said; but it had sworn. "Be bound," he said, "in heart and soul. I'll come for you before the hour of the night office."

"Do that," Tosti said, as bright as ever.

"If there is trickery—" Harold began.

"Not for my part," said Tosti.

Harold left him in deep unease. No doubt he should have stayed, overpowered and bound his brother while he still could, but he was too disconcerted to do anything sensible. He went away and prayed instead, prostrate on the floor of the earl's chapel.

Prayer did little to soothe his heart. Half of what he felt, he had no name for. The rest was too complex to understand.

Night came terribly slowly, and yet too deadly fast. Harold had fallen asleep at his futile prayers. He had slept through dinner; if God had mercy on his cowardice, he had slept through the night office as well.

But there was Tosti, impinging slowly on his consciousness. His brother had a length of cord in his hand, holding it out, smiling.

Harold wondered, with the perception of the half-asleep, which of them was the master here. He took the cord but did not bind the proffered wrists with it. "I'll trust you," he said, "at least to follow me to the cathedral."

"Ah!" said Tosti as if the prospect delighted him. "A splendid

place for an exorcism. This is much too unassuming; not to
mention excessively close to my very powerful wife. You don't
trust her, but do you fear her? You should."

"We are stronger than she," Harold said.

"You hope you believe it," Tosti said.

He held out his hand. Without thinking, Harold took it. Tosti
could have flung him to the floor, snapped his neck, broken his
hand—but he drew Harold to his feet and led the way out of the
chapel.

It was a strange procession through the darkness of Durham,
with the captive leading the captor, and no light to show the
way. And yet, even without moon or star, Harold could see. The
world was all shades of shadow, greys and blacks shifting subtly from formless into form.

Tosti was black on black. The cathedral was blacker still. All
the light was locked within. Not one ray, not one blessed beam,
was suffered to escape.

The postern opened to Tosti's touch. A gust of air blew past
Harold, thick with incense and cold stone. Holiness had never
blown so cold before, or felt so remote.

That was the demon, corrupting Harold by its proximity. So
he told himself as they ventured into the echoing vault of the
cathedral.

The high altar was walled away behind the screen of the
choir. Stigand was not there: Harold knew it without need to
see. He was in the Lady Chapel, with a handful of silent
priests, and a figure wrapped in a dark mantle.

That was no priest. Even shrouded, it was unmistakably a
woman, and unmistakably a queen.

A sigh escaped Harold. Maybe it was foolish, but Stigand
was merely a power in the realm. Edith was family.

Blood called to blood. Two of them against Tosti, surely,
could protect him from himself.

Tosti stood unbound by aught but a promise. Stigand turned
his back on him. As the dark-robed priests genuflected and
moved on past their archbishop, spreading as it were in battle
order about the altar, Stigand began the stately rite of the Mass.
"*Introibo ad altare Dei:* I will go up to the altar of God."

"To God who gives joy to my youth," Tosti chanted in a
chillingly sweet voice. It was not his own voice at all.

Stigand continued with hieratic calm, intoning the great words and suffering the eerie responses. Through the long melismas of the *Kyrie*, Edith joined her voice to Tosti's. The beauty of it was a white pain, power twisting against power.

The Mass was a structure as solid as stone and far more enduring. Tosti's fabric of airy fancy rippled against it, supple as silk. The holy words troubled him not at all. The consecration of divine body and blood won from him a grin of delight.

Stigand showed no sign of dismay. He continued the rite with unruffled devotion, accepting Tosti's responses as if they arose from true piety.

Edith's voice was pitched to blur and dim her brother's. The words she sang were edged like blades, cutting and thrusting at every word Tosti spoke. Tosti's grin never wavered, but it seemed to Harold that his face grew paler as the Mass drew to its end.

It was a battle, quiet but desperate, with Tosti's soul as the prize. Harold, caught up in it, realized only belatedly that the Mass had given way to something else. His Latin was good enough for common offices, but this was more.

"Out," Edith said, low and powerfully sweet. "Come out into the light. Leave the heart that nurtured you. Free the soul so terribly bound."

"Too late," said Tosti. "Years too late."

"It is never too late for salvation," Edith said as Stigand sang the closing psalm: *"My Lord is my rock, my fortress, my deliverance...."*

"Come," said Edith. "Come to the light."

"Go," sang Stigand. "Go in peace."

Tosti laughed. It was shrill—a yipping howl. Shadows leaped and spun. Darkness pressed strangling-close.

Tosti spun on Harold, quicker than sight—but Harold was too old a fighter to be taken off guard. He was aware, dimly, of Stigand and Edith chanting. For the first time the priests had forsaken their silence; their voices joined the others, a long sonorous roll of sacred Latin. But far more immediate were the hands groping for his throat, and the teeth bared, and the eyes with nothing human left to find, anywhere, all the way to the bottom.

There had still, somewhere in Harold's heart, been love for his brother, and compassion, and grief for what had become of him. But in that bitter battle, tooth and claw and no quarter given, love died. Tosti was gone—dead. This was an inhuman thing, a monster, a demon clothed in human flesh.

"Out!" Harold bayed at him: the cry of the hunter after the quarry. "Out! Out! *Out!*" In it was all his rage and grief and sorrow—the fullness of his heart.

It drove Tosti back. The thing within him did not leave; nor had Harold expected it. It was as much a part of him as a natural soul. If it left, the body would die.

Let it die. Harold pressed him hard, striking with fists, driving him back out of the chapel and down the echoing darkness of the nave. All the way to the door he drove the thing that had been his brother, flung open that massive gate as if it had no weight at all, and gathered for the last, the killing stroke.

Tosti lay limp in his hands. The eyes that looked up at him in wan moonlight were quiet. The wildness was gone from them. Almost, for an instant, Harold thought that after all it was Tosti; it was his brother.

That moment of hesitation, brief as it was, was all the opening the demon needed. It wrenched free and rolled, tumbling down the steps, out and away.

Harold leaped after it, but he was too slow. It laughed as it escaped, light and high and wild.

In that laughter were words. "Ah, brother! You should never have let me go. This will be the end of you—in the end. Unless . . ."

In the pause, Harold almost caught him, almost had him. But he danced away, grinning wide and white in the gloom. "Don't take what's given you," Tosti said, half chanting. "Don't give way to necessity. Don't do what you think you must do. Then you'll live. Maybe. For a while."

Harold dived for the shadow of him. But he was gone—utterly. Harold lay bruised, bleeding from a dozen tiny wounds.

Footsteps halted beside him. Two shrouded figures stood over him. Edith and Stigand.

He rolled onto his back even as Edith knelt beside him. Her hand was cool on his forehead. Her voice was cooler still, but oddly comforting. "He's gone. We'll not catch him now."

"That's grim news for England," Stigand said—as if Harold needed to hear it. The archbishop sighed heavily. "Ah well. He's out of Northumberland, for a while. We'll bring down a sentence of exile, and leave the rest to God."

"Amen," said Edith, but Harold said nothing. God had little to do with this. Harold had done a thing that he was already regretting, though what else he could have done, he could not imagine.

Leave it to God, he thought. Stigand was right in that much. Maybe God could mend it; maybe He would not. That was His choice, as was all else in this world.

❧ CHAPTER 40 ❧

The King of England was dying. The sickness had taken him in the autumn after Earl Tosti was driven out of Northumberland; it lay on him with increasing heaviness as autumn faded into winter. By the eve of Christmas he was too weak to rise from his bed, yet he insisted that he be carried to the Mass that he loved best of all in the year.

Archbishop Stigand sang the Mass, with a choir of sweet-voiced novices, and a phalanx of priests. The sight of them reminded Harold too vividly of the exorcism that had failed.

But this, in its way, succeeded. The king sat upright through the whole of it. His fading eyes warmed with the beauty of the words and the singing. He drew strength from it, enough to go to dinner afterward, although he had little appetite for the dainties that were set before him.

When dinner was done, he could not rise or walk back to his chamber. Harold carried him there, ignoring the servants who would have performed the office. He was terribly light, as if he were transforming already into air and spirit. As Harold laid the king in his bed, he knew that Edward would not get up again. This effort had been the last that he would make in this life.

In the days of his dying, Edward had said nothing of the heir in Normandy. Wise counsel would have sent envoys to fetch him, for the heir should be at the king's side when he died.

Harold knew the guilt of silence. His oath to William haunted the long hours of the deathwatch. He could feel the power of the holy relics under his hands, and the force of the words in his heart.

But he said nothing. He kept order in the king's chamber and the council hall; he saw to what needed seeing to, because everyone looked to him, seeing not only power but simple competence. They were all there: all the great lords and prelates of the realm, gathered for Christmas court, and waiting on the king's death.

The matter of the succession was now most urgent. And yet not only Edward or Harold failed to speak of William. No one did. It was as if a spell of forgetfulness had fallen over them all, even those who had stood in hall the day Edward proclaimed the Norman duke to be his heir.

"England needs strength," the lords of the realm said to one another. "England needs a king who can rule."

Their eyes fell on Harold more often as the king's dying went on. He could hardly deny that he had had similar thoughts. Who else was there, after all, if not William? Edward's nearest Saxon kin was his brother's grandson, whose name was Edgar: a pale, limp young man who was, it was generally suspected, somewhat simple.

"All kings of England have been of Alfred's line," Harold said on a long dark evening, while he and Stigand and Edith shared the deathwatch.

"Edgar is of Alfred's line," Stigand said. "He is also a weakling and a fool."

"Nevertheless," said Harold, "he has the most visible claim."

"Would you entrust this kingdom to the likes of him?" Edith asked.

"If there were a choice," said Harold, "no. But—"

"We have thought hard and long," said Edith, "and so have you. You know the choices. England looks to you already. It won't revolt if you take the crown."

"Not if you can help it," Harold said a little coldly.

She arched a brow. "Even without us, brother, they would choose you. You've done well with your inheritance."

"You know I can't do this," said Harold. "I swore—"

"You are in England now," Stigand said, deceptively soft.

"So I am," Harold said. Maybe, in saying it, he dared to contemplate what they were suggesting.

"What will England do," said Stigand, still soft, still quiet, "when faced with a Norman king? He speaks no Saxon. He knows nothing of us or our faith or any aspect of our kingdom. His arrival would be invasion, his taking of the crown usurpation. Long ago we succeeded in freeing the king from the bulk of his Norman obsession. The last of it, that embassy on which he sent you, was an aberration. It meant nothing. All meaning is here, in this room, at the heart of this kingdom. If we would preserve it, we must have a strong king who is—above all—Saxon."

"Perhaps, with ample help, Edgar—" Harold began.

"You know he can't do it," Edith said. "He can't hold the earls together, and he most certainly can't lead men against the invasion that will come, inevitably, once the king is dead."

"You can do that," said Stigand. "You alone of the earls can muster them all and hold against whatever comes."

"I can do it as regent," said Harold. "To be king—"

That was a capitulation, and they all knew it. Edith went in for the kill. "A regent is not enough. England needs a king."

"England needs a king."

The voice was weak but clear. Edward's eyes were open. They were fixed, not on his queen or his archbishop, but on Harold.

"I hear England calling," Edward said. "The earth groans with need; the defenses crack and strain. Darkness batters from without. England must have a king."

Harold opened his mouth, but Edith's glance stopped him.

Edward did not seem to see. He was focused far away from those walls or even the faces bending over him. "England must have a king," he said again.

"So it must, sire," said Stigand. "Will you confirm this as a king must? Have you the strength?"

"England must be strong," Edward murmured.

"Yes," said Edith, crooning the word. "Yes."

Perhaps this was how Edward had felt for much of his kingship: bound, swept onward by the will of his strongest servants. Harold should dig in his heels; should resist.

But Stigand met his doubts and fears and the ravages of guilt with what seemed to be perfect reason. "Whatever you swore to the duke across the sea, your oath to your king and to England both precedes and supersedes it. The king's will should be your will."

"Is it his will?" Harold asked. "Or is it yours?"

"In the end," said Stigand, "it is God's will."

There was nothing more that Harold could say. The king's bedchamber was filling with people, all come to hear the king, for the last time, name his heir. Harold was trapped beside the bed. Somehow Edward's hand had found his wrist and gripped it with strength that Harold had never known in him, enough to grind bone on bone.

Harold set his teeth and endured it. The oath he had sworn to William was ringing in his skull. His older oath of fealty to Edward was a far dimmer and feebler thing.

But the grip on his arm was real and immediate, and painful enough to make an offering on the altar of his guilt.

When they were all come, as many as could crowd into the room, Edward drew himself up along Harold's arm. With all the strength that was left to him, he said, "This I choose. This will be king. Serve him with honor, my lords. Help him to defend the kingdom."

No one was surprised. No one cried out against it, either. It seemed they had all seen what Stigand had: that there was no other, better choice.

They bowed to Harold. They gave him their fealty, there in front of the dying king. Edward sank down long before it was over: not yet, not quite, into death. The breath still rattled in his throat; life still clung to his body.

It no longer mattered. That was a cold thought, but kingship was a cold thing.

In time they left to continue their waiting, eating the king's food and entertaining themselves in his hall. Even Edith and Stigand had gone.

Harold stayed. It was not that he loved Edward; that had never been between them. But duty bound him.

Edward had sunk into his last dream. As often as not, Harold felt as if he dreamed with the king, wandering through a dim country full of half-heard voices, toward a light that he could barely see. At the gate of the light was a shining figure that, as he drew nearer, bore a remarkable resemblance to Edith.

This was Edward's dream; Harold would hardly have seen his sister as the angel at the gate of Paradise. Edward was very close now, and glad of it. His body was cold as he slipped away from it. The light was blissfully warm.

He turned at the edge of it and looked into Harold's face. His eyes were clearer than Harold had ever seen them. "I will wish you good fortune," he said, "and ask your pardon for what I've done to you."

"For what you've done?" said Harold. "What—"

"This will be the death of you," said Edward. "It's the best choice I can think of, now there are no choices left, but I have done you no service."

"We are all mortal," Harold said.

"We'll meet again," said Edward.

"But not too soon," Harold said.

"That is with God," said the king.

"Sire," Harold began. "What do you see? What is coming? What—"

Edward glanced at the angel who stood before the gate. It neither moved nor spoke, and yet he bent his head a fraction. "May God keep you," he said to Harold, "and the kingdom I have left you."

"Sire," Harold said. "Tell me what you see."

Edward was gone. Harold knelt on the hard chill floor beside the king's bed. The king's face was cold, his breath stilled. Of the dream there was nothing left but a faint dullness of the spirit.

King Edward lay in his tomb, wrapped in a shroud of pure white linen, with his crown on his head and his scepter on his breast, the sandals of a pilgrim on his feet. The stone lid grated as strong men drew it closed; even through the chanting of the last psalm, the sound of finality echoed through the abbey that he had built.

Already, even before the last notes of the requiem died away, the eyes of England had turned from the king who was gone, to Harold who knelt before the high altar. The Archbishop of York stood above him. In his hands lay the crown that Edward had worn.

Stigand was there, on the altar, watching with deep satisfaction. It meant a great deal that Archbishop Aldred had agreed to perform the crowning. While both York and Canterbury supported this choice, all of England stood behind it; all of England accepted it.

Edward was not even a full day dead. All this pomp and panoply was long prepared; but Harold doubted, somehow, that most of those who watched had expected to see him in the new king's place. If they had thought of it at all, they had thought it would be Edgar, the feckless boy, the last of Alfred's line in England.

The choir shifted from the requiem to the great anthem of the *Te Deum*—just as the kingship was passing from the frail old man to the strongest of the earls of England. Harold raised his eyes to the crown. It gleamed with gold and inlaid jewels, but its beauty was utterly without warmth.

He did not lust after it. It was only metal and colored stones. What it stood for—power, yes, but great labor and a heavy burden.

He could feel his oath to William like iron bands about his heart. And yet as the crown lowered, the bands snapped one by one—all but the last, which was like a chain stretching away into darkness.

He turned his mind from it. There were words to speak, a new oath to swear. For England he did it. For England, and for her Church, and for the people who had made her their own.

The crown was cold on his brow. It was not as heavy as he had expected. He had bent to take the weight of it; he straightened in some surprise, lifting his head. Fear was gone. Foreboding had shrunk to insignificance.

What would be would be. This must be; that was all he knew, and all he needed to know. The earth beneath him, the vault of Edward's abbey over him, supported and sustained him.

Walls of iron, William had called them. Walls of blessed grace. Under Edward they had grown weak. Harold would make them strong again. Then no power of Earth or Otherworld would dare to stand against them.

❧ CHAPTER 41 ❧

William felt the king of the English die.

He had been dreaming that he hunted in a green wood, hard in pursuit of a moon-colored stag. Harold the Saxon rode beside him.

Just as the stag came within bowshot, Harold spurred past William. There was blood on his horse's sides, deep rakes of the spur.

That was not like Harold, William thought with the distance of dream. The stag wore a golden crown about its neck. As William strung his bow and nocked and aimed, Harold overtook the stag. No arrow had struck the beast, and yet it stumbled and slowly, slowly, crumpled to the ground.

Harold bent over it with a long knife in his hand. Swiftly, deftly, he gutted and skinned the stag. The crown that had been about its neck he lifted in his hands, holding it up gleaming against the colorless sky. His eyes narrowed as if dazzled; his face was rapt. Calmly, with the firmness of decision, he set the crown upon his head.

William started awake. Mathilda was sitting upright beside him. Her face was as stark as he felt.

"He's dead," William said. No need to tell her whom he meant. "Harold's forsworn. He's taken the crown."

She nodded. "You're not surprised."

"I'm not anything," he said. "Yet."

"Will you let it go?"

"No." That came from William's heart. "By God and the old gods, no."

Anger was rising. More than anger. Wrath. It was not William alone whom this oath-breaking betrayed. It was the whole realm of Britain.

"This is war," he said. "I'm taking what's mine."

He thought Mathilda might say something to that, but she set her lips together. Wise of her. All that he had been and done, all that he had lived and fought and suffered for, had come to this. Nothing would stop him. He would have this. He was born and bred for it.

War.

Cecilia had waited for it all her life. It should not have been a shock; it was certainly not sudden. And yet it struck her with force enough to fling her flat.

After half a thousand years, the king foretold was coming back to Britain. But William was not thinking of it that way. He had been promised a thing, and the ally who had sworn to aid him had taken it instead. No lord in this world could let such a thing pass—not and continue to be a lord.

It was terribly simple, if one were a man and a fighter. A woman and an enchantress—such as she was in her youth and inexperience—found it rather more complicated.

Her brothers were given up to simplicity. Robert and Richard and young William were all determined to play in the war. They did not understand what could happen—that there would be blood and slaughter. That people would die.

Rivers of blood. Her dreams were full of them.

And yet she was not afraid. She had a cold heart, more than one person had said as she grew; and so she did. She had too much magic to indulge in fits of ordinary passion.

Extraordinary passion was another thing altogether. This war had been half a thousand years in coming. However it ended, either old Britain or the newer England would be gone. And either William or Harold would be dead.

Mathilda felt as if she had been holding her breath for her life long, and now it had all rushed out of her. The long waiting, the mysteries, the prophecies, the preparations and instruction, were all come to this.

It was not simple. It never was. Maybe it was inevitable that Harold, in England, in the king's trust, had found himself in the king's place.

But it was not his place, however logical it might be if one were a Saxon. Britain was beyond logic. The Old Things were the heart of the realm; their world touched only lightly on the world of men and their Church.

William had sent an embassy to Rome to ask that the Pope favor his undertaking. To sweeten it, he had endowed another abbey or three, and promised to honor the Church well once he was in England. It would be a great blow to the devout Saxons if he descended upon them under the papal banner.

In their way they were innocents. They would choke the heart out of the world and believe that they had made it holy.

William was the best hope Britain had. His anger at Harold was abiding; but it was a cold anger, the anger of a general in battle.

Mathilda watched him narrowly, as much as she could while he began to prepare his war. She had her own preparations, her own preoccupations, as winter thawed into spring.

When Easter was past, a great omen flamed across the sky: a bearded star, a comet. Artos' banner, the old folk called it. Saxons likened it to their gonfalon of battle, the flame-red wyvern, and reckoned it a harbinger of disaster.

So it was, thought Mathilda. But whose—that was the question.

"I have a gift for you," she said.

The comet was fading; the war was proceeding apace. She had been away from William for a month while he mustered armies. Their reunion would not last long: they were all gathered in the duke's fine new castle at Lillebonne for a great ceremony. William did not intend to make Edward's mistake. He would invest Robert as his heir, with full pomp; and Mathilda would take the title of regent in Normandy while William crossed the water.

It was not an office she had accepted lightly. Her heart was crying out to be with him, to sail across the sea, to fight at his side. But cold reason knew he needed her here. Normandy was the earth in which the roots of his mortal life were sunk; it gave him the strength to leap across the sea. She must guard it while he was gone.

She could still send part of herself, and so she intended to do. There had been no words between them since they went to bed, but as they lay together after a long night's loving, she let go a small part of what she had been keeping secret.

"Get dressed," she said, "and come out with me."

William had been hovering on the edge of sleep. He opened a bleared eye. "Now? It's the middle of the night."

"It's dawn," she said. And so it was: grey light glimmered through the open window, and the stars were growing pale.

He tightened his arms about her. "Can't it wait? Don't you want to—"

"No," she said, "and yes, but I need to do this. So do you." She slipped out of his grasp and reached for her shift.

He heaved a great sigh, almost a groan, but he also heaved himself out of bed. She took a moment while she combed and quickly plaited her hair, to appreciate the sight of him. He was aging well: thickening a bit here and there, but still strong, and still light on his feet for so big a man. There was a thread or two of grey in the short-cropped hair, but he was not losing it as so many men did as they came in sight of forty.

She always had liked to look at him, but she was defeating her own purpose—and he knew it. She tossed his shirt at him and pulled on a gown fit for walking in.

He was a fraction less cross once he had his clothes on, and beginning to be curious. Gifts were common between them, and mysteries frequent, but the two did not often go together.

They crept out like children, stepping over the maids and pages who were deep asleep, gliding down the stair, slipping through the crowded sleepers in the hall. Their fingers had laced together; Mathilda fought the urge to giggle. Lady and duchess, nigh on seven times a mother, and she had no more dignity than a serving maid.

The last stars were fading. Light was welling in the east, striding across the breadth of Normandy. Down on the river the fleet were gathered: long sleek-bodied dragon-ships, as fine as had ever carried their grandfathers a-viking.

One had come in the night, gliding under oar by other ways than mortal ships knew. Shipwrights of the Wood had made her. The riven oak of Broceliande was in her, and scions of the Druid oak of Falaise. The oak itself had given a branch to the prow, the graceful sweeping curve and golden gleam of a dragon's head.

Landsman and horseman William might be, but the old

seafaring blood was in him still. His eyes came alive at sight of that beauty of a ship.

"Her name is *Mora*," Mathilda said.

William drank her in from prow to stern, from hull to lofty mast. Her sail was furled, but it gleamed in the morning. Moonlight and starlight were woven in it.

There were more than human sailors in the crew, and more than mortal passengers. *Mora* shimmered with the mingled magic of an army of the Old Things. William saw them: they were reflected in his eyes. But he did not speak of them.

He clambered over every inch of *Mora*, inside and out, and lent a hand when the mortal crew stepped her mast and drew her up on the riverbank. Other hands were there as well, some visible and some not, and shapes in the river that made the great ship light, so that she seemed to leap from the water.

William was in love. Mathilda had had high hopes of the gift, but to see them fulfilled made her ineffably happy. She had put her heart in this ship, so that when he was in it they would never truly be apart.

He left the *Mora* with visible reluctance. But people were waiting, and there was an heir to proclaim and a great rite to perform. The ship would still be there when he could come back to her—just as Mathilda would, keeping Normandy safe while William took what had been his in life after life.

❧ CHAPTER 42 ❧

Harold rode into Canterbury on a night of wind and rain, blown in with the last of the light. His escort was no larger than it had been when he traveled fast and light as Earl of Wessex: he had left the royal following in Winchester, and had ridden without fanfare, answering a summons that even the king might not refuse.

The archbishop's house was dark and shuttered without but warm and dry and bright within—much like the kingdom Harold had found himself ruling. Stigand was still at dinner, dining quietly with a handful of his canons, a monk or two, and Edith.

They all rose at Harold's coming, even the archbishop. Edith left the table to embrace her brother and kiss him on both cheeks.

He held her at arm's length, taking her in. She was dressed as soberly as a nun; the unrelieved black did not suit her milk-and-honey beauty. It made her look older, and tired.

Still her eyes were clear, her face serene. She smiled at him. "You came quickly," she said.

"I was told it was urgent," said Harold.

"It is that," she said, "but there is time to be warm and rest, and to eat."

"I could eat," Harold said. "But tell me while I do it, why you brought me here when I'm needed in Winchester."

"Eat first," she said, leading him to a place at the table. Servants came quickly with food and drink.

He barely noticed what he ate. It was warm; it filled his empty stomach. The drink he did notice: it was wine mulled with spices, strong and fragrant. He drank it with care. He did not want to be addled in the head, not even here, with the man who above all had set him on the throne, and the sister whom he loved.

Loved, but did not completely trust. He had no reason for that; she had stood behind or beside him since he took her husband's crown. And yet he could not help but think that she had her own purposes, and those might not always be the same as his.

Tosti's betrayal had poisoned Harold's trust in the rest of his kin. No doubt that was exactly what the demon within his brother had intended.

Nevertheless, Harold chose to be prudent rather than to be in danger. He ate carefully, drank sparingly, then when he was done, set aside plate and cup and said, "Now tell me."

Edith glanced at Stigand. The archbishop tilted his head. The dining room emptied of all but Edith.

The fire flickered on the hearth. Now that there were only three of them, Harold could hear the wind crying without, and the drumming of rain on the roof. It sounded as if the wind had a voice, however inhuman.

Even if there were demons in the air, they could not enter this place. Perhaps that was why they waxed so shrill.

Stigand bent to tend the fire. When it was burning bright and high, he sat at the table across from Harold. Edith was still standing, wrapped in her dark mantle. The fire caught ruddy lights in her hair, but cast her face in shadow.

Stigand folded his hands on the table and leaned forward. "The siege has begun," he said. "The Danes are gathering a fleet against us. Normandy arms for invasion. The Pope himself is one of them: a lifelong and inveterate sorcerer. He is sending his banner to the Norman duke. Our allies in the Curia have failed to prevent him; some are dead, others imprisoned. We will have no help from that quarter."

"None at all?" asked Harold. "Nothing from the Church?"

"My Church here will stand behind me," Stigand said. "Some of it is corrupted, to be sure, but most of it is not. All who can be bound to obedience will be praying for the defense of England."

"Night and day," said Edith, "perpetually. God will shield us, and our holy men and women will be His instruments."

Harold searched for words to say. It was not that he lacked belief. He thought that he was a good Christian. But he was a man of war. He could not trust to prayers alone.

At length he said, "That's well, as far as it goes. Was it worth summoning me from Winchester in the midst of the spring muster? Was there no messenger whom you trusted, who could bring word to me of your efforts on England's behalf?"

He tried to speak softly, but he saw how Stigand bridled. Harold refused to regret what he had said. He was the king— and these two had made sure of it. They would have to accept that he would act, and think, as the king should.

Edith was more firmly in control of her temper than Stigand, or maybe she did not find Harold's words objectionable. "Of course we could have sent a message," she said, "and so we should, if that had been all we needed. But we need you. You are the anointed king; you are consecrated to the kingdom, and the kingdom to you."

Harold raised his brows. "That's not magic?"

"Magic is arrogance," Stigand said, "and binding of devils. This is a sacred rite. So was David consecrated to Israel, and Alfred to England, and many another king before the eyes of God."

That did not put Harold at ease, but he had no counter to it. "What do you want me to do?"

"Attend Mass tonight," Stigand answered.

"Attend . . . ? Is that all?"

"It will be enough," said the archbishop.

It was nearly midnight. The storm had risen to a crescendo. Harold knelt before the altar of Canterbury's cathedral. The choir was full; he could hear the breathing of the men who had come to fill the stalls, and feel their presence in his skin. But he could see only shadows. All of them were cowled, wrapped in darkness, with their faces hidden.

The altar was brilliant with candles. Cowled acolytes had lit them with long tapers, then glided away. By that light he caught glimpses of stone vaulting, flashes of gilding, fragments of painting on walls and ceiling. The windows were black, blank. Rain lashed them with relentless force.

As full as the choir was, there was no congregation but Harold. He was alone, without guard or escort. He had no weapon; his armor hung on a rack in the archbishop's house. He was robed in white wool over stainless linen, stiff and clean and new. The mantle that pooled about him was the color of blood. A heavy golden cross hung from his neck. A crown of gold weighted his brows.

The cross was heavier than the crown. His neck had begun to ache from holding it up. But he did not move to ease the pressure of the chain.

He felt odd, remote. There was a knot in his middle that he recognized, slowly, as the memory of his oath to William. It was walled off, enclosed like a worm in an oak gall.

He should be praying, but his heart was empty. He gave that emptiness to God, for what it was worth.

Just before the bells rang midnight, just as the wind's howl mounted to a shriek, the choir stirred, then stilled. Harold realized that he was holding his breath. He let it out in a long sigh.

At the end of that sigh, the choir began the psalm.

O God, with your judgment endow the king,
And with justice the king's son. . . .

Harold had expected a grand processional, an army of priests and acolytes with croziers and banners and censers, such as began every other high Mass in the cathedral. But there was only one acolyte, one censer; Edith bore it, dressed in white as Harold was, with a white cowl over her hair. Stigand paced behind her in vestments of white and gold, with miter and crozier and heavy cope embroidered with gold.

And yet, as they made their way down the long aisle, Harold felt rather than saw the processional he had expected. Out of the corner of his eye he could almost see them: every loyal priest and abbot and bishop in England, every monk and canon, even nuns and abbesses, joining in this Mass through the length and breadth of the kingdom. They were all here, embodied in Stigand and the widowed queen.

Just so were all the congregations of England, all the people great and small, embodied in the king. It was a most peculiar sensation: as if he were full to the brim and yet utterly empty.

No evil thing could come to him here. The bulwark of the Mass surrounded him. Every loyal soul in England defended him.

So must he defend his people. They were a weapon in his hand, a shield on his arm. He raised them as he would in battle.

The wind had veered. It had been howling from the south and

east. Now it roared out of the north. The voices in it had changed. Shrieks and howls had transmuted into the deeper, slower cadences of sacred song.

Harold lay prostrate on the paving. The stones were cold, but he barely felt it. The Mass was ending, and yet it went on, reverberating through his body. It had become a part of his blood and bone.

Slowly he rose. The whole weight of England came with him. He staggered, but then he steadied. The last psalm rolled over him. He could discern no words, only rhythm and sound. They held him up. They gave him strength.

"The Mass is ended," Stigand said, surprisingly soft, with no music in it. But the choir's chant went on beneath it. His words skimmed it as a gull skims the surface of the sea.

"Go," he said. "Defend the realm. Bring it back to peace."

Memory struck with the force of a blow. Another Mass, another cathedral; another figure lying alone. That rite had failed; the demon was still in Tosti.

And Tosti was coming back. Harold felt him. He came in dragon-ships, warships of the Danes. The wind of England's wrath blew hard against Normandy, but the Danes laughed at it. They rode it as they had ridden it for time out of mind, swarming toward the shores of England.

Prayer is not enough.

Harold shivered deep within. The cathedral was empty. He was alone. And yet England was still in him, all of it, and its invaders, too: Tosti his brother, William whom he had sworn to serve as his liege lord.

They were coming. War was rising. This was more than a siege. If he failed, if his defenses faltered, it would be invasion—conquest. And England would fall.

"Not while I live," he said. His voice echoed in the lofty space.

The wind had stilled. The rain had eased to a whisper, hardly more than the kiss of mist.

The great rite was not over. It would go on and on as long as England was in danger. But Harold was as free of it as he would ever be again.

He must go. There was the *fyrd* to muster, the kingdom to protect—and then a war to fight.

He genuflected and crossed himself, pausing to draw a

breath. Then he turned. The door was open, letting in the grey light of dawn.

Surely the Mass had not taken so long. But there it was; and there were his men, armed and saddled and ready to ride. Of Stigand there was no sign, but Edith waited, wrapped in a dark cloak, with a brimming goblet in her two hands.

She held it to his lips. It was full of mead, rich and sweet. Harold drank a deep draught. It tasted of mingled summer and autumn, and the green earth of England.

She lowered the cup. Her eyes were quiet, but they looked deep into him.

He met them levelly. He had nothing to hide from her.

It was she who looked away first, lowering her gaze as if to see how much mead remained in the cup. "Fare you well, my brother," she said.

Harold bowed his head. "Farewell, sister and queen."

She stiffened very slightly. Harold hardened his heart. Let her remember who they both were, and what they must do, both of them, before the kingdom could be safe again.

He left her standing there in front of the grey bulk of the cathedral, under the grey sky. The wind carried him away, back to Winchester and the army and the weight of kingship.

❧ CHAPTER 43 ❧

Harold was tired. He had stood on guard all summer long, month upon month, with an army as large as any that had mustered in England—and all it had done was eat itself out of camp and ship. Stigand's rite of warding had worked almost too well. The wind had never ceased to blow against the Normans; and there they sat in their harbors, powerless to cross the sea.

The danger was ebbing. Everyone said so—wise man and fool alike. Prayer and sacred vigilance had protected England against the Norman invader.

Harold had had to let his army go. Its term of service was over; there was nothing left with which to feed it. It rankled him to leave his coasts undefended, but Stigand's army of monks and nuns was still at it, still praying, still persuading the wind to blow. Another month and there would be no need of even that; the winter storms would begin, the tides rise, and the seas run too strong for any fleet to venture the crossing.

His people were celebrating already, declaring the danger over at least until spring, and the Normans defeated by nothing more than a steady gale. His fighting men were back among their families, his kingdom at peace. He should be content to settle at last to the less heroic duties of kingship: courts, councils, sitting in judgment.

And yet he was both exhausted and incurably restless. He was missing something; but he could not imagine what. Tosti had been nipping at the edges of England all summer and into the autumn. He had been making trouble in Flanders, had even ventured an invasion that Harold's fleet had turned back with contemptuous ease. Now he was with the Scots. That was close enough to keep a watch over him and be sure that his mischief remained safely small.

There would be a reckoning for Tosti; it was inevitable. But Harold hoped that it would not come too soon. Tosti was still Harold's brother; Harold could not help wishing, and praying, that somehow in the end, he could be restored to himself.

Harold woke from fitful, tossing sleep. His dreams had all been of marches and battles, ships sailing and armies advancing and fire running across a stubbled field.

That last dream stayed with him as he struggled to wake and focus. The harvest was in, the harvesters warm in their beds. They would be warmer yet when the fire reached them. Already it lapped at the thatch of the farmstead—even as a second, more potent blaze roared through a broken wall toward the rear of the house.

He found himself sitting up, looking about wildly for a pail, a barrel, anything, to put out the fire. But he was safe in his palace in London, where the only fire was the fire on the hearth. The curtains of his bed were still, the air cold.

People were talking outside, murmuring in soft voices. He caught a snatch of it: "No, don't wake him. He's been tossing all night. He's finally quiet. Let him sleep. There will be time enough after he's up."

"I'm up," Harold said, stumbling out through the curtains into the rather warmer, much brighter room. It was full of people, but that was nothing unusual in the king's bedchamber.

Most mornings he made sure to recognize each man and greet him by name, with a word or two for him to cherish because it had come from the king. This morning Harold was too badly out of sorts. When he looked at them, he saw them through a veil of fire. "Tell me," he said to the one who was closest, whose face was a blur and whose name he had inexplicably forgotten.

The man gaped and babbled, but someone else thrust past him. That one he did recognize even in his fog: his brother Gyrth, looking as if he had been up all night and riding through mud for most of it. He had been tending his earldom in East Anglia; clearly he had come to London in the kind of haste that made Harold's hackles rise.

Gyrth, thank God, knew better than to slip sidewise around the truth. "Norsemen," he said. "Thousands of them. Three hundred ships are sailing down from Scotland under Hardrada's command, headed for the Humber, burning and pillaging as they go. Northumbria and Mercia are raising forces against them."

Harold was abruptly, completely awake. Hardrada—the king of brutal counsel, the hard-bitten warrior, whose given name also was Harald; whose ambition was to plunder the world. Harold felt most peculiarly relieved. This, deep down, he had been waiting for. He was almost thankful that it had come at last.

His mind was perfectly clear. He gave the orders that were necessary. People leaped to obey them.

The wind that had kept the Normans at bay had brought this second and no more welcome invasion. If the wind shifted—

He had to pray that it would not. So would every loyal man and woman of God in England.

He was striding through the palace as he concluded the thought, seeking out horse and armor and weapons. Someone set a loaf of bread in his hand; someone else insisted that he take a cup of ale. He ate and drank on his feet. He would not sit at ease again until this war was ended.

"He's there," Leofwine said.

Both of Harold's loyal brothers were with him. Gyrth had ridden with him from London, refusing to stop or rest while there was a war to fight. Leofwine joined them outside of Lincoln, bringing the levies of the Midlands and a train of provisions, and news from the north.

"Tosti has made alliance with Hardrada," Leofwine said as they paused to rest and eat. "He met them as they sailed down past Scotland, and threw in his lot with them. They say he's sworn that if one son of Godwine can seize a crown, so may another."

"That doesn't sound like Tosti," Gyrth said.

"It isn't Tosti," said Harold. "Tosti died years ago. A devil walks in his body. If he comes for the crown, he'll take it only to destroy it."

His brothers glanced at each other. Harold never had told them what he knew, or what he had seen. That Tosti was not sane, they all knew; but not what had brought it on.

They elected not to argue with him. Time was passing. The sooner they came into the north, the more likely they would be to surprise the enemy. They ate, mounted, rode: pressing hard through mist and rain and brief glimmers of sun.

York had fallen. Harold's army halted in Tadcaster, three leagues south of it, setting guards on every gate and wall and ford, lest the enemy discover that they had come. Scouts and spies went out on horseback and afoot.

The news that came back was bad. The Norse king's fleet had come to land at Riccall; his horde of Norsemen had swarmed toward York, pillaging as they went. The earls of Northumbria and Mercia had gathered all the forces they could and ridden against them.

"There was a battle," said the scout who brought back the news. He carried a grim reminder: Northumbria's banner, tattered and half burned and clotted thick with blood. "Our people lost. The Norsemen have taken York. Now they've gone to gather hostages."

"Where?" Harold demanded. The scout gaped at him. The man was out on his feet; but Harold had no time to be merciful. "Where are they?"

"Stamford Bridge," said the scout.

Harold's brows rose.

"Yes, my lord," the scout said. He was one of Harold's own housecarls from Wessex: a good man, quick-witted, with keen eyes in his head. "They've left the fleet at Riccall and headed inland. Rumor is that some of them didn't even trouble to take their armor. Who threatens them, after all? There's no one left in the north to fight them. They're fat and happy where they are: they've looted your manor at Catton and settled with the spoils."

"That's a finger in your eye, brother," Leofwine said.

"Indeed," said Harold.

His eyes ran round his council: his brothers, the thanes and housecarls whom he had gathered on his wild ride north, a fair force of bishops and abbots who could fight as well as pray. They all waited to hear him speak. They would do as he bade them, fight as he ordered them. The long grief of Tosti's betrayal was still sharp, but it warmed his heart to see so many so loyal.

"Well, sirs," he said. "Shall we do unto the Norsemen as they have done unto us?"

The answer came in a long growl rising to a shout. "Yes. Yes! *Yes!*"

Harold waited until silence fell. Then he spoke again. "You heard Aelfric. They're off their guard; they're lazy with victory. They'll be looking for us late or not at all. We'll rest here tonight, then at dawn we'll go. We'll undo the victory and avenge the defeat."

Not one of them groaned or protested. He saluted them in honest respect. "Go on. Eat, rest. We'll have a hard ride ahead of us tomorrow, and a hard fight at the end of it."

They went like a sword to the scabbard, swift and obedient. Harold meant to follow his own order, but he paused. Without his willing it, his face had turned eastward. He could feel Tosti there, like a hand pressing on his forehead, and an ache behind his eyes.

Tomorrow, he thought. Or maybe the thought was Tosti's. Did the devil in him know what was coming? Would it betray what it knew, and destroy Harold's hope of surprise?

Harold crossed himself and breathed a prayer. God must protect him and all his men—or it was all lost. There was nothing Harold could do but hope, and rest as he could; then when morning came, ride to meet the enemy.

For all the cold and rain of the journey north, the next day dawned bright and clear. A last breath of summer wafted over them, growing stronger as the sun rose. Even so early the air was remarkably warm, and the night mist was already burning away.

Harold's men were up, all of them, and ready to mount their horses and ride. Both men and beasts seemed much refreshed by the full night's rest; they grinned as Harold rode along their line. Some of them were singing, and not all the songs were sacred songs.

Harold's heart was light. It was a good day to die—and a better day to win a battle.

Even as he took his place at the head of the line, the army began to move. Drums and horns were silent; their singing faded as they set out along the worn but still solid paving of the Roman road. This was an ambush; God willing, the enemy would never know what came upon him until the blow was struck.

* * *

York's grey walls rose stark and sheer before them. The gate was open as if in welcome. The road led straight through.

There could be death within, treachery, an ambush against the ambush, but Harold entrusted that as he had the rest, to the boundless mercy of God. His body stiffened as he rode toward the open maw of the gate; his horse jibbed in protest. He willed himself to be calm.

The way was open. People lined it. None of them was armed; no arrows fell from above.

Neither did the city cheer the coming of the king, as if they too followed his orders: be silent, be secret, give nothing away. But they bowed as he passed. Some reached out to touch his knee, his cloak, his horse's mane.

York might have surrendered perforce to the king of Norway, but it offered passage freely to the king of the English. Once he was free of its streets, he urged his horse into a ground-devouring gallop.

He knew this country: Catton was his, and Tosti had ruled it for ten years. Stamford Bridge was a handful of stone houses in the midst of open fields, clinging to the eastward bank of a deep swift river. Its advantage to an invader was both its nearness to York and its distance from the confines of the city. It was a crossroad, and its bridge was wide enough for a pair of horsemen to ride abreast, but narrow enough for one man to defend.

Harold would not have chosen it himself, because the land there was deceptive; the village sat down in a valley. By the time anyone there saw an army descending upon it, it would be too late to mount a defense.

But then Harold would have had his hostages delivered to the ships, and not left them leagues out of reach. These Norsemen were cocky. They did not know the new king of the English—and neither, it appeared, did their ally Tosti. Or maybe the demon was choosing to be a traitor twice over.

There were no guards, no scouts or outriders. All the Norsemen were in the valley, camped at ease in the fields on the far side of the river. Harold left his horse below the hill with his army and crept up to the crest with the scout Aelfric. Together they looked down on a scene of almost pastoral ease.

No man below was armed or armored. Most of them were sprawled in the grass with hats over their eyes, snoring in chorus. A hardy few braved the deep currents of the river, splashing and shouting. Desultory guards wandered yawning along the edges.

Near the center, Harold saw the king's tent with the raven banner over it, its tassels hanging limp in the noonday stillness. As harmless as it seemed, Harold shivered. That banner had raised terror in all the lands of the north: Land-waster was its name, raven of battle, bearer of victories.

The king himself sat in front of the tent, stretched at his ease, with a cup in his hand and a circle of men around him, playing what looked to be a game of dice. Even at this distance he looked enormous: a great, yellow-bearded, broad-shouldered man who towered over the rest.

Tosti, Harold did not see. He was there; his presence was distinct. But he did not present himself to view.

Harold drew back from the hilltop. His men had completed their preparations while he scouted the valley: gathered their baggage and set guards over it, entrusted their horses to the horse-handlers, and armed themselves and drawn up in ranks, ready to march.

Harold surveyed them narrowly, then nodded. "Good," he said. "Let's raise the dust as we go—let them think it's their hostages coming."

They shuffled willingly forward, raising a cloud of gratifying size. Harold swung back into his horse's saddle. The rest of the mounted men were waiting: his brothers, a handful of thanes, and the captains of his own household. They rode up and over the hill ahead of the rest, leading them down into the valley.

CHAPTER 44

Harold's plan had succeeded. The surprise was perfect. As he led the first of his troops down the hill, the Norsemen took notice, but without alarm: men woke one another, but few of them rose; swimmers climbed naked out of the water to point and stare.

Only slowly did it dawn on them that the parade of seeming hostages went on and on. A hundred nobles and their sons had been bidden to submit themselves to the Norsemen. Forty times that and more marched down over the hill, and every one of them armed and in armor, gleaming like ice in the sun.

No raw levies these, no farmers plucked from the fields with rakes and picks in hand and straw thrust in their shirts to protect them, however feebly, against blows in battle. These were housecarls of Wessex and Anglia and the Midlands, fighting monks and priests in armor, and thanes of the earldoms of the south, all trained and honed in years of battle.

They spread in ranks through the fields as they came, locking shields into a wall; their feigned prisoners' shuffle sharpened into the stamp of marching feet. A bowshot from the river's westward bank, they halted.

Harold rode toward the bridge with his mounted escort. On the far side of the river, men were running, scrambling, hunting for whatever weapons and protection they could find.

One man stood in the middle of the bridge. He was a huge man, perhaps even bigger than his king, and he had had the sense to bring his armor with him, if not his helmet. He had a double-headed axe as tall as a well-grown child, with a head nigh as broad as his shoulders, grounded on the planks of the bridge. He leaned on its haft, relaxed and at ease, waiting for the Saxons to venture the bridge.

Not yet, Harold thought. "Wait here," he said to his escort as they came within a furlong of the bridge. His horse scented a battle; it was suddenly restive, tossing its head and bucking lightly under him. He let it stretch into a canter along the riverbank.

Hardrada was coming. His men were drawing up in ranks to match Harold's; through the gap in the center, the king came riding on a great black horse. Just as he passed the foremost rank of his men, the horse stumbled. Its forelegs collapsed; it somersaulted end over end.

Hardrada fell rolling, remarkably agile for so big a man. His men gasped in horror; the ranks wavered. He heaved himself up, swaying on his feet, but obviously alive and unbroken. He was laughing, a deep roar of calculated mirth.

With equal calculation, Harold ignored both him and the omen that had so appalled the Norsemen. "Tosti!" he called out. "Tosti Godwineson!"

He reached the end of the Norsemen's line and wheeled his horse about, cantering back toward the bridge. As he drew near the center again, he saw a figure standing in front of the line.

He had seen no movement, heard no clank or rustle of men shifting to clear the way, and yet there it was: a man in mail with a helmet on his head, standing with his feet apart. The shape and stance of him were painful in their familiarity. So was the voice, light and mocking.

"Brother!" said Tosti. "You're looking well."

Harold set his teeth. What he had to say wanted to stick in his throat, but if he was going to win this battle, he could see no other way. "Tosti," he said. "You want your earldom back. Come back to us and send your friends away, and you can have it."

"You think so?" said Tosti. "Now that's tempting. But look here, I've brought my new brother to dinner; it would be terribly rude to send him home empty-handed. What do you have for him?"

The Norse king had recovered himself and his horse and come to stand beside Tosti. Harold looked him up and down. By God, he was big: Tosti's head came just to his chin.

"For him," Harold said to Tosti, "I have seven feet of good English ground."

Hardrada roared with laughter—genuine this time, if no less calculated.

Tosti did not laugh, but his voice was full of mockery. "He won't be asking for that much, brother—all he wants is enough space to put a throne on, and a crown for his head."

"What," said Harold, "you don't want it? I heard otherwise."

Tosti shrugged, a boneless ripple that made Harold's scalp creep. "Well, brother, it seems we'll be making our own dinner, since my friend is so clearly unwelcome. Won't you come and feed the ravens for us?"

Tosti was dead. Truly dead. Harold looked at him across the river and knew with cold certainty that this body must die and the thing in it be cast out beyond any hope of return.

He had done his grieving long since. What was left, now that he faced a battle as bloody as any he had fought, was an icy calm.

He turned his back on the enemy—not as foolish a thing as it might have been: they had no archers. His men were waiting. He swept out his sword and raised it high. The sun dazzled on the blade. He slashed it down.

The first rank of Harold's army charged the bridge. The lone man on it straightened, hefting his axe in his hands. As the first pair of Saxons sprang yelling upon him, their smaller axes up and swinging, his axe whirled about with breathtaking speed. It clove their heads from their shoulders, clean as an executioner's stroke.

The Saxons kept coming, but the Norseman was tireless. He wielded his axe as a reaper wields the scythe, cutting them down in swathes.

This was accomplishing nothing. Harold's horns called his forces back. Even as they withdrew in close order, Harold turned to one of his runners. "Find a boat," he said. The boy nodded, bowed, and ran.

While they waited for the boat, it looked like impasse: the Saxons held at bay by a single man, the Norsemen taking the time to firm up their lines. The man on the bridge took the opportunity to rest. There was no mark on him that Harold could see; he seemed barely winded.

It took less time than Harold had expected to find a boat. His scouts came back well within the hour, paddling what looked like a young lad's fishing boat.

It was big enough to hold a man with a long spear and two

men to guard him, though it rode somewhat low in the water. One of the guards rowed; the other raised a shield over the spearman.

The man on the bridge knew that something was coming, but from where he stood, he could not see what it was. He had no warning from his countrymen: the boat was hidden from them by the steepness of the bank. It slipped softly beneath the bridge.

Harold nodded to the men who waited for his signal. With a roar they charged once more against the lone defender.

The axeman braced for the onslaught. Harold, watching from behind the surge of his line, saw how the man stiffened; his eyes went wide. The axe dropped from his hands.

God had favored the spearman under the bridge: his spear had thrust up through the planks and spitted the enemy like an ox. He was still standing, but he was dead.

The first man to reach him swept him off the bridge, spear and all. He sank like a stone.

Harold's army poured across the bridge and spread across the field beyond, raising the shieldwall as they came. Inexorably they advanced toward the line of Norsemen. Almost none of those had shields or spears, but they were vicious fighters with knife and axe and sword. They hacked through shields and stooped low to stab at legs and feet.

Harold left his horse to graze on the far side of the river and sprinted after the last of his men, with his escort trailing behind. His sword was out, his spear in his hand. He aimed as straight as he could toward the center, where the Norse king was, and Tosti fighting beside him.

It was a vicious fight, and bloody: the grass turned swiftly to crimson mire. Harold slipped and slid as he pressed forward, hacking and stabbing, thrusting and smiting. Blades sang past him, thrust at him; he struck them aside or let them slide off his shield.

It was a kind of insanity. A sane commander found a hill to stand on, gathered his housecarls about him and his banner over him, and let his men do the fighting.

Tosti was baiting him by simply being there. Harold wrenched his mind back into focus. A lull in that part of the battle helped— and he gave due thanks to God for it.

He gathered as many men as he could, and his standard-bearer with them. On a rise of ground between the river and the thick of the fight, he took the stand he should have taken when the battle began.

It was a melee: clots of men entangled all across the field. Shields were cloven or flung aside; men were fighting hand to hand.

The tide of battle surged up over Harold's hill as it had surged over Hardrada. Harold's banner, the Fighting Man in his jeweled hauberk, floated in the wind. His brilliance mocked the Norse raven, black on white, that flew above the thick of the fight.

Harold charged down from the hill again, again, again. The strength of battle sustained him, but he was beginning to feel the strain. However hard he pressed, he could not break the wall of men about Hardrada.

He measured the line from his hill to the Norse king's banner. His eyes narrowed. His brother Leofwine was closest, leaning on his sword, catching his breath. "Someone in this army must have a bow," Harold said. "Send a man to find it."

Leofwine nodded. "You know," he said, "we should have brought a company of archers."

"We could have used a troop of Norman cavalry, too," Harold said dryly. "That's not going to happen, but it's not too late to remedy the other. Get together as many men as you can who have bows, and bring them up here. Tell them they'll be hunting a king."

Leofwine wiped his sword on the shirt of a dead Norseman and sheathed it. Even as the blade slid home, he ran down the hill. He was calling to men as he went, gathering his company of archers.

Harold would have occasion yet again to thank the God who watched over him: there was no need to send back to the camp. A good score of men had brought their bows and quivers to the fight. Once gathered together, bows strung, ranged on the hill within bowshot of the Norse king, they set to work.

The first flight of arrows was ragged. The second held together more strongly. Men began to fall. But the wind was blowing against the archers: their arrows fell short of the target.

The enemy had seen what Harold was doing and set about

storming the hill. Harold flung all his men against them, to win a few sorely needed yards for the archers.

One of them fell with a throwing axe in his throat. The rest closed up ranks and advanced, nocking arrows to strings as they went. The line of defense in front of them was holding—barely.

They took their time aiming. One took longer than the rest; eighteen arrows flew in their arc and dropped, again short of Hardrada's big fair head. The nineteenth caught a gust, or maybe an angel guided it; it lifted a fraction higher, flew a fraction wider.

Just as it fell, one of Hardrada's own men stumbled against him, mortally wounded. The king lurched backward. Maybe he heard the faint humming song of the arrow above his head: he looked up.

It caught him in the throat. His eyes and mouth opened wide. His hand clutched at the shaft as if to pull it out, as a man would do with an arrow in some painful but less fatal place: an arm, a hip, a shoulder.

Blood sprang from his open mouth. He went down like a tree falling, taking half a dozen men with him in a tangle of limbs and steel.

One of them was his standard-bearer. The raven began to fall.

A mailed hand caught it. Tosti raised it up, standing astride the king's body. His eyes were hidden in the helmet, and yet Harold felt them on him across the battlefield, as coldly mocking as ever.

That banner was victory. The man who held it would win the battle. So the Norsemen believed. Maybe it was pagan superstition; maybe not.

Harold had had enough. It was slaughter, this battle; the Norsemen had barely wavered when their king died. They would fight to the last man, to the last breath.

No, Harold thought. He could not even count the number of his men who had fallen—friends, retainers, loyal servants. Leofwine was with the archers. Gyrth he had not seen since they crossed the bridge, though he had heard the familiar voice shouting on the far side of the field. And all because of Tosti.

Be damned to prudence. What matter if a second king died today? If it drove back the Vikings forever and aye, such as Christians had prayed for since the first dragon-ship sailed out of the north, then it was worth the sacrifice. The words of the ancient litany echoed in his skull: *From the fury of the Northmen, O Lord, deliver us.*

From the fury of the Saxons, the Lord well might not choose to deliver the Norsemen. Harold swept his men with him down the hill, baying the battle cry: *Out! Out! Out!*

They struck the Norse line like a battering ram smiting a gate. It buckled; men fell.

Harold left the rest of that to his men. His eye was on Tosti. He would not stop or slow until he came there. Men who impeded him, he cut down and thrust aside. The thicker they swarmed, the harder he fought his way through them.

Tosti was laughing at him, leaning on the staff of the banner, sword in hand, safe from attack within the circle of the Norsemen. He had his foot on Hardrada's body.

That raised Harold's anger to a crescendo, and yet at the same time made it go cold. The world slowed its turning; the sun paused in the sky. It was much lower than he remembered. Night was coming.

He was exhausted beyond belief. He had one more good blow in him; that was all. It was his last and best; his gift to Tosti.

A giant of a Viking reared up in front of him, grinning a berserker's mad grin. Harold never even lifted his sword. He heaved up that great bear of a man one-handed and flung him in Tosti's face.

Tosti eeled aside, too swift and supple for a human man. But Harold had expected that. Tosti slid full into Harold's sword, driving it deep, up through the mail, beneath the breastbone, into the heart.

Its pulsing throbbed through the blade into Harold's hand. Pulse of life; but there was no soul left. Harold set his teeth and drove the blade home.

Hardrada's banner lay in a pool of blood. As Harold stared at it, he thought he saw the raven stir and spread its wings and take flight, leaving blank and bloodstained silk behind. Then he blinked; the raven returned to its place, painted in black on the white field.

He stooped. The staff was locked tight in Tosti's fingers. He left it there, wrenching the banner itself from its moorings. He hacked at it with his sword, tearing it, ripping it asunder.

The tatters of it hung limp from his fingers. He let them fall. They fluttered to the blood-soaked earth.

People were shouting, screaming: *Victory!*

They were shouting in Saxon. He heard them as if from far away. He knelt, heedless of the blood and entrails beneath him, and slipped Tosti's helmet from his head.

Harold had expected a demon's rictus, but the face was peaceful. The eyes were open; the thing that had lived in them was gone. It was Tosti again, his brother whom he loved, dead on the field beside the king of Norway.

Harold lifted the body in his arms. He did not care whether the battle had ended or whether it kept on raging. Hardrada was dead. Tosti was dead. God knew how many Vikings were dead. Saxons . . . it seemed their mail and shields had protected them. Not so many of those were gone.

Good, he thought.

He had to start thinking again. He was king; he could not indulge this grief. People came to take Tosti.

At first he fought them, but then he saw that they were priests. They would keep Tosti safe. He let them take him, with promises to look after him, and not dishonor him.

Hardrada would have his seven feet of English earth: here, where he had fallen, with nothing to mark his grave but the staff stripped of its banner. His great army was broken, running in rout. It was a victory, a triumph for the English. God had, indeed, delivered his people.

❧ CHAPTER 45 ❧

The Norman fleet sat at St.-Valéry on the edge of the sea. It had sat there for close on a month, while the wind blew relentlessly against it.

Mariners and the weather-wise had no hope to offer. The one soothsayer who had raised his voice had foretold disaster, then drowned in the storm that had struck when the new-built fleet sailed from Dives to this cursed harbor. Clearly, as William had thought at the time, he saw no further than his own fate.

William had paced a furrow in the shore beside *Mora.* His men were still in good order, but it had taken every scrap of skill and diplomacy and plain bullying that he had to keep them together. He would have to have a war for them soon, even if he had to invent one.

Summer was withering away. If they were still here when the winter seas began to run, it would be a bitter crossing, and probably deadly. But there was no stopping or changing the wind.

He woke one morning to the same ceaseless wuthering sound that had tormented him for the past month and more. He was past snarling at it. His son Rufus was waiting with a cup of ale and a loaf of bread to break his fast, and his second page, young Olivier, stood by with his clothes.

They both looked as if they were choking on a secret. William considered choking it out of them, but at this hour and in this mood, he might squeeze too hard. He ate and dressed in silence, belted on the sword that Rufus held for him, and ventured out of his lodging into the blasted wind.

His camp was pitched in and about the town, overlooking the shore and the beached fleet. From the house that he had claimed for himself, he could look down and across the long strand to his beloved *Mora,* with her gleaming sides painted green and bronze, and her golden dragon's head. Her inhuman passengers and crew slept deep inside her by daylight; at night, when the moon was up and the wind was wild, they came out to dance by the sea.

They were better protection for the ship than an army of mortal men. William was somewhat surprised this morning to see the shadow and the glimmer of them in the sunlight, flickering over the gunwales and swirling about the prow.

There was a mortal crowd on the shore near the ship. William saw the banner and began to run.

It did not matter how old they were or how onerous their duties or how nobly dignified they should be. When Mathilda saw William, the light in her face dazzled every man within reach. Then she was in William's arms, spinning completely about, and neither of them cared how many people were watching.

When at last he set her down, they were both breathless. William's evil mood was gone. Mathilda was here; all might not be right with the world, but if he had to, he could live in it.

She had brought a train of provisions and a late muster of men. She had also brought gifts: the Pope's banner, arrived from Rome at last, and a great lantern of gold and crystal. William's fingers tingled when he touched it: it was full of magic.

"For the crossing," Cecilia said.

William had not seen her until she spoke. She had hidden herself very well, melting into the shadow of the ship. It was a disconcerting skill.

"The wind is changing," she said.

Her head was up, her eyes on the sky. It was as blank as ever, and the wind was still blowing remorselessly from Britain. But the abbreviated figure beside her stirred, broad nostrils flaring.

The dwarf Turold, who was a boggart when he danced with his kin under the moon, had the same seeking expression. "Tonight?" he asked her.

"Tomorrow," she said.

He nodded. "And war in heaven tonight. We'll arm for it."

William's bad temper was coming back, but he had sense enough to know how little good it did to roar at the creatures of magic for being magical and therefore, too often, incomprehensible. He kept most of the growl out of his voice as he asked, "Are you saying we'll be able to sail?"

"Wait and see," his daughter said with maddening serenity.

William had been waiting for a month. He supposed he could wait another day, or two, or three or four or ten. It was all the same in the end.

The Guardians of Gaul stood on the shore under the stars. Cecilia stood with them, and Mathilda, and William rather less willing than they.

The Guardians had come with the fall of dark, wrapped in mantles, hidden and secret. It would have roused more interest than they cared to attract if the Count of Flanders and the Lady of the Wood had been seen together with the Prior of Bec and the Lady Melusine—particularly since Baldwin had sat at dinner that very night in his own hall in Bruges. Only Lanfranc was known to be there, having arrived two days before the duchess.

The wind was still blowing. The camp was as quiet as a gathering of so many men could be. Fires were banked, men in their tents or lodgings asleep. William had long since rationed their wine and ale to a miserly amount, to keep them sober and ready to sail.

He swallowed a yawn. He would much rather have been in his own bed with his wife in his arms. But if this turned the wind and got him out of harbor, it would be worth the trouble.

He moved ahead of the others, until the water almost lapped his feet. He could not see the isle of Britain from here; it was all darkness and glimmering water. But he could feel it. It was in him as Mathilda was, deep and solid.

When he turned his mind to it, it came clear. The walls of iron were higher and stronger than ever. The wind came from them. The winds of the world swirled about them, caught in them, funneled through them, so that they all blew against him, no matter how they began.

He spoke without turning. His companions would hear; they were what they were. "You could have taken care of this a month ago."

"So could you," said a woman's rich voice. He would wager that it was the Lady Melusine.

"We could not," Lanfranc said. His voice had a distinct edge. "The stars as well as the wind were against us. Tonight they turn in our favor. The defenses of England are down; the king's eye is turned from the coasts of the south to the northern shores. His wind has kept you in harbor but blown the Norsemen full upon England. He wages war, but not against us—not yet. Now let us turn the wind. Come!"

William felt the compulsion of that word, clear as a spur in the side; but it was never as strong as the call that rang out over the water, the cry of Britain against the bonds that strangled it. Maybe he was the only one who felt that. They were all of Gaul. Only he was bound to Britain.

Their magic commingled was a thing of breathtaking beauty. But Britain, faced with the force of it, saw invasion: saw them raising their working in a land across the sea, and their powers gathering to attack. Another power had already violated its defenses and trodden on its land, sweeping over the north of England. It was all the more determined to protect itself against the onslaught from the south.

William was the key to that door. He reached back and found Mathilda's hand. His other hand found Cecilia's. One was his heart, the other his blood.

The three of them wrought a shield for the rest. William made no move against the walls of iron, not tonight. That would come in time. Tonight he set about raising a wind of his own, driving back the gale from the isle.

It was slow. The air was a slippery thing, too insubstantial to grasp. It poured around his guard and sent outriders against him, sudden gusts and fierce whirlwinds that blasted him with sand and stones.

Warmth from the south, icy blasts from the north, met and clashed in a tumult of thunder. Clouds boiled; winds lashed. Rain poured down in torrents.

None of it touched the Guardians or the ones they guarded. William looked up at what seemed to be a dome of glass, with water streaming down it, lit by flashes of lightning. The sky had gone mad. There was, indeed, war in heaven.

It was out of his hands, and out of his power, too. He could only stand and watch, and let the battle roar and crack and rumble to its conclusion.

Slowly the storm faded. The clouds ran away to the north; the lightning walked across the sea, leaving the land behind.

The wind had shifted. It blew from the south, the warm and fragrant and beautiful south, straight for the shores of Britain.

The Guardians' protection melted away. A last shower of rain kissed William's uplifted face. Spirits danced in it, surrounding him with airy laughter.

They did love a good, changeful wind. William sighed and flexed his shoulders, which were aching as if he had been fighting all night with earthly weapons. He would not be able to let go this working, not completely, not if he wanted the wind to hold, until *Mora*'s prow touched the shore of Britain.

Cecilia's fingers tightened in his. He felt the surge of strength. As he turned to protest, she smiled.

He was too old a soldier to give way to simple charm, but Cecilia had a way about her that melted the hardest heart. She could be dangerous if she chose, with that face and that smile.

Nonetheless, she had taken a great burden from him. Some of it was still with him, but the rest was in her, barely ruffling the wide calm sea of her magic.

He took a moment to wonder at her. They had made this, he and Mathilda. Any breeder of horses knew how it could be, but it was still a marvel.

She tugged at his hand, imperious as the child she still was. "Come, Father. You need to eat, then sleep."

He did indeed. The Guardians stayed behind to continue a working of their own, a magic of guide and guard. They did not need him for that. He needed to rest, but not for too long. Today at last, God and the gods willing, he would sail for England.

Mora floated on the evening tide. Her mast was stepped, her sail furled, the crew ready to raise it at the captain's signal. Mathilda's lantern hung from the top of her mast, above the Pope's cross. The lamp was covered still; a pair of feys perched on it. They had orders, which they would obey, but they could not resist plucking at the edges of the wrapping, releasing stray beams of pure white light.

The wind had blown steady since the storm ended. William's army had roused with a roar. The fleet was ready, had been ready for weeks: provisions loaded, weapons in stores. All through the day, men and horses had streamed on board, filling ship after ship.

Now the tide was as much in their favor as the wind. The fleet floated at anchor, waiting for the signal. Men and horses were settled. They had all heard Mass, sung from the shore by the Pope's legate, and the Pope's banner had gone aboard *Mora* with great pomp and ceremony.

They were all ready to sail. Only William was still onshore, bidding farewell to his lady.

"When I see you again," he said, "I'll be king in Britain."

Or dead. But neither of them said that of all ill words.

"Go with the gods," she said, taking his hands in hers and kissing them one by one. "If you need me, call on me. Lanfranc will be with you. He knows the way."

"So do I," William said with a hint of a growl. His fist struck his breast over the heart. "You're in here."

That made her smile, though her eyes were brimming over. They had had countless partings before; some had lasted months. But this was different.

She could not fling herself into his arms and demand that he take her with him. She had to stay behind. If there was an attack behind his back, she must be there to stop it. Her father and the two Ladies would stand with her for the defense of Normandy. Lanfranc would go—and another of whom William did not yet know. Nor would he until he was well under way.

She kissed him until they both were breathless, and pushed him briskly away. "Go. You'll lose the tide."

He had never been so reluctant to go to a war as he was now. She thought she might have to hit him, but he shook himself, stooped for a last kiss, and turned to wade out toward *Mora*.

As he went up over the side, he glanced back. She gave him her best smile and her strongest face. He bowed low.

The sail ran up, bellying with wind. It was dark now in the twilight. In daylight it would be crimson.

High on the mast, the feys were loosed at last. They stripped away the coverings and freed the light.

It was a living thing. It blazed in the darkness, lighting the way across the sea. Men in the fleet gasped at the glory of it.

Turold perched on *Mora*'s stern, cloak billowing like wings in the wind. He set a horn to his lips and blew, a long, wailing call that echoed in the deep water. The earth of Normandy resonated with it. Mathilda's heart matched its rhythm.

She stood by the shore as the fleet sailed into the dark, gazing after it until the light of *Mora*'s lamp was long gone, and the wind had taken on a distinct flavor of dawn.

❧ CHAPTER 46 ❧

Mora rode the wind away from Normandy, with her lamp a beacon across the waves, and darkness ahead. The fleet followed the light of her, and the sound of Turold's horn blown at intervals to guide those farthest away.

William could feel them in his body as he did when he led men in battle. This was a greater battle than he had yet fought. He was going to claim what he had been born for, and call in the oath that the English king had sworn.

The walls of iron rose high before him. He had passed them before when he came to be named the late king's heir. Now they were higher, thicker, stronger; and they were armed against him.

The wind had failed, but the walls were a more potent barrier, and more deadly. Wind had simply kept him bound to his own country. These would catch him at sea, halt his fleet, and undertake to drown it.

Lanfranc came up beside him where he stood at the prow, close by the gilded dragon's head. So did someone else, a slender figure wrapped in dark wool. Her voice was as composed as ever, as if she had no slightest fear of her father's reaction to her presence on his ship.

"We can't break them down from here," Cecilia said. "We have to make a gate, then pass through and take the isle. Once that is ours, we can destroy them."

"They're wider than they were," Lanfranc observed. "We're not even halfway through the crossing."

"Then I would guess," said Cecilia, "that what we see is a feint of sorts. They've diverted their strength from elsewhere to focus it here. If we can go around it—"

"Too far," William said. The words that he had meant to say, of daughters who hid away on their fathers' ships until it was too late to send them packing, retreated before a greater urgency. "They've walled off the island along the whole coast of Gaul, clear up to Denmark and clear down to Spain. Maybe there's nothing to guard their backs, but we can't get there from here. Unless you know a spell or a road that will take us?"

"Not from here," Lanfranc said. Cecilia, perhaps wisely, was silent. "The straight tracks all lead this way—direct to the wall. The only way for us is through it."

"So we go through it," William said. "I can ward the fleet, if—"

"We will ward the fleet," said Lanfranc. "You must build the gate."

"But—"

"You are bound to Britain," Lanfranc said. "Just as with the wind: you alone have the power."

Just as with the wind. And just as, years ago, William had closed a gate to the Otherworld on Beltane night, now he must open one. It was all one, all the same long tide of fate and destiny.

Mora was running swift now, skimming the waves. The lanterns of the fleet were dropping behind. The walls of iron loomed ahead, invisible to the eye but overwhelming to the spirit.

One more magical battle. Then he could get his ships through and fight a much more comfortable war with mortal weapons.

In the meantime he had a matter to discuss with his daughter. But she had wandered off with some of the less canny of the ship's passengers. They were crowding the hull and the mast, pouring like mist through the mortal bodies and flocking about those who had magic, however faint or unacknowledged.

William leaned once more against the prow. A fey was perched on top of it, leaning forward with its hand over its eyes, peering into the darkness.

It was the fey he had sent to Mathilda years ago. It had never left her, even after he released it. And yet, like Cecilia, it was here.

Mathilda was looking out for him, whether he would or no. Even if she could not be here, she had made sure he had the two beings, apart from him, whom she trusted most in the world, and who were most closely bound to her magic as well as his.

It was as if she were here with him, resting warm against him in place of the cold curve of the prow, fingers laced in his and eyes gazing out over the lamplit glimmer of the sea. The rest of the fleet had fallen farther behind. They were calling back and forth, each with its own horn-call; Turold sent out *Mora*'s with tireless precision.

William had dallied long enough. With nothing but water under him, it might have been difficult to find the roots of his power. But *Mora* was wrought of oak from the woods of Gaul. The prow itself was a branch of the oak of Falaise. The ship was steeped in the magic of earth and air, and deeply intertwined with William's own blood and destiny.

In *Mora*'s embrace, secure as in Mathilda's own, William called up his power as she had taught him. He was aware dimly that the Old Things had gathered to him; that Lanfranc was at his back, and Cecilia. They had powers of their own to raise, protections to ward the fleet while William did what must be done.

Open a gate. Simple enough to say. In front of walls that had no substance yet were as strong as iron, sustained by the conjoined faith of a kingdom, he felt as feeble as a child with a dry stick in his hand, thinking to carve a gate in a mountainside.

A stick had its uses. Trimmed and fletched and fitted with a point of steel, it made an arrow that could pierce flesh and armor and penetrate to the heart. Or if one were a master archer, one could aim the arrow up over a castle wall, arm the arrow with fire, and burn down the castle.

William's eyes narrowed. Now there was a thought. But he needed a gate, not a gutted kingdom.

The wards were up: he felt the prickle of them on his skin, flowing back from *Mora* to the whole of the fleet. From where he was, they were like a shield, over which he could aim a weapon, and which he could raise or lower as he chose.

Simplicity had always been his best weapon and his most useful defense. He envisioned a stick in his hand, a peeled wand, glimmering in the night. Slowly, taking care to be exact, he drew the shape of a gate in the air.

The air resisted, catching at the tip of the wand. He set his teeth and persevered. It did not need to be elaborate. A simple opening would do, wide enough and high enough for a ship to pass through.

Where he touched the wall with his magic, he caught snatches of chanting, murmurs of prayer, and once the pipes of an organ rolling forth the notes of a hymn. The structure of it was as dense as a thicket, sharp with brambles and knotted with ingrown branches.

That was a trap. There was always a trap. He must see it as a wall: smooth and all of a piece. He would cut the gate in the wall, not hack his way through undergrowth.

He struggled to keep to his vision, not to be lured into the knots and tangles of that other working. Clean, clear, simple. First one line ascending, then another across, then a third down, the plain oblong of a door. No embellishment, no complexities.

The thicket withered and shrank into the waves. But he had succeeded too well: the wall was iron instead, smooth and impossibly hard.

Knife could not cut nor chisel carve that grim metal, but fire melted it—fire of the forge gathered into a searing point, so that it clove the iron as a knife would cut through cheese. Psalms and antiphons and fragments of the Mass dinned in his ears.

Behind him Lanfranc began to sing. He had a good voice, rather thin but true, and his Latin had a scholar's purity. After a moment Cecilia joined him with heart-stopping sweetness.

They lent William strength. Sparks flew; molten iron poured down the wall. But the shape of the door had come clear. The wall within it crumbled slowly to dust.

The way was open. *Mora* sailed straight for it. The rest of the fleet was a league and more behind. William groaned aloud. It would be hours before they were all past the wall, hours in which he would have to drain his strength of body as well as magic to keep the gate from shutting.

A flicker drew his eye upward. The fey had left the prow and flown up to the lintel of the gate, even as *Mora*'s mast passed beneath it. Flocks of its kin streamed in its wake. They swarmed along the frame of the gate, gripping it with fingers and claws and appendages for which William had no name. They lent it a shimmer that waxed rather than waned as the time passed. In their way they had become a part of it, woven into the substance of the wall.

That substance was changing. William's magic had cloven it, but the Old Things transformed it, spreading slowly but visibly from the flocks and throngs of them about the gate. Iron was transmuting into air: walls of air, impenetrable to hostile power but transparent to any friendly spirit that willed to pass.

And pass they did—so many that they streamed in clouds, far more than *Mora* could ever have carried. They were coming over the water from Gaul, skipping from ship to ship of the fleet, flocking together with those that had gone before them.

More met them on the other side. Dimmed, tattered, stunted, and poisoned though they were, still they welcomed their kindred home. And as they did it, they began to heal.

Dawn found *Mora* alone on the sea, and the shore of Britain before her, dark in the welling light. William was dizzy with too much magic and too little sleep. Sometimes he could feel the fleet far behind, slow but safe. Then he would know in his gut that the sea had swallowed it and there was only *Mora,* protected by her magic, to invade the whole of Britain.

His people—human and otherwise—were looking to him, prepared to panic if he showed any sign of fear. He put on the calmest face he could and called for his breakfast. "With wine," he said, "and spices."

It came quickly: bread baked in St.-Valéry the day before, cheese and apples from the rich stores of Normandy, and fish caught fresh out of the sea, with the wine that he had asked for. He ate every bit of it, though his stomach kept trying to reject it.

While he ate, Cecilia came to sit at his feet. He filled a bowl and held it out to her. She shook her head. He glared. "Eat," he said. "You've been working as hard as I have."

She sighed vastly, reminding him that after all she was very young, but she did as he told her. Her appetite was better than his, once she had got it going.

Youth, he thought. He had had it once, long ago. He did not recall that he had done much with it. Mostly he had tried not to get killed.

"So," he said as she finished her breakfast. "What makes you think you belong on this ship?"

"I do," she said, as composed as ever. "You need me."

"I need you safe," he said roughly.

"I'm safe here," she said. She set down the bowl; one of the dogs obligingly licked it clean.

She pulled the big shaggy head into her lap and rubbed the

beast's ears. William wanted to box hers. But he was cursed with a rational mind. He saw the advantage that she gave him: her strength, her self-control. She was a potent weapon.

He would not say that he gave in to the inevitable. Rather, he yielded to reason. "If you are hurt or killed," he said, "I will haunt you into your next dozen lives."

She smiled her quick smile, so much like her mother's, and said, "I'll be very careful, Father."

"You do that," he said.

She looked as if she might have said more, but a cry from the mast brought everyone to attention. "Sails!" the lookout sang. "Sails ho!"

They came up over the horizon, four of them at first, striped black or red or blue; then the rest behind, a forest of sails. The knot in William's gut let go; he breathed freely for the first time since *Mora* had left her companions behind. "Now we're ready," he said in deep relief. "Now we can begin."

❦ CHAPTER 47 ❦

The shore of Britain was unguarded. No Saxon shieldwall waited; no fortress rose to defend that stretch of coast, although it lay directly across from Normandy.

Still there were people waiting on the sand: two figures, motionless, wrapped in dark mantles that seemed to swallow the sunlight and leave nothing behind. Cecilia found that she was breathing hard, as if she had been running. She could taste the power in those who waited, sharp as heated metal, sweet as blood.

The landing that had seemed to take forever now seemed too swift to follow. Men swarmed over the sides of the ships, splashing through shallow water, sweeping them in toward the shore. *Mora* led as she had from the beginning: first to leave Normandy, first to touch the soil of Britain.

She leaped forward, borne on the sudden swell of a wave. Another, stranger wave rose inside her, as all her uncanny cargo streamed out of her. They ran like water across the sand, spreading as they went, increasing and multiplying, pouring away into the heart of Britain.

With their passing, the light was brighter, the air keener. The wind's song was no longer a lifeless whisper; it was full of voices, of music and singing.

The magic had come back into Britain. And yet it was a fragile thing, no more than a skin over a core of cold iron, until William's foot touched the sand.

He checked; his shoulders stiffened. Cecilia, still in the ship, caught the flicker of his astonishment, even as he stumbled and fell to his knees.

The land knew him as it would always know its king. He was bound to it; and it remembered. So, beyond a doubt, did he. The faltering step that could have been taken for a bad omen, he turned into homage: he stooped and kissed the earth, then leaped to his feet.

The two Guardians met him where sand met windswept grass. One was a woman, veiled and silent. The other was a tonsured monk with a long and unmistakably Saxon face and an equally unmistakable fire of magic wrapped about him like a cloak. "My lord," he said in not too ragged French. "Welcome! Welcome at last."

"Brother Wulfstan," William said. "It's bishop now, isn't it?"

Wulfstan bent his head. "For my sins, my lord."

"Oh, pride's a sin," said William, "and ambition is worse, but I'm sure God will forgive us all."

"So will the gods," said the veiled Lady. That she was a Lady, as powerful as Dame Alais in the Wood, Cecilia had no doubt at all. Her voice was low and sweet.

William bowed to her, as low as Cecilia had ever seen him bow except to her mother. "Lady," he said.

"My lord," she said; and that was carefully spoken. "Be welcome in Britain. What is yours is here for you to take."

"And so I shall," he said.

He looked about as if he had heard something or someone; but there was nothing that had not been there before in the tumult of landing. He frowned. "Something is strange," he said. "I smell blood; I hear men shouting, but far away. What is it? Who's coming to dispute my claim—Saxon Harold or Norse Harald?"

"At the moment, my lord," said Wulfstan, "neither. Godwine's son is in York, resting from a great battle. Hardrada sleeps in a bed of English earth."

William's brows rose. "He won? Harold won? Hardrada is dead?"

"It was a mighty victory," the Lady said. "Three hundred ships came a-viking. Scarce two dozen limp home again, carrying cowed and broken men. There will never be another king so bold or fleet so strong, sweeping down with the wind from the north."

Men nearby crossed themselves. Wild Norsemen their forefathers might have been, and they were still sea raiders at heart, but they belonged to Christendom now. Even if it was an enemy who had destroyed the terrible Hardrada, they gave thanks to God that he had done it.

So did William, but for another reason. "If Harold's fought that great a battle, he'll hardly be in condition to fight another. Let's not give him time to think. Let's get him here while he's still half dead on his feet."

"That can be done," the Lady said, "and you will do it."

William grunted. "That's always the way, isn't it? Well then, Lady, if you don't mind, I've a war to provoke."

"And we," said the Lady, "have one of our own. May the gods guard and guide you, my lord, and bring you to your throne."

Even as she finished speaking, William was in motion, seeing masts taken down and ships drawn up on the shore and secured, men and horses and supplies landed, camp pitched and, on the hill above the landing, claim laid to the old Roman stronghold that had guarded this coast since long before Artos was born.

Cecilia left him to it. That was his province and his duty. Hers was in another realm, and the sooner she got to it, the better.

The Lady and the bishop were waiting for her to come round to noticing them. Lanfranc was with them.

As her eyes passed from one to another of them, she felt a shifting inside her: as if the world had been all awry, but now it stood solid on its feet. Four pillars of magic: four Guardians of this realm as of every other in the world.

No one had ever told her how Guardians were made. It was a mystery. And no wonder, if it was as simple as this. There was no rite, no testing, no election; one simply knew. The earth underfoot, the air overhead, confirmed it.

There was also, Cecilia realized, no choice. She was inextricably wound within the fabric of this realm before she even knew that it had taken her.

"Now we are complete," the Lady said.

She sounded well satisfied. Cecilia was not so sure. She had come here of her own free will. She could hardly protest that now she was here, she was not only needed, she was indispensable.

"I don't know what to do," she said.

The Lady let fall her veil. She was not as young as she had been when Mathilda met her, when Cecilia was a child unborn, but she was still young enough to meet Cecilia's stare with a remarkable degree of understanding. "You do know," she said. "When you need it, it will come. For now, follow us; do as we do. The rest will come in time."

That seemed reasonable enough. The Lady began to walk down the strand. Cecilia followed. The other two brought up the rear. They were on guard, subtle but clear to her perception.

Behind them, the invasion proceeded apace. Where they went was another and no less deadly war. The walls of iron still rose high. The tide of magic rolled over Britain, but too often it caught in eddies, swirled about strongholds of twisted prayer, and lost itself in emptiness.

The heart of that void was far away from this place, north and east of it, and yet as close as the darkness behind her eyelids. There were Guardians of the Saxon rule, encamped in a place of great sanctity, which fed them with its power.

Cecilia saw through veils of time and distance to a vaulted hall—church or cathedral—and a choir of monks, and two who led the chanting: a man in archbishop's regalia and a woman in somber clothes like a nun. Yet she had taken no vows; Cecilia could see that. On her brow, like a flame, flickered the memory of a crown.

"Stigand of Canterbury," Lanfranc said in his cool scholarly voice, "and Edith, Godwine's daughter, late the queen of the English."

Cecilia nodded. When she looked about her, she saw that they had left the shore and the landing and entered a quite different place.

It was, she realized in no little startlement, a monastery. They stood in its cloister, warm in the shaft of sunlight that had brought them here. Voices were chanting within, just as they had been in her vision of the queen and the archbishop.

And yet whereas the vision had shown her those who raised and sustained the walls of iron, these monks sustained something else altogether. Their rite had the clarity of offices sung in certain holy houses in Normandy: where magic was welcome and its workings blessed, and the God of the Church encompassed the old gods of earth and water and air.

"Here," the Lady said, "we fight our own battle, so that your father may fight his."

That was familiar enough. Cecilia had come to do exactly this—though not from such a place or in such a position.

She would wager that her mother had known. Mathilda had a way of always knowing what her children were up to—and she had not only not forbidden Cecilia to sail on *Mora,* she had insisted that her daughter slip on board when her father's back was turned.

Cecilia drew a deep breath and let it go. She could do this. She had been trained for it since before she was born.

She followed the Lady up a stair from the cloister, into the airy summit of a tower. It was anchored to the monastery by bonds of stone and magic, but it was not strictly in the world.

Out of the corner of her eye the tall arches of the windows seemed to be the trunks and branches of slender silver-barked trees—birches or young beeches. But when she looked directly at them, they were carved of pale grey stone. The floor struck her likewise: a mosaic of many tiles when she stared down, but when she turned away, it seemed to be the leaf mold of a forest floor. Stars glimmered in the lucent blue of the ceiling, even while sun shone through the windows.

It was neither a cold place nor an empty one. There was a table spread, and beds made in alcoves, and couches and cushions for lounging in. As battlefields went, it was remarkably comfortable.

"Self-sacrifice has its place," Bishop Wulfstan said a little wryly, "but a soldier cherishes his comfort."

So, Cecilia could see, did the flock of spirits who gamboled in the vaulting. It was so much like home, and therefore so ordinary in her mind, that it was a long moment before she realized that this place was part of Britain—and both magic and creatures of magic had been shut out for time out of mind.

"Oh yes," the Lady said, for Cecilia's thoughts echoed here, brought to life by the power of the place. "Without your father, or you, we could not be here. It would have been a journey on mortal roads for us, and a cold stone tower at the end of it. By his living presence he brings the magic back to Britain, and opens up the straight tracks, and begins to make us whole again."

"And so we will stay," said Wulfstan with steel in his gentle voice, "however fiercely our enemies may fight against us."

Even as he spoke, wind buffeted the tower, rocking it underfoot. The pillars swayed; the vaulting threatened to crack.

Cecilia's hand sought the Lady's even as Lanfranc's sought hers. As they touched, their magic melded together, as beautifully simple as mixing paint on a palette. The color that came of it was indescribable, mingled brightness and beauty, shot through with the sternness of stone.

It was going to be a long battle. Cecilia settled to it, sinking roots in this earth of Britain and lifting up branches of magic to a sky that was now shining and free, now grim and grey as bars of iron. Mailed feet trod on her; blood nourished her. Cold sanctity strove to drain the life from her.

Across the distance of a town or a world, she met the chill blue eyes of Edward's queen. They widened. Edith saw or sensed her, though what it was that she saw, Cecilia could not be certain. A horned devil, no doubt, or a horror out of an old story.

Edith was strong. Cecilia could see the apparition herself, stretching greedy claws toward England's heart. She must, somehow, transform that vision; turn it into an angel of light, or better yet, into her simple, mortal self.

❊ CHAPTER 48 ❊

Tosti was buried in the earth of York, where he had hoped to be earl again, and perhaps even king. He had the city back in death, at least. Harold hoped he had his soul as well, whatever had become of it while the demon lived in his body.

The Norsemen were gone. Those who survived the battle and the hunt thereafter had taken what few ships they needed and fled. Harold had close on three hundred ships now, which he would send southward as soon as he had mustered crews for them. They were God's own gift for England's defense against the Normans.

On the third night after the battle, he went earlier than usual to his bed. He was still aching with bruises and the odd small wound; he could have slept for a week. Maybe, once the winter storms began, he would.

He felt a little strange. Maybe he was ill. It had begun in the morning: a sense that the sun was too bright and the air was singing. It had seemed to him as he heard the day's Mass, that a wave of light had swept over the cathedral, full of wings and claws and eyes.

Archbishop Aldred had been preaching from the book of Revelation. If it was a sickness coming on, that would explain the visions, and the strange, light-headed feeling, too.

As Harold tossed in his bed, unable quite to fall over the edge into sleep, he felt as if he lay in a boat on a gentle sea. Seabirds and strange fish circled him, peering in wonder, chittering softly among themselves. The room was full of them; they swarmed in the rafters and clung like flies to the walls.

Most of their chatter was simply noise, but he fancied that he caught a word here and there. All the words were in Norman French.

It was a fever dream. It must be. He tried to sit up, to clear his head.

Someone was sitting on the end of his bed. There was no weight there, but the figure seemed perfectly solid. It looked like a man, dark and wiry, with a clever fox face. He spoke in French, not quite Norman, but near enough. "Good evening, my lord of England."

Harold knew that voice and that face. They had vexed him in another dream or fugitive vision, one strange night in Brittany. "Geoffrey," he said.

The apparition bowed. "At your service," he said.

"You're not here," said Harold. "I'm in delirium."

"You're dead tired from a march that they'll be singing songs of for a thousand years," said Geoffrey, "and a battle that has so quelled the Norsemen's fury that they'll never rise again as they have before. You're perfectly well otherwise. And no, you're not seeing things. Or rather, you're seeing things that are really there."

"Such as you?"

Geoffrey arched a brow. "I'm a perfectly respectable haunting, messire. Why don't you ask instead why you're seeing the likes of us at all?"

"Because I'm going as mad as Tosti," Harold said somewhat tightly. "What was it that brought on the curse? Was it killing him? Burying him? Shredding the raven banner on the battlefield?"

"Not at all," said Geoffrey. "You're perfectly sane. We really are here. We landed this morning. Didn't you notice which way the wind is blowing? It's coming from the south."

Harold flung himself at the specter. It did not even trouble to flinch. He tumbled through it, catching himself against the bed's foot. Geoffrey spoke calmly from the middle of his back. "William has come. Or I should say Artos. Or Caswallon. Or Bran."

He was raving. Except that his raving made a ghastly amount of sense. "The beacons are lit," he said. "Tomorrow or the next day or the day after that, you'll get word. You'll know the truth."

"Where?" Harold snapped. "Where is he?"

Geoffrey smiled, patently indulging him. "You'll find him at Santlache." He rolled the word on his tongue. "Santlache . . . Santlache. Fascinating how your sandy pool will turn and shift, and Normans call it Senlac: Lake of Blood."

"Santlache. That's—"

"Straight across from his favorite port in Normandy," Geoffrey said, "more or less. You'll find him there. Have a care you don't find your death, too."

There was a cold knot between Harold's shoulder blades, but he refused to dignify it with his notice. "So? Why tell me? Aren't you one of his workings?"

Geoffrey flung back his head and laughed until tears streamed down his face. It was a long while before he had had enough of it.

When at last he had, he grinned at Harold. His cheeks were dry, the tears vanished. "Oh, no, messire. Our noble duke, king, lord of battles has hated me with a pure and stainless hatred since the moment he set eyes on me."

"So that's why," Harold said.

Geoffrey bowed where he sat. "My spirit was willing to destroy him, but my flesh was weak. I died; he outlasted me. Now I see what fate has written, and I think that I should like to see another story. It wants you dead and him on your throne. I would prefer the opposite."

"All to gratify an old enmity?"

"Why not?" said Geoffrey. "He may be the great fated king, but he's a stone-faced brute."

"And you were not?"

Geoffrey shrugged an infinitely Gallic shrug. "Ah well. I only have a scrap of advice to offer. Don't let him draw you. Give yourself time. Let him wear himself out trying to get you down there."

"What if I can't? What if the only sensible course is to hit him hard and fast, before he knows I've come there?"

"As you did with Hardrada?" Geoffrey shook his head. "Lightning doesn't strike twice, messire."

"Who says it can't?"

"Why, not I," said Geoffrey. "I'm only wind and will and a scrap of foresight. Watch yourself, king of the English. Be wise. Don't let either your pride or your temper control you."

Harold opened his mouth to counter that, but the apparition was gone. He blinked hard and rubbed his eyes, but it did not come back. There was no proof except his wavering memory, that it had been there at all.

* * *

Word came on the third day after that strange night in York. Harold was still there, still contending with the aftermath of the battle. His levies were ready to go home. He was minded to travel slowly back to the south, then settle to winter court in London. He even, rather cravenly, prayed that the visitation had been a lie or a sleight of the Devil whose son this Geoffrey had been.

It was with a sense of weary inevitability that he rose from dinner on the evening of the third day, to an outcry without. The watch beacons were lit. The Normans had come.

"We should wait," Gyrth said.

They had pressed the march from York to London, five hard-ridden days like an echo in reverse of the ride north. Scouts and messengers were waiting there, and all of them had the same tale to tell. The Normans were burning and looting and pillaging. William had strengthened the Roman fort at Pevensey, where he had come to shore, then gone on to Hastings and done the same on the cliff over the sea.

He had made no move to harry inland, or to take Dover, which was the city closest to his landing place. He was methodically, brutally, and thoroughly stripping Harold's own land of Sussex of its winter stores, then burning the storehouses.

"He's doing it deliberately," Harold's brother said. "He wants to provoke you. Let him do it. He's trapped on a spit of land with only a narrow way into the rest of England. Once he's used up his own stores and the ones he's stolen, there's nothing more for him to take. You can send the fleet to close him in from the sea, and levies from Sussex to close him off by land, and starve him out."

Harold shook his head. "There are too many *if*s in what passes for prudence. If he breaks out before we can stop him, if he goes rampaging up the coast, if he comes to take Dover or Canterbury or London, we'll be ravaged with war from one end to the other. Better to strike fast, strike hard, and end it soon."

"We're all exhausted," Gyrth said. "He's fresh; he hasn't fought a battle all year."

"He's soft," Harold shot back. "He's been waiting in harbor instead of fighting."

Gyrth shook his head. So did their brother Leofwine. But the rest of Harold's council, his thanes and captains, even his bishops and abbots, nodded as they came round to Harold's way of thinking. They were all eager to get this war over and this invader cast out as the Norsemen had been, and settle in for a long winter's peace.

In the dark hours of the night, while Harold lay awake, too troubled to sleep, the memory of Geoffrey's warning echoed and reechoed in his mind. More than once he thought he saw a flicker that might have been a ghost passing in the darkness, or heard a voice that could have been the dead man's. But he saw nothing clearly, and no apparition came to haunt him.

"I am not going to die," he said to the mocking memory. "I am going to win. England is going to be safe, and I intend to keep it so."

Was that laughter borne on a sudden gust of wind?

It was only the rattle of the shutters, and the lamp flickering in the draft that seeped through them. The room was cold: he wrapped himself securely in coverlets and shut his eyes, willing himself to fall asleep.

No matter what dreams came to vex him, his conscience was clear. He was doing as he must, no more and no less. Tomorrow he would ride to Hastings. Victory was waiting there, and an England free at last from any threat of invasion.

＊ CHAPTER 49 ＊

Harold was coming. He had taken the bait. William heard
galloping hooves in his dreams, and the tramp of feet as
the Saxon levies marched to the muster.

He kept up his raiding and pillaging, to be sure the trap was
securely laid. Even the greediest of his knights had been heard
to observe that they did not need the stores and livestock they
were bringing back, and were fast running out of room to put
it all. But William was not about to leave anything to chance.

He needed a battle, and the sooner the better. The Saxons
were riding high on their great victory, but it had sapped their
strength. Maybe it had also impaired their judgment.

He could pray for that. He was doing a great deal of praying
these days—and no matter who heard, either, as long as he or
she was or they were minded to answer.

"It's time," Etaine said.

Cecilia had come to know the Lady rather well since they
gathered in this place out of the world, which was tethered by
magic and by will to the monastery of St. Augustine in Canterbury. Old Saxon kings were buried there; their bones held great
power, though they might not have been pleased to know who
and what was making use of it.

It had been a waiting time, a time of standing watch and sus-
taining wards. The walls of iron were still high and strong. The
choir in the cathedral never wearied. As far as any of them knew,
or any common person who heard them, they were singing an anthem in praise of the victory against the Norsemen, and a long
litany for the defense of England against the Normans.

William was safe for the moment on his fist of land thrusting out into the sea. English ships were sailing to blockade him,

and English armies were mustering to fight him, but he was prepared for that.

The walls of iron were another matter. They could not come down for one man's trying—even if that man was William. The defenders in the cathedral were laboring to close those walls about the invaders, to crush the heart and spirit out of them, and leave them defenseless against Saxon steel.

The magic that had come back into Britain, the Old Things that had sailed in with the tide from Normandy, struggled like a flower planted in dry ground. They barely had strength to sustain themselves, let alone to help the king whom they had followed across the sea.

And yet the Guardians of Britain were complete. Cecilia and Lanfranc, with their coming, had restored the pillars of the wards.

Now it was time to bring down the walls of iron and raise the walls of air. Cecilia left the book that she had been reading, a book of old songs and tales borrowed from the monastery's library. It was full of magic and memory—pagan memory, the monks would say, but they had kept the book carefully nonetheless, and never destroyed it.

With those memories singing in the back of her mind, Cecilia followed Etaine and the others to the tower. It was a clear morning, golden with autumn; the air that wafted through the tall windows smelled of apples and honey and sun-seared grass. The chamber was more than ever like a clearing in a wood, surrounded by the whisper of leaves and the voices of birds and beasts and spirits of the forest.

This was pure Britain: the Island of the Mighty, stronghold of magic, most blessed homeland of the Old Things. The Guardians made themselves pillars of it: Lanfranc in the east, Wulfstan in the north, Etaine in the west, and Cecilia in the south from which she had come. Their powers flowed together. Their voices rose, each on its own, sustained note.

The sound poured out of Cecilia's throat. She was a reed, and the wind of the gods blew through her. The air turned crystalline. Walls began to rise, walls of air, walls of light, transparent and yet potent.

The clangor of iron struck a fierce discord. Crystal began to crack, light to dim. The leaves of the wood withered in a blast of bitter wind.

Cecilia called up the reserves of her power. She drew them from the earth, from the heart of Britain. She was aware, dimly and yet keenly, that each of the others was doing the same. Their fourfold harmony, their gathered strength, labored slowly to transmute iron into air.

It fought them. It turned to edged steel; it plunged deep into their hearts and turned them cold.

That was hardest for Wulfstan and Lanfranc, with their vows to the Church and their faith in the Christians' God. All that they did was pagan, apostate, sin and damnation. They were doomed; hell would take them, and heaven be forever denied them.

Etaine stood aloof, as one who ruled in her own realm as living goddess. Her strength did not waver, but neither did it bolster the others. It did not know how.

Cecilia had always been poised between worlds. Her father bent his knee to the Church because it was a power in the world, and William gave power its due. Her mother had taught her the orders of sacred observance in both worlds, and shown her how one could serve both the old gods and the new.

She could feel the fear and guilt that tormented the bishop and the monk. And yet she knew a little of the Lady's motionless calm. She brought them together and wove them into the working, transforming weakness into strength.

It would not be enough. The enemy was too strong. To secure the working, they needed a great power and a potent magic: the blood of a king. A royal sacrifice.

A king must die. There must be a battle; there must be blood. Nor, in the way of magic, did it matter from which king it came.

Of the two who would contend for rule of this kingdom, William was by far the greater power. Harold was king by necessity. William was king by right: the true king, the reborn, the fated lord of Britain.

If it must be, it would be. She was the gods' instrument. It did not matter what her heart felt or what she thought while she worked the great working. The threads were spun, the fabric woven. Now fate would stitch the tapestry, and ordain a king's death.

Harold had been riding for so long, in such a pitch of intensity, that he felt as if he had passed out of the world altogether.

When they stopped to rest and change horses, or to gather another company of mounted men, the rhythm of the gallop was still inside him. He barely noticed whether it was day or night.

And yet his mind was remarkably clear. He knew where he was and how far he had come, and how many leagues he had yet to go. He did not have all the forces that he would have liked: no trained cavalry; too few archers.

What he had would be enough. He had only to close off the Normans' advance by land and trust his fleet to block it by sea; then on the battlefield that he had chosen, both archers and mounted knights would be hard pressed to match the Saxons' shieldwall.

The last of the levies would meet with those whom he had swept with him on his way, on Caldbec Hill, by the apple tree that had stood, men said, since before the first Saxon set foot in Britain. It still bloomed in the spring and bore fruit in the autumn, small and wizened but famously sweet. So would this realm of England, once the Normans were driven out.

William, like Hardrada before him, would not be expecting the enemy so soon. Surprise once more would be Harold's most potent weapon.

Geoffrey's warning slipped away into the back of his mind. This was the best course, perhaps the only one. What did a ghost know of battle, after all? He was long past it.

Harold's army had ridden once again from day into night. League after league of green downs rolled away beneath their horses' hooves: Harold's own country, his beloved Sussex. Darkness loomed ahead. There lay the copses and thickets of the wood that stood like a wall between the downs and the Normans.

It was steep country, dense with oak and thorn, but passable if one knew the way. Even in the dark, scouts found signs of passage: levies making their way to the meeting place, the tree and the sandy pool that gave it its name.

Santlache. Harold could not restrain a shiver, or keep from peering through the whispering dark. Geoffrey had been a dream, that was all; a nightmare preying on deep fears.

Of course death was waiting at Santlache. Death was always the first to come to a battle and the last to leave. A great lord would die, but it would not be Harold. Harold would live to rule unchallenged.

And yet, as he followed his guides through the wood, he crossed himself and prayed. It was only wise, after all, to commend oneself to God before a fight.

The Saxons were coming. William's bones knew it, and his scouts confirmed it. They were slipping like hunters through Duniford Wood toward the gnarled and twisted apple tree and the sandy pool below it.

Harold knew how to pick a battlefield. He could hold the high ground, too steep for an easy mounted charge, and an uphill shot for the archers. Once those were weakened into impotence, arrows wasted and horses destroyed, he could sweep down with his shieldwall and drive the invaders into the sea.

William would have to lure the Saxons down onto easier ground, where his knights and bowmen held an overwhelming advantage. He had scouted thoroughly; he knew this place as well as one of his own castles. His men were on the alert. If there was to be a night attack, they were ready for it.

It was a long night. William dozed for a while, then woke with a start. The world was still, the wind calm. Far away, a night bird called.

Everything was waiting: the army, the stars, the earth underfoot. William was completely empty of magic—and yet so full of it that he had become it.

He would fight as mortals fought, with blood and sweat and steel. That was the gods' gift to him, but their price, too. Before the sun set, a king would die. Then at last Britain would be whole.

✤ CHAPTER 50 ✤

William was up long before first light. He was already focused on the march and the fight; he barely noticed until it was on, that his mail coat was back to front.

His heart tried to stop. Such an omen would have been bad enough at the best of times. On this of all mornings, with a score of squires, pages, knights, and priests hanging about, it threatened to breed disaster.

William's lips drew back from his teeth. He hoped it would pass for a grin. "Well, messires," he said, "it seems I'll be turning my coat today—from duke to king."

It was desperate and rather feeble, but they laughed at it. The tension abated; too many hands reached for him, eager to set his armor to rights, but his son Rufus beat them off with a fine flash of arrogance. "*There* now! We thank you all. My lord will be ready to ride directly."

All of them accepted the dismissal, and without undue grumbling, either. William was torn between wanting to put the young pup in his place, and indulging in a father's pride. He settled for a growl and a quick cuff that barely rocked the boy on his feet, and let Rufus and young Olivier make him fit to be seen.

The Normans marched at dawn from their camp by the sea. It was just over two leagues to Santlache, and they traversed the distance at a strong pace: first the Pope's banner with a processional of monks and priests, then archers on foot, then the heavy-armed foot soldiers, and last of all the knights and mounted troops.

They were in fine spirits. William, riding in the center of the cavalry, took a long breath and let it go. There came a time in every march when a man either had to give himself up to it or run away screaming. All his plans were laid and his forces prepared. There was nothing left to do but arrive at the battlefield and see what came of it.

Harold would be hoping for a surprise. William was going to turn the surprise against him.

He resisted the urge to call for greater speed. It was still dark; he would be a fool to risk losing the road simply to get there a few moments sooner.

Slowly the daylight grew around him. It was a clear morning, cool, with a hint of the perpetual British mist. It would be a good day to fight.

As the sun rose over the hills and marshes that rolled down to the sea, Harold came at last to the place of meeting. Somewhat over half of the levies were there; the rest were on their way. "They'll be here by midmorning," his outriders said.

Harold bit back the first, sharp words that came into his head. It would have to be soon enough. Meanwhile his own hard-driven troops had time to rest and eat a little and hear Mass.

He for one took more sustenance from the rite than from the bread and salt meat; as for rest, he would have that when the fight was over. There was no time to sleep, not with so many men still to come in, and so much left to do before the Normans came to the field.

"My lord!"

One of the last companies was tramping out of the wood. Harold sat under the apple tree, eating the small sweet fruit and scowling for the thousandth time at the map of the field. The Normans would have to fight as the ground forced them to fight. That was the drawback of their heavy armor and their massive destriers: unstoppable on the flat or on a downslope, but easy victims of their own weight on as steep an ascent as this.

And yet there must be something he was missing. There always was. When he heard his scout Aelfric's voice, the edge of urgency in it was almost welcome.

Aelfric was running up the hill. "My lord! My lord, look!"

Harold rose, as did everyone else who was with him. As soon as he stood erect, he saw what had brought Aelfric in such haste: sunlight glinting off Norman helmets.

They were coming in battle order, fully armed and obviously anything but surprised. Harold had let himself forget what William was that Hardrada had not been: Druid's son, mage and sorcerer. Even if he chose not to use his powers, he had allies with no such scruples.

Harold's troops were scattered, their order ragged at best, with more coming in at the run as word spread of the Norman advance. The bellows of their commanders overlaid the call of horns and the thunder of drums.

Harold's banners were up and gleaming for the army to rally round: the flame-red wyvern of England snapping in the wind, and his own Fighting Man aflash with jewels and gold, the better to be seen above a battle. In return William flaunted the Pope's banner, its blaze of white and gold the more mocking considering that Harold knew how strong a pagan William was.

Pagan, and very, very clever—and blessed in his allies. But cold steel cared little for a man's connections, unless those were standing before him as a shield. Harold had chosen the field; he had the whole of England at his back, whereas William had nothing but what was in his camp and his ships. Even his escape by sea was barred: English ships waited to cut him down if he tried to run that way.

William would know that all too well. He came on with terrible speed. His men were chanting as they came. All too soon the word came clear. "Oath-breaker! Oath-breaker! Oath-breaker!"

Harold's sight narrowed to a single luminous point. Full in the center of that was a knight on a dark horse with a silver mane, and on his crimson shield a pair of golden lions.

The invader. The enemy. The man who had persuaded Harold to swear an oath on holy relics, an oath that, yes, Harold had broken. It had been necessary. It still was. A Norman could not rule a Saxon kingdom; least of all a Norman who was both pagan—however skillfully he pretended otherwise—and a sorcerer.

The few levies who were still on their way would have to join the battle as they could. Harold called the rest together in close order, shield overlapping shield.

William heard the clack and clang of the shieldwall taking shape. What had been a scatter of separate companies, some waiting by their king's banner, others coming in from the wood, in a handful of heartbeats had become a living fortress.

Even as it took shape, it began to move, advancing down the hill with measured menace.

William's bowmen were ready: bows strung and arrows nocked, and quarrels fitted to crossbows. "Faces!" he roared at them. "Aim for their faces!"

A crossbow bolt could pierce a shield as if it had been made of linen. The thought was cold and clear, and borne out admirably as the first flight arced out from his line and up the hill. Shields buckled, even shattered; men stumbled and fell.

And yet for every man who fell, it seemed a thousand came on, and the archers' supply of arrows was not infinite. Trumpets were singing. William's infantry surged up the hill, scrambling over ditches and fosses, splashing through mud, mired in marshes, but pushing irresistibly onward.

They struck the Saxon line with a ringing crash. Behind in the center of the cavalry, William's hand slashed down.

Knights who had been riding almost carelessly behind the lines of foot soldiers, spears in rest or swords in sheaths, now came together. Some lowered spears; others lifted them to cast into the swelling melee. The knight foremost, whose horse looked as agile as a cat, couched his lance and dug in spurs and crashed through the shieldwall.

The hill was bloody steep. The wall was crumbling, but the men behind it were not giving way. They had axes—the terrible seaxes that gave their nation its name—and as well as spears and swords. Their few archers were no more than a nuisance; William's long line of them had done notably more damage.

His horse hurdled a deep fosse and landed full in the faces of a line of Saxons. William's knights were already mowing them down. His spear caught a big fair-haired boy in the throat. He wrenched it loose, ignoring the blood that sprayed his arm and side, and thrust at the next man.

That one was older and more in command of his wits. His axe hacked William's spear haft in two. William tossed aside the shards and went for his sword.

His horse stumbled. William shifted, balancing it with legs and weight. But something had gone out of it: life and will. William flung himself out of the saddle as the dead weight dropped and rolled, mowing down Norman and Saxon alike as it hurtled down the hill.

William lay winded. The taste of blood was in his mouth.

People were shouting. "The duke! The duke is down!"

If William had had any wind for it, he would have muttered a curse. Somehow he got himself to his feet. His beautiful Spanish charger was dead. The next one, he thought distantly, was never going to see a battlefield. Parades and processions, that would be all it knew.

People were still screaming that he was dead. The line was breaking; horses were turning. At least a score were in full, galloping retreat. They were starting to pull others with them. The battle hovered on the edge of a rout.

The knights near him, thank God, saw that he was alive. One of them swung off his horse and tossed the reins to William. William saluted him, still wheezing for breath.

Willing hands lifted him into the saddle. The horse was larger, broader, and significantly slower than the one he had lost. He had to jab it with spurs before it appeared to notice he was there.

It was a horse, and willing enough once it acknowledged his presence. He urged it on up the hill, with his banner close behind and his shield upraised so that they all could see it.

"It's a feint!" someone shouted. "The duke is dead!"

William had his breath back. "The duke is alive, damn your bloody eyes! What are you running for? Do you think that will save you? They'll hunt you down and slaughter you!"

"He's lying." That was a Saxon, baying the words in accented French. "The duke is dead!"

He sang it like a mocking antiphon. William kicked his borrowed horse into a lumbering gallop. He stood in the stirrups; he lifted his helmet, holding it high, and be damned to any arrows that flew.

They knew his face at least. Those who had been ready to run started to come to their senses. Those who are already running slowed. People were shouting, screaming.

William lifted his voice above them all in a bellow that would have him croaking hoarse for days. "Get back here, damn your eyes! Get back here and fight!"

They were still on the edge. He filled his lungs for one final, deafening roar.

But they were all stopping, turning, coming back. His brother Odo, armored in mail under priestly robes, had gone after them like a shepherd after the sheep. He whirled his rod of office above his head; now and then it cracked down on cowering shoulders or ducking heads.

The shrieks of panic died down. The broken line was mending. The Saxons had gained ground, but William was not as disturbed by that as he might have been. The farther down from the wood they came, the better for his knights.

The shieldwall had restored itself. It was all to do over again, with troops that had given way once and could all too easily do it again.

William refused to think of that. These were Normans. They were fighting mad—at themselves, and with a kind of backward glee, at the Saxons. That fury would carry them onward.

He signaled the trumpeters to call them all together, back into their ranks. The Saxons were crying victory. William's trumpets cried them false.

His control even then was tenuous, and could shatter at a word. He held it, and his army, together by sheer force of will.

There was a spell for that, he supposed, somewhere. But there was no magic in this place apart from the primal power of blood and death and voided bowels. Magic was all around them, watching, waiting, doing nothing to either aid or interfere.

All his life William had wanted to be simply what he seemed to be: William, Robert's son, thoroughly mortal and completely unmagical duke of Normandy. Now that gift was given him, just when he realized that a single great working could sweep the Saxons off this island and be done with them.

"It would not."

Cecilia was nowhere on this field, and thank every god for it. She was safe, Lanfranc had assured William shortly after the landing, and well away from the fighting. And yet he heard her as clearly as if she stood beside him, offering him a sip of wine and inspecting him for wounds.

He could see her, too: her face so much like her mother's, her eyes the same sea-grey as his. She was frowning at him. "There is no single power or spell that can break the walls of iron and destroy the ones who made it. Except one. And that is not—"

"What is it?" he demanded, not caring if people thought he had let go of his wits.

"It's not magic," she said. "Not in the way a spell is. It's the deepest power of all. Blood sacrifice. Blood of a king."

"That's not magic," he said. "That's ritual."

"Yes," she said. Or someone said. He felt as if hours had passed, but the sun had barely moved.

There was blood enough already on this field. Bodies of men and horses lay tumbled in the fosses and the fens. Ravens were circling. In a moment of silence, William heard a single, imperious caw.

All of his men were back, the lines restored with remarkably few ragged edges. He was bruised and aching, but his strength had come back with the last few stragglers of his army.

He hauled his horse about. "Up!" he roared at the trumpeters. "Sound the charge!"

Two of them did not obey. They were dead.

The rest were alive and had breath enough to do as he commanded. The brass bray of their instruments rang across the field. It even woke the dead: men who had fallen and seen no reason to get up, and wounded who sprang from the ground onto the backs of riderless horses.

They were an army again. William grinned so broadly his jaws ached, and flung them once more against the Saxon line.

❧ CHAPTER 51 ❧

The battle had no end to it. Saxons did not know how to stop.
Normans were damned if they would.

William was losing count of the horses who had died under
him. Three, he thought. Maybe four. It was not that he was
reckless; it was that he had to lead the fight. He was his men's
will and their heart. If he was not out in front of them, fighting
as hard as any, they would break; and this time, when they ran,
they would not come back.

The Saxons were beginning to give way. It was slow; they
rallied again and again. But the constant hammering of the
charges, the arrows falling in showers of deadly hail, had taken
their toll. Their shields were battered and pierced; the wall was
down in places, with no men alive or standing to fill the gaps.

William had gone past exhaustion. His lungs were burning;
his sword arm was leaden. The horse he sat on had stayed alive
for a good hour. When, in a lull in the battle, it was able to stop,
it stood with head down, sides heaving. Its neck was thick with
sweat and foam.

In the way of battles, the fight had gone off elsewhere for a
while. Someone was standing in front of William with a horse.
The animal looked almost fresh: it must have been brought up
from the ships.

He envied his spent horse as the man-at-arms led it away.
The fresh one was almost too fresh for him in this state: it
wheeled when he went to mount, and when at last he heaved
himself into the saddle, it half-reared and sprang off on its hind
legs.

He stayed in the saddle by habit and instinct, and a fair bit
of luck. Some of his weary men cheered, which set the horse to
prancing.

This charge, he let waver. He let the enemy drive it back. Men, under whispered orders, turned and fled.

But this was a sleight of battle. The Saxons fell into the trap: having seen one retreat, they had been waiting for another. A full thousand of them broke and ran after the fleeing Normans. Two tall men in golden helmets led them: Godwine's sons, there was no doubt of it. They even walked like their elder brother, and fought like him, with a ferocity that even a Norman could admire.

William lured the Saxons well down away from the wood. The rest of their army held to its position, gaining itself a respite.

When the pursuit had gone well out of their reach, the Normans turned on the would-be pursuers. Most of them had pressed the center hard, so hard that they failed to see how the flanks bent and curved. When they realized that they were surrounded, it was too late to break free. Their enemies closed in, fell upon them and destroyed them.

Harold stood in the center of the now sorely reduced shield-wall and watched his brothers die. There was nothing that he could do about it, not without laying the rest of his army open to the same fate.

He felt very little, except a remote sense that later, when he had time, he should grieve. He had traveled too far, ridden too hard, and fought too many battles. For all his famous strength, he was nearing the end of his endurance.

Those of his men who remained were dropping as much from exhaustion as from Norman steel. Somehow he kept on rallying them; he held them firm against the Normans and their relentless mounted charges. Even on what passed for level ground, they were barely reaching a fast walk now. But the weight of their horses was if anything greater than ever, and the sheer mass of them pressing against the weary shieldwall was breaking it down, man by man.

Even so, the Saxons were holding on. The last of the levies had come in only a little while ago; they were as fresh as anyone could be on this field. They filled the gaps with intact shields, barely wearied arms, and unblunted weapons.

William had no such relief. A few riders had come in before the last of Harold's reinforcements, bringing new horses for the duke and some of his knights, but unless William wanted to strip his ships of their defenses, there would be no more from that or any quarter.

Harold had only to persevere, to give no ground, to let the Normans batter themselves to death against an immovable wall. They had come fresh to this fight, but they had charged the Saxon line over and over, hour upon hour, throwing the full weight of men and horses again and again, without ever succeeding in driving their enemy back.

The sun was westering, the shadows beginning to lengthen. Even with his losses, Harold was still the stronger. Each charge might well be William's last. Then when he could not muster one more blow, Harold would move. He would fall upon the exhausted Normans as they had fallen upon his brothers, and annihilate them.

William could see that Harold was waiting him out. It was good strategy; he would have done it himself if he had had no cavalry, and held the higher ground.

As it was, this battle had to end soon. Not only was the sun sinking low; William's men were near their limit. Horses were beginning to die not only from spears and swords and the odd arrow, but from burst hearts and foundered feet. If there was going to be any hope of victory, it had to come soon.

He pulled his forces back, not far enough or fast enough to feign another flight, but to stop and breathe and gather for the last assault. As he had expected, the Saxons made no effort to attack. Their ranks drew together; their shields interlocked once more beneath a blood-red gleam of helmets and a bristle of spears.

He saw Harold in the first rank, precisely in the center: taller than the men around him, helmeted in gold, and above him his banners. So far the two of them had not crossed swords; the fight had driven William away again and again.

Now it was time. William signaled the trumpeters. For the last time, the brazen blare split the sky. For the last time, William's knights flung the weight of their horses against the enemy. William led the charge, such as it was: more a heaving thrust than a long crescendo and crashing impact.

It was a tiny sound amid the multifold clamor of the battle-field. And yet William heard it: the twang of a bowstring; the song of an arrow piercing the air.

That was nothing unusual. Flights of arrows had preceded the charge, as every time before. Yet this was different.

It came from his left wing. The men there came from Brittany: allies of older vintage than most men knew, and not all of them were human.

The arrow rose in an arc, one of many in its flight, and yet to William it could have flown alone. No one but William seemed aware of it. The battle was in full cry. Even while the world, and William in it, held its breath, he cut down a spearman who had thrust at his gut, and broke the face of a Saxon who tried to pull him from the saddle.

The arrow's song came to an abrupt end. It had struck home.

Harold had paused for breath in the midst of mighty slaughter. Most likely he never saw the arrow coming. And yet William knew somehow that he had. Like William, he had felt the shift in the world's breathing.

Whether that was true vision or simple lying fancy, Harold neither sprang aside nor raised his shield. The bolt pierced his eye, straight through into the brain.

He was dead before he began to fall. His hand, empty of will, caught the staff of the Fighting Man and struck it from the bearer's grip. It struck the earth before him; his body sprawled upon it, wrapped in it as if in a shroud.

The shock of his death rippled through the Saxon ranks. The shieldwall began to buckle. There was no man to lead them now, no single lord or commander to rally them against the charge.

They broke, shattering into a dozen smaller companies, giving way before the knights. Some withdrew in ordered retreat. Most simply turned and ran.

The Normans hunted them down. A great surge of joyous strength had risen up in them. Victory—this was victory.

William was borne along ahead of them. He could not think at all; he could barely keep his seat on this latest of gods knew how many horses. This place that had had the magic all swept out of it was suddenly bursting with it.

It crackled through him like a tree of lightning. Sparks snapped from his fingertips; as he turned his glance toward one of the dead rolling underfoot, the body puffed into ash.

He squeezed his eyes shut. He could see better that way. Lanfranc had a word for it. Paradox, that was it. Much of magic was a paradox.

The field had flooded with spirits. They were laughing, chattering, singing, as if the reek and gore of slaughter meant nothing at all. Only one stream of blood mattered to them. Only one body drew their notice.

The horse had borne William past it. It would stay, the flock of spirits sang. It would be there when he came back. He had things to do—many, many things. Many, many Saxons to hunt and kill, and magics to restore, and Old Things to return to their ancient places.

They were running away with him. It was not treachery, nor was it ill will. It was simple exuberance. But it could be the end of him.

With every scrap of will that he had, he brought himself to order. He straightened in the saddle; he firmed his grip on the reins. Slowly the lightnings shrank within him, until they coiled in his heart.

He was still riven with shocks as the land woke about him, but they no longer fuddled his mind. He could focus on the mortal world, and lead his army to the rest of its victory.

❦ CHAPTER 52 ❦

K ing's blood completed the working. King's blood freed
Britain at last: streaming down into the earth and bur-
geoning toward the sky.

And yet the walls of iron, even yet, refused to fall. As Normans hounded Saxons through the twilit wood and into the
dark, in holy Canterbury the Guardians joined their powers yet
again.

One child of Godwine still lived. One power yet remained
that could transform prayer into prison, and magic into emptiness. Edith's brother's death had devastated her—and roused
her wrath.

Stigand, who had been her master, had dwindled into her
servant. The choir that raised the walls and the power was
wholly bound to her will. She stood in the heart of the holy
place and defied the Guardians to cast her out.

Cecilia did not know what the others were thinking; they
were not as closely bound as that. Yet she knew what she
would do.

It mattered little where Edith was or what she did, if she did
it alone and arrogant and therefore unprotected. She was braced
for a direct assault. Cecilia aimed her attack at the choir.

Her mother had done something very like it long ago, before
she married William—when she traveled the straight tracks
from Paris to Falaise, and found herself in a monastery in
Britain. Indeed it was this one into which she had fallen, this
house of God in which Cecilia stood. It was no wonder that the
monks' offices were steeped in magic. Mathilda had freed them.

Cecilia had no angelic visitation to offer: her body was bound
within the Guardians' working. But she could give the cathedral's choir a new clarity of vision. Through her they could see

the world as it truly was, in all its splendor. They could look on their queen and see what she had done, and know the full measure of her delusion.

Their chanting faltered. Edith had been kneeling before the altar, praying with devotion as honest as it was misguided. She stiffened. The choir fell further into discord.

She rose, turning, searching shadows for the power that had invaded her sanctuary. "What is this?" she demanded. "Brothers, why do you stop? God needs you. Why do you turn your back on him?"

A few ragged voices tried to resume the antiphon. But too many saw too clearly. They looked about as if they had never seen a cathedral before.

Nor had they: not one such as this. Its walls were made of light. The airy wonders of God's creation danced in the vaulting and spiraled down the pillars. Unearthly voices chanted the *Te Deum,* wounding their hearts with beauty.

"Evil!" cried Edith. "Devilry! Snares and mockery!"

"Just so," said the cantor. Even in speech, his voice was sweet. "Come, lady. The office is done."

Edith would not move. "It is not done! It is barely begun. Do you not understand? England is invaded. Pray to God; beg him to cast the Normans out."

"We may yet do that," the cantor said. "But, lady, not tonight. Come with us. Come and rest."

"I will not—"

To her lasting shock, a pair of stout monks lifted her. The stouter of them stopped her mouth with a brawny hand.

Cecilia could not have done better than they. Without the structure of prayer to hold them up, or the queen to be their capstone, the walls of iron came tumbling down. Britain was at last and truly free.

All of Harold's Saxons were dead or fled. In the first light of dawn, the victors moved amid the wrack of battle, searching out the wounded and laying out the dead for burial. Little by little, as the day grew brighter, people crept down from the wood or up from the hills by the sea, to gather the Saxon dead.

William came riding back slowly from the wood. He had called off the hunt; better, he reckoned, to secure the victory here, and not try to challenge the whole of England.

His hauberk was spattered with blood, his horse stumbling with weariness. While he hunted, his people had pitched camp on the edge of the field. So did the victor always claim his victory: by sleeping at his ease where he had stared death in the face.

His horse halted abruptly, nearly falling to its knees. Knots of men were laboring on the field. Some were looting; William would see to those as soon as his horse would agree to move again.

A handful of young men with swords and axes had been sauntering among the corpses, pausing to hack at this one or that. As William watched, they halted. He could not hear what they said; they had drawn together, muttering fiercely among themselves—arguing, and from the look of it, coming close to blows.

One of them whirled suddenly, swung up his axe, and attacked a body at his feet as if it had been alive and armed to destroy him. Another tugged at something caught beneath the bleeding and now grievously dismembered shape: something like a cloak or blanket, but dangling from a broken staff. Jewels gleamed on it through the dullness of mud and blood.

William had no memory of leaving the saddle. He was halfway across the field when he realized that he had moved. An instant later, he had the torn and bloodied Fighting Man in one hand and the young idiot's throat in the other.

The thing that had bled so sorely on Harold's banner no longer looked like a man. Its limbs were hacked from it, its face destroyed. But those limbs were long, and a black arrow sprouted from the ruin of the left eye.

Such arrows had defended the Wood of Broceliande for time out of mind. One of the Old Things, sated with common mortal blood, had drunk the blood of a king.

The Old Things were neither docile nor servants. William would have to remember that. In the meantime, half a dozen of his mortal vassals grinned at him, too witless to be afraid. "Look, my lord!" one of them said brightly. "We found the Saxons' dog. He won't be yapping at your heels again."

William dropped the axeman, who fell gagging and wheezing at his feet. "Out," he said. "Away from here. Now."

Their grins turned to blank stares. William's fingers itched toward his sword. But there had been enough slaughter here, for a while.

"You are cowards," he said, "and drunken fools, and it would be no more than any of you deserves if I hacked you to pieces and left you to bleed to death. If you want to be alive by sundown, get out of my sight. Go back to the ships and find one to haul you back to the pigsties you came from. If I ever see your faces again, I'll take an axe to them."

They were, at last, alarmed, and well they should be. Even so, they were drunk enough to dally, maybe even to argue. William's hand dropped to his sword.

They blanched. The bold dismemberer of kings broke first, whimpered and fled. The rest were hard on his heels.

William spat, but the sick taste of disgust refused to leave his mouth. He was glad for many reasons that Harold was dead. But there was no honor in mutilating corpses.

Harold was gone. His soul had not lingered once it was set free. Others were still wandering, dim and confused; the living walked oblivious through them.

The land knew how to set lost souls at rest. William spoke the word it gave him, to give shape to the working. The power rose up through him and flowed from his hands, like a wind that caught the rags and tatters of human spirits and blew them softly away.

No doubt they would wake in the Otherworld, sore confused and looking for the priests' heaven. William stretched and sighed. He felt as if he had had a long night's sleep: nothing like the exhaustion of magic at all. In fact, he had never felt better.

"It's your land," a deep voice said.

The boggart Turold was standing in front of William. He had not been there an instant before. He had a bow slung on his back, and a quiver of black arrows. A company of his kin, boggart and fey and other, odder beings, hovered behind him.

"We've come to bury the dead," Turold said.

He was not speaking of the common corpses, Norman or Saxon, that were slowly being cleared from the field. "His kind waged war on us for five hundred years," the boggart said, "and all the gods be thanked that that's the end of them. But he was a good man. He would have been a good king."

That was as fine an epitaph as Harold could have wished for. William stepped back, expecting them to move in with picks and shovels.

They did nothing of the sort. They circled those broken

remnants of a body, laying hands on it, spreading wings across it. In the space of a breath they had covered it like a shroud. Its limbs drew together; as William watched, the arrow worked its way out of the eye, and the face found its shape again.

That was Harold beyond a doubt. William would not have been amazed if he had opened his eyes and greeted his enemy. But however fair his body seemed, the soul truly was gone out of it.

The grass was rippling under it: growing, curving like fingers, drawing it down into itself. Already its edges were crumbling; it was dissolving into the earth.

William was in no danger, and yet he had a sudden, powerful urge to be on the back of a horse. The beast who had brought him here had wandered down toward the fen, grazing as it went. It did not try overly hard to elude him.

Once he was in the saddle, he let the horse go back to its breakfast. With four iron-shod hooves between his magic and the ground, he was still inextricably bound to Britain; but the binding seemed less likely to swallow him whole.

There was nothing left of Harold, not even the mound of a grave. Britain had taken him as it took every man who would call himself its king—body or soul, it did not matter which.

Harold's body was bound but his soul was free. William's soul had never been free. He would always rule in Britain, and Britain would always rule him.

He signed the cross over the place where Harold's body had lain. It was not meant for defiance. The world was different now than it had been when Artos was king. The cross was rising, the Druid's sickle fading from the secret places and the sacred groves. The Old Things were as strong as ever, but even they were changing.

A new world, he thought. It seemed he was in charge of it. He turned his face to the sun.

It was warm for October, and bright. The walls of iron were truly and finally gone. The sun was more brilliant, the grass more lucently green. Magic had come back into Britain.

William breathed it in. The looters had taken advantage of his distraction and fled. Anyone who was left on that field took care to respect the dead.

He had work to do. His horse lifted its head obediently at the touch of the rein. He turned back toward the camp, where duty was waiting, and long labor, but not yet a crown. Britain was his to the bones of its earth, but even with its king dead, England would beg to differ.

He would take England as Britain had taken him—and rule it, too. He had no doubt of that.

ENVOI

❧❧❧❧

CHRISTMASTIDE

anno domini 1066

Dover had surrendered to William, and Canterbury had submitted without a fight. London had proved less easy to conquer, but one thing William had learned about Saxons: shown a proper display of strength, then given time to think about it, they nearly always yielded to reason.

It was not a trait he would have expected, having known Harold—but then Harold had been half a Dane. Common Saxons, it seemed, were much more sensible.

London had yielded to him upon persuasion. Now it was preparing to crown him king. Both priests and people had chosen Christmas day for the ceremony: quick enough, all things considered, but time enough as well to prepare a proper feast.

On the day of the solstice, King Edward's hall was hung with banners of silk and scarlet, garlands of ivy and holly, and sweet-scented boughs of fir and pine. It was a fine wet day on this windy isle, with hard rain and lashing of sleet.

The hall was warm and well lit; William's belly was full. He had sent half a roast ox and a vat of hippocras to the guards who had to brave the weather. They had sent back their honest gratitude.

His knights and squires, kept in for the third day by this spate of English weather, were losing interest in songs and games and tests of skill. They had begun to talk of foraying out into the city, rain or no rain, and seeking more varied entertainment.

So far William's orders had kept them out of trouble. If the weather broke tomorrow—and by the gods it had better—he would take the lot of them hunting, and wear them out with a long day's run.

He was twitchy himself, but as the day went on, he realized

that there was more to it than boredom. Something was coming. Good or bad—he could not tell. Only that this was a great feast of the old way, and strange things could happen, especially now that the magic had come back into Britain.

Cecilia had been waiting for him in Canterbury, safe and whole. Lanfranc was still there, looking after the city and tending to its church, since Stigand, who for lack of the Pope's censure was still archbishop, had slunk off elsewhere. Cecilia had come with him to London, and now was sitting in a corner of the hall, engrossed in a game of chess with a figure in a cowl.

It could have been any one of the clerks in this warren of a palace, or a monk from the abbey, or even Lanfranc come in secret from Canterbury. And yet William did not think it was a man at all. His hackles rose.

He could not leap up and charge across the hall—not without drawing every eye. But he could rise casually, exchange a smile with an archbishop and a word with a count, and make his way in easy stages to Cecilia's corner. By the time he came there, people's attention had shifted elsewhere.

The game was still going on. Cecilia was losing. That was not usual at all, and she was not pleased with it, either.

William had meant to wait until they were done, but in some things he had no patience. He laid his hand on the black-clad shoulder.

"In a moment," Mathilda said, tilting her head as she considered the better of two possible moves.

William bit his tongue. She took her time deciding. It was deliberate, he was sure.

Not only he had to struggle for patience. Cecilia was as close to a fit of temper as William had ever seen her.

At long last Mathilda chose. It was neither move that William had thought she would make.

He dropped down onto the bench and laughed. It had been far too long since he did any such thing; it made his sides ache, but it cleared his head wonderfully.

Mathilda was frowning at him. He grinned back. "You're not here, are you?" he said.

"Of course not," she said. "I'm safe in my bed in Rouen, where I'll wake in the morning and go about my business."

His heart sank, though he truly had known better. "You're only . . . not here for a night?"

"Solstice night," she said. "When the sun sets, retire to your rooms. Dismiss the servants. Dress to travel."

It had been long years since she led him on a strange adventure. William's heart leaped in most youthful fashion.

He should be afraid. There was always some terrible test or some awful price to pay for these nights of magic.

"Such as marrying me?" Mathilda inquired.

"That was most terrible of all," he said.

She showed him her teeth. Even after half a dozen children, she still had them all.

He could not kiss her; too many people would see, and there would have to be explanations. But it was not so long until sunset; then he could excuse himself. After that, only she knew what they would do or where they would go.

He had been conceived in the rites of the year's dark. Great magics were made then; great good and great ill could come of them.

Mathilda jabbed a finger in his ribs. "Go. Preside. Until sunset."

There were times when it was wise to be obedient, even if one were a king. William bowed, not so low as to require explanations, and went back to the high seat.

Nightfall came early in London on the winter solstice, but for William it seemed unbearably late. Somehow he endured until the sun was incontestably down, until all the lamps were lit and the last glimmer of light had faded from the high windows.

No moon or stars shone tonight. The rain had died to a whisper, but the clouds were impenetrable.

William had little trouble pretending he was tired and needed to sleep. Some of the servants hovered, as if they feared that he had taken ill. He was ready to heave them out bodily when they finally stopped dithering and left him alone.

He made sure the door was barred in more than mortal fashion. His riding clothes were hidden in the bottom of a chest, as if the servants were ashamed of them. He pulled them on with a faint sigh. Silks and jewels were splendid, and William looked rather well in them, but well-worn leather was more to his natural taste.

*   *   *

It was not Mathilda who came to fetch him once he was dressed to ride, but Cecilia.

William had not expected that. She was waiting for him to bark at her, but he was too old a dog to be predictable. He greeted her calmly, which made her stare.

She was his child: she mastered herself quickly, took his hand and said, "Follow."

William had barely had time to settle in the king's rooms, and it seemed that Harold had suffered the same affliction. Many of Edward's belongings were still there, and many that were older, and some so old that they might have come down from Alfred himself.

One of the passages appeared to lead nowhere. On the wall at the end of it, a shield hung. It seemed ordinary enough in shape and size, but some forgotten king—or perhaps a queen—had sheathed it in silver.

When last William happened on this corridor, the silver had been tarnished black, so that the shield seemed crusted with soot. Someone since had gone to a great deal of trouble to polish the face of it to a mirror sheen.

They approached it by witchlight, he and Cecilia. William was not a man for mooning in mirrors, and scrying in them gave him the grues, but he caught himself staring at their reflection. Cecilia was exactly as he saw her every day, slender and growing tall, with her smooth oval face and her wide-set eyes.

The shape that hulked behind her could have been a stranger's. Big, broad-shouldered Norman reiver with eyes like flint and a nose like a ship's keel. He looked a right bully. No wonder people blanched and ran to do his bidding.

Cecilia's fingers tightened on his. The face in the mirror softened remarkably. It looked almost human then.

She led him through the mirror. Her stride was so sure and her grip so firm that he never even thought to protest.

There was a moment of coldness, a sensation like silver and steel sliding over his skin. He felt a tugging at his power, drawing up magic from the earth. It was a great amount of magic, if it had come from a mortal body, but the land barely felt its passage.

They stood in whispering darkness. The air was neither warm nor cold. William could not tell what it was he stood on, whether it was living earth or hewn stone or nothing at all.

Cecilia was terribly young. Her power was strong but not yet perfectly trained. She was lost. They were bound in nothingness, trapped for gods knew how long. They could not—

Light grew in the darkness: moonlight, starlight, shining through the woven boughs of trees. They opened in a broad circle that leaped into sudden clarity: a soaring blaze of fire.

Amid the rumble of guilt for the injustice he had done Cecilia's skill, William thought that they must be in the Wood of Broceliande. It was remarkably like the place in which he had found Mathilda, where she had first informed him that she would marry him.

This was very like, and just as rich with magic, but it was clearly and potently in Britain. The power in it was ancient and yet raw with newness; patches of blight yet lingered, places where the tide of magic flowed past without touching or healing.

Yet here in this circle, the power was as whole and clean and luminous as the silver of the mirror. A mighty crowd of Old Things flocked to it, dancing round the fire, partaking of the feast that was laid all about the edges and under the trees, or gathering in swirls and skeins to laugh and chatter and sing.

At first he thought that he and Cecilia must be the only mortals there. But then he saw Mathilda, and Lanfranc behind her, and the Lady of the Lake with her veils laid aside, and Wulfstan the Saxon who had proved loyal to the ancient kingship and the magic of Britain. There were others with them, faces he committed to memory, names he would learn and remember later: not all or even most of noble rank, but all gifted with magic. All the magic of Britain was here, gathered in this place on this night.

"In a handful of days," Mathilda said as she came to take his hands, "your people will see you crowned by a Christian archbishop in Edward's fine new abbey. That's a proper crowning, and sufficient—if you were a mortal king.

"Tonight," she said, "you are king of the old realm, the great realm, the Island of the Mighty. King once, you were; king always and to be. And now, on this night, king who is in this age of the world."

Her hands were warm. Her eyes smiled. He was surrounded with wonders, and all of them, every one, with its eyes fixed on him, measuring him, making their choice. Great lords and princes of the Otherworld, unimaginably ancient sages, immortals possessed of power that he could only dream of, all bent down and bowed before him.

And yet, however deeply he felt the honor, before Mathilda he barely noticed them. They were no more or less than adornment for her, who for him was all the world.

They had come to the circle's center. The fire leaped to heaven, but its heat did not sear him.

The Lady was standing there, and beside her a being that he had seen in a dream or an old story: a tall man dressed in green and brown, with eyes the color of a forest pool, and the ivory tines of antlers springing from his brow. Even as William wondered if he should bow to the Lord and the Lady, they bowed low to him, so low that the Lady's forehead and the Lord's antlers swept the ground. As they rose, he saw that each held a crown.

That in the Lord's hands was of gold, that in the Lady's of silver. The gold seemed woven of leaves: oak and ash and thorn. The silver seemed made of water, with bright fish swimming in it, twined in a circle, a dance without end.

A slow smile welled up from William's center. Britain needed not only a king; it sought a queen as well.

He suspected that Mathilda had not known, or else had not thought of it. She had brought him here to be crowned in the old way, by the old folk of wood and water, and given the gift and the burden of the hidden kingdom. It had not occurred to her that the Old Things might be inclined to crown another with him.

She was hardly fool enough to refuse. Normandy needed her still; she would not abandon it any more than William would let her. But she bent her head to accept the crown of silver, even as the golden crown settled on William's brows. As she straightened, there was an odd look on her face, as if she had foreseen this long ago, but never known what it meant.

If any words were spoken from beginning to end of that strange and powerful rite, William was not aware of them. There was music and singing, and dancing that waxed wild, leaping and whirling and spinning about the two who stood hand in hand beside the fire.

Mathilda was trembling ever so slightly. William drew her closer to his side. She was not cold, not in the body, but he could sense that she was glad of his warmth.

"Oh, yes," he said softly beneath the skirling of the pipes. "It's a terrible thing you've got me into. Are you sorry now that you did it?"

Her eyes flashed up from the shelter of his side. "*I* did it? Am I the good God himself, to fashion a soul that refuses to wander off when its one life is done, but persists in coming back again and again?"

"You married me," he pointed out.

"As I recall," she said acidly, "you had somewhat to do with that."

"Maybe I did," he said. "Maybe I didn't know any better."

"You were certainly an ignorant young thing," she agreed too readily. "Do you think you're any wiser now?"

"I know I'm not," he said, "which I'm sure is why they've crowned us equally. You'll be wise for me—and teach me how to be a king."

"You were born knowing that."

"Maybe I need reminding."

"You certainly need reminding of something," she said. She reached up and pulled his head down.

"Well?" he asked after the kiss was done, when the dizziness had almost passed and he could breathe again. "Is it worth it?"

"What, the crown?"

"Everything," he said. "You. I. The world that's shaped itself around us."

She pondered that, eyes narrowing, lips pursing until he was sorely tempted to kiss them again. "Maybe not the fighting," she said. "The rest of it—yes. Oh, yes. Every bit of it."

"All of it?" he asked.

"All of it," said Mathilda.

❦ AUTHOR'S NOTE ❦

The union of William of Normandy and Mathilda of Flanders was one of the great love matches of the Middle Ages. It was also, in political terms, one of the most inspired alliances of its age—but from the novelist's perspective, there is far more interest in the fact that, at a time when love in marriage was regarded as not only unnecessary but actually sinful, these two were clearly lovers as well as political partners.

Their story lends itself remarkably well to historical fantasy. It is very unlikely that either William or Mathilda had any Druid blood or influence—the Druids were long gone, though there were clear remnants of pagan rite and observance all through the folk cultures of Europe. William, to be sure, was only a few generations removed from pagan Vikings.

Whether or not William's mother was anything more than the daughter of a tanner or undertaker in Falaise, she certainly was extraordinary enough to attract the notice of a duke, then to marry a nobleman of lesser but by no means low rank. It is also true that William's father abruptly and rather inexplicably decided to go on pilgrimage to Jerusalem, leaving Normandy to his only, and illegitimate, son. The usual reason given is that he was overburdened by the weight of his sins—including, we may assume, the sin that produced William.

The events of William's early life were even more harrowing than I have shown them to be—a long litany of narrow escapes, murdered guardians, and battles for control of the young and helpless duke. The battle of Val-ès-Dunes in 1047, when William was about nineteen years old, broke the cycle of helplessness and established William, at last, as a force to reckon with in his own duchy.

It is unlikely that William met Mathilda at the French king's court after this battle; in fact it is quite possible that they met for the first time when she arrived in Eu to marry him. The Church's objection to the marriage was real and vehement, and was not resolved until 1059—at least eight years after the wedding. The reason for the objection, however, is not precisely known. Consanguinity—canonical incest—is usually cited as the reason, but the connection between William and Mathilda is tenuous even by the standards of canon law. What other reason there may have been, or why the Church was so determined not to allow the marriage, no one knows for certain.

For the sake of the story I have altered the date of the marriage, setting it in the year after Val-ès-Dunes. In reality, it most likely occurred in either 1050 or 1051—shortly before the death of William's mother, Herleva.

I have taken few liberties with what few birthdates are known for William's children, except to choose the earliest plausible dates for some of them. I have also chosen to accept the count of surviving ducal (and later royal) offspring as nine: a very good Celtic and Druidic number.

The most dramatic departure from strict historical accuracy is, of course, that Cecilia was a sorceress. She was in fact sent as an oblate (an offering on behalf of her family) to the abbey of Holy Trinity in Caen—one of two sacred institutions founded in that city as expiation for the "uncanonical" nature of her parents' marriage—in the year of the Conquest, and in time became abbess. She did not sail on the *Mora*, and she played no known role in the invasion.

As for Harold and the Saxons, I have followed the historical timeline closely for the most part. Tosti may not have been possessed, but something did happen in Northumberland around 1065, when Tosti had been earl for a decade. There was indeed a rebellion, and Tosti was exiled. He was indeed married to Mathilda's aunt, Judith of Flanders, and he did indeed invade England twice in 1066; he died with Harald Hardrada at Stamford Bridge.

Harold's exploits—his embassy and capture in 1064 or 1065, the raid into Brittany and the dramatic rescue of William's knights from quicksand, and the almost superhuman feats of speed and stamina that he performed in the campaigns against the Norse and the Normans—occurred essentially as I have written them. They are all depicted in the Bayeux Tapestry. Where I have departed from the accepted account of, for example, the location and terrain of the battle of Hastings, I have followed alternative versions in the primary or secondary sources.

I am indebted for historical details and general accuracy to a large number of sources both in print and on the Internet. Most valuable have been the various renderings and transcriptions of the Bayeux Tapestry, and a number of scholarly studies, including David C. Douglas, *William the Conqueror* (Berkeley, 1962; renewed 1992); David Bates' book of the same title (Charleston, SC, 2001); Ian W. Walker, *Harold: The Last Anglo-Saxon King* (Stroud, England, 1997); and Jim Bradbury, *The Battle of Hastings* (Stroud, 1998).

Judith Tarr is a World Fantasy Award nominee and the bestselling author of the highly acclaimed novels *Pride of Kings* and *Kingdom of the Grail*. A graduate of Yale and Cambridge Universities, she holds degrees in ancient and medieval history, and breeds Lipizzan horses at Dancing Horse Farm, her home in Vail, Arizona. You can find her on the Internet at http://www.sff.net/people/judith-tarr.

Read on for an exciting preview of

KING'S BLOOD

the new historical fantasy by

JUDITH TARR

Now available in trade paperback
from Roc Books

anno domini 1087

Spring came late that year, lashed with wind and rain and sharp-edged with hunger. In corners where the queen could not hear, people muttered of signs and portents, and said prayers that had nothing to do with the Lord Christ or the good God, although many of them called on Our Blessed Lady.

Edith was small and quick and her ears were keen. When she went wandering, her nurses had long since given up trying to catch her. She might stay away for most of a day, but she always came back.

On the day the world changed, she had escaped to the top of the highest tower of her father's dun. The rain had stopped for the first time in days. The wind was fierce, but she was never cold. The people in the wind kept her warm: odd and insubstantial shapes and eerie voices, wrapping her about, singing her songs in their language and teaching her to see what their people saw. She was a blessed one, they said. She could see through the world.

Today she was feeling strange. It was not that she was hungry, although she had given her breakfast to a beggar at the gate. The wind was pressing on her, as if to push her down from the tower and out of the dun and away on the road. *South,* it sang. *South is your way.*

She clung to the wall, with the wind whipping tears from her cheeks, and glared defiantly northward. Beyond the roll of stony hills and winter-blasted heather, the firth was as grey as iron, flecked white with foam. The folk of the air swirled above her, shrilling their song. *You know the way. You know you must. It is fated.*

"I don't want to," she said, not particularly loudly. They could hear even if she said it in her heart.

They said nothing to that. She wished they had. Then she would have had someone to scream at. But the wind knew what it knew.

She could run away. But where would she go? Even if she could see what no one else would admit to seeing and hear what no one else could hear, and ride as well as a boy besides, she was still a child. There was nowhere she could go, that her father could not find her and bring her back to face something even more terrible than himself: her lady mother.

She drew herself up, there in the wind. They were looking for her; she could feel them. Her mother had remembered her. It was time.

The queen inspected her daughter with a hard eye. She was beautiful, was the Lady Margaret, tall and fair, and royal to the core of her. She waged war for the Lord Christ as her husband the king waged war for Scotland: with heart and soul and a fierce, deadly sense of honor.

Edith did not have the sense to keep her eyes lowered in proper submission. Staring at her mother was like staring at the sun; it could strike a person blind. But Edith was fascinated. Wherever Margaret was, the world was overwhelmingly solid. Edith could not see through it at all.

Margaret reached from her tall chair, taking Edith's chin in firm cool fingers and tipping it so that her face caught the light. The queen sighed faintly. "Well, child," she said, "I see they did their best, but that you are a wild thing, no one could possibly mistake. It's time to make a Christian of you."

Edith very carefully said nothing. There were no folk of the air in this cold, still room; no creatures at all but the queen and her ladies and the pair of little bright-eyed dogs that crouched watchfully at Margaret's feet.

The dogs might have had something to say, but they chose not to say it. Margaret, who reckoned them dumb animals, paid no attention. Having searched Edith's face, she let it go and folded her long white hands in her lap. "Tomorrow," she said, "you will go. The letters have been sent. Your aunt the abbess will be expecting you."

A shiver ran down Edith's spine. She could not help it then; she had to ask. "My aunt? You're giving me to an abbey? You're making me a nun?"

"We are offering you to God," said the queen. It was like a door shutting.

"But I thought," said Edith, not wisely at all, "that I was to be fostered, and when I was older, sent to be married. Not—"

"You are to be fostered." That was a voice Edith had not heard before. There were always maids with the queen, and nuns in veils. Edith had not been paying attention, not with her mother taking up all the light and air in the room.

This was a nun, or seemed to be. Her voice was soft. She seemed gentle and humble as a bride of the Lord Christ should be, but the small hairs on Edith's neck were standing straight up.

"Princess," the stranger said, "you will be tended and taught and shown the way to Our Lady's grace. Of that I can assure you."

Edith's heart was pounding hard. Her breath was coming short. She did not know why she should be feeling this way;

there was nothing frightening about the lady. She was like the folk of air—even here in front of the queen.

That was why she was so alarming. Because she could be here and alive and speaking with her own voice. Nothing from the other world could do that where Margaret was.

Which meant that this lady was very, very strong indeed. And she came from the place where Margaret wanted to send Edith. Which meant—

There was too much to think about. Edith's head ached with trying.

"Don't try," the strange lady said, so softly that only Edith could hear. "Just be."

That was exactly the sort of thing one of the folk of air might have said. It took the pain away, a little, but Edith did not object when her mother ordered her nurses to feed her a posset and put her to bed. "In the morning," the queen said, "if she is still vaporing, prepare a litter for her. She will go, whether it pleases her or no."

Edith did not know whether it pleased her or not. But even while she was carried off to bed, she knew that she would go—not because her mother commanded it, but because the lady was there.

The king was not there to see Edith off. Edith wondered if he even knew that she was going away.

If she had been a little younger she might have cried, but she was too old for that now. She blinked hard against the cut of the wind, and let her mother kiss her coolly on both cheeks and lay a blessing on her. Then she mounted her pony and waited while the guards took their places around her.

They were a strong escort. It was a long way to her Aunt Christina's abbey, all the way down into England. None of her nurses was allowed to go with her, though Nieve clambered on one of the packmules and dared anyone to stop her.

It took three men to do it, but they did it. The queen had commanded. They would obey.

Once Nieve was dragged off shrieking curses, Edith was alone in the midst of all those armored men, except for the lady whose name she did not even know. But the folk of air came and swirled about her and sang to her, and she forgot to be either lonely or afraid. They would never leave her alone. That was their promise. She knew they would keep it.

Once she had ridden out of the gate, she did not look back. For all her determination, her eyes were pricking with tears. She set her chin and kept her eyes fixed on the broad brown rump of the horse in front of her.

That was all she would see for much of that long ride: great tall horses around her and armored men on their backs, and the folk of air swarming so thick above her that they almost hid the sky. They told her stories as she rode, and sang songs in their eerie voices, and taught her to feel the land as she crossed it.

That was a wonderful thing. This was all one island, and Scotland was only the edge of it. There was England, with all its old kingdoms, and Wales, and Cornwall where the magic was strong.

She was going to England, where her mother's ancestors had been kings. New kings ruled there now: gross men, bad men, whom her mother refused to name. She would only call them *those invaders* and cross herself fiercely as she said it, as if the blessing were a curse.

And yet she sent her daughter there, because it was her inheritance. The abbey was a safe and sacred place, where Edith would learn to be she hardly knew what. But maybe not a Christian.

The folk of air were wildly excited that she was going there. She would be so strong, they sang; so wise. There would be no one wiser than she.

"It's good to be wise," the lady said.

Edith started so strongly that her pony almost shied.

For days the lady had said nothing. The guards walked wary of her, and spoke softly when they thought she could hear, but she hardly seemed to see them. Edith she seemed not to notice at all.

As soon as she spoke, Edith knew that that was not true. The lady had noticed every tiny thing. She could see the folk of air, and hear them, too.

She was wise. Britain was in her, or she in it—Edith could not tell which it was. She was very, very strong.

"I am a Guardian of the Isle," said the lady in her soft cool voice. "You will learn what that means—among many other things."

"Does Mother know?" Edith asked her.

The lady's brows lifted, as if she had not expected that.

"Mother thinks I'm going to Aunt Christina," Edith said, "to learn to be a nun."

"And so you are," said the lady, "but there is more to the world than some will admit."

The follow-up to *Rite of Conquest*
from
National Bestselling Author
Judith Tarr

KING'S BLOOD

Red William, the eldest son of William the
Conqueror, has inherited the throne and a kingdom
free of the Saxons. But his decision to abandon
magic causes the land to wither and die.

Now the fate of Britain lies in the hands of Edith,
princess of Scotland, and Henry, the youngest son
of the Conqueror. Both are gifted in magic, but
only the blood of the king can cleanse the land.

0-451-46045-6

**Now available in hardcover wherever books are
sold or at penguin.com**

EAU CLAIRE DISTRICT LIBRARY

R081

EAU CLAIRE DISTRICT LIBRARY

National Bestselling Author

JUDITH TARR

"A MASTER OF HISTORICAL FICTION."
—*BOOKLIST*

"HER CHARACTERS ARE AS ENGAGING AS HER NARRATIVE IS ENCHANTING."
—*PUBLISHERS WEEKLY*

House of War

0-451-52900-6

Kingdom of the Grail

0-451-46004-9

Available wherever books are sold or at
penguin.com

r099